Ruthless Havoc

Ruthless Havoc

Montana Mayhem
Book 2

Millie Copper

Written by Millie Copper

Edited by Ameryn Tucker

Proofread by WMH Cheryl

Cover design by Dauntless Cover Design

Also by Millie Copper

Montana Mayhem Series

Unending Havoc: Montana Mayhem Book 1

Havoc in Wyoming Series

Havoc in Wyoming: Part 1, Caldwell's Homestead

Havoc in Wyoming: Part 2, Katie's Journey

Havoc in Wyoming: Part 3, Mollie's Quest

Havoc Begins: A Havoc in Wyoming Story

Havoc in Wyoming: Part 4, Shields and Ramparts

Havoc in Wyoming: Part 5, Fowler's Snare

Havoc Rises: A Havoc in Wyoming Story

Havoc in Wyoming: Part 6, Pestilence in the Darkness

Christmas on the Mountain: A Havoc in Wyoming Novella

Havoc Peaks: A Havoc in Wyoming Story

Havoc in Wyoming: Part 7, My Refuge and Fortress

Nonfiction Books

Stretchy Beans: Nutritious, Economical Meals the Easy Way

Stock the Real Food Pantry: A Handbook for Making the Most of Your Pantry

Design a Dish: Save Your Food Dollars

Real Food Hits the Road: Budget Friendly Tips, Ideas, and Recipes for Enjoying Real Food Away from Home

Join My Reader's Club!

Receive a complimentary copy of *Wicked Havoc: A Montana Mayhem Prequel*. As part of my reader's club, you'll be the first to know about new releases and specials. I also share info on books I'm reading, preparedness tips, and more. Please sign up at:

MillieCopper.com/Wicked

Who's Who

Rochelle Bennet: Her son is missing. Her husband, Dale, was murdered as she watched. She and her daughters were taken captive, then sold to the highest bidder. He said he wanted a family to love. But Fred Lassiter's vision of family included control and abuse. Now that Rochelle and her girls are free again, she's on a mission to find her son and bring him home.

PJ Cameron: A close friend of Rochelle Bennet, PJ is committed to helping her find her teenage son. As a professional outfitter, he brings many skills to help on their journey, including a team of two half-draft horses and a wagon. But as they reach populated areas, will the wagon be a help or a hindrance?

Robyn Sorensen: After losing her only child last summer, Robyn was recently widowed when her husband was killed in a massacre. She now wants nothing more than to go home to the loving arms of her parents.

The Hoffmann Family: Kimba and Rey Hoffmann, along with their three children—Nicole, Nate, and Naomi—fled Denver after the bridges exploded. They are invaluable members of the group and are committed to helping the other families reach their homes. Kimba's and Rey's former careers, as clandestine government operatives, provide them with useful skills for the journey.

The Dosen Family: Away from home when the attacks started, Jennifer and her three sons are determined to return to their small ranch outside of Great Falls, Montana. Eighteen-year-old twins Atticus and Asher and sixteen-year-old Axel all trained with the Bakerville militia alongside their mom. Will a few months of training be enough to see them safely home?

The Dawson Family: After her husband's atrocious acts made her family an outcast, Victoria Dawson and her two sons, Brett and Jameson, need a fresh start. They'll be joining the Dosen family in Great Falls—if they can make it there.

The Monroe Family: Skinny and malnourished, Leanne Monroe and her two children are last-minute additions to the group. Eight-year-old Sebastian has a ready smile for everyone, while his twelve-year-old sister, Sadie, keeps to herself.

Donnie McCullough: A bit of a rebel, Donnie is determined to help Leanne Monroe and her children make it to their aunt's home.

Tamra Nicholson: Twice-widowed mom of two daughters, thirteen-year-old Beth and seven-year-old Debbie. Her first marriage was built on love and trust—her second one, convenience and security needed at the end of the world. Turns out, what she thought was security, was nothing more than a lie. Now safe in the small town she grew up in, and a new Believer, she and her daughters hope to build a new life.

Rochelle's Story

Chapter 1

"This is not what we agreed to." She slaps her palm on the table.

I let out a breath through my nose. "We've discussed how this could happen."

"We *discussed* my children riding in the wagon until we separated."

"If you'd let Rochelle finish— " my good friend PJ Cameron says, his tone calm and reasonable.

"Oh, by all means, *Rochelle*. Please finish. Finish telling me how you are condemning my children to death."

I force a smile. "We agreed we'd use the wagon as long as it was safe. We always knew it could make us a target. And with the new information— "

"This isn't new information. I told you how things are out here. We're targets, even without the wagon," Leanne says, her green eyes boring into me. "My children are not well enough to be on their feet all day."

"I understand."

"No, you don't. You didn't watch your children slowly starve, wasting away day by day until . . . you have no idea what they've been through. And now you expect them to walk eight or ten miles a day? They can't do it."

"We know Sadie and Sebastian, and you, have had a rough time. We'll still have the horses. PJ and I, even Donnie, have all agreed riding double for short times will work fine. The children are small. They won't stress the horses. You can ride, no problem. Even Robyn, with the injury to her shoulder, might not be able to walk all the time."

"And I have no say in it, as usual."

PJ leans back in his chair. "Sorry, Leanne. We agreed that, in matters of security, Rey and Kimba have the final say. And since I own the wagon, I'm adding my two cents. The wagon stays in Joliet. They'll keep it in a garage— "

"Fine, whatever." Rising in an angry rush, she knocks over the chair, shoots us one final hateful look, and stomps out of the room.

"That went well," PJ mutters, scrubbing his hands against his bearded face.

"She's concerned for her children," I say. "I get it. You know that's the entire reason we're here, my concern for my son."

He puts his hand on top of mine. "We're going to find him, Rochelle."

I drop my eyes. "I pray he's healthy and waiting, knowing I'm doing my best to get to him. But if he's not . . . if I can at least have answers one way or another . . . it'll be better than not knowing."

It's been over nine months since five passenger airplanes were shot out of the sky, setting off a cascading series of attacks and striking fear into the hearts of every man, woman, and child in the United States. Each attack compounded on the one before, causing an avalanche effect of disaster.

The coup de grâce was a nuclear attack. Not only were port cities destroyed with ground detonations, but a high-altitude nuke wiped out our power grid and most cars with an electromagnetic pulse. The EMP destroyed communication and set us back well before the Industrial Age. Some say we're living in the 1800s again, while others insist we're in medieval times. The violence surrounding us certainly feels medieval.

The day the EMP hit, my husband Dale, two daughters, and I were on our way to Shepherd, Montana, to get our son Christopher from summer camp. In hindsight, we should've gone after him the night of the first attacks. But we thought it was just a flash in the pan. An isolated event. An inconvenience that grounded air travel.

When we finally realized it was substantially more than an inconvenience, it was too late. After the car stopped running, we started off on foot. We had just set up camp when a group of men assaulted us. They killed Dale, then took my daughters and me hostage. I blink my eyes to put aside the emotions threatening to rush over me.

"I know it's going to be harder on us without the wagon," PJ says. "When we find your son and separate from the group, we'll have just the two horses. One of us will be on foot."

"I'm thankful your family gave us snowshoes."

"Not sure we'll need them much longer. We've had some beautiful days since we left the lodge on the mountain. What was that? Two weeks ago?"

"We left March 15."

"And today is . . . ?"

"April 1." A pang of regret courses through me. Yesterday was my oldest daughter's birthday. Kerryanne turned fourteen, and I missed it. I hope her day was wonderful—as special as it can be in our current circumstances.

"Huh, April Fools' Day. Seems fitting," PJ says.

I give him a fleeting smile. "Most years, it snows well into April, sometimes even May."

"Yep. And we've seen more snow this year than I ever remember, but it has to melt off sometime. A warm day and a good wind, we'll find ourselves in mud, especially at this elevation. We're about three thousand feet lower than our mountain home."

"How long do you think it'll take to get to Camp Ah Nei from here?"

"Joliet to Billings was only an hour or so by car, back in the days when cars were a thing." PJ waggles his eyebrows at me. "But with the trouble between here and Billings, we're smart to go around, taking the small back roads. Here to Fromberg's two days. Then from there past the little town of Edgar until we reach Chief Plenty Coups State Park, we're looking at a minimum of five days, probably more like seven. Another ten to reach Lockwood, where we'll drop off Robyn with her parents. Then two, maybe three, to your son."

"So . . . three weeks?" I ask, my voice filled with hope. Three weeks until I can see my son again.

He tilts his head and meets my gaze with his deep brown eyes. "If we can travel every day, yes. But if we get another storm like the one we had in Bridger a few days ago, we'll need to wait it out. And you know what Atticus thinks."

"That we're going to be stuck here a few days because of the weather coming in."

"Yep. These spring storms are common, even in normal weather patterns."

"And this year has been anything but normal."

"Right. There might be something to the theory of nuclear winter." He tilts his head and lifts his hands.

"All I know is I want to find Christopher and get back to my girls. I hated leaving them in Bakerville. Sure, I know it was the right choice, the safe choice, but I miss them."

"It'll probably be two months before we make it back."

"It should at least be spring by then."

"Should be." PJ nods.

What he doesn't say, what neither of us is willing to speak aloud, is a lot can happen between now and then. I left my daughters at our mountain home, with a good friend, for this exact reason: the danger of being away from the safety of the group. Even groups aren't always safe.

Several weeks back, part of our community, those who had chosen not to move up to the mountain, were attacked. Five children hid, living through the ordeal. Those children were taken in by PJ's brother and his wife. The trauma they've experienced . . . the rest of the community, including the children's parents, were slaughtered. Robyn Sorensen, part of our traveling group, lost her husband in the attack.

Around the same time of the murders, the president—who we hadn't heard from since before the EMP—announced he's making strides to get the lights back on. They're starting in cities that weren't destroyed by the bombs. Undoing almost a year of chaos won't be easy.

I shudder to think how many deaths our country has suffered. What will the United States of America look like in the future?

~~~~~

"We'll see you in a couple weeks," my friend Tamra Nicholson says, wrapping me in a hug.

"Probably closer to a month," I say.

As Atticus predicted, we've been stuck in Joliet, where Tamra's parents live, for too many days as another storm swept through. This one, though not a cold arctic blast like we'd experienced the week before, was a wet snow that dumped at least a foot in the first twenty-four hours, then continued to storm off and on for several days. When it finally let up, we waited another couple of days before leaving. There was just too much new snow to make travel safe.
~~~~~

Finally, today, April 9, we're packed and ready to head out. It's still cold, but not bitter. We're all dressed in multiple layers, helpful for taking off as the day warms up.

"Whenever it is, don't worry. My dad has no trouble keeping the wagon until you return. And I can't wait to meet your son."

I wipe my eyes before clearing my throat. "It's the same as it was for you—not knowing what you'd find when we reached Joliet. I miss the days when we could pick up a phone or send a text to ensure our loved ones were fine . . . even being able to mail a letter and receive one in return. This world is so different."

"Maybe they'll bring back the Pony Express. It sounds like the most recent update from the White House—wherever that may be right now—is encouraging. They're making headway."

"Are they?" I ask, thinking back to a few days ago when the info came over the functioning ham radio the town of Joliet has. It was another extremely vague announcement from the president.

"Well, who knows?" Tamra says. "Either way, I think things will start to turn around. And who says we need the president or the government to make it happen? Look at how well they're doing here, in Joliet. Just like back on the mountain, they're making it work. And when the snow melts, they're going to join with the towns of Fromberg and Bridger. Maybe Belfry will even be part of the cooperative. They can start their own mail service between those towns at least."

I think back to the towns she mentioned; we've traveled through all of them on this journey. Between Bridger and Fromberg, they'd cleared the snow from the road by using scoop shovels and a four-wheeler with a plow attached. The two towns are already working together for mutual survival. Adding a town on either end—Belfry to the south and Joliet to the northwest—sounds smart.

"Maybe Bakerville will become a part of their co-op too? It's not *that* far between Bakerville and Belfry."

"See? Lots of possibilities, which can all start at the local level." Tamra pulls me into another hug. "Don't forget to walk once in a while. You don't want saddle sores."

I let out a hearty laugh. "That's the last thing I need. But with three pairs of pants on, I should be okay there. When Leanne or one of her children need a rest, I'll walk Lucky. It'll be fine."

"Yeah . . . " She raises her eyebrows at me. Leanne's reaction to leaving the wagon in Joliet is no secret. Even though we were in the separate dining room, her voice carried through the entire house. And her stomping around afterward only added to the drama.

"Let's hit the road," Donnie McCollough bellows from atop his horse. "As the Duke would say, 'We're burnin' daylight.' Time to get a move on!"

Several people wave as we travel past houses on our way out of town. With the horses and backcountry ski gear, I'm sure we're quite a sight. While those with ski gear managed to have a little fun when we left the ski resort outside of Bakerville, we've been on what is essentially flat land for most of the trip.

The skis were made suitable for walking by adding skins, strips of material attached to the undersides, providing traction for flat stretches and moderate climbing. They're reminiscent of snowshoes but not as easy to maneuver.

We wanted snowshoes for everyone, but our mountain community wasn't willing to part with them. Understandable, since that's how everyone gets around when there's several feet of snow on the ground.

Providing the backcountry ski gear was a good alternative and has made our travel easier than it would've been without it. The addition of three utility sleds allows us to tow necessary supplies instead of carrying everything on our backs or in our saddlebags.

The sun is already shining bright, even though it's only been up a short while. God has given us a beautiful day for traveling. And even the memory of Leanne's hatefulness isn't putting a damper on my excitement to be on the road again.

The forced weather delay gave her children several days to recover from our journey thus far. It was also helpful for Donnie McCullough and Robyn Sorensen, who were both injured a few weeks ago when we were attacked while traveling through Bridger, Montana.

On the way to my son's camp, we'll be stopping in Lockwood, Montana, which is east of Billings, to take Robyn to her parents' house. From there, our group will continue on to Camp Ah Nei, slightly northwest of Shepherd, Montana.

Once PJ and I have Christopher, we'll return to Bakerville, Wyoming. The rest of our group will continue northwest. Leanne Monroe is going to Lewistown, Montana, where she has an aunt, while the Dosen and Dawson families are heading near Great Falls.

Jennifer Dosen and her three teenaged sons, commonly referred to as the *A Boys* or the *A Team* since each of their names begins with an *A*, have a small cattle ranch east of Great Falls. They invited the Dawsons to move up with them. It was a nice invitation, considering Victoria Dawson and her two sons, sixteen-year-old Brett and fourteen-year-old Jameson, are no longer welcome in Bakerville.

Jon Dawson, Victoria's husband and the boys' father, attempted to overtake the legitimate town council, murdering several in the process. Even with his death, and the death of most of the people who attempted the coup, many blamed Victoria. She insists he'd gone crazy and, in his insanity, made poor choices. That's an understatement for sure.

Because of a commitment made long before I met them, Kimba and Rey Hoffmann, along with their three children, are traveling with the Dosens to ensure they make it home. From there, the Hoffmanns seem unsure of their plans.

While they enjoyed their time living with the people of Bakerville and have made many close friendships, Kimba and Rey feel a sense of duty to help with the country's rebuilding efforts.

Both have a rather interesting history, if rumors can be believed. It seems Kimba and Rey met when they were working as clandestine government operatives—Kimba for the United States and Rey for Britain.

They've talked about going back to Denver, where they lived before the attacks, or possibly west to Spokane, Washington, which is reported to have started reconstruction. Wherever they end up, their skills with firearms and thinking on their feet makes them huge assets on this trip. This has already been proven with the difficulties we've encountered on our journey.

I glance over at Robyn. Her arm is still in a sling from the trouble we had in Bridger. She dislocated her shoulder when trying to escape the grasp of a captor. Thankfully, it doesn't seem to bother her much as she uses only one pole while skinning instead of two, her tall, full-bodied frame having little trouble with the movement.

Leanne, who rode in the wagon with her children during our journey from Bakerville to Joliet, seems to have taken to skinning without any issue. She doesn't even struggle with the gliding motion, moving almost like a dancer. Even her children do well with it, but they tire quickly and both welcome rides on the horses.

We find out quickly there's some logistics to giving them breaks from walking. Someone needs to carry their skis by attaching them to their backpack. The collapsible poles need to be stashed. It's always several minutes of fussing, but it's necessary and gives me or PJ time to get our snowshoes on so we can walk alongside our horses.

Both eight-year-old Sebastian and almost thirteen-year-old Sadie Monroe were severely malnourished after walking from Oregon to Wyoming. Leanne too, she's little more than skin and bones, even after the extra care and food given by the people of Joliet during our weather-forced stopover.

Not only are they physically affected by the trek, but Leanne's also rumored to have been mentally affected. I've heard she was a kind and caring person before. Whether it was the threat of starvation or something more, she's now bitter and calloused.

When she looks to be tiring, I offer her a ride. Her nonverbal response leaves no doubt in my mind of her opinion about my offer. She juts out her chin and digs in harder, never wavering or looking weary for the remainder of the day. With the excellent weather and everyone well rested, we make good time, setting up camp about a mile outside the small town of Fromberg.

One day down. How many days ahead?

Chapter 2

The past several days blend together as we make our way east. Yesterday, Victoria Dawsons youngest son, Jameson, started complaining about feeling bad not long after breakfast. A short while later, he was feverish and pale. Although it was not yet noon, Rey made the decision to call it a day and set up camp.

Jameson's fever broke around dark, and he slept fine through the night. Starting off this morning, he seemed back to his usual surly teenage self. We're thankful it doesn't seem to be anything serious. I can't even imagine what we'd do if we needed a doctor out here in the middle of nowhere.

Today is not only sunny but has a warm wind—a Chinook—blowing from the mountains. The wind died down shortly after lunch, but with the sun still shining, it's a gorgeous day.

The route we're on, from Edgar to Pryor, was little traveled in previous times. Now, with the way things are, the snowy ground shows no tracks of anyone traveling through. Even the few scattered ranches appear vacant.

With the trackless snow, we stay between fences on either side of what we assume is the gravel road. We've seen one car abandoned on the side of the road, but desolate is certainly a good word to describe this area. And that's how we like it. Fewer people means less chance of running into trouble.

We take a long lunch break, making sure Jameson has time to rest after his ordeal yesterday. We've only been walking a short time when he starts looking pale again and his mom asks if we can stop for the day. Even though we still have several hours until sundown, we take one look at the boy and quickly agree.

"How about the meadow?" Kimba Hoffmann asks, pointing to a wide spot.

"I'm not sure it's a meadow," PJ says. "Might be a pond."

"A stock pond on private property?" she asks.

"Could be. Or it could be on public land. There isn't a fence here, and the gazetteer shows it checker boarded. I think we'll be fine if we stay close to the road."

"Yeah, well, you might think so, but the landowner might disagree with you," Donnie says.

"Yep, for sure. We can keep going until we find a place that we know is public land."

"No need on my account," Donnie says. "I'm okay with bending the law a bit."

"No doubt," I mutter.

Like Leanne, Donnie has his own peculiarities and opinions on things. And he, too, is less than pleasant to be around. To be fair, he's had a rough trip so far.

When we were attacked one night while staying in a small house off the highway, he was shot in the hand. The bullet went through, doing some damage, and left him without full use of it. And at the incident in Bridger, a bullet grazed his skull just above his ear, knocking him out, leaving a gnarly looking scar, and giving him a doozy of a headache.

Leanne and Donnie, who are similar in many ways, seem to be forming a bond. The glances and touches between the two of them have become more apparent as we make this journey.

Leanne, widowed when her son was just a baby, may be headstrong and difficult, but she certainly could use a little happiness. And if equally ornery Donnie can give that to her, then great. I like to think there's someone for everyone, and Leanne and Donnie certainly seem to be two peas in a pod.

"We'll check it out." PJ pats his horse's neck. "I'll make sure there's a solid edge for setting up camp."

"Do you want to take one of the radios?" Kimba asks, motioning to her hip. Our single pair of radios have been useful while on night watch or times our group has separated. We were blessed to have access to a cache of batteries and other useful items early in our journey.

"You want Lucky and me to join you?" I ask, motioning to the gelding I'm riding. Both Lucky and PJ's horse, Titan, are half drafts—crosses between Quarter Horse and Percheron. They both have a wonderful disposition and were great not only working together to pull the wagon but are also a dream to ride. I'm especially partial to Lucky, a beautiful, dappled gray with the sweetest face. Titan, PJ's chestnut, is also amazing.

"Nah. Go ahead and walk around a bit. It'll be good to stretch if this place doesn't work out."

"We could just camp in the middle of the road." I motion with my hands. "There's no one around but us."

"True. But somehow it feels smarter to get off the road, or at least what we think is the road."

I give him a smile and dip my head in agreement. PJ Cameron is a good man. He reached out to me in friendship when I felt terribly alone, not only alone but embarrassed about the things I'd allowed. The things I'd done to keep my children sheltered, fed, and clothed.

Last summer, in the moments following Dale's murder, I thought our lives would also end. That we'd be shot too. I take a deep breath as the memory of that day washes over me.

I let out a scream.

A hand smacks me across the face. "Shut up!"

A strip of tape is put over my mouth and then a bag is put over my head. My hands are tied behind my back, then I feel hands go under my arms. I'm yanked along, my heels dragging in the dirt.

Whimpering from nearby gives me hope my girls are with me.

Soon, I'm lifted in the air. I land with a thump on something hard. There's another thump, then a lighter one.

I groan and move my body around until I can find both of my daughters. Then I let out a breath, trying to stay calm while waiting and hoping we'll soon be able to escape.

An engine roars to life. We're in a pickup truck. Bouncing around, with my hands bound, blind to my surroundings and unable to speak, I lose all track of time. When the truck starts to slow, I make grunting noises, trying to let my girls know we'll be okay and everything will be fine.

Their responding noises sound less than convinced.

I'm yanked out of the truck, landing hard on the ground.

Rough arms grab at me. "Get a move on it. Fall again, and you'll be sorry."

"You okay, Rochelle?" Robyn asks, bringing me back to the present. She gives me an inquisitive look.

"What?" My breath is ragged.

"Are you sick?"

I lift a hand to my forehead. "Oh . . . yeah, sure. Just . . . " I shake my head. "Is your arm okay?"

"Better each day. It could've been worse."

"Definitely." I let out a slow breath, willing myself to calm down.
She gives me a long look. "You sure you're okay?"

"Just . . . memories."

We stand in silence for several minutes. I glance around, watching the others in our group as they stretch or talk quietly.

"You ever been through this area before?" Robyn asks.

"Never. You?"

"Once. We went to the state park at the end of the road. It's not far from my parents' house, so we met them there for Mother's Day once, the year Bradyn turned one. He was just learning to walk and hated being in his stroller while we explored the grounds." She gets a wistful smile. "He always had so much energy. Just like his dad. Go, go, go. That's how they both were."

I give a nod as my eyes fill with tears.

"Losing both of them . . . " She bites her top lip and shakes her head. Her voice hoarse, she says, "It's so hard. When Bradyn died, a part of me died too. He was so young, only three. That was the hardest part, he'd barely began to live and he . . . "

She shakes her head again. "Then Garth died in the massacre. I'm just praying my parents are okay. I don't know if I could bear it if I get to Lockwood and they're . . . you know."

I swallow hard to clear the lump from my throat. "I know. The unknown is part of what makes this so hard."

"Right. You have it, too, not knowing if your son's still where you left him, safe at camp."

"We're going to be okay, Robyn, no matter what happens. You and me, we're fighters. Survivors. We'll be okay."

She shrugs. "I don't know if I'm much of a fighter."

"Are you kidding? I saw you when that guy was holding you hostage in Bridger. You looked like a warrior. And when Kimba said to drop, you dropped like a rock."

"Yeah. And look what it got me." She motions to her arm. "All those self-defense classes we took, I always thought I'd know exactly what to do. But when it came right down to it, I was scared stiff. But I do appreciate you thinking of me that way. I want to be strong. It's just . . . it's hard sometimes."

I know she's right. We've all had at least minimal self-defense training, not only the adults but the children too. While living with the Bakerville community, even the youngest kids learned basic combat skills to protect themselves.

Almost everyone aged fourteen and older were part of the junior militia or full militia. Robyn was part of the militia last summer, until her son died and her mental health took a nosedive.

I was only added to the militia after Christmas, when I was finally able to pass the psych exam. Up until then, they thought the things I'd been through were too much for me, that I'd be unreliable for team members who were counting on me.

I'm better now, though there's still times when the memories of those days seem to overwhelm me, when I'm taken back to the brutality.

Flashbacks.

Although they don't occur as often as they used to, they still happen on rare occasions. Since we've been on the road, Kimba and Rey have kept up with our training, focusing on hand-to-hand combat plus a variety of exercises and drills with our handguns and rifles.

"It's hard for all of us. The way things are now . . . " I say. "I try to remember how the Bible tells us not to worry about tomorrow, how each day has enough trouble of its own."

"I guess it does. And I know that was a favorite verse on the mountain. It was often mentioned at the support group I was in."

"A group Sylvia Eriksen led?" I ask. Sylvia is my close friend and is currently taking care of my daughters. She's also been instrumental in helping me come to terms with the things my girls and I have gone through.

"Yep. She seemed very fond of the verse. I think she shared it with all of her groups. It's good she's watching after your girls."

"Very good. They love her."

"And I'm sure they'll do well with her. She really seems to understand the hurt so many of us are feeling with the way the world is now. I know there's often talk of cowboying up and just accepting how things are, but . . . " Robyn lets out a sigh. "It isn't always easy, especially with the loss of people we love. How do I forget my little boy? My husband?"

"You don't. *We* don't. None of us forget the things we've gone through, whether it's since the lights went out or before. Plenty of people had problems before the attacks. Those didn't just go away. In some cases, the change in our world really brought those problems to a head.”

“Maybe so. With the way Bradyn died so quickly . . . we might’ve still lost him if things were normal. But Garth wouldn’t have been murdered. All the others he was with—our friends and people we’d known for years—they’d still be alive too.”

One thing I’ve found in my prayer and Bible study is there’s nothing certain in this world. There never was. Life could always change in an instant.

This happened in my life before the apocalypse, when my dad died suddenly. My mom followed him not terribly long after.

Since the lights went out, things seem to change daily. None of this is new. We can see many Biblical examples of uncertainty and change. While I can’t deny the unpredictability of our world, I’m coming to understand God is in control.

Robyn is still mourning, and rightly so. It’s best to tread gently and acknowledge her grief. “Would you like to talk about your husband? Or your son?”

When she looks at me, her eyes are shimmering. “I appreciate the offer. Maybe after we get camp set up, we can walk around a bit? You must be sore from being on your horse all day.”

“That’s the truth.” I chuckle. “I’ve always loved to ride, but this is certainly different than working cattle or pleasure riding.”

“It must’ve been wonderful having a real working cattle ranch. Garth and I only had a small herd, just enough to supply our own food and a few more each year. We didn’t have the acreage to support a real ranch. But we did love what we were doing. And we had kind of a niche since we marketed as grass fed.”

“Smart to have a niche market. Dale and I— ”

“What’s he doing?” Robyn interrupts as she points toward PJ. He’s off his horse and walking along the tree line on the far side of the frozen pond.

“I’m not sure.” I shake my head. “He must’ve found something that caught his attention and he’s taking a closer look.”

Seconds later, PJ hops back on Titan and immediately brings him to a trot. As soon as he’s within shouting distance, he hollers, “We need to move!”

Rey instantly barks out orders, which includes telling me to take Sebastian Monroe on my horse. With his skis already off, I hand them to one of the teenage boys in our group. Sebastian folds down the ski poles, tucking them in a loop on his pack. His sister, Sadie, is making similar preparations, handing her skis off to another teen so she can ride with Donnie.

"What is it?" Kimba asks as soon as PJ reaches us.

"Tracks. Humans. At least three people. Maybe more. They're fresh, within the last few hours anyway."

"Let's move, folks," Rey orders. "You see any houses or anything?"

"Nope. Didn't smell any smoke either. But with the way Titan was acting, I'm fairly certain someone is still nearby."

"Atticus, you're with me. Kimba, get everyone out of here, double time." Rey and the oldest of the A Boys quickly move into a defensive position, each taking a knee to make themselves small with their rifles at the ready.

"Asher, you've got the lead," Kimba calls to Atticus's minutes-younger twin. "Go now! Everyone— "

The snow next to Rey poofs up a fraction of a second before a large boom sounds through the crisp air.

"Go! Go!" Rey calls out. "Atticus, do you see them?"

"I don't have them!" he answers.

"Grab ahold, Sebastian!" His arms wrap around me as I urge Lucky into a trot, faster than I should be going on this snowy and unfamiliar road.

Those on skis take off at a near run, or as close to a run as the awkward skis and skins will allow.

Another shot sounds off as I continue my getaway. Donnie, who has Sadie on his horse, is by my side. PJ stays with the skiers, somewhat shielding them from the gunfire, his pistol at the ready.

As we round a bend in the road, safe with a hillside between us and the shooting, I ask Donnie, "Should we stop?"

"Take the girl too," he demands, as another couple of shots sound off. "Get these kids out of here, and I'll help cover the skiers." He pulls his horse next to mine and tells Sadie, "Scoot over with her."

With wide eyes, Sadie shakes her head.

"It's okay," I say. "Put her on the ground, Donnie. Then I'll help her up."

He lets out an aggravated sigh before helping her slide down. Her feet are barely on solid ground before he rides off.

Help getting her on the horse would've been nice.

"Sebastian, I'm going to get off and get your sister on. You just sit tight."

"Are we . . . is it safe here?" he asks, as several rounds echo along the walls of the hillside. It sounds like our people are shooting back.

"We're sheltered by the hill."

I have Sadie in the saddle when the A Boy who's leading the skiers and dragging one of the sleds pops around the corner; the older Dawson boy is pulling a second sled directly on his heels.

Instead of getting on Lucky, I say, "Sebastian, hold on to your sister. Sadie, hold the saddle horn. We're moving now."

Leanne comes around the bend with Jennifer Dosen by her side, helping pull the rope on the third and final sled. Both are moving fast and breathing hard.

"Are they okay?" Leanne calls out.

"We're fine, Mom," Sebastian answers.

"Everyone else?" I ask.

"I think everyone's okay," Robyn replies after rounding the corner. She flinches at another shot from the distance. "They're going to cover Rey and Atticus so they can join us. We need to keep going."

As she's talking, more from our group reach the safety of the bend. Jameson Dawson, who was already looking a little pale from his illness, is ashen. His lips are pulled in a tight line. How much farther can he go without stopping?

"PJ?" I ask.

"Helping Kimba," someone answers. I don't take the time to figure out who as I stumble into a drift of deep snow, filling my boot and covering my insulated pants with the powder.

"You okay, Mrs. Rochelle?" Sebastian asks.

"Fine. I'm going to get in line behind the skiers."

I'm moving toward the end of the line when PJ rounds the bend.

"Everything okay, Rochelle?" he calls out.

"Where are the others?"

"Right behind me."

The other two A Boys round the bend, running on their skis. Kimba and Rey are right behind them, with Donnie and his horse bringing up the rear.

"Let's keep moving!" British-born Rey says, his accent more prominent from his excitement. "I think they were just trying to scare us off. Let's not stick around to find out."

"Scare us off?" Robyn says. "It worked. I'm scared."

PJ rides next to us. "Sebastian, you shimmy on over here so Rochelle can get back on her horse."

I stop moving as Sebastian puts out his arms. In what could be a circus act, PJ grabs him and plops him at the front of his saddle. Seconds later, I'm on Lucky with Sadie, following PJ.

"I can't . . . I don't think I can keep going," Jameson Dawson mutters.

"Someone handle his gear," Donnie orders. "The kid can ride with me."

Once Jameson is on Donnie's horse, Gordie, we move at what I'd call speed walking . . . if they weren't all flapping on their skis. The sun has dropped behind the horizon when Rey finally declares we've gone far enough.

"You're sure?" his twelve-year-old son, Nate, asks.

"As sure as I can be. It's too dangerous to keep going with the sun sinking."

"There's going to be a moon tonight—a half," Nate offers.

"Your dad's right," Kimba says. "It's too dangerous. And everyone's exhausted. Let's set up." She turns to Rey. "On the edge of the road?"

"Right here." He moves to the north side of the road. "Triple sentries tonight. Remember, we're not alone."

"We're lucky they didn't hit us," Jameson says.

"Either they were terrible shots, or they just wanted to scare us off." Atticus says, rubbing the scruff on his chin.

"They were scaring us off." Rey nods. "They were excellent shots. And they were well hidden. I only caught a glimpse of one, and just for an instant."

"Same here," Kimba agrees. "They were good for sure. And we weren't lucky—we were blessed. God is definitely watching over us today."

"Not just with them," PJ says. "It's good we didn't try and camp there. The reservoir was bigger than I thought, and when Titan and I were trotting back, it was cracking behind us. These warm days and the Chinook are starting a slow melt. A few more days like we've had, and we might start seeing bare ground again."

"'Bout time," Rey says. "What is today? April . . . "

"Twelfth," Kimba answers. "Well into spring. It's time for less snow."

Chapter 3

None of us slept very well after being shot at. We stopped early today, choosing to stay at Chief Plenty Coups State Park on the Crow Reservation, not only because we're all lagging but because it looks like it'll snow again.

We chose this route specifically after asking in Fromberg and Joliet what the best way to reach the towns of Lockwood and Shepherd are. Each response was the same. Not only is this a less-populated route, but they haven't had the troubles the city of Billings and the stretch of Interstate 90 between Laurel and Billings have faced.

In the days following the original attacks, there was considerable looting and violence. After the EMP, things became even worse. Between Joliet and Billings, there's even a known group of bandits, looting and killing. It's definitely smart to avoid the area.

Even though no one has any real information about Lockwood or Shepherd, the town nearest Camp Ah Nei where my son Christopher is, one of the people in Joliet recently traveled through Pryor, Montana—a town adjacent to the state park—and said they were starting to trade. They even had something like a farmers' market set up at the old school.

There are several families living at the state park, using the historic home and other buildings. We experienced several tense minutes when we first arrived here, as we feared we may be shot at again. Thankfully, those first moments gave way to new friendships.

After telling us we're welcome to set up our tents, a short man with a wild, blond, bushy beard says, "Hey, we're going after geese. I've never seen so many geese in my life. Feel free to join us if you'd like. We'd love the company."

Yesterday, after being shot at, it was too late to do any hunting. With game prevalent through this area, not only geese but also deer and small game, such as rabbits, we're taking advantage of it and harvesting as much as we can and then drying it over a fire so we can have it later. We suspect we'll find a food desert when we reach the more populated areas.

PJ, Donnie, and Brett Dawson take our two shotguns and go with Blond Beard, who finally introduces himself as Gus. While, as Gus said, the geese are plentiful, they're not my favorite. The dark, greasy meat is too gamey for my tastes. But tastes and preferences are a thing of the past.

When the lights went out and the grocery stores closed, food became little more than nourishment and fuel. And the meat provides substantial calories to keep us going.

Calories are especially important with the cold temperatures and the amount of walking we're doing, since our bodies are working harder to stay warm. And in the case of the malnourished Monroe family, they're likely still experiencing a calorie deficit.

Shortly after the goose hunters leave, another man and woman from Gus's group say they're going deer hunting. They invite us to join them, and Atticus and I take them up on their offer.

"We'd better hurry." Atticus motions toward the sky.

"More snow," the lady says, dropping her shoulders. "Hasn't anyone got the memo it's spring?"

I give a slight laugh. "No kidding. I've lived in Wyoming my entire life and have never seen a winter like this. We've been living at a higher elevation and expected the snow there, but down here . . . " I lift my hands. "We thought it'd be minimal."

"Ha! It's never ending," she answers. "I can't wait to get out of this place."

We toddle across a beaver dam to reach the other side of the creek, not an easy task with the slick wood. How will we get a deer back?

"We're going to sit up there." The man motions to a crop of boulders on the hillside. "Maybe you can get things moving."

"Sure," Atticus says. "Just know what you're shooting at." He gives a smile to soften the words.

"Absolutely. We're very conscious of wasting bullets. We're precise."

As they head off hand in hand, Atticus and I wait in the thicket so they have time to get in place. When we're confident they're set, we slowly start moving. After only a hundred yards or so, we find a well-pounded trail in the snow.

"Fresh?" I mouth.

Atticus gives a brief nod, then motions for me to take the lead. We slowly make our way through an open space in the brush, moving as quietly as possible.

I'm just about to step into a new clump of underbrush when Atticus lays a hand on my shoulder. I turn to where he motions.

The brush is moving slightly. I catch a glimpse of gray fur, the right size for a deer. Atticus steps back, hiding himself, as I quickly follow and then move down to one knee, my Remington 30.06 rifle pulled tight against my shoulder.

The movement of the brush is now accompanied by the sound of breaking twigs. A doe whitetail deer steps out, followed by a buck with barely visible antlers.

I take in a deep breath and silently release the safety. I take a second deep breath and feel myself steady. On the next breath, I hold the exhale while gently squeezing the trigger. The doe jumps and spins while the buck lurches forward before dropping.

"Whew," Atticus says. "Good job!"

With my heart still pounding from the adrenaline, I nod my thanks. "Now how are we going to get him across the creek?"

Hearing the shot, the two from Gus's group quickly make their way toward us. Though Atticus offers to do the eviscerating, I do it myself.

"Let's go this way." The man motions toward the main road in the distance. "It's a longer walk but we can use the bridge. Much easier than the beaver dam."

"I can't believe you got one," the lady says. "We're out here almost every day and rarely even see a deer."

Later, Gus tells PJ he thinks they're not out there hunting as much as they're looking for time alone. Private time is rare in the close quarters of the three families sharing the five-room historic house that formerly belonged to Chief Plenty Coups, the last of the traditional chiefs of the Crow Nation and the namesake of the park created in his honor.

The home, which was previously a museum until the lights went out, is really a six-room house—three rooms up and three down—but one room, the Ceremonial Room, is not used by request of the residents of Pryor, the town the state park sits next to.

They offered Gus and his family, plus two other couples, use of the home and park when they were stranded in the area last fall, with the express request to stay out of the Ceremonial Room on the second floor.

"We're just happy to have someplace to wait out the weather," Gus declares while we skin the deer and pluck the geese. They've converted the Park's Visitor Center into a space for processing wild game. Though the space is unheated, it's much better than being out in the wind and snow.

"Not using the room isn't too big of a deal. John Plainfeather and his wife, they've been really good to us—to everyone around here. The town has really banded together, even bringing in those living on the outskirts, any who wanted to move into town. Shoot, they've even brought in the livestock. There's cattle and horses in any fence that'll hold 'em."

"You have any trouble with feed?" PJ asks.

Gus nods. "The winter's been hard. They shovel the snow and move them around as best they can. We've had cattle here, will again soon. With the warm wind, we should see some melt soon. At least that's what everyone says. I pray they're right. You having any trouble feeding your horses?"

"Some," PJ answers with a nod. "We left home with hay, and also found several bales along the way, but now we're down to scraping the snow."

"Yup. Sounds 'bout the same. My wife, kids, and me, we're starting home as soon as the weather breaks. Even though we've got just about everything we need—except a doctor, that's one thing we're missing, but we make do—it's not home. It'll be nice to get home."

As Atticus and I work on skinning the deer, Gus talks about their plans for traveling. I only half listen, paying attention to my knife.

Before the apocalypse, my husband Dale hunted. I'd go with him, but rarely did any of the actual work of gutting or skinning. As part of the hunting team on the mountain, I learned to do it all.

Where Dale used to hang a deer for several days, and an elk for a couple of weeks, these days we get the skinning done, let it cool, and then move right to butchering.

Even on the mountain, where we needed at least two elk a week to keep our people fed, we didn't hang them for any length of time. We also culled cattle, sheep, goats, and pigs from the livestock people brought up the mountain. Same thing—hang the carcass until it was cool, then move on with it. We didn't want to risk any shrinkage or the meat freezing solid before we could cut it for use. And use it we did.

We practiced nose-to-tail methods to avoid waste. Organs, bones, muscle meat—all of it. We did avoid eating the elk brains, due to the possibility of Chronic Wasting Disease, a prion disease affecting cervids. The spinal column was also avoided for the same reason. A few in the community would've preferred all bones and organs were discarded because of CWD, but they were overruled. Besides, CWD isn't known to affect humans. Of course, neither was BSE, the prion disease found in cattle, which did jump to humans and is known as mad cow disease.

In addition to not using the spine and brain of elk, the community didn't hunt deer at all due to the number affected by CWD being so high. This part of Montana is also known to have CWD in deer.

But we need food.

PJ and I killed two deer on the mountain before leaving, processing the meat into jerky for travel. While the hunting crew didn't kill deer for community-wide use, there was no restriction on people harvesting for personal use. Our traveling group decided it was worth the risk of possibly consuming CWD-positive animals.

It's better than starving.

The biggest concern, which PJ and I discussed, is deer with the disease are carriers of it, and it'll spread easily to other deer and even elk—any cervids. Wild game is now our main source of protein. If the cervids die off because of CWD, what will we eat? We need a healthy deer herd to continue to feed us until things return to normal.

Apparently, the people living at the state park and in the town next door also have no such qualms of the possibility of eating prion-infected deer. We split the deer, and I offer them the heart while keeping the liver for our use. They also ask if they can have the hide for tanning and the goose feathers. It's an easy yes since there's no way we can take either with us while traveling.

"Looks like you guys might be stuck here for a day or two," Gus says. "The snow doesn't seem to have a mind to let up any time soon."

I glance at Atticus, who gives a weary nod.

"We'll let this deer hang overnight and cut it in the morning," Gus says. "You all can join us for dinner tomorrow night. We'll have a feast."

"Doing steaks?" PJ asks. "We can bring some from our supplies too."

"Nah, no need. My wife Ginger'll take care of it. We'll have enough."

Our tents, set up by the old farmhouse with our horses in a stand of trees nearby, are weighted down by the wet snow. I'm ready for this weather to end. It's so wet, we can't even keep a fire going, so we have a cold dinner in our tents.

Ripping off a hunk of jerky, Robyn lets out a sigh. "I'm getting anxious. Getting to my parents' house is starting to feel real, like we might actually make it."

I pat her hand in agreement. "I'm excited too. I can't wait to hold my son. I wonder how different he'll be now. It's been almost a year."

"He's fifteen?"

I let out a sigh. "Yeah. His birthday was October 5. Fifteen. It doesn't seem possible."

"I hope my parents are okay," she says wistfully.

"They're how old? Midfifties?" I ask.

"Dad's fifty-seven. Mom's sixty. They were both in great health, no medications or anything, so that's something. You know how we lost so many people who couldn't get their regular meds."

I give a nod. I don't really know since many of them died before I was an official part of the community. But even over the winter we had a few who passed due to age or frailty.

"My parents are so cute. They've been married forever but are still great together. My mom is so fun, almost like her namesake, Minnie Mouse."

"Your mom was named after Minnie Mouse?"

"Well, not really. Her real name is Miriam, but everyone calls her Minnie. Minnie and Von—that's my dad. Great names for great people. I can't wait to see them."

We spend several minutes in silence, each of us lost in our own thoughts.

"Should we read from the Bible?" Robyn asks. "Even though the others aren't with us . . . I'd like to. Would you?"

I give her a smile. We've developed a habit of reading a passage and then praying each morning before we leave for the day. And since we left Joliet, we've started finishing our day with a reading and prayer.

Bookends. That's what Kimba calls it. Starting and ending our day in the Word.

Not everyone in our group enjoys it. Leanne and Sadie often step away. Most of the time, Donnie goes with them. Occasionally, Jameson Dawson too. Surprisingly, Leanne is okay with her young son staying and participating.

I dig my Bible out of my pack. "What would you like to hear?"

"I don't know. I'm not very good at knowing the different verses, not like others in our group. You?"

"Not really. Should we just do what Kimba does when she's stumped for something to read? The Proverb of the day?"

"Sure. Today's the thirteenth of April, so Proverbs 13?"

I start reading. When I get to verse 18, Robyn stops me. "Can you read it again?"

"Whoever disregards discipline comes to poverty and shame, but whoever heeds correction is honored."

"That's one we should have Kimba read," she says. "Jameson Dawson really needs to hear it."

I give a slow nod. "He certainly has some attitude. And needs correction."

"His mom— " She shakes her head. "I know she's having a hard time, but she's shirking on her parenting duties something awful. And he takes advantage of it."

I go back to reading. A few passages later, the famous—or infamous, depending on your viewpoint—verse of whoever spares the rod hates their child comes up.

"See?" Robyn asks. "I don't think it's saying to beat your kid, but we should discipline them. We really need Kimba to read this."

"You and I may not think this verse is permission to beat a child," I say. "But I'm sure you could find many people who think it is."

"What are you saying?"

"Nothing. I'm just making a point. Victoria and Jameson do need to hear this passage, but unless they're ready to hear it . . . I don't think either will grasp the meaning."

We're both silent for a few moments. I'm mulling over the trouble with the Dawsons. I know they've had it rough. The things Victoria's husband did would be hard for anyone to move past. And her struggles are evident.

When I first met her, she was a well-groomed and attractive woman. Even though the EMP had hit, and the lights were out, she still wore makeup and nail polish. Her hair was combed and styled. She spoke in a slightly clipped manner with just a hint of an accent I couldn't quite place. In the weeks before Jon Dawson staged his coup, she started falling apart.

Now she'll go days without even combing her hair or cleaning up. Her hygiene is definitely lacking, to the point Jennifer Dosen mentioned it to her—not only because of odors but because there's a fear her skin could start breaking down from bacteria and she'd develop an infection. Something like that could be deadly in today's world. She no longer tries to hide her accent either. There's a definite Southern sound.

"Yeah, well, maybe," Robyn says, bringing the conversation back where we left it. "But something needs to be done about him. Jameson is trouble. He's almost as bad as Donnie. No, I take that back. Donnie can be a total snot, but he doesn't have a temper. Jameson runs on his emotions and flies off the handle over every little thing. He's— " She lowers her voice. "Sometimes he scares me."

"Jameson?"

She nods vigorously. "There's too much of his dad in him. And you know exactly what his dad did. He's a killer."

"And you think Jameson— "

"He's a bad seed."

After several beats of silence, as I consider how to respond, I decide to finish reading the Bible section. Closing The Book, I say, "He's still a child. While I agree he needs discipline and correction, I don't think he's like his dad."

She gives me a shrug. "Maybe he isn't. But he still scares me. He gets an angry look so often. Even though I'm taller than him, he's stronger. If he turned on me, he could hurt me. You too, probably. I'm glad Kimba and Rey have us doing the martial arts training. And the shooters training. I just wish my arm would finish healing so I could better participate."

"You think you need it to protect yourself from Jameson?"

"No, not just him. Also from things like what happened in Bridger. I know it's only a few days until I get to my parents' place, but it's a good idea to know how to . . . to defend myself, with a gun or with my hands. Don't you think?"

I agree, and I also agree the combat training we had on the mountain is important to keep up with. We've grown lax on our journey. Being attacked while on the road woke us up. Rey and Kimba have drilled into our brains to keep going until the threat is eliminated. I think we've all come to a point of understanding it's us or them.

Stop the threat or die.

Well, most of us. Victoria Dawson isn't interested in the training and won't touch a gun. Sebastian Monroe and Naomi Hoffmann, Kimba and Rey's youngest child, get self-defense training and have been taught how to use the .22 rifles, but not the handguns.

Jameson, who was all gung-ho on all of it, tried to skip training. According to him, he knows all he needs. He proved his point by punching his brother in the gut, which earned him a reprimand from Rey. Jameson clenched his fists before stomping off.

Robyn and I move on to talking about other things—her parents, my children, and anything else that comes up, even circling back to Jameson.

As our conversation begins to lag, she says, "We should pray. I'll do it." She asks for help with our travels and for her parents to be well before thanking God for getting us this far. She finishes with asking Him to help her be patient with Jameson and to not be so scared of him. After our amens, we chat a few more minutes before drifting off.

The next morning, the snow has stopped, but there's at least another foot on the ground. PJ has one of the rocket stoves going, cooking the deer and goose livers for breakfast. Nourishment, I remind myself, as my stomach curls at the smell. Butchering the deer goes quickly with the help of Gus, PJ, Atticus, and me.

"Yep, we'll have a real feast tonight," Gus says. "Ginger's excited to have you over."

When showing up at the appointed time, I'm slightly shocked at the historic home. There's no kitchen—not a real one, anyway—and the only heat is from a fireplace in the front room. The walls and windows are covered in a variety of fabrics and clothing to help insulate.

There's not much furniture, just a couch and a couple of chairs, but most everyone sits on piles of clothing on the floor, poofing the items up like beanbags. Even though it's warmer now than it has been during the long winter, even warmer than yesterday when the storm came up, it's not warm in the house.

"Welcome, welcome." Ginger flutters her hands, motioning us inside. "I'm so glad to have new people to talk with. We all are." She gestures at the other two women; one is the woman who went hunting yesterday. "It's especially nice to have other ladies here."

Over a dinner of deer roast, stewed goose legs, stewed wild rabbit, corn mush, and stewed dried plums—all cooked in the open fireplace—we visit.

"So you're going to Billings?" Ginger asks.

"Lockwood," Robyn answers. "My parents are there."

"Lockwood?" Gus asks, alarm lacing his voice. "Is that— "

"I think it is," one of the others from his group says.

Ginger nods. "It was Lockwood."

"What was Lockwood?" Rey asks. As is his habit when meeting new people, his British accent gives way to a Midwest American intonation, something left over from his previous profession as a spy, I guess. It seems both he and his wife Kimba are chameleons of sorts.

Gus tugs on his beard. "They were talking about Lockwood at the farmers' market last week."

"The week before." Ginger smiles.

"The week before," Gus says. "Jared Goes Ahead— "

"No." Ginger shakes her head. "It was Marvin Bird Hat."

"Okay. Anyway, he said they had a couple come through talking about troubles in Lockwood. I'm sure it was Lockwood."

"It was," Ginger says patiently.

"Right. We're not from here, so it's sometimes hard to keep the towns straight. Did I tell you we— " he motions to Ginger and their three children, all under the age of eight " —were on vacation when things went crazy?"

"Us too," the man we hunted with yesterday says while his wife gestures her agreement. "Them too." He points to the final couple, a quiet pair who've yet to add much to the conversation. "All of us were on vacation and are now being treated like family by the townsfolk."

"Yep." Gus smiles. "We thought it'd be smart to get off the main road. Figured they'd maybe even have fuel. But anyway, that's how we all got here, stranded now until we can walk out. Maybe the president— "

"Lockwood?" Robyn asks, urging him on.

"Oh, yup. Marvin had to show me where it was on a map. Not even forty miles away from here, where it's peaceful and quiet with everyone helping everyone. Not there, though. They've got trouble. The couple called it a siege."

"A siege?" Robyn asks, leaning forward. "Meaning?"

"That part was a little unclear. Seems there's some sort of barricade around the town."

"Maybe they're keeping out the riffraff," PJ suggests. "We've seen that in our travels."

"That's what Marvin thought." Gus bobs his head. "But the couple said people can't leave either. And the ones controlling the barricade are some sort of gang members."

"Warlords," Ginger declares. "The woman said it was like a foreign country, with guns mounted on the back of pickups."

"Really?" Rey asks, his voice dripping with skepticism.

Kimba gives a slight shake of her head.

Ginger shrugs. "She said the people who live there— " She breaks off and looks at Robyn.

"What?" Robyn prods.

"They're being kept hostage. Used as slaves. The warlord or whatever is making a play to takeover Billings from whoever is in control now. Lockwood is the staging area."

"Who *is* in control of Billings?" Rey asks, while Robyn seems to shrink within herself, a tear running down her cheek.

"As far as we know, it's a divided town," Gus says. "There's several different factions in charge, depending on the area. Even the legitimate government has a piece. It's quite the mess for sure. I'd steer clear."

"My parents . . . " Robyn lifts a hand.

"We'll figure it out." Kimba pats Robyn's leg. "Right, Rey?"

He gives a slow nod. "We'll do what we can."

Chapter 4

The storm kept us at Chief Plenty Coups for an extra day. We've been back on the road for two days and have been making good time. The warm wind at our back seems to spur us on. On to what, we don't know. The news of Lockwood hangs over us.

"Mrs. Rochelle? What's today's date?" Sebastian asks as he helps me set up the last tent. We've taken to dividing up duties around camp. The youngest children, Nicole Hoffmann, and I set up camp, while PJ, Donnie, and Jennifer goose hunt. Rey and Kimba patrol the area to ensure we're alone. Everyone else is gathering water from the partially frozen creek, while the horses enjoy a patch of fresh grass as they're secured to highlines—a length of rope stretching between the trees along the creek.

"Do you remember what Kimba said this morning? It's April 17."

"I like that we keep a calendar." He gives me a wide smile. "When we were walking with Mr. Ben before—you know, before we got to Wyoming—we didn't know what day it was. In school on the mountain, the teacher had someone change the calendar each day. That was my favorite part. It's nice to know what day it is. I hope there's school in Lewistown. Do you think there is?"

"Probably of some sort. The towns we've been through on this trip have school for those your age. Gus and Ginger's little boy said his mom teaches him, right?"

"I liked it at the Chief Plenty Coups place and the town next to it. It's pretty there, and everyone was nice. Too bad my mom didn't want to stay. We'd be done walking."

"It'll be good for you to get to where your family is." I smile and pat his shoulder.

"I guess." He drops his head. "I don't know my aunt, though. My mom used to work there over the summer when she was young."

"She worked for your aunt?" I ask, crinkling my brow.

"Mm-hmm. She and her husband own a hotel. But her husband died, so now it's just Auntie taking care of it. Mom said it was a little like the lodge we lived in on the mountain, but much nicer. She helped clean rooms or worked in the restaurant. She talked about it a lot, and we were always supposed to visit but never did. Not after I was born anyway. She took Sadie there a couple of times, but that was years and years before my mom had me."

"Years and years, huh?" I ask, raising an eyebrow at the whimsical boy. He certainly has a way of telling a story.

"She was as old as me when I was born." Sebastian gets an odd look on his face. "I mean, um, almost."

"Sadie?" I let out a light laugh. "She's twelve and you're eight. What's twelve minus eight?"

"Oh, um, four."

"Right. Maybe we should work on some math while we're traveling, have school on the road."

"I just forgot how old she's supposed to be."

"What do you mean?"

He shakes his head. "Did you see the little animal Asher is whittling for me? It's going to be a horse. He looks a little like your horse."

"I didn't see it, but I know he's very good. I'm sure he'll make it look just like Lucky." The A Boys all find things to do to occupy their time when we're sitting around, not that spare time is abundant with keeping watch, preparing meals, and gathering water. But the three of them always have some project going.

"He's going to teach me how to whittle too. I'm going to make a present for Sadie for her birthday."

"That sounds wonderful. When's her birthday?"

"In May. May 19. We should be in Lewistown by then. Maybe we can even have a cake for her."

I give him a small smile. "That'd be nice."

"What if Mom's auntie doesn't like me?"

"Oh, they'll like you. You're a wonderful boy."

In a very quiet voice, he asks, "What if she doesn't like my mom anymore? She's not very nice, not like she used to be."

I drop to my knees and meet his eyes. "She's family. She'll remember the love she has for your mom, and maybe that love will help your mom too. I know things have been rough for her, for all of you, and it's hard to remember how things were, how we used to be before."

"She needs God again. She doesn't like Him anymore because of the bad things that happened, the things she had to do to keep us safe."

I choose my words carefully. "We each need God."

Like his mom, I had my own time of rebellion when I thought God had turned His back on me, leaving me and my girls to survive on our own during terrible circumstances.

"When bad things happen, it's hard to not blame God for allowing those things. I did that too. My daughter Cheyre helped me to remember how much God loves me."

He gives a vigorous bob of his head. "I pray for my mom. For Sadie too. But I don't tell them. I don't think they'd like to know . . . you know, since they're mad at God."

"Praying is important."

"The snow melted a lot today," he says, abruptly changing the subject as he looks around.

Yesterday, the warm wind started in the afternoon and blew all night. When we climbed out of our tents this morning, there were new drifts and plenty of bare ground. By midday, those near the end of the skinning track were seeing pavement, as the tracks disturbed what little snow remained on the asphalt and the road absorbed the heat from the sun.

After lunch, the skis were attached to the sleds, and everyone changed into insulated boots for walking. Because of the occasional drift or ice patch, they continued to use their poles for balance.

"It sure did. How'd it feel to walk instead of being on the skis?"

"Weird. One of my boots hurt my foot a little."

"Was it rubbing?"

"Maybe." Sebastian shrugs.

"Have a seat and take your boot off." I motion to a bare spot on the ground that looks fairly dry.

"Will it be harder to get water without the snow on the ground?" he asks as he unlaces his insulated boot.

"Easier. With the creeks thawing, we'll be able to just dip it out. There're lots of creeks around here, so we'll have it made."

"I know that's what Mom and the others are doing now, but what about in other places? Between here and my auntie's house, there aren't many creeks. Mom says it might be dry like the desert."

"It'll be the rainy season soon. That'll help. You'll be able to collect rainwater, which, in many ways, is much easier than melting snow. Plus, we usually have snow in April and even into May, so there's a chance of more. We'll probably figure out a way to collect it since spring snow has a high water content and doesn't always stay on the ground for long."

"Less snow is good." He smiles. "It's not as cold, and our tents won't always be wet. Mom makes us take our boots off outside, but our pant legs still have snow on them. And the tent is always wet in the morning. Condensation, that's what Mom calls it."

"These dry days have been nice. Maybe the tents will even dry out. Mine's starting to smell like mildew." I make a face, which Sebastian mimics. "And as warm as it is, we won't need to wear as many layers. That'll be nice too."

I motion to the rope strung between two tents, weighted down with snow pants and parkas. The jackets were shed early in the day, with almost everyone wearing a sweater while walking.

The three sleds being pulled by the A twins and Brett Dawson were overloaded with winter gear, crammed wherever they'd fit, with skis strapped on top. PJ made a comment about looking like the Beverly Hillbillies, which was lost on the young men.

Once we're on fully bare pavement, using the sleds will become a challenge. There're already discussions about what we'll do for alternatives.

"Sadie gets too cold." Sebastian's voice is low as his eyes travel to the other side of the camp. His sister is with Nicole and Naomi Hoffmann, sitting by the small camp stoves as they cook meat from the deer over the grill grates.

With the cold nights, we decided to freeze it and thought it'd be okay for a while. But after last night and today, it became obvious we wouldn't be able to keep it frozen. They'll cook it past well done to remove as much moisture as possible so it'll keep. It won't be like our smoked jerky, but it should still give us several days of freshness if it's kept deep in our packs and cool.

"Sadie doesn't have enough fat, that's why she's so cold. Mrs. Jennifer always makes sure we eat, all three of us, so we can put on weight. And I think I'm getting stronger. I'm walking more now and don't need to ride. Do you think so?"

"Definitely. You and Sadie are both walking more. But any time you need a ride, you just tell me. Lucky likes you and your sister a lot."

"Okay. Mom doesn't like us being fussed over. She doesn't like Mrs. Jennifer doing it. Mom should probably ride more, but you know she doesn't want to. She likes to be strong. I like Mrs. Jennifer giving us food. She's a nice lady, and so are you."

"And you are a sweet boy." I pull him into a hug. "And it's definitely working. There's more of you to hug than there was when we left the mountain just a few short weeks ago. Must be all the geese we're eating." The words are barely out of my mouth when a shotgun sounds in the distance, followed by a second retort.

"More geese?" Sebastian asks.

"Most likely. Want to try your boot and see if the adjustments I made help?"

He spends a few minutes getting his foot back in the boot and walking around.

"Seems good." He nods.

"Great. If it bothers you again, let me know. We don't want you getting a blister. Should we help the girls? We need to get all the meat cooked tonight."

"At least some of it's still frozen," he says, as we walk over to his sister and the Hoffmann girls.

"How's it going?" I ask Nicole.

"It's going okay. Should we dig a firepit? It sounds like they got a goose. We could cook it in the pit."

"I think they got two gooses." Naomi holds up her fingers.

"Geese," her sister corrects.

"Probably a good idea," I agree. "I'll get it started."

Our fires are a double-hole system, often called a Dakota fire pit, having one hole for the fire and the second for a draft, with a tunnel connecting the two. Digging down through the snow and into the ground is the first obstacle. In some places, the ground is so frozen we can't get a decent hole, and digging two becomes nearly impossible. But once it's dug out and the two holes are connected, it burns efficiently and creates little smoke. Both are important.

Using as little firewood as possible is helpful, and not attracting attention with our smoke is part of our plan. Combined with camping off the road and, when possible, avoiding towns or people, we're able to be stealthy.

Now that we're getting closer to Lockwood, and there's the possibility of the town being in peril, we're talking about additional security measures. The closer we get, the more houses we expect to see. Houses always make us nervous.

This road from Pryor was much more populated than the previous road we were on. Earlier today, we went through a little enclave of a dozen or so homes. There wasn't any sort of sign indicating it was a town. We came down a hill, and there it was. A man stepped out of his house, shotgun by his hip. With a snarl to his lip, he said, "Just keep walking, and there won't be any trouble."

We did, and there wasn't.

Our plan for Lockwood is to camp outside of town and send in a group of scouts to determine the situation. Those staying in camp will forgo the fire and not hunt. Building up our food stores now for those times is also important.

"We'll be ghosts," Rey said, borrowing a term from Scruff. We traveled with Scruff for several days until he was injured in the Bridger incident—when Robyn hurt her arm and Donnie was shot in the head. Scruff was shot in the leg, requiring weeks or maybe even months of healing. He stayed in Bridger, encouraging us to continue without him.

While we were at Chief Plenty Coups, Robyn took her arm out of the sling. She's considerably better but still has a limited range of motion before it causes her pain. She's doing some gentle stretches with it, but I'll often hear a gasp of discomfort with her movements.

Donnie still complains of an occasional headache, and the scar on his head is puckered and pink. And his hand still looks awful. I've noticed he doesn't use it much, obviously favoring his other. At least he wasn't shot in his dominant hand.

I'm digging the draft hole for the firepit when a scream pierces the air, followed by cries for help.

"On the ground!" I order the kids, as my hand goes to the Glock 20 on my hip.

Nicole follows suit, pulling the pistol from her holster and moving onto a knee, muzzle aimed at the ground in low ready.

My rifle is in its scabbard inside my tent. I look to the cluster of trees where the horses are. All three have their ears back, looking in the direction of the cries for help. To their right, Kimba is sprinting toward us.

I lift a hand. "We're okay. It wasn't us."

She puts the radio to her mouth, motioning as she speaks. "Who was it?" Kimba asks when she's close enough not to yell.

"Must be the water gatherers. With the hill between us and them . . . " I lift my hands.

"I'll find out. You're okay here?" she asks, her eyes darting from me to her daughters.

"We're okay, Mom," Nicole answers, while I nod my agreement.

I point to her radio. "Where's Rey?"

"He's coming from the east. Have any of the water gatherers returned?"

I give a slight shake of my head. Suspecting Kimba's asking about her son, I specify, "Nate's still with them. How about our hunters?"

"Don't know. Send them toward us if they appear," she says as she turns to leave.

"Where do you want us?" I ask, while Sadie, her voice barely a whisper, asks, "Are we under attack?"

"I don't know what's happening. Stay here and be ready. We'll figure out what's going on." Then Kimba runs off.

"Is the meat almost done?" I ask.

Sadie is staring at Kimba, straining to look beyond, maybe in the direction of where her mom is.

"Sadie?" I ask. "Can you keep the meat cooking? As soon as it's finished, take it off and don't start a new batch."

"Y-yes. Okay."

"Is my mom okay?" Sebastian asks.

"Kimba and Rey will find out."

"Shouldn't we help them?"

"You heard my mom," Naomi says, sounding older than her seven years. "She told us to wait here."

Please, God, please keep us safe. Help our friends with whatever is happening there. I send my silent petitions heavenward. "We'll be ready if they need us."

Sebastian moves close to his sister, his bottom lip quivering.

"We're okay," Sadie whispers.

Within a few minutes, PJ, Jennifer, and Donnie come into view across the field. From their casual stride, it's obvious they didn't hear the calls for help.

"Should I run and tell them?" Nicole asks.

I chew the inside of my mouth as I consider the best course of action. "Let them come to us. Without another radio to contact your parents, it's best we stay here, where your mom left us."

She gives a shake of her head. "Them too?"

"No. Us. They'll do what they must." With my eyes on PJ, I wait until he lifts his head, then I wave my arms to capture his attention. He turns to Donnie, handing off the goose he's carrying, before breaking into a run with Jennifer by his side. Carrying two good-sized geese, Donnie does more of a fast walk.

"What is it?" PJ asks, out of breath.

I shake my head. "We don't know. There were calls for help."

"What? Who was calling for help?" Jennifer pants.

"Our people? I don't really know."

"My mom!" Sebastian cries. "I think it was my mom yelling."

Sadie eyes are wide as she pulls her brother toward her.

Taking several steps, Jennifer cries out. Her three sons are part of the water crew.

"Wait," PJ says, reaching for her arm. "Where are Rey and Kimba?"

"Kimba was here," I answer. "She called Rey on the radio."

"What's up?" Donnie asks, as he approaches camp.

PJ quickly fills him in.

"Let's go." Donnie hefts the geese to his other shoulder.

"Slowly," PJ says. "We don't know the situation or where the Hoffmanns are. Let's approach with caution. Rochelle? You're okay?"

"Fine. Leave the geese."

"Don't worry about them right now," Donnie says, giving me a look like I'm daft.

"We won't. I was just reminding you you're still holding them."

He drops the birds to the ground. "You think someone fell in?"

"Fell in?" I repeat.

"The creek."

I shake my head. "I don't . . . I didn't think of that."

"Get the meat off the heat and start warming up some water," Donnie says. "If someone went for a swim, they'll be chilled to the bone."

Jennifer's eyes go wide. "Let's go."

"Here they come." PJ motions toward the north as a head pops over the knoll. "It's Kimba and Nate."

"Where are my sons?" Jennifer breaks into a sprint, with Donnie right behind her.

"Do you see my mom?" Sebastian asks, jumping to his feet and stretching onto his tippy toes.

"Is my brother okay?" Naomi asks, copying Sebastians movements.

PJ starts toward the group. Yelling over his shoulder, he says, "Hot water is a good idea."

Since they were gathering water, they took one of our sleds and the empty containers. We only have a two-gallon jug and a couple of individual bottles that get carried in the backpacks.

"You want me to get the soup pot?" Sebastian asks.

"Please," I respond, watching as Jennifer meets Victoria Dawson, her youngest son leaning heavily against her. Atticus is right behind her, carrying someone. I squint slightly to make out who it is.

"That's my mom." Sebastian quickly stands.

"Just wait," I say.

"Is she— "

"She doesn't look good," Naomi says. "She's all wet and just . . . limp."

I take a deep breath. She doesn't look good. Not only is she wet, but so is Atticus.

"Please, Lord, please. Let everyone be okay," I whisper.

Louder, I say, "Hurry. Let's get the water going. Take the meat off, and we'll work on it later. Nicole, can you get another fire going? I was working on the draft hole. Finish it and get it burning." I get to work as I give the orders, quickly grabbing the soup pot and a small tea kettle, filling one then the other and getting them over the heat as soon as Sadie has the meat pulled off the grill.

"Nate?" Naomi cries, running to her mom and brother as they get close to camp. "Are you hurt?"

Nate nods. "Cold. Robyn . . . she's not so good."

My eyes dart to Kimba, who gives a small shake of her head.

My breathing turns shallow. "We have water started. Is . . . Leanne?"

Kimba sends a small smile to Sebastian and Sadie. "She's a hero. She wouldn't get out of the water until she had Robyn. Brett and Atticus are helping her. They'll all be here shortly, and everyone will love something hot. Victoria's the only one who didn't fall in."

"The ice gave way. We thought we were on the bank, but— " Nate shakes his head. "Victoria grabbed me and didn't let me float away."

"You're okay, right?" Naomi asks.

"He'll be okay." Kimba touches her young daughter's cheek. "He needs dry clothes and a hot fire."

"Yeah," he replies through chattering teeth. "It's not as warm when you're wet."

PJ's carrying Robyn. Leanne is now mostly upright, attempting to walk as she leans heavily on Rey. She's a terrible ghostly gray, and her lips are almost white.

"Rochelle?" PJ calls as he stops at my tent, the one I share with Robyn. "Can you help me with her?"

"Is she—?" I ask as I hustle toward him.

"She's breathing—now."

"Now?"

As bad as Leanne looks, Robyn looks much worse. Her breathing is so shallow I can't even see her chest move.

"Are you sure?"

"Yeah. But . . . " He lowers his voice. "She was under too long. I don't know . . . " He shakes his head.

"Do you want to put her in the tent?"

"Get dry clothes and her bedding. Let's put her by the fire."

I quickly grab my quilt from the tent and put it on the ground. PJ gently lays her on the blanket.

"Should I help?" PJ asks.

I start to unzip her soaked sweatshirt. "Send Kimba or one of the other women over, please."

Victoria, guiding her wet sons to the tent the boys share, assures me she'll be right over to help. Jennifer promises the same.

I cover Robyn with part of the quilt, then remove her shoes and socks. Once the other women have made sure their sons are in dry clothing, the three of us work together to keep Robyn covered while removing her sodden garments. We put dry sweats and a shirt on her, then wrap her in her dry quilt.

"I'll hang the blanket to dry," Jennifer says.

"Should one of us crawl in next to her?" Victoria asks.

"What?" I ask.

"Body heat. It'll warm her better."

"I don't know. Let's move her by the fire."

While we were changing Robyn, Rey started a huge fire, not bothering with the small firepit.

"Will she be okay?" Nate asks after PJ and Rey position her near the flames.

"We're praying she will be," Kimba answers.

"Atticus gave her mouth-to-mouth."

My eyes dart to Atticus. He's wearing a dry jacket and has another draped across his lap, his hair slicked back and wet, as he sips from a metal cup. The rest of those who were wet look similar to him, with blankets, sleeping bags, or coats draped around them. All look not only damp but also exhausted, and most are shivering.

"Should she have tea?" Naomi asks.

"She'll choke." Donnie shakes his head. "She's unconscious. Maybe in a coma."

I look to Kimba. Her eyes are moist. "Other than trying to warm her up, I don't know what to do."

"Now's a good time," Leanne says through chattering teeth, "to see if that God you all keep praying to cares enough to do something."

Chapter 5

A new day dawns overcast and cool with a slight chilling breeze, the mountains in the distance sporting a fresh coat of snow. I'm back to wearing my heavy coat and a stocking cap as I sit by the fire for breakfast—fried goose and a cup of peppermint tea.

It's been three days since Robyn fell in the creek and nearly drowned. As Leanne suggested, we've been praying for a miracle. I'm hopeful our prayers are being answered. Yesterday, Robyn finally stirred. It wasn't much, just a slight moaning sound and some weird rapid breathing. Then, several hours later, I looked over and her eyes were open.

"Robyn," I said. "Hey, are you awake?"

Her eyes opened a little wider, then fluttered a few times before she went back to her dreamland—or wherever she is.

While everyone in the Bakerville militia was given basic first aid training, it was focused on gunshot wounds and falls that resulted in sprains or broken bones. We were given extremely limited information about hypothermia, with most of what we learned concentrating on how to stay warm in cold weather and avoid frostbite. We had zero training on drowning.

Kimba and Rey, from their previous careers in clandestine government services, know slightly more than the rest of us, as does PJ from a lifetime of hunting in subzero temperatures. But caring for a near-drowning victim is entirely new for all of us.

When Atticus gave her mouth-to-mouth, it took a few breaths, but she responded well by expelling the water she'd taken in. But the amount of time she was under . . . I just don't know.

Everyone who was there agrees it was several minutes. We all fear the worse: she was under so long that her brain may have been deprived of oxygen. Brain damage! That was bad enough before the EMP, when she could be treated in a hospital. But what do we do here in the countryside, set up in tents?

The day after it happened, Rey and Donnie walked back to the hamlet where the man had told us to keep walking. Our hope was they had a doctor there who'd be willing to help us treat her, or at least tell us how to help.

The guy was plenty gruff when Rey and Donnie first showed up, but after learning of our situation, he softened. They don't have a doctor, though. And he told us going to Billings would be a waste of time with the way the city is in turmoil. The nearest town, Pryor, which we'd already passed through, also didn't have a doctor. Our best bet, according to him, was to go back to where we came from. Rey didn't tell him we've been walking for weeks.

When they returned to camp, we decided we'd pack up the next day and keep going, trying to get her to her parents' place in Lockwood. We don't know what we'll find there, if the city is truly under siege, but we must do something to find her help.

Leanne started coughing that evening. Within an hour, she'd developed a fever and the chills. We can only assume she has some sort of infection or pneumonia from her time in the freezing water.

Just in case it's something contagious, we've kept her children in a different tent and limit who cares for her. Donnie insists on helping her with anything she's comfortable with. Besides him, it's mainly been Jennifer taking care of Leanne, with Victoria filling in as needed. Not that there's much anyone can do for her.

While the medical team on the mountain sent us with a first aid kit, it's basic and doesn't include antibiotics, an item in short supply. They sent us with a generous amount of pain relievers, but we've gone through most of those from the gunshot wounds Donnie received.

We have something that would help reduce her fever, but letting her body do its best to fight the infection seems to be the best course of action for now. Besides, she refused the pills, saying her children may need them before they get where they're going.

Everyone else is recovering from the ordeal without incident. After Nate Hoffmann's brief description of what occurred, the details were filled in by the others. Everyone thought they were on the bank, on solid ground, when they were really on a sheet of ice. There was no advanced warning, just a loud groan filling the air before the platform immediately gave way.

They were using a bucket-brigade method to retrieve water, with three of them—Atticus, Robyn, and Brett Dawson—dipping in the containers and then handing to people behind them. Victoria was placing a water jug on the sled, having just taken it from Nate, when the ice moved. She was on the edge of the crack, stable enough to keep her balance. With quick thinking on her part, she grabbed Nate by the arm as he dangled in the water. Everyone else was already in the swift-moving creek.

The only reason we didn't lose anyone was because the water wasn't overly deep, plus there was plenty of brush and trees growing along the edge of a gentle bank just downstream from where they went in. And everyone was helping each other.

Leanne saw Robyn slide under a slab of ice on the other side. As Victoria pulled out a sopping wet Nate, Atticus and Brett helped the other boys to the edge, making sure they had ahold of solid branches. Atticus told Brett to stay with them, as Victoria offered a hand to drag them out, while Atticus went back for Leanne and Robyn.

Leanne was hanging on the ice shelf, wiping her saturated hair out of her eyes. "I can't find her," she said. "It's not deep, but she must be stuck or . . . I don't know."

Atticus went under, unable to see anything in the murky water. When he came back up, gasping for air, Leanne said, "I'll go again. We'll take turns."

Leanne found a foot. Pulling her up, she passed her off to Atticus, who took her to the treed area where the rest were able to get out. He thought Leanne was behind him, but she was so exhausted from the efforts and the cold, she was clinging to the ice shelf.

Brett, still standing in the creek to help as needed, went after Leanne, dragging her to the gentle bank.

Rey and Kimba showed up shortly afterward to help everyone get back to camp.

With Leanne sick, we've lost any hope of traveling as a group. While we may be able to move an unconscious Robyn in the largest of the three sleds, it's doubtful Leanne could handle much movement. No one voices it, but I think we all know—including Leanne—things aren't looking good. She needs a miracle.

Barring the miracle, our plan is to separate. Several of us will continue on to Lockwood, in hopes of finding help for Robyn, while the rest remain with Leanne. Today, Rey and Kimba are scouting for a better place for them to stay.

"Rochelle?" Victoria calls from my tent, where she's sitting with Robyn while I take a break. "Her eyes are open!"

I stumble to my feet and race the few yards to the open tent flap. As I scoot inside, I call out, "Robyn!" I'm excited to see my friend's beautiful green eyes again. While the color is as lovely as ever, when I say her name, I only get a flutter of her eyelids, just like before.

"Robyn?" I try again, touching her hand. Her usually expressive eyes are dull, staring at something unknown. I get a sudden memory of a baby doll I had as a child. When I sat her up, her eyes opened but they were, of course, blank. Doll eyes.

"I don't think— "

"She's not awake," PJ says, kneeling just inside the tent. "Her eyes may be open, but . . . " He lets out a long, slow breath.

"Maybe she just needs a little more time," Victoria suggests. "Sleep is healing, right? Isn't that what they say?"

I drop my head. "Maybe so. Can you help me with her?"

"Time to change her?"

I give a slight nod, then quickly look to PJ. He gets the message and backs out of the tent, zipping it to give us privacy. The tiny tent is too small for the three of us, but Victoria's help will make it go quicker.

Although Robyn's unconscious or whatever, her basic functions seem to be intact. Her breathing, which was slow at first, seems fine now. And her heart rate is somewhat normal, maybe a little slow but not terribly so.

We can also give her broth and water without trouble. She seems to know to open her mouth when her lips are touched, and she even swallows most of the time. It's sometimes a messy process, but I think she's getting some nourishment and fluids, at least based on what's coming out. Not a lot there either, but some.

I'll admit, I was shocked to discover she's still urinating. I realize now that I should've expected it and prepared for it from the beginning. After the first time she soaked her dry clothes, I tore up my bedsheet, folding it to make it as thick and absorbent as possible.

Other than rinsing out our undergarments and socks, we don't really do laundry while on the road. Yeah, we're pretty much filthy, with less than pleasant aromas.

After falling in the creek, the clothes being worn dried out and still stunk like mildew and dead fish. Everything got washed. I even took advantage of being here for a few days and washed my own disgusting clothes.

And now, with Robyn's new needs, we're cleaning the make-do diapers over the campfire in a much too small pot, using too little of our precious soap just to try and keep the stench down and prevent additional illness.

Robyn's eyes are shut again when we begin our task of making her more comfortable. As we work, Victoria asks, "Any change in Leanne?"

"Nothing good."

"Do you think . . ."

I shake my head. "I don't want to think about it."

"What will we do with her children?"

"I heard Kimba tell Rey that Leanne made her write down her aunt's name and address. Then she made Kimba promise she'd take them there."

"So, she knows?"

I swallow hard as tears fill my eyes. I shake my head in lieu of answering.

"And what about her?" Victoria lifts her chin toward Robyn. "Do you know where her parents live?"

"Other than in Lockwood?"

"Right. Do you know their address—or their names?"

"Von and Minnie."

"At least those aren't common. Maybe we'll be able to find them. Assuming . . ."

"Assuming we can figure out how to get her there . . . the sled seems like a terrible idea to try and take her that far."

"Not only that," Victoria says, "but what if the rumors are correct? If their city is under siege, then what do we do? It was different when she was well. She could've decided on her own what was best, right? Now someone has to decide for her." Victoria shakes her head. "We don't even know if her parents are alive."

"It's a risk. This entire trip is a risk. When we left the mountain, we all knew we were going into the unknown. And we knew it could be dangerous. Look at you, Victoria. You took such a leap of faith. Have you ever even been to Great Falls before?"

"Simms."

"Pardon?"

"They live west of Great Falls, in a little town called Simms."

"Okay. The way they talk about their place, I guess I knew it wasn't *in* Great Falls since they have cattle."

"Right. And to answer your question, I have been to Great Falls. But never to Simms. Jennifer said their place sits on the Sun River."

"It sounds lovely."

"Yes . . . but . . ."

I stop what I'm doing and look at Victoria, waiting for her to continue.

She shrugs. "It's really for the boys. My boys and her boys get along great, even after what happened. Jennifer . . . she . . . I don't think she blames me for her sister's death. But I think she believes I could've stopped Jon from doing what he did. Oh, she tells me she's forgiven him and wants me and the boys to stay with them, to have a fresh start, but . . ."

I give a slow nod. "But you don't believe her?"

"How can I?" she whispers. "My husband is responsible for not only the death of her sister but also many others—all innocents. Even his death in the process wasn't justice for many people living on the mountain. They'd happily have me serve any sentence they could think of."

"Jennifer isn't like some of the others. I'll admit, I don't know her well, didn't really know her at all until we started planning this trip, but I believe she's a woman of her word. If she says she's forgiven your husband, she has. And if she says she wants to help you and your sons, she does. She's . . . " I take in a breath while I consider my words. "Jesus shines through her."

With moist eyes, Victoria meets my gaze. "I've never really understood that phrase. I mean, I've known lots of church people. Jon and I even attended most weeks. That was . . . I hate to say it, but it wasn't because we wanted to be there. I didn't anyway. It was a networking event for Jon. He thought people would think better of him if he was a churchgoer."

I make a noise of agreement.

"But with Jennifer, I can see it. I can see Him, see Jesus through her. Even when . . . it wasn't long after her sister was killed that she searched me out, asking if I was all right. We'd been friendly before, close enough to talk regularly anyway. And her sons, they were there right away for Brett and Jameson. I think— " She abruptly stops talking and takes a clean washcloth, dampens it from a water bottle, and starts wiping Robyn's face.

"You think . . . ?"

"You experienced it, too, right? The glares and . . . and judgment? The way some of them would go out of their way to say or do hurtful things?"

"The people on the mountain?"

She dips her head, seeming to shrink into herself.

"Yeah, some," I answer. "Even though most people knew my girls and I were brought there against our will, there were still some who seemed to blame me for Fred's disappearance. For the men he killed."

"They blamed you for . . . for what exactly?"

I lift a shoulder. "I'm not entirely sure. I think— " I take in a breath. "I think there were some people, friends of his, who didn't believe . . . um, who found it hard to believe . . . "

"That he was involved in human trafficking? That Fred Lassiter purchased you and your children and forced you to marry him?"

I tilt my head to the side as my eyes fill with tears.

"I'll never understand people. Even with the evidence . . . " She shakes her head. "Will you stay in Bakerville after you return with your son?"

"I'm not sure. We have our place in Lander. Christopher may want to run our ranch."

"If I were you, I'd go home to Lander in a heartbeat. Bakerville's too cliquish. We lived there for three years and were still outcasts. Even though Jon was running for County Commissioner before this all happened, before the attacks and everything falling apart, we weren't really a part of the community. We'd moved from Prospect you know. That was where his support was from, especially since he was still working there."

Victoria continues talking about their life before the attacks and how she never really wanted to move to Bakerville but, when her husband bought the land and started building their new house, which sounds more like a mansion than a house, she kept quiet.

"I thought I was doing the right thing, being the dutiful wife. But it's brought me nothing but trouble. And now, with Jameson . . . " Victoria's voice drifts off as we continue our duty.

As we finish with Robyn, Victoria crosses her arms. "It wouldn't have mattered anyway. Jon didn't listen to me. He was in charge, and that was that. But now, I'm the one who decides what we're doing. Brett and Jameson talked with me about it, but I'm the one who made the decision to accept Jennifer's offer." Her eyes are hard. Determined.

"It'll be a new life for you."

She lets out a slow breath. "Yes. And I'm grateful for it. Do you think this is God's work?"

"What do you mean?"

"Rochelle!" PJ hisses. "Walkers on the road."

Victoria's eyes go wide. "What do we do?"

"One of you stay with Robyn. We need the other one in with Leanne while Jennifer takes the children to hide. The rest of us . . . we'll do what's needed."

"I'll go to Leanne," Victoria offers.

"Do you want my pistol?" I ask. "I have my rifle." I motion to the scabbard sitting next to me.

Her eyes go wide. She shakes her head and motions with her hands as she unzips the tent. "I hate those things. Besides, maybe they're friendly."

"Let's pray so," I whisper as she scoots out. As I begin to rezip the tent, my hands are shaking so badly I struggle with the process. Should I leave it open? Then I'd have a quicker escape if needed. But what about Robyn? I can't just leave her here.

Other than those in towns or communities, we've seen very few people on this trip—very few groups on the road since we left the mountain. Of course, we never did see the people shooting at us between the small town of Edgar and Chief Plenty Coups State Park.

With the weather warming and the snow clearing, we talked about this, about how we're likely to see people on the road and how some may have nefarious intentions. Jennifer reminded us we need to show hospitality to strangers, as we may be entertaining angels.

Donnie quickly rebutted, while stroking the scar above his ear, saying that strangers have guns. And many have no qualms in using them.

With the tent door half open, I sit next to Robyn, my Glock on my lap. "Don't worry, my friend," I whisper. "I won't leave you."

The wait is grueling. Even with the chill of the morning, nervousness brings a trickle of sweat to my brow. The wind is rustling the tent fabric, but it's suddenly stifling hot. I focus on keeping my breathing even, and just as I'm about to unzip the mesh-covered window, a shadow crosses the fabric. My heart instantly beats faster.

"We're okay," a youngish male voice says. "They're friendly."

"Thank God," I say.

"Yeah," Axel, the youngest of the A Boys, answers. "And one of them worked in a hospital. He's going to check on Leanne first, then he'll see Robyn."

"A hospital? Really? How . . . that's amazing."

"A miracle." He smiles.

My eyes fill with tears. "Did you hear that, Robyn?" Her eyes are open again, slight slits as she stares into nothingness. "There's a nurse or maybe even a doctor. We'll get some answers about how to help you."

"Oh, and Rochelle?" Axel says. "We'll have some weather soon."

"Snow?"

"Maybe. Atticus thinks so. Right now, it feels like rain. But the temp's dropping, and the wind's picking up."

"Atticus seems to know these things."

"Yeah. Our dad called him the weatherman. Even when he was young—younger than Sebastian—he seemed to know."

"Did someone go after the children?" I ask.

"Asher did. They're on their way back now. I can see them."

A few minutes later, a man sticks his head in the partially opened flap of my tent. His watery blue eyes show the exhaustion his voice carries. "I'm David. May I come in?"

"Please. Do you want me to step out? It's pretty tight in here."

"I might need your help," he says as he undoes the flap. "We'll make it work."

I have my doubts when I see the size of him. He's tall, well over six feet, and bulky. Bulky in today's world is unusual. Either he's been eating a lot better than most of us, or he was considerably overweight to start with. I'm leaning toward overweight, based on his jowls being visible—even under his full black and gray beard—and the thickness of his forearms. His broad forehead is ruddy and chapped, while around his eyes the skin is pale from sunglasses or maybe goggles.

"It's getting cold out there," he says once he's scrunched inside.

I glance out the open door to where PJ and Rey are moving our largest sled to Leanne's tent. "What's going on?" I motion in their direction.

"You guys are moving. We stayed in an abandoned house up the road last night. It'll be better for her than the tent."

"Okay . . ." My eyes search out PJ, who sees me staring. He gives me a slight nod.

"Now then," David says, "what's your friend's name?"

"Robyn Sorensen. Did they tell you she was under water for several minutes? She wasn't breathing when— "

"Yes, I've heard." He turns to her. "Hello, Robyn. Let's see if we can figure out what's going on with you."

He continues to talk with her as he gives her a brief exam. I split my time between watching him and peering out the tent door. They're piling the sled with quilts and sleeping bags. A woman stands nearby with a teenage boy and girl. She gives me a tentative smile when she sees me looking at her.

"That's my wife and children," David offers.

"Have you been walking long?" I ask.

"Just started again a couple of weeks ago. Found a place to hole up over the worst of the winter. You?"

"Same," I answer. Before we left the mountain, we decided to not share any information about the ski lodge or our people there. Vague responses when questioned is our best option for keeping our community safe.

He pauses a moment, as if waiting for me to provide more, then turns back to Robyn.

After a couple of minutes, he says, "Okay, Robyn. We're going to get you into a comfy bed soon. You just keep resting for now." He begins to back out of the tent. "I'll do a more thorough exam once we get to the house."

"You're coming with us?" I ask, following him out. The camp is being torn apart, with all the tents except Leanne's and Robyn's already collapsed.

"For now." He gives a solemn nod. "A few hours delay won't matter much."

Angels unawares, I think as I give him a smile.

"Ready to go?" Donnie calls out, sitting atop his horse at the edge of camp.

David makes his way to his feet and lifts a hand.

With the sled holding Leanne hooked to his waist harness, Rey begins to move, with Asher by his side.

David turns to me. "See you in a bit. Try and make Robyn's ride like they have done for Leanne." He and his family fall in behind Rey and Asher.

How in the world will we ever fit Robyn on one of the smaller sleds? She's a couple of inches taller than Leanne and weighs more.

As if reading my mind, PJ walks over. He puts a hand on my shoulder. "They'll come back for her. That's the only sled sturdy enough to carry a person."

"Looks like everyone's almost ready to go."

"Yeah. We're trying to get there before the storm. I'll stay with Robyn. You go with them."

"I'll stay." Our eyes meet. My stomach does a little flip when he gives me a small smile. He reaches for my hand, giving it a squeeze. "I meant to ask if he was a nurse or a doctor. Do you know?"

In a low voice, PJ says, "Pharmacist."

"What? And we let him— "

"We don't have many choices. And Kimba seems to trust him, thinks he really is who he says he is."

"Well, that's something."

Kimba does seem to know things. She used to think of it as her intuition or gut feeling. Now she believes it's God leading her. The more she prays and reads her Bible, the more she feels His presence directing her paths.

"But a pharmacist . . . we need a doctor. What does he think about Leanne?"

"What we thought. Pneumonia. Bad. He wants to get her off her back. And you won't believe this, but he has antibiotics."

"What?" My eyes go wide. "You're right. I don't believe it. And he's willing to share them?"

"Already gave her the first dose. He even gave Kimba the rest of the pills and instructions. Said it isn't exactly what'd be prescribed, but he thinks it'll work. We'll know in a few days."

"Wow. I don't know what to say."

"Thank you, Jesus." He squeezes my hand. "That's what I've been saying. And praise the Lord."

"You guys okay?" Kimba calls out.

"Fine," PJ says, lifting a hand.

"Asher should be back with the sled soon," Atticus says. "You better get a move on if you want to beat the weather."

Once the group is gone, I turn to Atticus and ask, "How much you think we'll get?"

"Snow? Hard telling. Earlier I thought maybe a drizzle of rain—and it'll start off as rain—but as cold as it's getting and as dark as it is over there . . ." He motions toward the Pryor Mountains in the distance, completely obscured by heavy, gray clouds. "I think it's going to be a good one. I just hope it doesn't get too cold."

A shiver runs through me. "Well, I'm cold now. I'm going to get my jacket and start getting Robyn ready. It looks like they left the blankets and a couple of sleeping bags for her. Should we put her inside one of the bags?"

"Good idea," PJ says.

"And wrap her in a tarp," Atticus adds. "She'll need it."

I get her changed and redressed on my own, not the easiest of tasks, then move her into the sleeping bag. PJ helps me take down the tent.

"There's Asher now."

I look in the direction PJ is pointing and see Atticus's twin jogging while carrying the sled atop his head.

"Huh," PJ says. "That's different."

Atticus shakes his head. "At least he's hustling. We're going to get wet before much longer."

Once Asher reaches us, it takes only a few minutes to get Robyn settled in the sled and the remains of camp broken down. The twins take off while PJ and I get our horses.

The house at the end of a long driveway off the main road is in view when the rain starts.

"Is she okay?" Asher asks, pointing to Robyn. "Her eyes are open."

"Stop for a minute," I say to Atticus, then ask Asher, "Can you check on her?"

He pales slightly before nodding. "Tell me what to do."

"Just . . . is she breathing?"

He kneels down. We've positioned her on her side, and he tentatively places a hand near her nose. "Yeah. She seems fine. She's just . . . staring."

"Okay. She does that. I think she's fine."

"Should we cover her better?" he asks.

Nestled in the blankets so only her stocking-cap-covered head and face show, with the tarp around her to keep the rain off, I'm not sure what else we can do.

"Let's just try and get there before that cloud opens up." PJ motions to the rapidly approaching weather. "Looks like it has a bellyful of rain."

We've just turned down the driveway when PJ's prediction comes to fruition.

"Go on, Rochelle," PJ says. "No sense you getting completely soaked. I'll stay with Robyn."

"There's a barn," Asher says. "Donnie put his horse in there."

I tap Lucky's flank to bring him to a trot as I make a beeline for the small house with a trail of curling smoke climbing from the chimney. A larger barn is visible behind the house, and beyond is a line of trees.

Donnie must have been watching for us. He steps onto the covered front porch and motions me toward the barn, directing me like I'm an airplane on the tarmac. Shoving his hat down, he fast walks to the barn and slides open the large door so I can ride in.

"It's almost dark as night out here," Donnie says. "Can't even see the others."

"We'd just turned onto the driveway when it started coming down. PJ told me to ride ahead."

"Yup. Makes sense. I'll take care of your horse. Go on in the front door. Get warmed up."

"I appreciate it. Is Leanne any better?"

He lets out a loud breath. "No change."

Chapter 6

After getting Robyn inside, dry, and set up in the second bedroom of the compact home, David the Pharmacist checks her again. This time his wife assists while Kimba stays in the room, partly as nurse's aide and partly as protector. While it was decided the new family is not likely a threat to us, full trust is no longer freely given.

I change into dry clothes in the tiny bathroom, then move to a spot by the fire. The cold rain practically chilled me to the bone. Even though we've been traveling and have been out in the elements for almost a month, it's been a dryer cold—the cold Wyoming's known for. This wet, damp cold seems to seep in and settle.

Several days of moving Robyn and being hunched up in the tent probably didn't help anything. I'm achy all over and appreciate the warmth of the fire. Rey, the A Boys, and the Dawson brothers are in the barn, having determined the small house already had enough people in it. The two small bedrooms and single bath, combined with an open front room containing the kitchen, eating area, and living room, is certainly cozy.

Seventeen-year-old Nicole's on the couch, talking with David's teenagers, while her younger siblings, Nate and Naomi, sit on the floor nearby. Jennifer and Victoria are at the two-person table talking quietly. Of course, in this small space, it's easy to hear most of their words, no matter how softly they speak.

"It's really coming down," PJ says, sidling up to me. He, too, has changed out of his soaked garments and is now wearing sweatpants—not a normal look for him. Usually, he's in heavy lined work pants or, on milder days, western-cut Wranglers. While he certainly wears his jeans well, I'm not hating the casual wear. His tall, lanky frame seems well suited for just about any clothing choice.

"I hope David can do something to help them," I whisper.

PJ gives a slow nod as he tugs on the edge of his mustache. "I think, now, they at least have a chance. All those prayers for a miracle we were sending up . . . looks like they were heard."

"By sending us a pharmacist?" I ask, cocking an eyebrow.

"Why not?"

Not long ago, I was in such a funk—a black hole, really—I had little hope or belief God was even there, let alone He would hear my petitions or act on them. When my daughters and I were kidnapped and purchased by Fred Lassiter, I was convinced we were on our own, that no amount of praying would save us.

When Fred took us from the awful place he found us, where the men there did what they wanted with me while threatening the same to my young, innocent children, I expected things to be bad.

But he surprised me. "All I want is a family to love and a wife to grow old with," Fred said. I felt a flare of hope. I'd never love him. How could I? *He bought us.*

But if he didn't hurt us, didn't hurt my girls, that was all that mattered. And at first, he was kind and attentive. If I hadn't met him under such awful circumstances, I may have even been able to enjoy his companionship.

But then I got to know the real Fred Lassiter.

His kindness was like a coat he took off and on to suit his needs. He was not kind. Not loving. He was manipulative and evil.

During the time of turmoil, when things were truly getting scary with Fred, it wasn't me doing the praying. I was too broken. Too defeated. It was my youngest child, Cheyre. She was faithfully praying that we'd be saved, that we'd be rescued. In the end, it was also Cheyre who was responsible for our rescue.

I give PJ a smile. "We both know they're heard."

"Indeed. Sometimes we don't hear the answer, though. This time . . . " He lifts his hands.

"Thank you, Jesus," I whisper.

"I don't think we can say it enough today."

"Leanne?" I ask. "She do okay getting here?"

"As far as I know. Sadie and Sebastian, along with Donnie, are in with her now. David thinks it's bacterial and not viral, so she isn't contagious."

"Is she well enough for them to visit?"

"It's more of a . . . " He tilts his head to one side. "Rey said David thought it might be good for her to have some time with the children. In case the medicine . . . " He lifts his hands.

"Oh. That makes sense."

"He thinks she might've got some water in her lungs, which led to pneumonia. Guess he was surprised Robyn hasn't been coughing and spiking a fever too."

I nod silently, thinking to myself, *That's all she'd need.*

"Yup," PJ says. "Prayer works. Best we stick with it."

Victoria moves from the table with a ladle in her hand. "Just going to give the soup a stir. It's really starting to smell good."

I give her a weak smile. While we were camped, they brought in several more geese, and she's cooking the legs. "Anything useful in the cabinets?"

"No food. They'd been picked clean. But we did find some clothes in the bedroom Leanne's sleeping in. And David's wife told us there're dandelions growing in the yard. Jennifer says her mother-in-law used to forage for salads, and that maybe there's lamb's-quarter too. As soon as the weather let's up, I'm going after some. I don't even really know what lamb's-quarter is, but it's edible and it's fresh."

"Kind of bitter." PJ makes a face.

"Doesn't matter to me," Victoria says.

He shrugs. "My mom used to add the early spring dandelions to salads at my grandpa's insistence. He said his mom swore by them, calling them a spring tonic. 'Cures what ails you.'" PJ lets out a small laugh. "I can hear him now."

"I've never eaten either," I say. "Of course, there's lots we eat now that I never would've eaten before."

"No doubt." Victoria grins. "I'm just excited to have something green. *Anything.*"

The door to the second bedroom opens with a groan. David emerges first, followed by Kimba. I search her face for a clue about Robyn's condition.

"Soup smells good," David says. "Broth will be good for both of them. My wife's going to stay in with Robyn while we talk about her condition."

"Should we get Rey and the others?" I look to Kimba.

"I'll brief them later," she answers.

"Should we . . . " I motion to the children.

"Up to you." David looks to Kimba. "I'm okay with my children staying."

"Nate, take Naomi to the barn," Kimba says. "Nicole, I'd like you to stay. You may be needed to assist as a caregiver."

A look of fear passes Nicole's face as she gives a tentative nod.

Nate makes several noises to indicate his displeasure at being told to leave. "We're going to get wet."

Once they're gone, PJ asks, "What do you think about Robyn?"

David gives a slight shake of his head. "Without being able to run tests—and understanding I'm a pharmacist in a small hospital where we stabilize people who are severely injured before shipping them to Billings or Denver—I can only give my best guess."

"Is she in a coma?" I ask.

"Not a coma. The way she responds and opens her eyes is hopeful. It's more of a semi-vegetative state."

Victoria gasps. "She's a vegetable?"

"Not necessarily. She may be starting to wake up and this is part of the process. When the brain goes without oxygen it can be damaged mildly or severely. The first area of the brain to suffer damage in near-drowning incidents is the cerebral cortex, which is responsible for the brain's highest conscious functions, including memory, speech, and voluntary movement. With being under water for so long, this was probably affected. That and the bump on her head may be causing issues."

"The what?" I ask.

"There's a lump on the back of her head. She may be having effects from it as well. We just really don't know without being able to do brain scans."

"Will she be okay?" I ask.

"She exhibits some posturing— "

"And that is?" PJ asks.

"You know how she keeps her hands clenched into fists? And her feet are rotated inward?"

"Yes?" I ask.

"That's part of it. It's a sign there may be some damage to her brain. There was some response to stimuli. I kept repeating her name, and she'd open her eyes for a moment or two. That's a good sign. Plus, she's reacting to pain. Both are encouraging." He looks around the room, making sure we each understand what he's telling us.

"What kind of pain?" I ask.

"Nothing traumatic. I poked her with a safety pin. She moved away from the pain, which is what I hoped to see. She doesn't rattle when she breathes. She's not running a fever. These are good things. Plus, her bodily functions seem to be working as they should. You're keeping her clean, turned, and well hydrated. You were smart to do those things. Kimba said she's even had a bowel movement?"

"Just the one," I say quietly.

"Her skin breaking down may become a concern. Keep her dry and reposition her every few hours. You've been doing that?"

"I think?"

"Good. You don't want bed sores, those could lead to infection. You'll also need to exercise her muscles and joints so she doesn't lose her range of motion. Lift her arms and legs, bend her knees and elbows, move her hands and feet. Just be gentle. And give her all the fluids she'll tolerate. Ideally, she'd be on an IV and have a feeding tube. You'll need to be very conscious of not letting her get dehydrated, and also of not letting her blood sugar drop too low, which might be a challenge with the way things are."

"But she'll be okay?" Victoria asks. "She's going to wake up from this . . . vegetative state and be fine?"

He lifts his hands slightly while shaking his head. "There's a lot we don't know about the brain."

"But opening her eyes, that's good," I say. "You said that's good."

He lets out a long breath. "We can hope."

Sadness washes over me. "That doesn't sound very promising."

"You're keeping her comfortable. That's important."

"Keep her comfortable and wait for her to die?"

"Or get better," Victoria says quickly. "She might get better."

"Like I said," David says in a calm, patient voice, "there's a lot we don't know about the brain. Without the ability to run tests, you just need to take it one day at a time."

"The lights are on, but no one's home?" PJ asks.

"I guess you could think of it that way. For now. I know you're trying to get to her parents' home. When Leanne's well enough to travel, you should continue with those plans."

My eyes dart to Kimba. She tilts her head toward David. "About that, did you happen to travel by Lockwood?"

"Lockwood? Where's that?"

"Just up the road, outside of Billings. We heard a rumor there's some trouble there."

"Sorry. No. We were in Bismarck last summer when everything went down. Spent the winter in Miles City, Montana. We started traveling again the first of March. It was too soon, though, been slow going."

He looks to his children; one of them shrugs while the other nods. "At least the worst of the weather seems to be over now. We took a wide berth around Billings, dropping south at Pompeys Pillar. Not much good seems to happen in the larger towns and cities. Did you guys hear the airplanes? See the helicopters?"

"What?" I cry out, while the others do the same.

With a big smile, David says, "Yep. Heard the first airplane one night after we finished walking. Must have been, what, two weeks ago?" He looks at his children.

His son answers. "Sounds about right."

"It was a few days later when we started seeing the helicopters. We were somewhere south of Interstate 90."

We spend several minutes talking about this exciting news and what it means for the country's recovery efforts. David doesn't know much. They've done some speculating but haven't met anyone who knows what's happening—haven't met many people at all, in fact.

"Why do you have antibiotics? And why'd you share them?" I ask.

With a wry smile, he asks, "You ever have a kidney stone?"

I shake my head while there's a chorus of nos.

"My dad did," PJ says. "It put him in the hospital with not only pain but a nasty infection."

"Yep. I'm susceptible to them. Probably due to my rather large girth." He gives a slight laugh. "Or my former girth. I'd also get a nasty infection." He motions toward PJ. "When we travel, I take pain pills and a blister pack of antibiotics—self medicating . . . um, with a doctor's approval, of course. I don't recommend it, but I do it. Anyway, I made sure to find extra as soon as it was obvious things were going downhill."

"But you're willing to share?"

"Seems the apocalypse diet is helpful for not only losing weight but keeping the kidney stones away. I haven't had an attack since fall. I do drink an insane amount of water now, which is probably helping. And I have a full treatment for myself just in case."

"Are kidney stone antibiotics the same as what's used for pneumonia?" Victoria asks.

"It should work. It's not what she'd be given if there were more choices. And they'd take a sample and grow it to make sure she's on the right stuff. Sometimes . . . well, sometimes the wrong antibiotics can cause harm too. Right now, we can only do what we can do. If these work, you'll see an improvement within a few days."

"And if we don't?" PJ asks.

David shakes his head. "If they work, you'll know. Finish the full course and then she'll still need rest. It'll be a couple of weeks probably before she's able to travel."

"What about the coughing?" I ask. "She's miserable." I don't add how we're all miserable since her coughing means no one sleeps much.

PJ agrees with a nod. "Don't s'pose you're carrying cough syrup?"

"Sorry. No. But I was talking to her son—smart boy. He said that when he started getting a cold once, before the lights went out, his mom gave him vitamin C drinks. Then the sister said that while they were traveling with another man, he'd make them tea out of pine needles. Said it'd keep the scurvy away. She asked if it'd work the same as the vitamin C drinks."

"Sadie spoke to you?" I ask, unable to hide my surprise.

He shrugs. "Um, yeah. Her mentioning the pine having vitamin C reminded me of an article I read about using pine needles as an expectorant."

There're several exclamations of disbelief, including from me. When we were living on the mountain, one of our nurses was knowledgeable on alternative medicine and wildcrafting.

My daughter Kerryanne, who wants to go into medicine for her apprenticeship—a path each of our youth choose when they turn fourteen—shared some of the natural remedies taught during a short class.

I don't remember her mentioning pine needles, but living in a forest, I'm sure it was something being utilized. What else didn't we learn about that might have made things better for us on this journey?

"Why didn't Sadie mention the pine needles to us?" Victoria asks. "We could've all used some vitamin C these last few weeks."

David nods. "Yep. Same here. Most of my knowledge is pharmaceuticals, but I've picked up a few things here and there when talking with people or reading various articles. But it's all theoretical. I wish I would've put some of it into practice. One of the few natural things we've used since the collapse is willow bark. I knew about that from my own studies as a precursor to aspirin. It helps with the pain and fever."

Kimba shakes her head. "They used a few alternative medicines where we lived before, but I didn't pay much attention. I even knew about willow being the early aspirin. I guess we were so focused on finding a doctor with commercially prepared medicines that we just didn't think. The few pills we had in our first aid kit, we've already used them for other . . . incidents."

"Understood." David shakes his head. "This world is ripe for incidents. Anyway, there's a couple of willow trees on the creek behind this place. Probably not the preferred variety used by herbalists, but they'll work. We've been taking a little bark off the young shoots when we've found the trees on our journey. We chew it to get the juice out, then spit the pulp. Tastes terrible, but it does the job.

"My wife gave Leanne a piece already, making sure she didn't choke on it in her weakened condition. For her, a tincture would be best—less work to get the relief. But that's not really an option right now. You could try a tea like the pine. Just remember, it's medicine, so don't overdo it. One other thing, make sure you're all practicing good hygiene. Wash your hands after caring for Leanne or Robyn. The rest of you don't need to be getting any bugs."

"You'll be leaving soon?" I ask.

"As soon as the weather breaks."

"Where you headed?" PJ asks.

"Home. Powell, Wyoming. Couple of weeks, and we'll get there. Kimba said you folks came out of Wyoming. You happen to know anything about Powell and the situation there?"

"Talk with Donnie," PJ says. "He's the other one on the horse. He went through there and Cody a couple months back. From what I understood, they're doing okay. But, uh . . . " PJ looks at David's teens. "Steer clear of Wesley and Prospect. Both are having troubles."

"We plan to get on Highway 310 near Fromberg and going through Frannie, Wyoming. Is that way okay?"

"Fromberg to Bridger is fine," PJ says. "After that, we don't know. Donnie may have more information. Check with him."

"Our oldest daughter is still at home." David chews on the long bits of mustache hanging by his lip. "She didn't want to vacation with us, decided to stay and work. Had a summer job at McDonald's. We've been worried sick. After seeing what's happened in some of the towns we've traveled through . . . we've been thinking the worst."

"There're bad things happening in many places. Some of us have seen some things too."

"As I said, we've been worried sick."

I drop my eyes. Worry is something I'm familiar with—worry over Christopher being okay and worry over leaving my girls in Bakerville. Giving my worry over to God is something I'm still working on. It's not easy.

"The broth is probably ready," Victoria says. "I'll take some to Leanne."

"And I'll feed Robyn." Jennifer moves from her spot at the small kitchen table.

I start to protest when she raises a hand and says, "You rest. You've been taking care of her for days." Victoria turns to David. "You, sir, are an answer to prayer. At least now they both have a chance."

"Keep praying," David says. "They'll need it. And do the things we talked about for Robyn. You have your hands full."

After my own bowl of goose meat and broth, I take my quilt to a spot near the fire. Using my arm as a pillow, I turn on my side and face the wall.

I'm exhausted. Caring for Robyn has been physically and emotionally draining. And David's assessment gives me little hope she'll improve much in the next few days. We'll be taking her home in a near childlike condition.

Assuming we can even get her home.

If Lockwood's under siege, then what do we do?

Chapter 7

As Atticus predicted, the rain turned to snow, keeping David and his family with us overnight. Checking Leanne before leaving, he was cautiously optimistic. That's the phrase he used. Cautiously optimistic.

Her fever was down slightly, and she seemed to be breathing easier. He reminded us not to push, to let her body heal before we started moving again. And even then, he didn't think she'd be able to walk much, if at all. It could take many weeks for her to get her strength back.

Unfortunately, there hasn't been any real change with Robyn. Like David said, she does stir when we talk to her. I can tell her to open her eyes, and she will . . . eventually. I didn't try the pain things he did, but I assume her response hasn't changed. As PJ said, the lights may be on, but she's still not home.

David reminded us about positioning, fluids, and avoiding bed sores before he left. He also reminded us to keep praying.

It wasn't long after the family left when Jameson Dawson said we should go forward with our plan to split up. Donnie could stay with Leanne and her children, and the rest of us could get going again— deliver Robyn to her parents, find my son, and then maybe Donnie could meet up with them somewhere and they could continue the journey together.

Jameson's suggestion was given serious consideration, but in the end, we took a vote, and the majority chose to stick together.

During our time here, we've been doing what we can to not only care for Robyn and Leanne but to also nourish ourselves. There's still plenty of geese and even ducks. With the rain continuing off and on, the hunting seemed to get really good between the storms.

The snares we had going for rabbits, plus box traps resulting in several Eurasian doves, were also not negatively affected by the weather. A little larger, and with more meat than a mourning dove, the Eurasians were spectacular.

Nate Hoffmann, who took charge of the snares and trapping, discovered that setting up the trap and then finding a place to hide gave him an opportunity to harvest the doves with his slingshot in addition to using the trap.

He, along with the other children, made slingshots in school. Learning how to use it seemed to come easier for some, and Nate is one who excelled at the sport. He's continued to hone his skill on our journey, landing birds and even a rabbit with the homemade weapon.

The rubber band, made of a black piece of innertube, has already been replaced once with a strip he brought along. Additional tubing is on our list of items to salvage.

The biggest food treat during our time at this small house was two tom turkeys! We cooked one of them outside over an open fire, roasting it on a pseudo spit. After so many weeks of boiled and dried meat, it was amazing.

The other turkey, more geese, and a mule deer were added to our dried foods by slicing the meat thin and hanging it on wire—found in the barn—behind the woodstove and in an outdoor smoke pit PJ put together with rocks and freshly cut green branches.

Because of the increased humidity, compared to what it was over the winter on the mountain, we used some of our precious salt as a dry rub for the wire-hanging jerky. I'm not sure it was needed, though, since the meat was well dried and brittle in half a day.

And the results were much superior to our attempts at dehydrating over the small pit fires. The smoked meat was beyond amazing, giving us new flavors and an almost gourmet taste.

Behind the house, hidden by the line of trees, is a creek with plenty of fish. Adding fish to our diet was a welcome addition, and the extra was dried along with the other meats in the smoke pit. And Victoria, as promised, harvested bitter greens from the large lawn behind the house.

I'll admit, the first bite was harsh, but after that, I really liked them. We've had such a lack of variety in our diet, living in this little house seemed almost abundant. I feel much healthier than when we arrived. And we managed to dry a wonderful amount of food, food we know we'll need while making our way through the Billings metro area where hunting may be impossible.

After the snowstorm when we first arrived, we only had one other snow event, which didn't amount to much. With a warm wind and rain several days in a row, the ground is now essentially clear, which is good in many ways but bad in another. The sleds won't do well on bare ground and will be worse in mud. And that's mainly what we have right now: mud with patches of snow and the occasional dry spot.

After finding the few clothes in the house in those first hours after arriving, we performed a more thorough search of not only the house but also the barn and outbuildings. While there wasn't a great haul of anything, there were many miscellaneous items we could use: clothing, towels, children's socks, which fit both Sebastian and Naomi, and other odds and ends. The best find was a toiletry bag with small hotel soaps, shampoos, and lotions. Soap and shampoo were something we desperately needed.

Although I thought the best find was soap and shampoo, others had their own favorites. Kimba was ecstatic over a sports bra in the back of the closet.

And a box of books on a dusty shelf in the garage brought out *oohs* and *ahs* from almost everyone, and even brought tears to Sadie's eyes. There was a wide variety of genres and reading levels. I found a cozy mystery that I thought looked good.

Whenever she wasn't doing chores or helping salvage, Sadie spent her time reading aloud to Leanne. One day, I stopped to listen and was impressed with her wonderful reading voice. She didn't stumble over words, and she provided just the right amount of inflection.

"She's something, isn't she?" Kimba whispered as I listened in on Sadie's storytelling.

"More than she appears to be, for sure."

"Quiet and reserved—scared even—yet my guess is she's brilliant. A prodigy maybe. There's a lot going on in her head."

Sadie lifted her head just then, catching us eavesdropping. One side of her mouth lifted in a slight smile as she gave us a nod. Definitely more going on in her head than it would first seem.

"Do you need anything?" I asked.

She shook her head and went back to her reading.

Kimba touched my shoulder and motioned me down the hall. We were working on the kitchen, checking every nook and cranny to see if there was something lifesaving we missed.

Salvaging for any usable items has become an important part of our journey. Even though most places had been picked over by the time we got to them, there was always something. The big find in this house were three cartridges of 9-millimeter ammo under a drawer in the bathroom. Three rounds are a goldmine in today's world. Though PJ and I are carrying 10-millimeter Glocks, what PJ calls bear guns, most in the group have 9-millimeter pistols.

The reasoning is exactly this. It's common and was, at one time, easy to find rounds. The ammunition was relatively cheap, and the popular caliber meant we had a decent amount of it on the mountain. It was a round that was required to be contributed to the community stores when moving to the safety of the ski lodge.

I know some people grumbled about having to give up a portion of their popular-caliber ammunition, but it really did make sense. Kimba and Rey were smart to stick with as few calibers as possible. And the community was generous in outfitting us for our journey, giving excess weapons and ammunition.

While streamlining calibers worked out pretty well for the handguns, there're still a few revolvers—like Donnie's giant .460 Smith & Weston Magnum—and the long guns are an assortment, though that's based more on the specific uses of each gun than anything.

The A Team came up with an idea for moving Robyn. At first, we discussed converting the sled into some type of travois by adding poles and dragging it along. The new plan is much better, definitely a more comfortable ride.

Using the wheels from a riding lawn mower in the barn, they built a low platform large enough for her to stretch out comfortably—using wood that was part of one of the outbuildings and sanding it smooth so she wouldn't get slivers—then added low walls to keep her from falling off. They tested it by pulling each other around, using one of the harness systems from the sleds.

And to haul our stuff, they found a three-shelf utility cart covered with old painting supplies and other things. I'll admit, I was surprised the people rummaging through this place before us ignored the utility cart. Maybe they couldn't see what it was because of all the junk on it, but for us, it was a great find. Three feet high and just shy of three feet long, with a handle on one end to make it easy for pushing, it seems sturdy enough.

The rapidly melting snow not only means the sleds won't work for hauling our stuff, but the skis and snowboards are also obsolete. After a rather intense debate, they were determined to be more of a hindrance than a help.

We'll no doubt have more snow, but with how much the ground is warming, especially the pavement, it's not likely it'll stick for any length of time. In the end, it was decided hauling the skis and boots for just in case didn't make sense.

I think the A Boys were most disappointed about leaving the skis, especially the youngest one. They'd spoken many times about how it might be winter again before they reach home. Rey and Kimba agreed, saying while it was possible they'd be on the road for many more months, lightening their load could help with faster travel.

Besides, the miles they put on their gear had taken a toll. They were never designed to be used for skinning day in and day out. The bindings were loose, and the skins were deteriorating. Best to leave these behind and find new ones if the need arises.

PJ, Donnie, and I are each keeping our snowshoes. Being on the horses has a few advantages. The snowshoes will attach easily to our packs, plus their smaller size will make them less of an issue. PJ and I discussed stashing ours somewhere to pick up on our way back to Bakerville after we find Christopher, but we didn't want to feel committed to return by this route.

In addition to food gathering, processing, and preparing for our journey, we've used this downtime to continue to hone our self-defense skills. Daily training of defensive maneuvers both with and without weapons have given me new confidence. Blocking, kicks, punches, and escapes—including not only getting out of being grabbed but forward and back rolls—have been the focus for hand-to-hand combat.

We've also done several different shooter drills with both handguns and rifles. Quick drawing from our holsters has been my favorite. Kimba and Rey really know their stuff and gave many helpful tips.

"You're doing great," Kimba said after we finished one day. "You've got a fast hand. Steady too. Keep practicing. You never know when you'll need a quick draw."

As before, Victoria sat out. And Jameson rarely joined us, thinking it was dumb. His behavior didn't improve during our time at the house.

It became so bad that Rey and Kimba had a talk with his mom about it. Victoria was extremely defensive, insisting we were making more out of it than needed. "All teenage boys have attitudes," she said.

"Maybe so," Rey said. "But it's not something we can have now. Here, at this house, it doesn't specifically endanger us. But once we get back on the road, it may."

It was Donnie who stopped any semblance of negotiations. "Get your kid under control, or I'm going to knock him into next Tuesday."

Now I feel like we're completely walking on eggshells around both Jameson and Victoria.

A few days after we arrived at this little house, I was talking to Robyn while getting her dressed, and I said something like, "Robyn, you're doing so much better. I think soon you'll be talking up a storm and feeling just fine. I'm so glad you didn't get sick or have a cough. Aren't you?"

I almost fell over when, in a slurred voice, she said, "So glad."

It wasn't much, but it was something! Since then, she's made more noises—not all of them good. Sometimes she cries like she's in pain or does the strange breathing she did right after the near drowning.

Leanne finished her antibiotics and has been slowly regaining her strength. The pine needle tea also seemed to help her cough. We're all drinking it now, knowing the addition of vitamin C is important in our limited-variety diets.

Yesterday, after more than two weeks in this little house, Leanne declared herself well enough to travel. What she actually said was, "If I'm forced to remain in this way-too-small house one more day with all of your stinking bodies, I might fall over dead from lack of air."

Yep. She was better. And she wasn't wrong.

The house had a serious funk, partly due to too many people in too small of a space and partly due to the increase in Robyn's fluids. Fluids in means fluids out.

And doing laundry hasn't been easy. We cut a second sheet to use and have been using the towels and clothing we found, but we'll need a better solution. While at the house we can at least muddle through laundry, I don't know how we'll manage on the road.

My new prayer, in addition to Robyn's full recovery, is that we can easily reach her parents. If all goes well, we're only a few easy days away from Lockwood. But even that hangs over us. With the town under siege, what good will it do to reach it?

This morning, after our Bible reading, Kimba announced the date: Thursday, May 7. We've been gone for almost two months. Since David's family left, we haven't talked to anyone else.

We did see a group walking on the road a few days ago. But they kept going, walking cautiously and keeping their hands visible.

We've been so isolated, we have no idea what's happening away from this little house. Are there more aircrafts? Has the president spoken again? These questions, and the fact we're finally going back on the road, resulted in a hearty discussion over breakfast as to what our new government should look like.

"You'd have thought," Donnie said, "the tax money they'd been collecting forever would've put safeguards in place to prevent this from happening." At this, he used his arm to encompass everything.

Of course, we all knew what he meant. How was it even possible to have coordinated attacks on such a wide scale? Someone was certainly asleep at the wheel to allow it. And we didn't even retaliate . . . at least as far as we know. The president has said nothing about any kind of retaliation in his addresses. They nuked us, and we let it happen.

"You ready?" PJ asks, jarring me from replaying the conversation in my head.

"I'm ready. She'll need help getting on Lucky." I motion to Leanne, who has just walked out of the house and is on the covered porch. "I'm not sure— "

"They'll help her."

I give a nod, then walk Lucky to our gathered group. I'll lead my horse while Leanne rides. After so many days of not traveling, the idea of stretching my legs sounds amazing, so I volunteered the first ride.

Even though PJ, Donnie, and I each offered her to ride the horse any time she was tired when we were in Joliet at Tamra's parents' house, she didn't take any of us up on it. She even argued yesterday, insisting she was well enough to walk. PJ and I discussed maybe she has a fear of horses. Donnie told us she loves horses. They've talked about how she'd been around them growing up and when she worked at her aunt's hotel.

There's no longer any doubt that Donnie and Leanne have a romance going. While she's been sick, he's constantly been by her side—feeding her, helping her, anything he could do. I've seen them holding hands and caught a few quick kisses pass between them. While both are often brusque with the rest of us, they seem entirely comfortable and loving toward each other.

Looking at her pale face, just from getting herself dressed, packed, and out of the house, I don't think she even has the strength to sit in the saddle, let alone move on her own. Rey easily puts her atop Lucky. As soon as she's in the saddle, her body seems to mold to it.

She strokes him along the neck, cooing soothing words as she does. "You are a gentle giant, aren't you?" She's completely relaxed and in perfect posture. Yeah, she's been on horses before.

I smile up at her. "Ready to go?"

I receive a rare fleeting smile in return. The friendly expression quickly disappears, her usual grim countenance back in place. "Let's go."

Standing at his shoulder, I move my hand forward. "Come, Lucky."

PJ and Donnie are riding their horses while the others—minus Robyn and Leanne, of course—are on foot. Robyn's well cushioned by blankets in the new cart, with Atticus wearing the harness. His twin's pushing the well-laden utility cart carrying our supplies.

With the skis and ski boots left behind, the bulk of the items on the cart are extra things. We discussed leaving the heavy winter coats, but even early May can be cold. Especially once the sun goes down.

The jackets and extra footwear are on the cart. Most of the food is carried in personal backpacks, with extra on the cart, along with bedding and anything else that didn't fit easily in the packs. There's a stamp on the cart indicating a max weight of four hundred pounds. I don't think we're quite to the maximum, but we certainly gave it a good try.

The three of us with horses are each outfitted in similar manners. When PJ arrived in Bakerville last fall, he and his group had shown up well supplied. With their livelihood and lifestyle revolving around horses, he'd brought everything we'd need to be well equipped for this journey, allowing our gear to ride on our horse.

Saddlebags, which hang down on either side at the back of the saddle, hold dried food along with a few miscellaneous things in one bag, with Lucky's grooming supplies plus a pair of nippers and a length of thin rope in the other. The center back bag has a spare pair of underwear, additional socks, an extra bandanna, and more dried food.

I didn't overfill it, so my tent and bedroll, wrapped in a length of plastic tarp, can fit under the gently curved cantle at the back of the saddle.

On the front offside is my scabbard holding my loaded 30.06 rifle, with an ammo sleeve on the buttstock holding an additional eight rounds. On the nearside, I have a pommel bag with additional rifle and pistol ammo. PJ has a nearly identical setup. Before leaving the mountain, PJ and I made sure we were matched in calibers, allowing us to share ammo. He, too, carries a 30.06 rifle and a 10-millimeter handgun.

My Glock is on my hip, with a second magazine in a pouch on my belt, along with an additional pouch for a multitool. A sheathed stiletto knife is tucked in my boot. My heavy jacket is cinched to the front of my saddle, tied with a front string from either side.

In my small backpack is a change of clothes, nightwear, a few toiletries, two water bottles, more food and ammo, and my snowshoes tied on the outside. Keeping the backpack from bulging at the seams helps with my weight being correct when riding.

I'm wearing a lighter fleece jacket and have changed from insulated riding boots to regular lace-up boots with half chaps. The chaps are like a gaiter covering the lower leg to prevent chafing while in the saddle. They also help with warmth.

My insulated boots are currently on the cart. I'll need to decide about them when we separate. But for now, I'm not yet ready to part with them. While it's warm and sunny today, winter may still try to get in a few licks.

After about an hour of walking, my pack starts feeling heavier than it should. I'm about ready to call for a break when Atticus does it for me.

I look up at Leanne. She's pale and exhausted. She starts to speak but ends up giving a hearty cough. She quickly turns her head into the pit of her elbow. When she's finished, she clears her throat. "I had no idea sitting could be so exhausting."

"Remember," PJ says, at Lucky's side after ground tying his own horse, "you're setting the pace today. We'll stop as often and for as long as you need."

"Yeah, 'cause I haven't slowed us up enough."

It's not the first time she's said something similar in the last few days. From previous experience, I choose not to respond. And I definitely avoid mentioning anything about how she saved Robyn. It's been brought up before and, according to Leanne, letting her die would've been the humane thing to do.

I know Leanne's not the only one who thinks this. There have been several conversations along a similar vein. Donnie referred to it as assisted suicide, but it's not. Robyn isn't aware enough to be assisted. We'd be the ones choosing to end her life. That's murder.

Donnie shot back with, "Not murder. A mercy killing. I mean, look at her."

I turned on him. "You stay away from her. We're taking her home to her parents."

In typical Donnie response, he uttered several choice words and phrases before stomping off. Sometimes, he's like a spoiled little boy.

We take a two-hour break; Leanne sleeps for most of it. With Victoria's help, I take care of cleaning Robyn. We move her out of the cart, letting her stretch on a blanket-covered tarp, exercising her arms and legs for several minutes to stretch the muscles.

Several people choose to hunt during the break. It's been decided this is one of our last hunting opportunities, as we're getting close to Billings and expect to see an increase in houses. What we're not seeing much of is geese. The nicer weather is likely partly responsible.

With the hunting and trapping we've done while on the road, plus the provisions we brought with us, we'll be okay on food while getting through the populated areas, as long as we can do it quickly. As if an omen of things to come, our hunters return empty handed.

As we're loading up to go, Rey asks, "How're the carts holding up? Moving easily?"

"No problem," Atticus answers. "This thing is pretty slick. It doesn't corner great, but other than that, it's good. Seems sturdy too."

"This cart's fine too," Asher says. "But my arms go to sleep pushing it."

"Let's make sure you're switching off before that happens," Rey says. "Atticus, I need you in top form, too, so you do the same."

Donnie, PJ, and I have been making sure to choose soft ground for the horses. Each of the three horses are barefoot. When we left the mountain, there was so much snow, the chances of freezing the shoe and snow balling up under their feet was too high to risk leaving with horseshoes in place.

On my ranch at home, our horses were almost always shoeless. We, of course, cared for their hooves, keeping them trimmed and cleared of any debris, plus having the farrier come in every couple of months for a proper reshaping. We're doing the same here and taking time to check their hooves each time we stop.

There's something amazing about caring for an animal who you've developed such a relationship with. When we first started talking about this trip, around the first of the year when I thought it'd just be PJ and me going off to find Christopher, he introduced me to his string of horses. He, his brother, his dad, and his grandpa, who died the year before the attacks at the age of ninety-nine, all had a love of horses, resulting in quite the collection.

His grandpa used horses to work cattle back when their ranch was a commercial operation. His dad focused his horses on the hunting outfitting business and a summertime dude ranch type enterprise. He even used the chuck wagon and horses to take people on multiday trips like the pioneers. They have a beautiful group of horses, but I immediately fell for Lucky.

It's midafternoon, and I'm walking again while Leanne rides. It's been a day of slow progress, and based on the way Leanne's slumping in the saddle, she's tired again and it's time to start thinking about a break. Or maybe just be done for the day.

When we were traveling in deeper snow, we took it very slow, figuring any forward progress was better than nothing. Leaving the mountain, we expected the valleys and the basins to have less snowpack, and they did, but there was still enough to keep us leery of one of the horses stepping wrong.

When the melt started, we quickly became spoiled, picking up the pace and going from traveling only six or seven miles a day to around ten. Today, according to the mileage markers, we're at less than four.

"Walkers ahead!" Donnie calls out, motioning in the distance.

"Which way are they headed?" Rey asks.

"Can't tell yet," Donnie answers. "But with the way our luck goes, no doubt they're heading toward us. And there's half a dozen of them or so."

Rey motions us to stop. "Off the road."

"There." Kimba points to the east. "That terrain looks like we'd have an advantage. And it's high enough we should be able to view their approach too."

"Good call, love. Let's move."

Though we'd like to think the walkers are friendly, we know better than to make any assumptions. The spot Kimba chooses for our hideout—and defensive location—is several hundred yards across the semi-barren, mud-laden landscape. The A twins each take an end of Robyn's cart, lifting her in the air and carrying her. Axel Dosen and Brett Dawson grab the utility cart, lifting it through the mud. All the boys are struggling by the time we reach the halfway point. The mud isn't making it easy for anyone.

Nicole hustles to the utility cart, slipping along the way. "Jameson, help me with this so Axel and Brett can help with Robyn."

He gives her a dirty look and mutters a few things but does as Nicole asks.

"Good thinking," Brett says, as he moves from the utility cart to Robyn. Together, the four of them heft Robyn higher and make their way to the knoll.

When we reach the hideout, it's really little more than an elevated mound with a crevice on one end. But it's fine for keeping the children hidden and using to shoot prone. It's also muddy as all get out.

"Half a dozen heading this way," Donnie declares. "They saw us, too, based on the way they're pointing."

Rey shakes his head. "Can't ever be easy, can it?"

"What about the horses?" I ask, as I help Leanne dismount.

"I'll take them," Donnie says from his saddle. "Those trees over there should give us some protection."

"Looks like a creek." PJ hands Titan's reins to Donnie. "They could use a drink after you cool 'em down."

I remove my rifle from the scabbard, then hand Lucky off to Donnie too.

"Got what you need?" Donnie asks.

"Yep."

"Ammo?"

"I'm set."

He makes some sort of grunting noise in acknowledgment before clicking his mouth to get Gordie and our half drafts moving.

"We should've sent the children with him," Leanne says.

"This is a precaution," Kimba answers. "I think we'll be okay here, but . . . " She turns to her daughter Nicole. "If things start to go bad, you and Nate get your sister, Sadie, and Sebastian to Donnie and the horses. If you stay behind the hillside, you'll have cover."

"Donnie? Mom . . . " Nicole shakes her head.

Leanne crosses her arms. "He's a good man. He'll make sure you're okay. Sebastian, Sadie, you know that's true."

Sebastian nods while Sadie lifts a shoulder. Although Donnie is gruff and opinionated, he does seem to be kind to the children. He and Sebastian get along especially well, which is a good thing if Donnie and Leanne plan to move forward with their developing relationship.

"Let's get set up," Rey says. "Victoria, you stay with the children. If they need to move, you go too."

Victoria dips her head. Being the only adult unarmed, and making it clear she has absolutely zero use for any type of firearm, doesn't help the children much as far as defending them. But Donnie would need a second adult. Good man or not, he'd easily be overwhelmed. And for defense, Nicole Hoffmann has both a handgun and rifle.

Nate also has a rifle, the .22 Robyn was carrying. While we were staying at the little house, Rey and Kimba took both Nate and Sadie through the paces of training and becoming comfortable with the light rifle.

Nate has shot before, on the mountain, but it was a first for Sadie. Even though she's still timid and unsure, she does seem to be comfortable with the .22, enough so both she and Nate are part of the watch team. Rey said, as we get closer to town, we'll have three on at all times and they'll need to take their turns.

The group on the road is now close enough they're easy to make out. Rey was wrong, though. There's seven of them, and three are small in stature, likely around Sadie's and Nate's age.

"I don't think they're a threat," I say.

"Maybe not," Rey responds. "We'll know soon enough. If they do something dodgy— "

"Like attack," Kimba interjects.

"Yeah. We'll have our answer then for sure," Rey says. "But I think Rochelle's right. We'll be okay."

It's several minutes before the group is almost parallel with us and a couple of them begin waving their arms.

"What are they doing?" Jameson Dawson asks.

"Trying to get our attention," PJ answers. "Guess they want to have a little chat."

Rey lets out a long, frustrated sigh. "They couldn't just walk on by and let us get on with our day?"

"What's the plan?" Kimba asks.

He turns to his wife. "I'll talk to them, love. Make sure you shoot them before they can shoot me."

"Sure, baby," she says with a snort of a laugh.

"That's what I keep you around for— " he gives her a wink " — your amazing sharpshooter skills."

"Huh. I thought it was because you love me desperately and find me irresistible."

"Moooom . . . " Nicole says with an exaggerated eye roll.

Their banter brings a hint of a smile to my lips. I'm sincerely grateful for both Kimba's and Rey's skills with not only firearms but all tactical matters. And Kimba, an absolutely beautiful woman, knows how to use her looks to her advantage, even getting us out of a jam several weeks ago. It's good to have a former spy around when you need one.

While the rest of us stay in our spots and provide backup for Rey, he makes his way to the now-waiting walkers. With them so near, it's clear they have a child around Sebastian's age and two tweens—eleven or twelve.

One of the two women may even have a baby tied to her chest, based on the way she's standing and swaying back and forth, plus the odd shape of her clothing.

The men who did the waving are both holding their hands well away from their sides, trying to not look like a threat.

When Rey's within shouting distance, he stops and calls out to them. "Is there something you need?" he asks in his American voice.

With the quiet of the countryside and the way sound travels, we have no difficulty hearing Rey, but the response from the walkers is fleeting. I pick up a couple of words. *Traveling. Distance. Quiet.*

"What'd he say?" Jameson asks.

"Shh," PJ says. "We'll find out later."

"No troubles when we came through," Rey calls to the walkers. "As far as we know, there haven't been any changes."

This time I hear *Billings* and assume they're asking if that's where we're headed.

"Near there," Rey answers. "You know anything about Lockwood? We heard there might be some trouble."

The two men look at each other. This time the other one responds. *Tell. Soldiers. Careful.*

"You don't say?" Rey yells. "The military, huh? The US military?"

Uniforms. Hundreds. Lockwood. Airplanes. Then one of the ladies yells out. *Better. Long.*

"Good, good," Rey responds. "So, you think it's safe—for now at least?"

This time I catch only one word. *Enough.*

After a few more minutes of back and forth, not amounting to anything new, they say their goodbyes and start walking again. Those of us keeping watch begin whispering about what we think we know.

"Wait." Kimba lifts a hand. "Stop talking and stay alert until this is over. Rey will update us."

Rey stays in place. Waiting until the walkers are well down the road before returning to us.

"That's good news, huh?" Rey asks us with a smile.

"Couldn't catch it all," PJ says.

"You'll need to fill us in, babe." Kimba slings her rifle as she stands.

"Seems the military swooped in, and Lockwood's no longer under siege."

Everyone begins talking at once, asking questions and expressing excitement.

Donnie rides up and asks, "What's all the hoopla about?"

"The Army is here!" Jameson pumps his fist in the air.

"Maybe," Rey says. "Although, it's more likely the Marines. They can operate on US soil without issue. The guy had no idea, though. Just said they're uniformed, they're in Lockwood, and have most of the trouble under control."

"But with the airplanes and helicopters, it's probably the Air Force, right?" Jameson asks.

"Don't know. Marines have an aviation unit. We'll know more when we get there."

"How bad was it there?" I ask, worried about whether we'll even find Robyn's parents alive and able to care for their severely injured daughter. "Do they have doctors?"

"He didn't say, just that they'd been stuck there a couple of months after stopping for the weather."

"Great." Donnie smacks his hands together. "Let's get going. The sooner we get Robyn home and find Rochelle's kid, the sooner Leanne can get home . . . and the rest of you, of course."

"Oh, of course." Kimba shakes her head at him.

"We're done for today," Leanne says. "I'm done. I'm ready to rest."

Donnie's rough demeanor softens. "Sure. Of course. I forgot how exhausted you must be."

Leanne meets his eyes with a small smile before lifting her hand for him to help her stand. They stare at each other a couple of extra-long moments.

I glance over at Sadie, who drops her shoulders and shakes her head. I guess she's not overly enthusiastic about the budding romance between her mom and Donnie.

Chapter 8

With the news that the Lockwood siege has ended, our movements seem light as we pack our camp the next morning. Even the horses seem to feel the excitement in the air as we get ready to leave. We have hope—hope we can get Robyn home and cared for. Even with the hope, I'm still forcing myself to banish the worry over finding her parents.

Robyn may even feel the difference too. She's been fidgeting a lot since sundown last night. The weird rapid breathing and the moaning, even crying sometimes, meant little sleep for me last night.

And not just me. Donnie makes a point of whining about his lack of sleep from her noises.

Jameson adds his own disapproval at being kept awake, going over the top about how much he needs his sleep.

In usual Donnie form, he points a beefy finger at Jameson and says, "You're young. Get over it and stop your whining."

I hide my smile at his antics. Apparently, he can complain, but no one else can.

"She's obviously not well," Leanne says, directing her comment toward Donnie. "It's not like she's doing it on purpose. Everyone needs to cut her some slack."

Leanne gives a slight smile and pats her new beau on the arm. I'm surprised by not only what she said but also by her friendly demeanor. I'm really beginning to like this new, less grumpy Leanne.

Looking around as the final preparations are made, PJ says, "I have a Bible verse for today. I spent some time looking for this one last night. It's one I'm sure we're all familiar with, but I couldn't remember exactly where to find it. I just knew it was in one of the Gospels. Thankfully, it was in Matthew, so it didn't take me too long to find it since I started there."

"Do you want to read while we finish?" Kimba asks, tying a string around her pup tent to hold the poles and nylon together.

PJ clears his throat. "'Therefore do not worry about tomorrow, for tomorrow will worry about itself. Each day has enough trouble of its own.' Like I said, it's from Matthew, chapter six, verse thirty-four."

I give him a smile. He knows worrying is something I struggle with. We've talked about it many times—just last night even. My heart fills as I realize he spent time looking for this verse specifically for me.

"Seems to be a fitting one for sure," Rey says. "It's probably one we should've been thinking on each day of this trip. Worry has been our constant companion."

I bite my lip as I finish tying my bedroll behind my saddle. I've often let my thoughts run away from me when I think about my concerns over finding Christopher, about my girls still in Bakerville. Have they moved off the mountain back to Bakerville proper to begin growing the crops we'll desperately need for next winter? Are they safe? And now, with our latest worries of Leanne coming so close to death and Robyn being in her semi-vegetative state . . . it's so easy to get wrapped up in worry.

Each day does have enough troubles. Especially traveling as we are. We need to be diligent, need to be attentive to what's happening around us. We're getting close to Lockwood, then we'll go on to Shepherd, Montana, near Christopher's camp. Worrying about what we'll find in Lockwood or Shepherd won't help. It won't change anything, and it won't keep us safe for today.

"We ready?" Rey asks, looking around.

"Looks like it," Kimba answers. "PJ, would you like to pray before we go?"

He gives a moment for the movement to stop and for those wishing to participate to bow their heads. "Father in heaven, we come before You without a church or a place of worship but knowing You are here with us. We ask You give us a sense of peace and help us remember Your words from the gospel of Matthew. Let us not worry about what will happen tomorrow. Let us focus on today as we travel these roads. Keep us safe from harm and hidden under Your wings. We pray these things in Jesus' holy name, amen."

A barely audible "amen" escapes Leanne's mouth.

My eyes dart toward her.

When she sees me looking, she narrows her eyes and turns her head. She's riding Gordie, Donnie's horse, first today. She strokes the neck of the beautiful buckskin before asking Donnie if he can help her up.

Climbing in my own saddle, I give a slight shake of my head. Although she tries to keep it up, I can see Leanne's brusqueness fading little by little. Perhaps coming so close to death made her realize what she's missing in life by being angry all the time. Or maybe it's her new relationship with Donnie. Whatever it is, I like it and hope it continues.

About half an hour into our day, the rumble of a motor breaks the near silence.

"Is that a car?" young Naomi Hoffmann asks.

"Off the road!" Rey orders. "To those trees!" He points to a small grove on the left.

"But . . . a car!" Naomi persists.

"Go!" Rey motions her and everyone to move.

At the tree line, Kimba says, "Nicole, take the children farther back."

PJ and I, along with Donnie leading Gordie, with Leanne perched in the saddle, go with the children. While humans can easily hide behind trees and make themselves small, the horses don't have the ability. And though this cluster of trees will provide some concealment, it's not as dense as we need for hiding.

As the sound of the vehicle increases, Kimba motions for everyone to stay down. Seconds later, the rumble reduces without a vehicle coming into view.

"Did it stop somewhere?" Nicole asks in a whisper.

I shake my head.

After several minutes, Rey stands. "I guess we're close to the junction of the highway and are hearing the car from there."

"Really?" I ask, not even attempting to contain my excitement.

This road we've been on since leaving Pryor, aptly named Pryor Road, has gone on forever. Or at least it feels like it. From our map, we know it's only a little over twenty miles from Pryor to the junction of US Highway 87. Three days, that's how long we thought it'd take to reach this point, four at most.

Because of the incident at the creek, we've been on this never-ending road for over three weeks. Sure, most of that time was in the little house and not *actually on* the road. But it still feels like a big deal to reach the junction.

"But why'd we have to hide, Daddy?" Naomi asks as we make our way back to the rest of the group. "I wanted to see a car."

"We've talked about this before, munchkin. It's best to keep a low profile and not let people see us when we can avoid it."

"But a car— "

"Naomi," Kimba says, a warning in her voice.

She lets out a huge sigh. "I guess."

There's a new spring in our step as we make our way back to the pavement. Around a gentle bend, the highway, running perpendicular, comes into view.

"All right!" one of the A Boys calls out. The celebration continues as we reach the junction and see a big, beautiful green sign on Highway 87, declaring "Billings 11."

Even Leanne's smile is evident when her son Sebastian says, "We're getting closer to Auntie's house, Mom. Won't be long now!"

Eleven miles to Billings means it's slightly less to Lockwood and Robyn's parents. Before her accident, she'd looked at the map with us, showing us Johnson Road, the route she takes to get to her mom and dad's place. "They live in a little mobile home near the fire department," she'd said.

Our plan is to turn off Highway 87 at Johnson Road and find the fire department. From there, we'll start asking people if they happen to know a couple named Von and Minnie in their late fifties to early sixties.

But last night, Rey admitted the military being in place could complicate things. Of course, with them there, it means the siege is over and we can enter Lockwood.

"All right, folks," Rey says. "We're all excited. But as we know from just a few minutes ago with the car, we need to be extra diligent. The snippets we've heard about the situation in Billings and Lockwood is concerning, and people may have become desperate. Plus, this close to a major city, we should start seeing an increase in homes."

"I'm surprised we haven't already," Donnie adds. "They're still a lot more scattered than I expected."

"But with the military there," the youngest A Boy says, "they should be fixing things, right?"

"Ha!" Donnie scoffs.

Last night, after we set up camp, we thought we heard an aircraft. It was far off, and I wasn't entirely convinced it was a plane, but it was definitely a motor of some sort. Just like the car, we never saw it, but it gave us hope our world may soon return to normal.

Gave most of us hope.

Donnie is convinced the military is staging some sort of take over. "I read all about these plans," he said. "It's the Deep State, you know. I betcha they're behind all of this. That's why we didn't retaliate. The president—he's probably part of them too. Bought and paid for."

"Deep State?" Victoria asked. "Isn't that some kind of conspiracy theory?"

"It's not a conspiracy if it's true! They're part of the New World Order."

He's back at it today. "You all are completely oblivious to what's really happening. I told you last night. Deep State. New World Order. Remember? Wake up and smell the coffee before it's too late. Don't trust any of them."

As we continue our walk toward Billings and Lockwood, Donnie starts up again about his theories on why we're in this mess. He's adamant the military isn't swooping in to save us, that they're going to make it worse by putting us under martial law and then taking advantage of our weaknesses.

"I have a hard time believing the men and women in our military don't want the best for our country," PJ says with a slight clip to his words.

"Oh, I agree." Kimba lifts a hand in the air. "Those serving—most of them, anyway—do it out of love of country. They're not the ones who are the issue. I'm concerned about those pulling the strings. The puppet masters."

"Well, I guess you'd know," Donnie mutters. "Weren't you one of those? Part of the covert operations controlling others?"

"Me?" Kimba laughs. "Nope. I was an employee and nothing more."

"Sure," Donnie answers with a cruel laugh. "You know what I think?"

"I'm sure you're going to tell us, mate," Rey says, his voice light.

"I think the government has been overtaken," Donnie says. "The FBI, CIA, DOD, and all the other alphabet soup groups have been infiltrated by the Deep State, along with higher ups in the military and Congress. And yes, even the presidency! You think you weren't part of it, but shoot! You guys were even behind 9/11, right? Or knew about it at least and did nothing to stop it."

Rey lets out a slow breath. "Where'd you get your information?"

"The internet, of course! It's all there for those who care to do the research."

I stop myself from laughing by pretending to cough. Donnie's always struck me as a cowboy, one who would prefer to spend his time in the open air with his horse, not sitting in front of a computer going down rabbit holes.

"That's why they pulled the plug! Too many of us knew the truth. The gig was up, and they had to act. Take us down. Cripple us. Strand people away from home and then launch the nukes. They knew we'd kill each other. Now the UN—you know that's who's probably in Lockwood, not our military but the United Nations. After all, our military can't even operate on US soil, right?"

"We talked about this." Kimba's voice is patient, like Donnie's a toddler she's explaining something to for the first time. "The original Posse Comitatus Act doesn't apply to the Navy or the Marines, but a statute was added later to include them. And military can support civilian law enforcement under certain circumstances. Also, they can be used to prevent an invasion."

"Blah, blah, blah," Donnie says. "Sounds to me like they can do whatever they want."

Kimba forces a smile. "We don't know if it's actual military in Lockwood or National Guard."

"Or the UN!" Donnie declares loud enough to cause his horse to flinch. "Oops. Sorry, Gordie. You okay, Leanne?"

"I'm fine, but you should probably take a breath . . . or two." She rubs Gordie's neck. "Besides, I want the military to help. Whatever it takes to put this to an end—Marines, Navy, Army, Air Force—does it matter? Shoot, bring in the Coast Guard if they can get our lights back on and stop the killing."

"Yep, I s'pose you're right." Donnie gazes up at her. "It's just . . . this all seems so senseless. The deaths. The destruction. If it's not an inside job, I'll be surprised."

"Do you really think we'll ever know?" Leanne asks. "Besides, does it matter? It doesn't change anything today."

"It could change the future," Kimba says softly. "If Donnie's right—and I'm not saying he is—then the United States we knew may not return. The talks the president has given on rebuilding, we only assume he's talking about our country being as it was."

"Our country was a mess." Donnie nods. "We like to think it was going along smoothly, but was it really?"

"I happen to love this country," Rey says. "I may not have been born here, but I love it like it's my own. The day I became a citizen— "

"I didn't know about that. I thought you were just here on a green card or something."

Rey shakes his head. "I've seen some things that make me realize how good we had it, or should have it. The United States Constitution was written in a manner completely different from anything tried before."

"That's just it." Donnie raises his voice again. "Too many people think it's no longer valid because of *when* it was written. Some people say the US was an experiment, and it was good while it lasted, but it's time to move on. Boy, that's one good thing to come out of all this. Those social media giants are gone, and we don't have to read the drivel put out by people who'd write complete dissertations on their posts in opposition of whatever they had their knickers in a bunch about."

This time, I don't even attempt to hide my laugh. I didn't even know Donnie knew what a dissertation was, let alone how to properly refer to it in a humorous manner. There's certainly more to him than meets the eye.

Rey, also laughing, says, "I'll agree with you on that, friend. I do miss having information available at my fingertips, but the rest of it I can do without."

As the road takes us into a canyon with trees along the hills that are scarred from a past fire, Rey makes a stop motion. "I don't like the way this is closed in."

"Good place for an ambush," Kimba agrees.

"Atticus, you take point. Brett, get in the harness and pull Robyn. Jameson, you have the utility cart. Everyone else spread out. Keep your rifles at the ready. Leanne, you okay until we get through this?"

"I'm good." She's already gone much farther this morning without a real break, other than when we were hiding in the trees from the car noise, than she did at any one time yesterday.

"Okay, you all know what to do. Don't bunch up. Watch for movement. PJ and Rochelle? Can you each take one of the youngest children?"

Naomi walks to my horse and puts her arms up. The youngest A Boy helps her sit at the front of my saddle, while his older brother helps Sebastian get in front of PJ.

"Slow and easy." PJ motions to Atticus.

We fall in behind Donnie at the end of our walkers. Kimba is directly in front of him, while Rey and Asher fall in well behind our horses. The canyon continues on for several miles. At our slow pace, it takes us over two hours before we finally get to the other side. When we reach the open space, Atticus motions to a shack off to the left, long ago abandoned and none too sturdy.

"Yep," Rey agrees. "Looks like a good rest stop."

Our break extends for several hours after having a cold lunch of dried meat followed by naps for some while others take watch. Everyone's exhausted from the stress.

I care for Robyn, getting her cleaned up again and talking to her. When I hold her hand and squeeze, she returns the pressure. "You're going to be okay," I assure her. "Soon, we'll have you with your mom and dad."

Her eyes open, and for the first time, there seems to be a spark of recognition.

I squeeze her hand again. "You ready to see your parents? Your mom? Your dad?"

"Mom," she says in a wobbly voice.

"That's right. Your mom. She loves you and will help you get well. We all love you and want you to get well."

"You too." She closes her eyes.

"C'mon back, Robyn. You can do it."

"Do it," she mutters, her eyes still closed.

I drop a kiss on her forehead. "Soon, Robyn. Soon, we'll get you the help you need."

Restarting our trek, we only make it about a mile when the entire landscape opens up.

"Oh!" Leanne exclaims from her place on Lucky, as many others gasp or make similar expressions of wonderment.

"Wow, that's beautiful," I agree.

"I didn't realize we're on a mountain," Leanne says.

"Me neither. But . . . wow."

Billings is in the distance and is at least several hundred feet lower than where we're standing. The entire view is truly breathtaking.

"Downhill is good." Nicole smiles. "Better than uphill."

"For sure." I nod my agreement.

"It's good," Kimba says. "But from what we can see here, it's a long descent and curvy. What do you think, Rey? Call it good for today and find a nice, flat spot to set up camp?"

"That's probably best. We'll want to be well away from the road. This close to civilization, there could be more traffic, both on foot and by car."

"I was thinking about that." Donnie pulls off his hat and runs a hand through his hair. "I'm kind of surprised we only saw the one group of walkers yesterday. I thought there'd be more."

"Yeah," Rey agrees. "I've thought that too. That's another reason to camp away from the road. We're getting close, so let's try and remember to stay attentive and cautious. Carelessness is how bad things can happen."

Chapter 9

"The bugs are out this morning." Kimba swats at the air. "They bother you much?"

"None made it into the tent, but I could hear them trying. The buzz is annoying. I'm not sure—and maybe my imagination is running away with me, and hope is taking over—but I think Robyn heard them too. She made a face and then lifted her hand in a swatting motion."

"Every day, every hour even, she seems to come back to us a little bit more. God is truly good." Kimba puts an arm around me and gives me a side hug. "Did you get much sleep last night?"

"Yes. Some," I answer.

Since I'm Robyn's main caregiver, I haven't taken watch or done anything but stay with her each night. I was given one of our precious headlamps so I can be hands-free when I tend to her in the dark, making things so much easier. Truly, it's not the light that's precious, it's the battery powering it. How much longer will we have conveniences like batteries?

There're so many things we considered disposable that we took for granted. I've been on the lookout for a new toothbrush. The one I've been using is showing its wear. Soon, I'll need to come up with something different.

Jennifer and I were talking about cutting washcloths down to cover our index fingers, then maybe stitching up the sides to resemble something like a finger puppet. That might work as something like a toothbrush.

Dental floss is another thing we need. I haven't used that in months. And I'm down to the bottom of my toothpaste. Dental hygiene is definitely something we're going to be fully lacking in soon.

"You have everything packed up?" Kimba asks. "Should we get Robyn set and take your tent down?"

"I'm ready. This is a beautiful morning, even with the bugs."

"It is. And it's nice to not have rain for a change. Snow all winter long followed by a wet spring . . . " Kimba shakes her head.

"Yeah. With the clear sky, I feel like I can see forever from here. I can't get over how the valley looks. So crisp and beautiful. Except . . . "

"Except the trail of smoke at the west side of town." Her finger points to where my eyes landed. "The fire started during the night. Sadie was the first to see it. Nicole said she was super nonchalant about it when alerting her and Jennifer about the flames. Sometimes . . . I wonder about that girl."

"She's still young," I say.

Although seventeen-year-old Nicole was a member of the militia on the mountain and regularly takes watch on the road, Sadie's completely new to all of it. At her young age—she'll turn thirteen in a week or so—and being new to our mountain community, since her family only arrived on the mountain the month before we left, she doesn't have the training the rest of our youth has.

Our community's junior militia membership didn't start until age fourteen, but even the very young—those around age five—start learning necessary survival things as part of their schooling: fire starting, outdoor cooking, traps and snares, self-defense moves, and even the basic use of light rifles.

Until we were at the house while Leanne recuperated, Sadie seemed to have little knowledge, or even interest, in survival skills. I half wonder how she even made it halfway across the country with her lackadaisical attitude.

She's still not overly enthused, but she's willing to do what's needed, especially with Leanne and Robyn unable to take watch and Victoria's refusal to carry a weapon. Victoria is willing to stand on sentry duty, and she's often added when we need a third pair of eyes, like now when we're camping so close to civilization, but she'd really be kind of useless if anything were to happen and she needed to respond.

Her son Jameson is almost useless also. He's declared he's tired of being on watch so much and would be more than happy to give Sadie all his shifts. He's touchy about everything and seems to be getting worse every day. I hope he gets his stuff together soon. They still have a long way to go after we separate. And we know how dangerous things can be. Even when we think we're safe, it can change in an instant.

"What do you think it is?" I ask, lifting my chin toward the smoke stream.

"Hard telling. I've never been to Billings and don't know what's there. You?"

I shrug. "I've been there several times but not enough to know for sure. That looks like the area around the zoo, maybe. I don't know, though."

"I wonder what the zoos are like?" Kimba asks.

"Maybe like that wolf refuge outside of Bridger? They turned the animals loose?"

"Releasing the wolves is one thing, releasing a whole slew of different animals from captivity . . . " She shakes her head. "I can't imagine what that'd do to the ecosystem."

"It probably wouldn't be good," I agree.

"Well, let's get finished packing. I think everyone feels the excitement from being so close to Billings."

"Is it excitement or nervous tension?"

"Good question."

Though Nicole was excited about going downhill yesterday, once we start, it's not as easy as we thought it'd be. Leanne rides with me first, and I walk Lucky. We haven't gone far before my toes start to hurt. Naomi also mentions her toes hurt, while Victoria feels the decline in her hips.

Leanne's gotten most of her strength back and is sitting much better in the saddle. Today, she's not the issue with making good time, the decline is.

To keep the utility cart under control, there're two people holding the handles. There're also two people with Robyn, one in the harness and the other bent over at the back of the wagon, holding it to control the descent. We trudge along, stopping even more often than usual, as what we thought would be an easy stroll takes its toll on our bodies.

With Leanne still on Lucky, I hand the lead rope to Donnie, allowing him to pony my horse while I take a turn at the back of Robyn's wagon. The hunched-over position is less than comfortable.

"Look alive," PJ says. "There're people at the house on the left."

The house, which resembles more of a compound, thanks to the multiple buildings, has a curl of smoke escaping from the chimney.

"You see anyone?" Rey asks, adjusting his tactical rifle so the three-point sling provides easy access for firing.

"Not yet."

"Pick up the pace. Let's get past them before we stop again. Naomi, you and Sebastian keep moving, but walk close to the side. If things go bad, I want you flat in the ditch."

As we move past the compound and start around a corner, out of the direct line of fire, Rey says, "We're still too close for a break, but I want Brett and Axel to take Robyn. Victoria and Nicole, you're on the utility cart. Switch quickly."

"Get the feeling back in your upper body," Kimba tells me as I'm released from my position. "You need to be ready in case things get dicey."

"We're okay now, right?"

"Too many houses. And even though we haven't seen anyone, I find it hard to believe they're empty. Look at that one over there." Kimba motions with her chin to a place on the left, farther down the hill. "No one's in sight, but it doesn't really look empty, does it? Not like so many other places we've gone by that you could *tell* no one had been around them for months."

"I don't— " I lift my shoulders, wincing from the sudden motion. "It looks the same as the rest to me."

"Movement ahead." Atticus motions with his head, keeping his voice low.

Kimba repeats what he says so those behind us can hear.

"Where?" Rey asks.

"At that house." Kimba gestures toward the same place she told me wasn't empty. "I just caught it too."

Naomi lets out an exaggerated sigh. "I'm going to need to stop soon."

Several people shush her, as Atticus asks, "What do we do? There's nowhere to get off here."

We're pretty much sitting ducks, with an upward slope on our right and a drop off on our left.

"Keep moving," Rey orders. "Stay loose but ready. Walk with purpose, but don't try to be intimidating. We're just trying to get where we're going. We're not a threat to them, so don't let them think we are. And if you're not already, start praying."

We make it past that house without incident and take a short break around a bend.

Staying on alert, Rey looks at each of us. "This is what we can expect from here on in. We all knew this would happen."

Leanne makes a noise of disgust. "We didn't expect to have Robyn nearly comatose. Or having me . . . " She lifts her hands. "Me the way I am."

I smile down at Robyn as I brush the hair away from her face. She moves her head in the direction of my hand. Her eyelashes flutter but don't open.

"This might work to our advantage," Kimba says. "We have injured people and children. This close to civilization, I'd like to think these people are friendlies."

"Possibly," Rey agrees. "It makes sense that any bad element would've already moved on or moved into the city. These folks here are just trying to get by. They see us walking, the way we are— " he motions to Robyn " —and they give us a pass."

"You really believe that?" Leanne asks, her eyes wide and her voice dripping with venom. She'd been much more kinder and calmer in recent days, that I'd almost forgotten just how hateful she can sound.

"Maybe." Rey offers her a smile.

"You're wrong. And foolish. The people out here are just like the people everywhere else. They'll kill you for mere morsels, for the shoes on your feet. Don't believe for a minute there are *good* people anywhere."

"No one is good, except God alone," Jennifer says, meeting Leanne's glare with a compassionate look of her own. "But with the blood of Jesus covering those who believe, we're given grace."

"Oh, puh-leeze. I'm not talking about that babble. I'm talking about the fact people would just as soon shoot you as look at you."

"Wait a minute, Leanne," PJ says calmly. "When my brother and his group found you, squatting in one of the houses belonging to someone with them, they didn't shoot you."

"Given the chance, they would have. The only reason they didn't was because they knew the people I was with. You folks have no idea what it's like out here. Even on this trip, we've had it relatively easy and have only been shot at a few times. This . . . stress . . . you're feeling now, I lived with it—my children lived with it—day in and day out for months."

I drop my eyes and concentrate on Robyn again. The difficulties Leanne and her children faced are widely known, or were at least spoken of often on the mountain. Ever since her arrival, a month before we left the mountain, Leanne was immediately like a square peg in a round hole, going out of her way to be difficult and argumentative.

Her and her children were so frail, she was excused from work duties while she recovered from her ordeal. But that didn't stop the rumor mill and the name calling. I'd heard her referred to as the heathen atheist on more than one occasion.

At first, I found it humorous, considering there were several people who considered themselves agnostic or atheist in the community. Wyoming has long had a live and let live philosophy, to go along with our tagline of the "Equality State" after championing women's rights and being the first in the country to give women the right to vote.

Of course, there's more to that story. *There always is.* And it turned out there was more to the nasty comments about Leanne.

Seems she'd go out of her way to tell people they were stupid for attending the twice-daily church services at the ski lodge. And she had even more awful things to say to those who were part of the women's or men's support groups, Alcoholics Anonymous, survivors of abuse, et cetera.

I was never on the receiving end of her indignation, but Sylvia Eriksen, who's caring for my girls while I'm on this trek to find my son, leads several of the women-only groups and received a severe tongue-lashing after inviting Leanne to join.

Leanne made it abundantly clear that anyone so weak they needed a support group in today's world deserved a bullet in the head.

I guess she doesn't realize many of us in those groups have been at rock bottom and considered being the ones to self-inflict that bullet. I doubt any of us haven't considered ending the emotional suffering we've gone through. But not now. Those days are over for me.

The things that happened to me in the awful place where Fred bought me and the things Fred did—his systematic abuse and forcing me to marry him—are part of my life.

I find no shame in banding together with others who've had similar experiences and finding a way for us to work through those atrocities. End of the world or not, mental health is still important. And I refuse to be bitter and miserable like Leanne.

While some things may be out of my control, such as what we may encounter as I search for my son, I will focus on what I *can* control. And I'll let today's trouble be sufficient for today.

I clear my throat. "I can't even imagine the things you went through while on the road."

"That's right. You can't," Leanne snaps.

"I think you're amazing, Leanne."

She narrows her eyes. "Don't mock me."

I shake my head and lift my hands. "I'm not. We all see it. You're a warrior. You've done everything to protect your children." I motion to Sadie and Sebastian sitting next to her.

Sadie drops her eyes, while Sebastian nods vigorously and says, "My mom will do anything for us. Just like when she— "

Leanne puts a hand on his arm and gives a small shake of her head.

"I know she will," I say quickly. Sebastian has hinted several times about the things his mom did. "And what she did for Robyn . . ." Tears fill my eyes. "If that's not a warrior, I don't know what is."

"I made her a vegetable." The venom is back in Leanne's voice. "You think I did her a favor? The favor would've been letting her die."

"Do you believe that?" Kimba asks. "If she were your child, would you think that? You've given her a chance. She's still breathing, and each day she seems to make some improvement. At least her parents will have their daughter back."

Leanne snorts.

"If they're even alive," Donnie says. "We might be stuck with her. And then what?"

"She'll come home with me." All heads turn to Jennifer. She nods. "We'll take care of her."

"Yeah, super," Donnie says sarcastically. "Great. We'll haul the vegetable halfway across Montana. If you folks were really the good Christians you claim to be, you'd— "

"Enough, Donnie," Rey says. "You've made your feelings on the matter known."

"I think he's right."

My head snaps in the direction of the voice.

"Jameson!" Victoria says, chastising her son.

"Well, he is," Jameson says quietly. "We should've left her."

Rey gives Jameson a hard look before saying, "Let's get going again, get down off this mountain and find a place to hole up for the night. Tomorrow, we'll find her parents."

95

Chapter 10

"Everyone knows what's happening today?" Rey asks, making eye contact with each of us gathered around. "Jameson?"

Jameson rolls his eyes in a manner only a young teenage boy can accomplish. "I'm not an idiot."

"Dude," his brother murmurs.

"Well, I'm not. Same as every day. Stay quiet. Keep watch. Do whatever I'm ordered to do. That pretty much sums it up, right? I don't know why I can't go with you and do something different for a change."

Leveling his gaze, Rey keeps an even tone. "We're not putting you, or anyone else, in any more danger than necessary. Stay here and help keep watch."

"And don't do anything stupid to cause trouble," Donnie says.

"Are you calling me stupid?" Jameson spins on Donnie.

Donnie crosses his arms. "If the shoe fits."

Rey lifts a hand. "Enough. Jameson, listen— "

"No! I'm tired of listening. I'm tired of you, *all* of you, ordering me around like you think— "

"Jameson," Victoria whines, her tone exhausted and resigned. "You will not speak to Rey that way. What he— "

"Fine. I don't care. I'll be a good little robot soldier. Just go find someone to take her off our hands." He points to Robyn. "Then we can get back on the road and get on with our *special* new life." He glares at his mom as he says the last part.

She drops her head, her shoulders collapsing.

What will my son be like when I find him? When he left last summer for his fourth consecutive year at the camp, he was a happy and helpful young man, always willing to do what was needed on our small ranch and always being a champion for his younger sisters.

I pray he's had an easy time of it and the things of this world haven't affected him, that he hasn't been left scarred and resentful like Leanne. Or timid and almost feeble like her daughter, Sadie, who does little more than move through her day on autopilot. And I certainly pray he isn't angry like Jameson. That'd be terribly hard to handle.

On the mountain, Jameson didn't seem to be nearly as bitter as he's been in the last several weeks. Is Donnie's influence adding to his angst? Losing his dad, especially under those circumstances, surely left a giant hole in his heart. That was evident when we left home, showing a melancholy more reminiscent of Sadie's manner.

The anger, though, that suggests Donnie. At least Donnie usually knows how to keep his under control—not so with the young Jameson.

"Rochelle, you ready?"

"What?" I ask, blinking my eyes.

"We're making our final checks." PJ touches my arm. "You have what you need?"

"Yes." I shrug. "We're taking only the clothes on our backs, right?"

"Pretty much," Rey says. "No use risking losing things."

"Walking in there like lambs to slaughter . . . " Donnie shakes his head. "You're making a mistake."

"It's a risk," Rey agrees. "But we don't know what kind of rules the military implemented. If martial law's in place, they could very well confiscate our weapons and may not give them back."

"You should stay here."

"We've discussed this, Donnie."

"And I still think there's no reason for you to go. Let them go." He points to me and PJ. "Make them take her with them." He jerks his thumb in Robyn's direction. "We'll separate here, and they can— "

"Not happening."

"I'm not opposed to it," PJ says. "Neither is Rochelle."

I nod my agreement.

Last night, after settling into a vacant house on the outskirts of Lockwood, we started this discussion. The suggestion of separating now is valid and makes sense. Although the original plan was for everyone to accompany us to Shepherd in search of my son, Donnie pointed out Leanne is still weak. The extra time on the road may take a toll on her.

They could keep going from here to Lewistown and avoid the extra days it may take to find Christopher. PJ and I could make our way to where we believe Robyn's parents live, then head to Shepherd from there.

The big reason we rejected this plan is the unknown. If martial law is in place, we could lose not only our guns but also our horses. Walking in with nothing is safer. Rey going with us, though, risks the rest of the group losing him, arguably their strongest tactical advantage.

"PJ, Rochelle, and I are going to walk down Johnson Lane. We're going to figure out what's going on and do our best to find Robyn's parents or someone who may know them. If for some reason we aren't back by the day after tomorrow, the rest of you will figure out a way around Lockwood and Billings, continuing on to Lewistown. Right?"

"Right." Kimba wraps an arm around her husband. "It's the smart thing to do. And I agree with going in unarmed and looking unthreatening."

Donnie snorts. "I already told you what the smart thing is."

"Some things aren't negotiable, Donnie. This is one of those things. When we return, then we'll discuss splitting up. I'll agree, since PJ and Rochelle seem okay with it, that part has merit. Leanne— "

"I'll do what's needed," she snaps. "You made it clear from the beginning that my children and me joining you was at your convenience. That hasn't changed. If you think you need to go with her to get her son, then do it."

"Can we discuss this later?" I ask. "Let's take care of Robyn first. One thing at a time."

"Does she need anything before we go?" PJ asks.

"Victoria knows what to do. Leanne's also going to help." I give the woman a smile.

Even though Leanne seems to be returning to her acrimonious self, she was agreeable when asked if she could assist Victoria in caring for Robyn while I'm gone so that Jennifer and Kimba can be available for guard duty.

I am a little paranoid, though. While I don't believe either Leanne or Donnie would follow through with their hints of a mercy killing, I did ask Kimba to make sure neither of them are ever alone with her.

We finally make our escape from the house. On our way out the door, Rey jokes, "Getting out of there was like getting out of Beirut."

While I don't entirely get the reference, I do laugh. Leaving was a challenge.

Even after we thought we had things sorted and Robyn was ready, Donnie and Jameson wouldn't let it go. It was like a tag team match of which one could be the most annoying and get their point across.

Donnie wanted PJ and me to go alone, while Jameson didn't think he should have to stay behind.

"Let's pray." PJ stops at the end of the driveway. "I think . . . we need to pray."

"All right." Rey gives a slow nod. "Should've done that with everyone."

PJ reaches for my hand, then bows his head. "Father God, we ask You to guide us on this endeavor. Help to keep us safe and keep those at the house free from harm. Let us find Robyn's parents and return their child to them. Please touch her body, her brain and heal her. Give her Your strength to come out of whatever it is plaguing her. We ask these things in Your Son's holy name, amen."

Donnie was right about one thing: as we walk along the road in this area that's becoming increasingly populated with each step, I do feel like a lamb going to slaughter. Or a sitting duck. Definitely some kind of prey animal with predators salivating and waiting for their chance to pounce.

I attempt to keep my breathing even, staying alert but not on edge. Dropping my shoulders, which had managed to creep up to my ears, I lift my face to the sun. Spring has finally reached Montana. It's still chilly in the early morning, common for the season, but it feels like it'll be a warm day.

This morning, we left the house as soon as it was light enough to see. The sunrise over the mountain was breathtaking, painting the landscape in pinks and purples.

As my anxiety increases, I return to that memory, remembering the beauty of the new day. Isn't there a Bible verse about that? About how we may be outwardly wasting away but inside we're renewed with each new day, and we shouldn't lose heart?

I give a quick glance toward PJ.

With his well-worn ball cap pulled low on his forehead to shield from the morning sun, he catches my eye and gives me a wink.

My stomach gives a little flutter.

We've gone about a mile when the houses, now forming subdivisions, all show evidence of being lived in. "Shouldn't be long now," Rey says.

"Long until what?" I ask.

"That's the question. My guess would be a roadblock. Probably right around that bend in the road." He juts his chin a hundred yards in the distance.

As usual, he's right.

Another fifty feet after the corner, we find several cars across the road. One's an old small-size pickup truck with some kind of gun mounted in the back—just like the rumors we heard. I feel myself tense. I'd be even more nervous after seeing that truck if there weren't at least a dozen military vehicles scattered about.

As we watch, one sputters to a start and slowly moves down the street. I feel like Naomi with her excitement over hearing a car. Even though we had a few pickup trucks and even an old diesel car on the mountain, motorized vehicles are a rarity. Maybe we'll even see one of the planes or helicopters while we're here.

Even though I'm nervous—not just nervous, scared—I smile at the half dozen men and two women in camouflage uniforms. They look amazing, all in their spotless, light-colored camo with shiny boots. The men are even clean shaven. The women have their hair tucked up tight without any stray curls. And they're clean. I swear I can smell the soap and shampoo wafting from their bodies.

A man standing behind a table, with plenty of armed guards surrounding him, holds up a hand. "That's far enough. What's your business?"

Earlier, we decided I'd be the one to do the speaking. I clear my throat. "Hi, uh, yes, my name is Rochelle Bennet. We're looking for someone. Is there a registry or something?"

"Are you trying to find family?"

"Yes, exactly." I vigorously bob my head and smile.

After being asked about firearms, and assuring them we don't have any on us, Rey asks if they're confiscating them.

"Anyone going into the aid station must be unarmed."

"What do you do with them?" I ask.

"Lock them up over there." He points to what looks a lot like a bear box used in campgrounds. The large metal box has a hasp lock on it with a padlock in place.

"And then you give them back after they're done in the aid station?" Rey asks. "Even if they're staying in town?"

"For the most part. However, we take that on a case-by-case situation."

"We haven't been in any areas with a military presence. Or heard much on the radio lately. Has martial law been declared?"

"Again, it's case-by-case. There was some trouble here, so our rules are in line with that."

"Thanks, Sergeant . . . um . . . Gunnery Sergeant?"

He lifts his head slightly in acknowledgment, then motions us to come forward. He asks for each of us to give him our driver's license or other identification. When I tell him mine was taken from me months ago, he gives a sympathetic nod.

"We get a lot of that."

He records my name and my last official address at my home in Lander, Wyoming. After getting info from the men, he says, "Put your packs on the table, then take several steps back."

Three more soldiers move to the check in station. A female soldier searches my pack while two men take care of PJ's and Rey's. I flash back to the last time I flew and having TSA check my bag after they saw something suspicious on the x-ray screen. The something suspicious was a package of trail mix.

Once each of the inspectors declare our bags as clear, the sergeant motions us to step back. "Now you'll have a physical search. Please put your arms out to the side."

The female soldier steps next to me. Even though we left our guns behind, each of us has a knife tucked in our boots. Discussing this earlier, we'd decided to play dumb if the knives became an issue.

The woman gives me a small smile before starting the pat down. She's much nicer than any TSA screener I've ever had. The pat down goes quickly. She does pause a moment when reaching my left boot— the one with the five-inch stiletto blade in its sheath—but doesn't say anything about it.

After we're cleared, the sergeant calls out, "Private Romo!" A very earnest looking young man around Atticus's age runs over. "Take them to the aid station."

We walk only a few yards before PJ asks, "So, do *you* think this town's under martial law?"

I glance at him, wondering about his question since the sergeant at the checkpoint has already said martial law wasn't declared, just that they have rules.

"Nah," the private replies. "Not Lockwood."

"Billings?" I ask.

"Parts of Billings are still no man's land. They're making headway."

"What does that mean?"

"We'll be traveling up 87 toward Roundup," Rey says in a rush. "Is that area clear?"

"You can ask in the aid station." The young soldier shrugs. "They get daily reports. They'll also help you get your travel papers."

"Travel papers?" PJ asks.

"It's not what you think. It just helps move you through the checkpoints."

"That sounds a lot like what I was thinking."

Rey taps PJ on the shoulder and gives him a look, then turns slightly to the soldier. "So, we can find the family we're looking for at the aid station?"

"If they currently live in Lockwood, there should be a record of them. Here you are."

He points a half a block up the road to a line snaking through a parking lot of a building that's clearly a fire station—or was before things fell apart. There must be close to a hundred people waiting. And it's completely silent.

"It moves quickly once they take care of the leftovers from yesterday. Looks like they just made that call and then will be starting on today's line."

"Thank you." Rey offers his hand to the man.

The soldier hesitates a moment before reaching out to shake it. "Uh, you're welcome."

"Will we need an escort when we leave?"

"They'll help you with all of that. You can even get a meal if you need one." He turns and picks up his pace, returning the way we came.

"What do you think?" PJ asks quietly as we continue our walk to the aid station.

"Better than I'd hoped." Rey switches to his normal voice after using his American one since we reached the checkpoint.

"The soldier was nice." I adjust my pack as we reach the end of the line. "He didn't seem nervous."

"Marine," Rey says. "They don't like to be called soldiers."

"What?"

"The military that's here—at least all we've seen so far—is the Marine Corp. If they were Army, you'd call them soldiers. But they're Marines, so you call them . . . " He lifts up his hands.

I let out a loud sigh. "Does it really matter?"

"To them it does." Rey chuckles. "Years ago, I was given a serious tongue-lashing for not knowing the difference."

"How can you tell?"

"Uniform and insignia."

"So Donnie was wrong then?" I ask. "This is a legit operation, and we're not being overtaken?"

"So far, so good. Let's see what happens next. Keep your eyes and ears open. And let's not discuss our personal business with anyone who isn't in a need-to-know position."

"And then we're vague, right?"

"Right."

Chapter 11

Reaching the parking lot of the fire station now turned aid station, we take our place in line behind a young family with a baby who can't be more than a month old. Having a baby in this world would be scary.

We had two on the mountain, and both births went well. The first was PJ's niece, born on Thanksgiving. The second arrived in January. Thankfully, we had well-trained nurses who were able to assist with the uncomplicated births.

Many in the line are lying on the pavement parking lot, looking like they've been there for hours. Some are covered in thin blankets and others wear only light outerwear, but a couple have plush sleeping bags. Such a variety of survivors.

As the Marine said, within a few minutes, the line begins to move. We wait about an hour outside before arriving near the door.

During our wait, we talk occasionally with each other and those around us. Many have had a rough time of it, which is evident in the way they look and speak. There're several children who remind me of Sadie, fearful of everything and almost seeming crushed. Women and men, too, but it's mainly the children that bother me.

I think again about Christopher and how he's endured. I pray he's been sheltered from the worst of it at his remote camp and will be much like the young man I left there almost a year ago.

If he's alive.

I shake my head to banish the unwanted thought. He's alive. He has to be. Wouldn't I know if he wasn't? As his mother, wouldn't I *feel* it?

Moments after moving inside, where the shade is a welcome relief from the morning sun, PJ whispers, "Who's this?" He tilts his head toward a woman walking across the room.

She stops and talks with a man, both in uniform but not the military camo of the other Marines. These two, and the rest wearing uniforms in this building, are dressed up. They're wearing blue slacks, or even skirts, and white shirts. Definitely sharp looking. It's a complete contrast to those, like us, filling the aid station in hopes of assistance.

The people needing help are tattered and downtrodden—and in need of bathing. Outside, the sour smell of sweat was lessened by the light breeze. In here, it reeks. I wonder if I'll ever get used to the smell of unwashed bodies so prevalent in this new world.

"Are they officers?" I ask, admiring the crisp uniforms.

"Don't think so," Rey answers. "I'd say Air Force, but they look so . . ."

"Young?" PJ offers.

He's right about that. They're as young as the Marine who walked us here, some even younger. One boy looks about the age of my son Christopher, with a face full of active acne.

"Maybe they're ROTC or something." As one of them walks near us, I squint at his name tag.

Rey crosses his arms. "Huh. That's interesting."

"What'd his tag say?" I ask. "Civil Air Patrol? Isn't that something they used in World War II?"

PJ shrugs while Rey says, "It's still around. It's mostly volunteers who help out during times of emergencies. They have programs for youth—they call them cadets."

When we're at the front of the line, they again ask for ID, and I again explain my issue of not having any. Then we're each given a card. The men get a green card, mine is yellow. I'd noticed several other women with yellow cards, and all the men I'd watched received green cards.

I'd determined green was for men and yellow was for women, but then I saw a few women get green cards too. There are a few other colors, but I've yet to determine why they've been issued. Their reasoning for who gets what is a pattern I haven't fully comprehended, other than the orange given to the children. It seems all of the children ahead of us had orange.

After our cards, or as I'd heard them referred to, checkpoint documents, we're then shuffled off to the next table. We've watched the procedure enough while in line to know what to expect. And what not to expect. They're all business. Someone ahead of us asked how Billings is faring and what the death toll is. That conversation was shut down quickly.

"Your business here?" the young woman at the next table asks us.

"We need to locate Lockwood residents."

"Their names?"

"Von and Miriam—she goes by Minnie."

She gives me an expectant look. "Last names?"

I shake my head. "They're my friend's parents. She's injured and unable to speak. I only know their first names through our previous conversations."

"Where is she?"

"Too injured to travel. We were on our way here when it happened. We're just trying to get her home to her parents."

"Do you have other business?"

"Such as?"

"Do you need lodging or to sign up for the meals?"

"Meals?" PJ asks.

"Visitors can receive up to three meals while moving through the area."

I glance to Rey, who gives a slight shake of his head. I look back to the woman. "We might want to take the meal option, but not today. I'd like to take care of my friend first, find her folks and go from there."

She motions with her arm. "You'll need to go to the fourth table down. The one with the orange tablecloth."

"Thank you." I give her my best smile.

The table with the orange cloth has another long line. And it's immediately evident this is the table for those with more difficult issues.

Or troublemakers.

The other tables, for simple person searches or those registering to live in the confines of Lockwood with proof of ID or other evidence they live here, or even tables for simple aid packages, all seem to move quickly. Not the orange table. It has the most workers, all adults as opposed to youth or cadets, and they aren't taking any guff.

A traveling man in front of us discovers this the hard way. He raises his voice, and suddenly two burly guys appear out of nowhere. He's quickly escorted out of the building.

Unfazed, the woman behind the table calls out, "Next."

Over an hour later, when it's finally our turn, things go much better than I had even hoped they would. While they're a little apprehensive about Robyn not being with us, they seem to understand the nature of her injuries and how we couldn't risk bringing her here without knowing what we may find. Providing her driver's license, which I grabbed out of her pack before we left, seemed to help.

Thankfully, with names like Miriam and Von, it wasn't too difficult to locate them on the resident list, even without a last name.

"They're alive?" I want to jump up and down. Celebrate. Instead, I take a deep breath and attempt to tamp down my excitement.

"Assuming it's the correct Miriam and Von." The lady gives a slight smile.

Minutes later, one of the cadets is escorting us out the door and turns us over to a Marine, handing off paperwork the woman provided.

Clawson, according to the Marine's name tag, motions to another Marine before saying, "If you'll stay with me, we'll get you where you need to go. It's nearby."

I smile as I think of how right Rey was for us to go to where we thought her parents lived. While Lockwood city center would've been straight north from the house we stayed in last night, from talking with Robyn, I knew her folks lived on the east edge, near the fire station— the same one being used as an aid station.

As Clawson walks next to us, with the other Marine at our rear, I can't decide if I should feel protected or under guard. We weave through the even larger crowd of people waiting for their turn inside the aid station.

PJ takes my hand, keeping me close.

We cross the road and walk along the shoulder, a hedge of shrubs lining the way and providing a sound and sight buffer for the houses on the other side of what was likely a busy thoroughfare. From studying a map of the area, I know the junction with Interstate 90 is only a few blocks away.

As we walk single file, PJ asks the Marine, "Have you been here long?"

"We liberated Lockwood almost a week ago."

"So, you've been here a week?" I ask.

"Something like that."

"We need to go to Shepherd after this. Do you know . . . is it okay up there?" I ask, unsure if I really want the answer.

"Where is that, ma'am?"

"Northeast. I usually take I–94 to Huntley and get off there."

"Huntley is under Army authority. That's really all I know."

My heart soars at the news. Huntley is awfully close to Shepherd, only about five miles apart. If the Army's in Huntley, then surely Shepherd is also okay.

"Army, huh?" Rey asks.

"Yep."

"They've been given permission to be active?"

"The reconstruction efforts will take all able bodies," Clawson says. "Even some not-so-able bodies. You planning to volunteer?"

"Haven't heard the details," Rey says. "What are the requirements?"

"Humph. Not much."

"We're trying to help some friends get home. After that, my wife and I plan to do our part. What about farther north? Up Highway 87 to Roundup?"

"Where's 87?" he asks, as we move from the shoulder onto a side road.

"It goes through the east side of Billings," PJ offers, "over by the Metra Arena, where they used to have the Montana Fair."

"Oh, yeah. They've set up an aid station there. That area is developing."

"Developing?" I ask.

"There's still some pockets with issues. You'll likely have a specific route to follow."

"But it won't be a issue?"

"Everyone in your party will need to be checked in and have passes issued. But it shouldn't be a problem, especially with the green passes."

I raise my eyebrows. "The men's passes?"

"Pardon?" he asks.

"They got green. I got yellow. Are the green for men?"

A slight smile plays at his lips. "No, ma'am. The green shows they presented valid ID—or what we assume is valid in today's world."

"And since I don't have a driver's license, my card is yellow? There were lots of women getting yellow cards. Are you saying— " I break off my words as the memories of exactly why I don't have identification washes over me.

Very few women were given green cards, at least when I was paying attention to the cards being handed out. Most had yellow. A few, both men and women, had red cards. Had the yellow-card women also been kidnapped and abused? I shake my head to move the thoughts aside.

PJ reaches for my hand, taking it gently in his. The warmth of his rough, calloused palm spreads through me. He gives me a gentle squeeze.

We walk in silence for many minutes, taking a street across from the fire station and then turning down a side street. We're definitely in a trailer park, which is where Robyn said her parents live. My heart rate increases with the anticipation of finding them. Part of me feels badly that, when we do find them, I'll have such terrible news to deliver.

Although each day, each hour really, we see increased responses from Robyn, she's nowhere near well—nowhere near the woman she was before the accident. Her need for full-time care, at least right now, will be a burden on them.

But she's alive. Their daughter is alive and may one day be the woman they knew.

I glance back at the Marine that's still many paces behind us. His scary looking black gun's held in low-ready position as he swivels his head around. He has a blank but earnest look on his face and betrays nothing.

Where there'd been several uniforms stationed in various places on the main road, other than our escorts, this area is without a military presence.

"This is it." Clawson motions to a single-wide mobile home. "Wait here." He gives the other Marine a pointed look and lifts his chin, receiving a nod in return.

The second Marine stays near us, looking even more ready and fierce than he was before.

Clawson gives a firm knock on the door of the trailer, its faded white and yellow paint betraying its age. While many homes in this community are newer, this isn't one of them.

The entrance at the side of the house does have a large, newer-looking covered porch, and there're even several pots of flowers growing on the deck. I give a small smile at seeing the blooms.

Almost everything now is things of use. Seeing something that's simply for beauty is great. Sure, we've seen some wildflowers popping up in the last days as the snow fades away, and we did find that wonderful crop of dandelions at the house where David helped us, but these domestic flowers in a pot are something new.

As I look closer, I notice a few other containers with things growing. Maybe they've put together a small container garden to add to their food supply.

I glance to other houses nearby and see the same thing. I then realize all of these small front yards have been dug up, the dirt freshly turned. Taking a deep breath, I inhale the heady scent of the rich soil.

"They're planting gardens." I point to the fresh dirt.

"Yep." PJ smiles. "Good to see Victory Gardens making a comeback. Better eating than grass."

"Do you think the military brought seeds in? They wouldn't have the seeds saved from last year like we did back in Bakerville, right?"

"Maybe some. My guess is a few people already had gardens when this started. And some may have planted late, after it all started, hoping for some sort of harvest. Then they saved what seeds they could."

The door of the trailer opens slightly.

Clawson's voice carries as he asks, "Von and Miriam Hardy?"

Hardy. I search my memory to see if Robyn ever mentioned that as their last name, her maiden name. I'm sure she didn't.

I strain to listen for the response from the other side of the door. I also try and get a glimpse of the people in the house, but I can't see inside with the door closed and Clawson in the way.

"Do you have a daughter named Robyn?" Clawson asks.

The door is immediately thrown open. A gray-haired man, slightly stooped with age, steps out. He practically bowls over Clawson, who takes several quick steps back. Right behind the man is a tiny woman of similar age, her white, thin hair pulled into a severe bun.

Robyn said her dad is in his late fifties and her mom's in her early sixties. They look closer to eighty. Are we at the wrong house? If not, what happened to them to make them look so aged? And how will they ever care for Robyn?

With the couple now on the same side of the door as Clawson, his voice drops, making it difficult to hear. Clawson points in our direction.

Von shakes his head; Minnie's shoulders drop and her hands go to her face. Von gives me a look that I can't quite interpret. Anger? Confusion? Both. And something else. Hope maybe.

Von pushes past Clawson, ignoring him as the Marine calls out, "I have a few more questions, sir."

"You know my daughter?" the old man asks as he reaches the bottom of the steps.

I step forward to meet him, as PJ whispers, "Careful, Rochelle."

Giving him a small wave of my hand, I continue my motion. "I'm Rochelle Bennet. I know Robyn from Bakerville."

"Where is she? Our grandson?"

My smile falters. I'd been so focused on getting Robyn home that I'd failed to remember the death of her son, Von and Minnie's grandchild. "Uh, Robyn, she was injured. She isn't mobile, and we're on foot. We weren't sure what we'd find here, but she's safe with our friends. You can come with us to get her." I look to Clawson, who gives a slight shake of his head. "Or we can bring her to you."

"And Bradyn?" Minnie asks as she steps next to her husband.

I bite my top lip. "I'm sorry. Bradyn— " I swallow hard as emotions overwhelm me.

PJ steps forward. "I'm so sorry to tell you this, but your grandson and son-in-law have both passed."

A cry escapes the woman as the man turns to her, wrapping her in his arms. "I knew. I told you, Von. I knew something bad happened. I could *feel* it."

Von holds her as she cries, making soothing noises. After a minute, he lifts his head, his eyes filled with tears. "But Robyn's alive?"

"As Rochelle said— " PJ puts a hand on my shoulder " —Robyn was injured. We've done what we can for her, to get her here, but she's not . . . " He lets out a loud breath. "She had a near drowning."

Another crying noise escapes Minnie.

"Where is she?" Von asks.

"First," Clawson interrupts, "we need to verify the information."

"Verify?" I ask.

"He told us we're supposed to make sure it's really Robyn and not some type of scam." Von Hardy crosses his arms, giving us a hard look.

"Scam?" PJ sputters.

"Why would we be here trying to . . . " I lift my hands. "What would we have to gain by lying?"

"We've heard a few things." Minnie touches her husband's arm. "People are trying to get access to the town and on the official rolls. They're desperate."

Rey shakes his head, while PJ mutters under his breath about the things desperate people do.

"I showed her driver's license at the check station," I say, reaching inside my pants pocket to pull it out. I watch as Clawson flinches.

"Easy." Rey lifts his hands. "She's just getting the identification out. We've already been frisked and are unarmed."

"Oh!" I cry out as I throw my hands in the air. My stomach drops as I realize he was close to drawing his weapon. "I . . . I'm going to reach in my pocket, um, okay?"

Clawson gives a nod. "Go ahead, ma'am."

I attempt a smile and nervously bob my head. After removing the license, I pass it to Robyn's dad. "Her husband was Garth. I don't know their exact wedding date but know it was in November. You all were still living in Arizona then, where she and Garth met while he was there for a horse auction. They had an online romance for only a few weeks. Then he drove down and asked you if he could marry her. The wedding was small, more of an elopement really."

Minnie gives a small smile. "They were anxious to get married and move up here. She couldn't wait to start their life together. Live on the ranch. Have a— " She chokes back a sob. "Have a baby."

"That's what she said. They were married on Saturday morning in a park and left the next day. You weren't very happy with them, but you did your best to hide it. And then, when she was pregnant with Bradyn, you moved up here so you could be nearby. Bradyn's birthday is around the same time as their wedding anniversary, within just a few days. I want to say November 15, but . . . " I lift my hands. "I'm sorry I don't remember for certain."

Robyn's dad looks to Clawson. "It'd be hard for her to know this information without knowing my daughter. Especially since there isn't internet right now. Let's go get her."

"We'll make those arrangements." Clawson nods.

"I'm going too." Von straightens his bent frame.

"No, sir. That won't be advised."

After much back and forth, Von finally acquiesces. "Fine. As soon as she's inside the barricade, we want to be notified so we can be with her. You'll take her to the medical tent?"

"Most likely the school building. That's where the main medical is operating. You may wish to prepare for your daughter's return. Get a room ready or whatever."

Robyn's mom reaches for me, hugging me tight. "How bad is she? Will she— " She swallows back another bout of tears.

"She's not really conscious." I choke back my own emotions. "She was under water for several minutes and also bumped her head."

Another gasp escapes Minnie, while Von curses under his breath.

"We've been caring for her the best we can, but we don't have a doctor or any real medical knowledge. She does . . . I told her we were bringing her to you. She seemed to understand that and had a bit of a reaction. We met a pharmacist along the way. He was somewhat helpful."

Von crosses his arms and narrows his eyes. "A pharmacist?"

"Uh, yes." I bob my head up and down. "He was amazing—very helpful. He gave us great info and saved the life of another person in our group, the one who rescued Robyn."

"Humph. Corporal, I hope you'll have a real doctor evaluate my daughter."

"We'll do our best, sir," Clawson answers.

Von shakes hands with PJ and Rey before grasping my hand. "You've given my wife and me hope. Thank you for that."

Minnie embraces me again. "And thank you for taking care of her."

Chapter 12

After saying our goodbyes to Robyn's parents, Clawson and the other Marine escort us back to the aid station.

"I wasn't sure they were the right people," I say once we're far enough away the Hardys won't hear.

"Why's that?" Clawson asks.

"Robyn told me they were younger, in their late fifties and early sixties. They look much older than that."

"Some of these people have had a rough time. Aged 'em quick. Food was scarce while they were under siege, and they had to work— much harder than people their age should be working. It was almost like a concentration camp here. Those two are in better shape than most. At least they survived."

"What happens now?" I ask when we're within sight of the old fire station.

"A team will be put together. Then you'll take us to their daughter. She'll be brought in, but—I'm sure they told you—we won't permit the rest of you to stay unless— "

"We're not staying. I'm looking for my son." His eyebrows shoot up as I add, "He was away from home when everything happened. I've been trying to reach him since the day of the EMP, but . . . it's been a challenge. Then we had to wait for the weather to improve."

"And you think he's in Shepherd?" Clawson asks. "Is that why you were asking about the town earlier?"

"Yes, exactly."

"And then you're heading north?"

"He is." I point to Rey.

"Rochelle will find her son and take him home. The rest of us are just trying to get home too. Or to friends' homes."

Clawson turns to look at Rey. "I'll report on the situation with your friend. Then I'll see what more I can find out about your route while we wait for the squad to assemble."

"Thank you," Rey says. "We appreciate the help. Will you be going out with us?"

"Not likely. How long has their daughter been unconscious?"

Rey motions for me to answer.

"Almost a month. She's been getting slightly more responsive. She opens her eyes, but . . . we don't know if she's in a coma or what."

"You've been carrying her?"

"We made a wagon."

We step across the street to the parking lot of the aid center. "Hobert will wait with you." Clawson points to the second Marine. "I'll report and then return with the plan. They'll likely send a Corpsman with you."

"A Corpsman?" I repeat.

"You have Navy personnel?" Rey asks.

Clawson gives him a strange look. "We always have a doc with our units. There are medical officers too. Even a few civilians that they've put into service."

"Do you have a hospital?" I ask.

"One of the schools has been converted. One of the hospitals in Billings is being revamped for use too."

"Was there trouble at the hospital?"

"Yep. Seems to be a nationwide issue. I doubt there's many hospitals fully standing anywhere."

I shake my head.

"Don't worry, your friend will get the best care we can give her. Wait with Hobert." He motions to his partner before leaving us and disappearing into the crowd. The line that was long when we left appears to have doubled in size.

"Where do you think all these people came from?" I ask. "We didn't have anyone else walking on the road with us this morning."

Rey looks to Hobert. "Do they have a tent set up where they're housing refugees?"

"That's correct, sir. If you need lodging, you'll need to return to the line for assistance."

"No, we're good. Thank you."

"So the Navy's here too?" I ask. "Seems a little far away from the water for them."

"Marines don't have their own medical personnel," Rey answers. "They use the Navy for physicians."

"Is a Corpsman a physician?" I ask.

"More like a physician assistant. Or a Medic in the Army. I've also heard some of them called Devil Docs."

"Devil Docs?"

"Yeah, it's a term of endearment."

I look to Hobert, who gives a slight nod.

As we wait for Clawson, I take a long drink of water as a trickle of sweat worms its way down my back. From the crispness of the morning, it's warmed considerably. We've all taken off our sweatshirts and stashed them in our packs, but even my long-sleeved T-shirt feels like too much. I've shoved the sleeves up to my elbows, but it's little help.

I tilt my ball cap so it covers my face better. A sunburn is the last thing I need. I wish we would've brought cowboy hats, which would provide a wider arc of protection, but the ball caps pack better. When we left the mountain, we were wearing stocking hats and gaiters pulled up to cover our faces, the ball caps shoved in our packs.

Back in February, when PJ and I began discussing this excursion and gathering supplies, we knew we'd be in a variety of conditions. We chose to leave around the first of spring to ensure we'd be back before the next season of winter. We'd be traveling in snow, rain, the heat of summer, and then the coolness of fall and possibly snow again.

Although it isn't many miles from Bakerville to Shepherd, only a little over a hundred, not knowing what we may find along the way meant we needed to be prepared for just about anything.

Then, when Jennifer Dosen asked if she could join us for part of the trip, breaking off when it made sense for her and her sons to continue on to their home outside of Great Falls, Montana, our plans adjusted. They adjusted more each time someone new joined our expedition.

The addition of Leanne and her two children only a few days before departure resulted in the biggest changes.

Originally, we planned for our two groups to separate in Joliet, Montana, after dropping off Tamra Nicholson and her girls. Then the Dosen, Dawson, and Hoffmann families would head west while PJ, Robyn, and I went east.

Leanne's need to go north up US-87 to Lewistown was out of the way from the rest of our destinations. That was when Kimba suggested we change the plans slightly and they would stay with us until we found Christopher. For them, it's a detour adding in several days of travel.

While I welcome the help of going after Christopher, especially since we have no idea what his situation is, I now agree with Donnie. Leanne, though doing much better, really has no business being on the road a day longer than necessary.

Donnie was the last person to join our journey. And the only reason he's even here is Leanne. His entire life, including his brother, is back in Wyoming. In the beginning, I think Donnie only came along because of his crush on Leanne.

We accepted him into the group because of what he brought: another body for defense. For Donnie, it hasn't worked out too well. He was shot in the hand when we were attacked near the Montana and Wyoming state line, then a bullet grazed his head in Bridger. But his crush on Leanne now seems to be reciprocated, so that's something at least.

Thinking of the new romance between Leanne and Donnie brings a smile to my face. He's gruff and short with most people but softens considerably when talking with Leanne or one of her children. At first, he was also somewhat friendly with Jameson, seeming to want to take him under his wing. But as Jameson's surliness increases, Donnie's patience with the boy decreases.

Jameson certainly has issues. Many are no doubt brought on by what his father did in his attempted takeover of our community. But I've heard he had a sense of entitlement even before that. He constantly grumbled over duties he was given.

At almost fifteen, he was expected to continue with modified education, be a part of the junior militia, and start as an apprentice for a future career track. While he was more than happy to be part of the militia, he balked at the limitations of the junior militia, believing he should be allowed on the regular group. When the group moved up the mountain last fall, he refused to go to classes or choose a training program.

And his dad, a member of the community council before he became a rebel leader, allowed it. Not only did Jon Dawson allow his son's misbehavior, but he also worked to pass a resolution removing the education and apprentice program and giving a fast-track option for youth under sixteen to become full militia members. The debate was intense but ultimately failed.

Some believe Jon Dawson's downward spiral began around that time. Others think it was well before that, over the summer when the first discussion of moving to the mountain for winter began. He was originally against it, stating it was best to stay in Bakerville where everyone lived.

The debate of moving went on for some time, with him always being the main holdout. Then, one day, he agreed, saying after much consideration he realized that everyone being close together was the only way they could make it through the winter.

That's when they started working on the rules of moving up; the biggest rule was everyone was required to contribute usable items to the good of the community. The list of usable items was long and included all food, livestock, fuel, generators, and more.

Many in the community refused, deciding they'd rather take their chances in their own homes than give up things they'd worked so hard for over the years.

Robyn's husband was one of those. He was happy to share with his neighbors, but he drew the line at being forced. Working out a compromise, he donated a good portion of supplies so Robyn could move to the ski lodge where the medical team—including a psychiatric nurse—would be residing. With the death of her son, he felt she needed the support they could offer.

There were a couple of other men who moved their families up, but for the most part, entire households stayed behind, including two of the Bakerville councilmembers.

Both of the councilmembers had been in favor of moving to the mountain until the forfeiture list, constructed by Jon Dawson, came out. Those councilmembers also had livestock and goods they were happy to share but refused to relinquish on demand.

On the flipside, there were other ranchers and farmers willing to move their cattle up the mountain and donate all their crops to the community to feed them for winter.

Even though Dawson had been adamant that anyone staying behind shouldn't be allowed to have crops from the farmers who went up the mountain, arrangements were made to leave a portion of the sugar beets, corn, barley, potatoes, pumpkins, and more with those staying in Bakerville proper.

When the massacre of Robyn's husband and the others happened, our entire community was devastated. Dawson and his rebellion had occurred only a few weeks before, resulting in not only the death of all but three of the rebels, but also several from the mountain community. Then to find out over seventy members of the original town were slaughtered and all of their livestock and most of their goods taken . . . it was sobering. We'd likely all be dead had we not moved to the mountain.

Of course, I had no voice in whether I moved to the mountain or stayed in Bakerville proper. I was still a captive when the plans for moving began. Fred and I had our sham of a marriage only days before. I faked being the happy bride for my children's and my survival.

The day before the wedding, Fred beat me so badly my body hurt with every movement I made. He'd been careful not to mark my face, focusing on my back and my head.

Afterward, he begged my forgiveness, telling me he was just nervous about the wedding and, once we were man and wife, it'd never happen again. I wanted to believe him, to think that maybe it could be true. But deep down I knew he was lying. How could he ever treat me with respect and love when he purchased me from a brothel?

"Rochelle?" PJ touches my hand. "You okay?"

I blink my eyes, bringing myself back to the present. "Just thinking about how hot it is. I should've brought that tube of zinc for my nose. At least there's a little wind and it's not completely stifling."

Rey wipes his forehead. "Yet. I almost miss the cold. This parking lot isn't helping much, with the sun reflecting off the pavement."

"You have a bandanna?" PJ asks. "It might keep the sun off your neck."

"Here comes Clawson." Rey motions with his head.

Clawson weaves toward us. A rough-looking man grabs for his arm. Clawson stops, gives a nod, and takes a step. The man blocks him, putting his body in front of Clawson.

Standing next to us, Hobert immediately stiffens.

Clawson turns to face the man full on. I can't hear him, but I'm able to read his lips. "*Step aside, sir.*"

The response from the man is loud enough it carries on the light breeze to where we are. "I'm done with this line. Get someone to help me now!"

Heads turn toward the outburst, with many calling out, "Yeah," or shouting other words of anger about having to stand in the hot sun.

"Not good," Rey says. "Let's move, get away from this powder keg."

PJ takes my hand as Rey motions to the line of shrubs across the street.

We've taken a couple steps backward when the man who stopped Clawson takes a swing at him. There's a scream and then several others jump on top of Clawson. Hobert is moving toward the assault, when Rey tells us to run. We're on the other side of the road, moving into the shrub, when the first shots are fired.

"Who's shooting?" I ask, stumbling into the shrubs.

"Marines," Rey says. "Get down. We should be okay here."

"There's children in the line," I cry as I watch several people go down. "They're going to kill them!"

PJ wraps an arm around me. I bury my face in his side. After what feels like an eternity, the shooting stops and only crying and screams fill the air.

"There's no blood." PJ whispers.

"Not much anyway," Rey says. "Rubber bullets?"

I tentatively lift my head to look over the carnage. While there's still plenty of distress, one man that I saw go down is sitting up, holding his leg. Like PJ said, there doesn't seem to be any puddles of blood. A few people have bloody lips or other various cuts—and there's a couple of people not moving—but it's not what I expected.

A female voice on a megaphone calls out, "Return to your tent or your home. If you are here on a day pass, go to the nearest checkpoint. The aid station is closed until tomorrow. If you require medical assistance, stay where you are."

"What does this mean for us?" I ask.

Rey groans. "We're done for the day. They'll clean this mess up, tend to the injured, get people under control . . . yeah, we're done."

Making our way out of our hiding spot, we find Hobert leaning over Clawson. He doesn't look good, having taken many blows to the face and torso. My first thought was he's dead, but then I hear a slight moan.

Hobert points. "Go to the barricade for instructions."

At the checkpoint, we're told to keep our passes, and we're given an additional pass to show tomorrow. "The doors to the aid station open at 0900. If you arrive before they open, you'll have an opportunity to go in first with this pass."

"What about my friend's parents?" I ask. "They're expecting their daughter to come home today."

"I'm not sure of your situation or what that means. They'll have to wait until tomorrow, same as you."

"Do all three of us need to return tomorrow?" PJ asks.

"I wouldn't know." He gives us a curt nod and calls out, "Next!"

Chapter 13

Rey and PJ left before daybreak this morning. Walking back last night, PJ suggested I stay at the house today. I started to decline, but then realized I've done what I needed to do: contact Robyn's parents.

It's better for me to be the one caring for Robyn anyway. While she's doing well, and there were no issues yesterday, I feel better being the one in charge of her care. I'm sure it's some kind of a control issue on my part, but that's fine. I can accept being a control freak if it helps Robyn get well and if it keeps her safe.

Plus, she's rapidly improving and even seems to realize what's happening. It's an answer to prayer that she's finally coming around.

Last night, when Leanne and Victoria were briefing me on Robyn's day, Leanne said, "Robyn, lift your arm." She wrinkled her brow and then her right arm went up.

"Robyn!" I cried as tears filled my eyes. "You're doing so good. And you know what? Your mom and dad are okay. You're going to be with them soon."

"Mom and Dad," she said in a garbled voice.

Her hands are still clenched in fists, what David the Pharmacist called posturing, but maybe that's something the doctors will know how to treat. I did the stretches last night, massaging her hands and feet to try and release the tight muscles, all the while talking to her about her parents and how excited they are to see her.

When it was time to reposition her last night, I said, "Robyn, can you roll on your back for me?" I was so excited when she moved in the correct direction, I started crying again. And then she had tears running from her eyes!

"How's she doing this morning?" Jennifer asks as she enters the bedroom.

"Good," I say. "She's still responding to commands—muttering more too."

"Is she still thrashing in her sleep?"

"Yeah, that's also increasing. And the weird breathing too. I'm glad we're here at the house. She's moving so much more that, if she was still in the wagon, she could hurt herself."

"Did you tell them she's completely immobile?"

"The aid station people know she'll need a stretcher. I made that quite clear. The Marines have vehicles, so maybe they'll bring one of those."

"And you're sure her parents can take care of her? They sound rather . . . " Jennifer lifts her hands.

I shake my head. "I don't know. But with the medical care they have there, she's better off with them than us."

"No doubt." Jennifer glances toward the open bedroom door. She moves her head closer to mine and whispers, "I still think Leanne should be checked."

When we returned last night, we talked about Leanne going with them this morning so she could see a doctor. Donnie said he'd go, too, and let her ride Gordie. But she was adamant about staying here. She believes the medicine David gave her was enough.

While it's true she's considerably better, and I no longer worry about the illness taking her life, she still has little energy and wheezes when she breathes.

"You did say pneumonia can take a long time to recover from, right? You said your sister was sick with it?"

Jennifer tilts her head to the side. "It was many weeks before my sister had her energy back and didn't wheeze on occasion. And she had proper medical treatment, even staying in the hospital for a day on IV antibiotics."

I give a nod. When she brought up her sister with the group last night, it caused an unexpected reaction. Jennifer's sister, Nina, was among those killed during the attempted coup on the mountain led by Victoria's husband.

Bringing up Nina's name, Victoria shrunk into herself, looking ashamed and distressed. Her son, Jameson, narrowed his eyes and scowled. A few minutes later, after the conversation shifted to another subject, Jameson was still on edge, to the point he was snapping at others and picking fights.

I understand teenagers can be difficult, with their hormones raging as they move from childhood to adulthood, but this is really becoming excessive.

So much so, I'm beginning to look forward to splitting off from the group. Whether we do it after we find Christopher or separate here, Jameson's mood swings, combined with Donnie's gruffness and

Leanne's animosity, make for some stressful times. Add in the continual fear of being shot at or attacked . . . my adrenals are on constant overload.

At least when it's just PJ, Christopher, and me, part of the stressors will be eliminated. Or if we do separate as soon as Robyn is situated, and it's just PJ and me . . . my face reddens at the thought of traveling alone with him.

I can't deny I like him. More than like him.

He's a kind and considerate man with a good heart. A heart for God. And he's easy to look at with his lovely brown eyes, wide shoulders, and quirky smile.

Like me, he's known heartache. His wife and child were killed in a car accident several years ago, which almost took the lives of his nephews too. His willingness to accompany me on this journey to find Christopher is partly born of that loss.

And while I don't consider us a couple or even dating, I can't deny there's an attraction.

He knows all about my history, from losing my husband, Dale, who was brutally murdered, to being kidnapped and forced to do terrible things until Fred Lassiter "rescued" us and made me his unwilling bride.

When PJ and I first became friends, I was embarrassed. Even though PJ joined the Bakerville community after the truth about Fred was discovered, he'd heard the stories. Some were truthful, detailing what really happened. Others were blown up and elaborate. What Fred did to me, and where he found me, was no longer a secret.

When Fred's bad deeds where exposed and he was taken into custody to later escape, killing his guards, several people blamed me for it—for the deaths and for "making Fred the way he was."

They actually thought it was my fault he searched me out and purchased me. Like I was a willing participant in the event.

Maybe it's because PJ didn't know Fred. Or maybe it's just because of the type of person PJ is—a kind and generous soul who's been nothing but considerate of all I've gone through.

And PJ's made it clear he'd like more than friendship whenever I'm ready. He's also made it clear that, even though we may travel alone, nothing will happen between us.

"Maybe Leanne will be okay," Jennifer says, bringing me out of my thoughts. "She finished the antibiotics. With Donnie's extra attentiveness, he'll make sure she gets enough rest. What a couple they're turning out to be!"

I let out a snort. I put my hand over my mouth while Jennifer also laughs, then I say, "She *is* a little less uptight than she was before. Plus, I think she brings out the best in him. And he's really good with her children."

"He's not good with Victoria's son."

"What do you mean?"

Jennifer pauses a moment as her nose crinkles in thought. "The way Donnie is . . . Jameson's emulating him."

"Meaning?"

"Watch him—Jameson, I mean. He seems to study Donnie. Atticus is the one who told me about it. But Jameson only studies the churlishness. On those occasions Donnie is . . . " She stops for a moment. "I don't know . . . considerate? When he's not being a jerk, Jameson doesn't seem to notice those times."

"Hmm. Now that you mention it, I think you're right. I do see a lot of Donnie in Jameson. I guess it'd be normal for someone in his position to look for a role model. But lately, Donnie seems to want nothing to do with Jameson. Do you think someone could talk to him, ask him if he could be . . . I don't know . . . not be a jerk? Tone it down?"

"Ha! I don't think Donnie would be very receptive. We'd be better off talking to Leanne and having her approach him, but . . . " She again lifts her hands in a *what can we do* motion.

"Yeah. Would Leanne be any more receptive than Donnie? But I think it's worth a try. She's softened some."

"Has she?" Jennifer asks, tilting her head. "Or is it just because she hasn't felt well and doesn't have the energy to be her usual ornery self?"

"Maybe. But she doesn't even grump when we do Bible reading like she used to. And I'm positive I've heard her whisper amen a few times after our prayers. Even this morning."

"That'd be an answer to prayer," Jennifer agrees. "You need any help with Robyn? I'm happy to— "

Our conversation is interrupted by a raised voice from the front room. I crinkle my brow. "Speaking of Jameson."

Jennifer lets out a long breath. "I wonder what he's worked up about this morning?"

"Hard telling."

There's another outburst. "Don't you tell me what I can do and what I can't do," Jameson yells. "I don't take orders from you!"

"That's enough," Jameson's brother, Brett, says. "Everybody needs to— " His voice is cut off by the slam of a door.

"Another fun day ahead." Jennifer shakes her head. "He was a snot yesterday. I guess, today, he's trying to outdo himself. At least when we're on the road he seems to know enough to keep quiet. I wish he'd remember that for here."

"We definitely don't need him drawing any attention to us."

Several hours later, Leanne pokes her head in the bedroom door, saying, "You should get some air. The kids and I were going to play a card game. We can do that in here with Robyn while you take a break."

"Thanks, Leanne." I smile. "I appreciate it."

I'm in the small, fenced yard behind the house, soaking in the sunshine, when the backdoor opens so hard it bounces against the house. Jameson spills out with his mom hot on his heels.

"Listen here, young man," Victoria says, wagging her finger at him. At fifteen, he's already several inches taller than her and outweighs her by at least twenty pounds. Even so, she stands tall, no longer the shrinking violet she often is.

Firmly, Victoria says, "I don't *care* if you believe this should be your day off. You lounged around yesterday, doing nothing. Today you will— "

The sound of the slap reaches my ears at the same time I see Victoria's face turn to the side. She cries out.

My eyes go wide as I move toward them.

"Don't talk to me like that!" he screams at the top of his lungs.

"Jameson." His mom's voice is a horse whisper.

"Shut up! I'm sick of you! It's your fault. All of it! It's your fault my dad went nuts and killed everyone. You constantly nagged him. Everything is your fault." His face is inches from hers. She takes a step backward, and he moves with her. "You didn't give him the respect he deserved! But you will not— "

"Jameson." She reaches for him.

"Don't you talk to me! I want nothing to do with you!"

Victoria sees me standing behind him. She gives a slight shake of her head.

He whirls around. "Keep your nose out of our business!"

I lift my hands in a surrender motion, while moving my right foot back slightly. "No problem, Jameson."

He curls his lip at me. "You're nothing but a . . . a hooker! A troublemaking hooker." Rushing me, he raises his hands and pushes me at the fronts of my shoulders, giving me a hard shove.

As I go down, I tuck my right leg behind my bottom and pretend like I'm moving to sit on the ground. I lift my left knee up and reach back with the same arm. Looking slightly over my left shoulder, I do a back roll, keeping my head out of the way and my body round until I'm on my knees.

From there, I quickly scramble to my feet and yell, "Stop!" while putting my hand up in a halt gesture.

He lets out a roar, puts his head down, and runs at me like a bull.

I spin around as I get out of his way. I stick out my foot, tripping him as he sails by.

From the ground, he calls me several choice names.

"What's going on?" Atticus asks, as he comes out the back door.

"That . . . she attacked me!" Jameson yells, pointing at me.

"What?" I sputter.

Brett Dawson steps out behind Atticus. Looking at his mom's red, tear-stained face—the imprint of a hand evident. "Mom? What happened?"

She shakes her head and makes a few blubbering noises.

"I told you what happened." Jameson crosses his arms. "That crazy kook attacked me for no reason."

"That's not true!" Sebastian yells, sticking his head out the back door. "I was watching from the bedroom window— "

"You'd better shut up, kid," Jameson growls.

Sebastian shrinks back slightly before squaring his shoulders. "No. I won't. You're a bully, and I'm not going to let you . . . let you be that way." Sebastian turns to Brett. "Your brother hit your mom. I heard them arguing, and then he smacked her across the face."

"He didn't mean to." Victoria's voice is quiet. "It was . . . it was a mistake. An accident."

"Nope," Sebastian says. "He did it on purpose. Then he said bad things to her. Then he attacked Rochelle, pushed her to the ground. But I guess he forgot that she actually pays attention when we work on our self-defense, because she— "

"Thank you, Sebastian." I give him a small smile. "You should go back inside now."

He opens his mouth, then shuts it quickly before stepping back inside.

I turn to Brett. "This is family business. I was . . . in the wrong place at the wrong time."

"You're going to pay for this." Jameson moves toward me, his voice a harsh whisper. "You and the shrimp."

Atticus takes several steps toward the teen. "Step away from Rochelle."

"Please don't make this worse, Jameson," Victoria whines.

Jameson turns to his mom. "Sure. Take her side. I'd expect nothing less from you." He spins on his heel, moving toward the gate at the back of the yard.

"Are you hurt?" Atticus asks me.

Shaking my head, I turn toward Victoria. "You okay?"

"Fine," she snaps. "Like you said, this is family business. Brett, please come with me to talk with your brother."

Before they walk away, Brett gives me a small shake of his head and mouths, "*Sorry.*"

After they're gone, Atticus quietly asks, "Are you truly all right?"

"He didn't hurt me."

"But he knocked you down?"

I tilt my head to the side. "I'm not sure what we can do to help him."

"We've talked to him—Brett and me. He doesn't want our help, told us to leave him alone. But if he's slapping his mom and attacking you, we have to do something about it."

"Like what?"

He shakes his head. "I don't know. But my family invited them to live with us. He was . . . difficult then. But not violent. They can't stay with us if he's violent—he can't stay with us like that. There's too many dangers from outside influences. We can't be looking over our shoulders at home too."

I'm back in Robyn's room, trying hard not to be overly emotional about what happened. In a surprising show of support, Leanne wraps me in a hug. "Are you okay?"

Donnie barges in before I can answer. "What just happened?" he bellows.

Sebastian again speaks up, giving exact details of everything, including how I moved when he charged me and how Jameson was left gasping for air.

I drop my eyes in shame. I'm feeling pretty rotten about tripping a child. And that's what he is: a child. He may be almost full-grown and the size of a man, but he's still a kid.

"He hit his mom? Then attacked you?" Donnie asks, wrinkling his brow. "The kid needs a serious talking to about how to treat women."

"You should've heard the things he said," Sebastian says. "He used bad words."

"Humph. That boy needs to learn some manners and some respect."

"And who's going to teach him about respect, Donnie?" Leanne asks quietly. "His dad is dead and, from what I've heard, didn't seem to have much of a grasp on common courtesy. He needs someone to take him under his wing and really teach him. Teach him to love the way— " She stops midsentence, then drops her eyes.

"Love the way what?" Donnie asks.

When she looks up, her eyes are filled with moisture. She whispers, "Love the way Christ loves."

Donnie gets a strange look on his face. "I thought you said you were done with that?"

She nods. "For me, it's too late. But for Jameson, he needs it. And . . . " She chews her lip. "And Sebastian and Sadie, they need to know God's love too."

"Mama?" Sadie whispers.

"We'll talk about it later." She gives her daughter a weak smile.

"What do you want to do?" Donnie asks. "Beat him over the head with a Bible? Because that kid's not listening to anything you have to tell him about anything—especially God. Shoot, when I was his age— "

"When you were his age," Leanne says, "it wasn't the apocalypse, and your dad wasn't killed while trying to take over a town. Whatever happened when you were young, when any of us were young— " she motions to include herself and me " —things were different. I don't have the answers or know what's best. But we need to set boundaries, and he needs to observe them. Otherwise . . . " She shakes her head. "Where's Kimba? Does she know?"

"She and Asher are still on guard duty, walking the perimeter. I'm sure Atticus told her."

The rumble of an engine interrupts our conversation.

"Are they here?" Sebastian asks.

"We'd better get ready in case it's not friendlies." Donnie moves from the bedroom.

Chapter 14

After a few tense moments of uncertainty, a large military vehicle comes into view. Seconds later, it's parked in the driveway, and well-outfitted and well-armed Marines spill out the back and gather around it.

I break into a smile when I see PJ. He, Rey, and three of the Marines are soon in the house.

"Robyn's in the back room." I motion for them to follow me.

PJ and one of the Marines stay in the hallway, while the other two come with me.

"Are you the doctor?" I ask, pointing to the one carrying a medical bag. *Brilliant, Rochelle.* "I mean, you must be, right?"

"I'm a Corpsman, ma'am. I'll evaluate her and then we'll transport her to the infirmary."

"So, you're not a Marine?" I ask, remembering the brief lesson from yesterday.

"Navy." He points to his insignia, which means little to me.

"And her parents will be notified where she is? They'll be able to see her?"

"That's my understanding." While he talks, he sets up an IV bag. "You've been keeping her hydrated?"

"As best we could. We don't— " I motion to the IV bag and shrug. "We started with spooning water and broth. But she can sip from a cup now. She's not . . . Robyn's not really awake."

"Is that right, Robyn?" he asks as he kneels next to her bed. "Have you been taking a long nap?" He turns to me. "The report said she had a near drowning. How long ago?"

"Almost a month." I look to PJ. "April 17?"

"Sounds right." PJ nods.

"She didn't do much those first few days, then she slowly started doing new things. But since we've been in this house, she does more than before."

He gets the IV started, which causes her to flinch and make a noise indicating pain. He talks soothingly to her the entire time, always telling her what he's doing and that she's doing great.

At one point, she mimics him, repeating, "Doing great."

After a few minutes, he tells the Marine with him that they're ready to transport.

"We're not staying here," I say. "Can I tell her goodbye?"

"Go ahead."

PJ steps out of the room while the Corpsman moves away from the bed.

I push her hair away from her face. "You're going to be okay now. They have real doctors to take care of you. And your mom and dad will be there to help. I don't— " My voice cracks. "I don't know if I'll see you again. Maybe we can stop by after we get Christopher, but I'm not sure if they'll let me go to the hospital. Know that I'm always thinking of you and praying for your full recovery."

When I stand, the stretcher has already arrived. They gently move her onto the transport. As they carry her out, our friends have positioned themselves to be able to say their own quick goodbyes. The Corpsman and the Marines are all patient and move slowly, allowing for our tearful parting. I'm standing in the front yard, PJ's arm around my shoulder, as the big truck fires up.

"She's going to be okay now, right?" Sebastian asks from his spot a few feet away from me.

"They'll do their best," Leanne answers.

I glance around at our group. Everyone—even the Dawson family—is watching as she leaves. Many eyes are moist, but there's also hope surrounding us.

I wipe at my own eyes. "I think she'll be okay. She'll be well cared for, and her parents will be with her. And we'll keep praying."

As everyone files back into the house, PJ reaches for my hand, giving it a supportive squeeze.

I squeeze back. "Tell me she'll be okay, that we're doing the right thing."

"We are." His voice is husky. "They're much better equipped to care for her than we are. Speaking of, Rey and I saw Hobert today."

I give a nod, remembering the Marines from yesterday. "Did he say how Clawson is? Was he hurt badly?"

"A couple of cracked ribs, a broken nose. Could've been worse. Hobert . . . he seems to be a good guy. Some of the stuff he said—and didn't say—has Rey wondering."

"Wondering about what?"

"Um, Mrs. Bennet," Jameson Dawson interrupts. "I'd like to— "
He takes a deep breath. "I'm sorry for behaving so poorly toward
you."

PJ's eyes dart between the teen and me.

"Thank you, Jameson. I appreciate your apology and accept. Did
you . . . have you spoken with your mom?"

His back stiffens. "I told her I was sorry."

"That's good." I offer him a small smile. "Did the two of you talk
about ways you can prevent this in the future."

He narrows his eyes at me. "Like you said before, this is family
business."

"What's going on here?" PJ asks.

I wave him away. *Later*, I mouth. "It is family business. But as long
as we're all traveling together, there needs to be boundaries. There's
never an excuse for any kind of abuse. We all want to help you with
what you are going through, with what you've— "

"Look, I said I'm sorry." He turns and stomps off toward the house.

"What happened?" PJ asks, his hands clenched.

"His mom got after him for something. He smacked her. When he
realized I'd seen it . . . " I lift a shoulder. "He pushed me."

"Pushed you? And he hit his mom?"

I give a nod.

"And then he gives a halfhearted apology? Humph." He takes a
step toward the house.

I grab at his arm. "Don't make it worse."

"Worse? That little punk has been a menace for weeks. I've spoken
to him. Rey's spoken to him. His mom does nothing but wring her
hands. We should've seen this coming."

The front door pops open, Rey strides out with fire in his eyes.
"Have you told him?" he asks me.

I give a combination shrug and nod in response.

Arms crossed, PJ points. "He pretended to apologize to her."

"I think he meant it."

"No. It was a lame apology." PJ turns to Rey. "What are we going
to do about this?"

"We planned another meeting tonight to discuss our next steps,
whether going with you or separating here. We're doing it now. Axel
and Asher will take watch. They've already expressed their concerns
on the Jameson situation to their mom and brother."

"I'm sure," I mutter.

Within a few minutes, we're gathered in the living room. Because of the limited seating, most of us are on the floor, including Jameson, his mom, and brother. At least Jameson has the sense to look ashamed.

The younger children, along with Sadie and Nate, are in one of the back bedrooms with a board game. Nate, who, like Sadie, is beginning to take sentry duty, thought he should be included in the conversation.

"This is more than sentry duty talk," Rey said. "You'll be caught up on anything pertinent."

As soon as everyone's gathered around, Jameson clears his throat. "I want to start by saying how sorry I am. I've apologized to my mom and Mrs. Bennet, assuring them it won't happen again."

Standing against the wall with his arms still crossed and his brow furrowed, PJ speaks up. "You gave something resembling an apology to Rochelle, but when she asked if you figured out a way to control your temper, you had nothing but a smart-mouthed response."

His apologetic demeanor disappears. "I *said* I was sorry. And since you two won't be with us much longer, I don't really think you have a say on anything."

"Back up a bit." Rey motions with his hands. "First, we're going to deal with the issue of your behavior." Jameson opens his mouth to interrupt, but Rey rushes on. "Today is not the first time we've had trouble with you. We've spoken to you about it. When we left the mountain, it was agreed there'd be certain behavior standards followed on our journey.

"You've been given a lot of latitude. We all know you're hurting— you, your mom, and brother. The things you've been through would be tough for anyone. We all know that. We understand. But the pain you're feeling is not an excuse for raising your hand to anyone. Not your mom, and not Rochelle."

Jameson has the sense to lower his eyes as he mutters, "Yes, sir."

Rey glances to Kimba and gives a slight nod.

She returns the gesture before taking over the conversation. "What can we do to help you? Victoria, you and Brett also. We know this is hard for all of you. And we still have several weeks, maybe months, of travel ahead of us before we reach Jennifer's place."

With her eyes directed to the floor, Victoria asks, "Are we still welcome there?"

"Of-of course," Jennifer sputters, looking to Atticus, who gives a raise of his eyebrow and tilt of his head.

Though Atticus and Asher are twins, Atticus is older by several minutes and has taken the role as head of the family along with Jennifer. Asher, who's always happy to do what's needed, doesn't seem at all bothered by not having a leadership position, whether in his family or in our group.

Atticus clears his throat. "We won't remove our invitation to have you join us. Truth is, we need you as much as you need us. Us working together will be mutually beneficial."

"See?" Jameson hisses.

"See what?" Atticus asks. "We've never hidden this. Remember? You were with Brett when the five us—you, your brother, my brothers, and me—started talking about it. We didn't even include our moms until we'd ironed out the details. In today's world, it's too much work. We offered you a new start, with the understanding we'd all be working together. We'll need to add a few more people too. You know what it was like on the mountain."

"Oh, I know exactly what it was like," Jameson roars.

Victoria makes a shushing noise. "Jameson, please. Brett, can you . . . "

With a shake of his head, Brett puts a hand on Jameson's shoulder. "We did agree. Both of us. He's just— "

Jameson shrugs the hand off, giving his brother the side eye.

"Like Rey said," Brett continues, ignoring the glare, "he's still hurting. We all are. But he's going to do better. Right, brother?"

With a roll of his eyes, Jameson gives a noncommittal shrug.

"It's my fault," Victoria says. "I shouldn't have nagged. He was upset and took it out on Rochelle. It won't . . . I'll do better."

In a soft, kind voice, Kimba says, "If I didn't know better, Victoria, I'd think you might be assuming Jameson's behavior as your own." She softens her words with a smile. "Regardless of what you did or said, he put his hands on you. On Rochelle. And that is unacceptable. I think Jameson knows that." She turns slightly toward him. "Don't you?"

Jameson drops his head and whispers, "Yes."

"It can't happen again. We're in a daily struggle—a daily threat from outside forces. All of us, we need to be a team. We need to have each other's backs. You've been put in a position of needing to do adult things—being part of our defense team, hunting, all of it. And we need to know we can count on you. If it's too much, say so now. We can change things around so you have less responsibilities."

"I like sentry duty. Hunting and running the snares is fine. It's the other stuff I don't want to do."

"Let's discuss duties after we figure out how many of us there will be," Donnie says. "I think there should also be consequences to actions. Before, when there was law enforcement and things were normal, Rochelle could've had you arrested for assault."

Jameson responds with a sour look.

"Your mom too, for that matter," Donnie continues. "But with her being your mom and all . . . I did know of a kid misbehaving like you are that was turning abusive toward his parents, and he had to go to a mental hospital."

"I'm not crazy." Jameson slams his hand on the floor.

"Never said you were. I'm just telling you about another kid and what happened to him. I like you, Jameson. I think you have real potential and a good sense of humor."

A fleeting look of pride passes Jameson's face.

"I'd like to help you," Donnie says. "All of us would. But the bottom line is, we can't have you as a threat."

"It won't happen again."

"Fair enough." Donnie swivels toward me. "I don't think this conversation is over, but we should figure out what we're doing. Rochelle? What's your plan?"

I glance to PJ.

He's still standing with his arms crossed, but he looks less angry. He lifts his chin. "You want to go it alone?"

Tears fill my eyes. "I don't . . . I'll admit . . . " My voice quivers. Why am I being so emotional about this? "I think it's best."

"You're sure?" Kimba asks. "You don't know what you may find."

"It's best to get Leanne home."

"Don't put this on me." Leanne glares at me.

"I'm not. We spoke with one of the Marines yesterday— "

"And several more today," PJ offers. "I haven't had time to tell Rochelle, but we did clarify that the military, whether it's Marines, Army, or those Civil Air Patrol folks— "

"They're not really military," Rey clarifies.

"Exactly," Kimba says. "Rey and I were talking about them last night. They're good for what they are: helping in an emergency."

Donnie grunts. "I'd say this qualifies."

"True," PJ acknowledges with a lift of his hands. "Anyway, there's also some Air Force around. But the point is, they've got I-94 secured from the I-90 Junction to Huntley. And get this, I-90 is good from there all the way west to Laurel."

Cheers go up as Donnie asks, "What's that? Around thirty miles?"

"A little less, but close." PJ smiles. "They're making sure there aren't any pockets of aggression."

"Pockets of aggression?" I repeat.

"That's what he said."

"Hobert said that?"

"Not Hobert. Another guy."

"What about from Laurel to Joliet?" I ask. "Isn't that where they were having some issues and why we went to Chief Plenty Coups? If they cleared that, we could get home a lot quicker."

"I asked. He didn't know, said we'd have to find out from someone manning a checkpoint near there. Said he only gets the thirty-thousand-foot view. And I don't think he likes that much."

"Meanin'?" Donnie asks.

"He's new," Rey says. "He joined up to help with reconstruction. I got the impression he was some sort of CEO in his previous life and thought he'd be given an officer position. He wasn't. And from what I could gather, they're given most of the benefits but wear a different patch and are called Auxiliary Marine. It seems to be made clear it's a short-time gig until they're no longer needed. Not a regular enlistment."

"But they're actual military?" Kimba asks. "Trained properly."

"Abbreviated training. And . . . " Rey strokes his beard. "It sounds like a few things are different. It was obvious who the short termers are compared to the regular Marines. We did talk to Hobert. Did PJ tell you?"

"Only about Clawson's injuries." PJ's words come out in a rush.

Rey raises his eyebrows at him.

PJ gives a slight shake of his head.

"What are you two not saying?" Kimba asks.

Rey lets out a long, slow breath. "Might as well tell 'em, mate. They need to know."

"Need to know what?" PJ asks. "What we think we know is nothing more than a rumor. What we see . . . things are looking up."

Kimba's eyes drill into PJ before darting to Rey. "What rumors?"

"Corporal Hobert was considerably more talkative today than yesterday," Rey answers. "The things he said, or more correctly *didn't* say, make me think the reconstruction isn't going as smoothly as they'd like. The Civil Air Patrol is taking the lead in this area, and the Marines and Army have their noses out of joint."

"Okay? Civil Air Patrol is known for helping out during disasters. We just talked about that."

"Right. That's true. But Hobert and a few others, including Clawson, think things might not be entirely on the up and up."

Kimba smiles. "Or they have their noses out of joint. Marines aren't exactly known for being accepting of other branches."

"Civil Air Patrol isn't a branch of the military," Rey reminds us.

Kimba waves her hand. "I suppose the disagreements are to be expected. And maybe there is some truth to it. Did you find out if they're accepting civilians for the reconstruction? Or are they just enlisting them?"

"Well, there're doctors," PJ says. "We heard about those. Nurses too. And engineers are working on getting the lights back on."

"There're regular workers also," Rey adds. "Plenty of grunt work's available, especially on the burial crews and clearing out houses."

Kimba gives a visible shudder. "Not exactly what I had in mind."

"No, but it's necessary work."

The Hoffmanns have a plan to deliver the Dosen and Dawson families to their ranch, then check on friends living in Bozeman, Montana. After that, they've made it clear they wish to help with the reconstruction efforts.

PJ and I have talked about this a few times, wondering if their particular skillsets as former cloak-and-dagger government employees would be useful in rebuilding at the end of the world.

Like Donnie has said before, the government spies should've been the ones to find out about the attacks before they happened and to stop them—not let our world fall completely apart.

But the truth is, even though we've all heard the rumors about their former careers, we still don't know the details. We've been on the road with them for just shy of two months, and neither talks about their life before.

"So . . ." Donnie says. "PJ and Rochelle will head to Shepherd, and we'll go on to Lewistown. Sounds like a plan."

"Hold up, mate. I don't think that's been decided. While they're willing to go it alone, I'm not sure it's the smartest move."

"Leanne shouldn't travel more than necessary." Donnie turns so he's looking at her. "Right?"

Leanne lifts her hands. "Being here these last few days has helped. My breathing is better. And I'm getting some of my strength back."

"Too bad we don't have better food." Jennifer shakes her head. "That'd help you regain your strength quicker."

As we expected, the wild game this close to the city is played out. While we know it wouldn't be smart to use our guns, we'd still hoped to use the snares, box trap, and slingshot for small game or birds. So far, we've come up empty. Other than a few songbirds flittering around the trees, we don't even see anything. No livestock either.

Yesterday morning, while walking into town, I thought I heard a rooster crow in the distance, but that's it. The meat we dried before leaving the mountain and on the trail are our main food source, along with a few dandelions and other greens.

"You said they have meals?" Donnie asks. "Did you get any more info on those?"

"Yep. We can go to a checkpoint, then get set up at the aid station," PJ says. "We also found out there's camping along the route through Billings. You can have one meal a day and camp while making your way through the city. And like the interstates, Highway 87 is clear through the other side of the city."

"What about getting to Lewistown?"

PJ shakes his head. "All we know is it's good until the city limits. You hear anything else, Rey?"

"Not about Lewistown. But the Navy doctor said the Air Force took control of Great Falls in the early days. Even before the EMP, the base was battening down the hatches."

"All right!" Atticus pumps his arm. "I knew they would. Did you ask about their planes? Were any of them spared?"

"PJ did." Rey dips his chin. "The guy didn't know anything specific but said there have been planes flying in and out of Billings. He thinks some were from Malmstrom. The Civil Air Patrol seems to have quite a few planes too—according to him."

"So they were EMP hardened?" Kimba asks.

"Seems so. Some at least."

"At least there's some. And you saw military vehicles, so we know they've got those too. Plus, they have some communications, right? The reconstruction might go smoother than we'd hope if they've solved transportation and communication issues."

"I'm surprised Malmstrom wasn't targeted," Jennifer says. "When we started hearing about the nuclear ground strikes, I was sure Great Falls would've been hit . . . you know, with the ICBMs."

"Malmstrom, Minot, and Warren in Wyoming are all intercontinental ballistic missile launch facilities. Why weren't they hit? And why didn't they strike back?" Kimba asks.

"Maybe they did." Donnie claps his hands together. "We don't know. They're probably lying to us about that too."

I cover my mouth with my hand to hide my smile.

Jennifer doesn't bother with subterfuge and lets out a hearty laugh. "Oh, Donnie. You're a riot."

"I'm serious about this!"

"Yes, I know. Maybe they aren't announcing it over the radio, but we'll know when we get home. I'm sure the grapevine is up and running. It'll be the talk of the town."

"Yeah, probably," Donnie agrees. "But Kimba's got a point. Why weren't they hit?"

"We've been talking about that." Atticus motions to the Dawson brothers. "Asher and Axel too. When my family was in Meeteetse, Wyoming, several peoples' phones had started working—not ours, and we couldn't reach our caretaker at home either." Atticus shrugs.

"When the alerts went off, it said there were missiles on the way. Then it wasn't long until the phones went dead. I know we assumed the missiles were coming from overseas, and maybe the EMP ones were. With the chatter we heard on the ham radio while we were on the mountain, it sounded like the coast cities were hit first, right?"

A chorus of maybes and agreements follow. I'm in the maybe camp, not really knowing what happened. After the community moved up the mountain, they had a working ham radio. While we did get some news through the radio, the town council filtered what we were told. The info was sketchy at best.

And if I'm being honest, I was so wrapped up in my own world of despair that I didn't much care what was happening in California or New York. I cared about getting through each day, keeping my girls safe, wondering how my son was, and not losing my mind over all the terrible things I'd experienced.

"Right." Atticus nods. "What if those weren't from overseas? Maybe they were launched from nearby ships or were even just *there* in the city and detonated, not coming in as a missile at all."

"You think we'll ever know the truth?" Donnie asks. "I'm telling you, they're behind this. The Deep State."

"I'm not sure I want to get meals from the aid stations," Leanne says, easily steering the conversation away from Donnie's theories. "You said they don't allow weapons in the aid stations, right? We'd have to unarm to get our passes?"

"That's what they said at the checkpoint by the fire station," Rey answers. "I can only assume it's that way at each checkpoint and aid station."

"Nope. No way." Leanne shakes her head. "What if something happened like when you were there yesterday. We could be attacked with no way to defend ourselves."

"Getting you a good meal might be worth the risk." Donnie touches her arm. "And your children—none of you have recovered from your prior ordeal."

She pulls her arm away and widens her eyes at him. "I don't agree. Being unarmed is just asking for trouble."

"They weren't armed when they went yesterday. Rey and PJ went back unarmed today."

"Exactly! What happened yesterday? There was a fight and— "

"There would've been no advantage to being armed yesterday," Rey says calmly. "It might have even caused us additional troubles. The children and Leanne getting meals would make sense. Those who don't need a meal can stay outside and wait. The weapon rules are a little . . . loose. No weapons in the aid stations or for meals, but walking through and in the campgrounds doesn't seem to be a problem once you have the pass. We could go in groups to get the passes, that way someone's always with our stuff."

"Will they allow that?" Kimba asks.

"At the one we went through, I think they would. I'm not sure about the ones we'll use as we head north."

"Wait." Leanne puts up a hand. "Just so I understand, everyone goes to the checkpoint, then from there to the aid station for a pass to either pass through Billings or get their services? There's no traveling through without the pass?"

"That's what they said." Rey nods. "A pass is required."

"Papers, show your papers," Donnie taunts.

Leanne shoots him a look. "That's dumb. We have to show ID to walk through a town?"

"Martial law, though they insist it's not." Rey lifts his hands. "As near as I can tell, there's no local law enforcement, just the military. And I've no doubt they're in charge."

"I've been saying it all along." Donnie smirks. "Told ya so."

With a grim nod, Rey says, "Not much we can do about it." He turns to me. "You're sure you're good to go on your own? You and PJ?"

I glance to PJ, who gives a single bob of his head. "We're good. I agree with Donnie."

"You do?" Donnie asks, his eyes wide.

"Uh, about you guys not being on the road any longer than necessary."

"Oh, yeah. That."

"Sorry, mate." Rey laughs. "Sounds like you're on your own with the other stuff."

"I'm not sure I'd say that." Kimba gives her husband a wink.

"Ah, my darling wife. You're always keeping me on my toes." Rey looks around the room. "Unless anyone has any opposition to separating, that's what we'll do."

Jennifer raises her hand, and Rey motions for her to go ahead. "I know it's the smart thing to do. But I feel like we're letting Rochelle down by not doing what we agreed."

I put my hands to my chest. "Oh, not at all. When I first started planning to go after Christopher, I thought I'd be completely alone. PJ offering to help was great, then when all of you joined us . . . it was more than I ever imagined." My voice catches. "You've all . . . we're family. Even with the difficulties. I'm so grateful to all of you."

I look around the room. "You've helped me so much. Now I think we've gone through the worst of it. With the military here, it should be safer. And they're gaining more ground every day."

"You act like the military is a bonus." Donnie shakes his head. "I wouldn't trust them."

Chapter 15

"Look at that sunset."

"It's amazing, for sure," PJ says. "Big Sky Country definitely lives up to its name at sunrise and sunset. Wyoming too. Our sunsets are just as impressive. Looks like we're going to get more rain."

"Of course we are. Even so, I love this time of year. The long days just really . . . " I give a shrug. "They just fill my cup."

PJ raises his eyebrows at me. "Is that right?"

I let out a small laugh. "I had a friend who'd say that. I like it but so rarely have a chance to use the phrase. I thought you might appreciate it."

"That I do." He chuckles.

"I wonder how she's doing."

"Who's that? Oh, your friend?"

"Yeah. Gail. We were roommates in college. She lives outside of Cheyenne. Will we ever be able to find out if our friends and loved ones survived?"

We're camped at a park in Huntley, Montana, one of the lodging areas set up by the Army. Like in Lockwood, there was a checkpoint as we exited the interstate. Unlike Lockwood, there's no aid station here.

We used our passes we were given before, but they were only given a cursory glance. Then we were told the rules of being in Huntley, which is essentially don't cause trouble.

We weren't frisked, our bags weren't checked, and we weren't even asked about our weapons. There're no meals or any offer of assistance and no obvious patrols around the campground.

We arrived late afternoon and decided to stop for the day. I'll admit, I would've liked to kept riding. I'm ready to be reunited with my son.

We ended up staying an additional day after Robyn was taken away by the Corpsmen. Although I was anxious to get on the road, everyone was, PJ and Rey started vomiting shortly after our talk about the trouble with Jameson. Fever and chills followed.

We thought they had food poisoning from eating something at the aid station, but they insisted they didn't eat anything but what they'd taken with them.

PJ was sick through the night and into the early morning hours, while Rey didn't seem to improve until afternoon. Around noon, PJ said he was well enough we could leave. But his pale face told me otherwise.

Thankfully, no one else became ill. PJ assures me he's feeling fine after his bout with the stomach troubles, but I'm not convinced. He still looks a little peaked.

We left the house at daylight this morning. After goodbye hugs and well wishes, the rest of our group headed north, while we went east. Separating was bittersweet. The last several weeks have allowed us to grow close, almost like family.

And like family, it hasn't always been easy.

Jameson's misbehavior was over the top, but there have been the occasional snide or rude comments caused by being with the same people day in and day out. Donnie was often uncaring of who his words might affect. Victoria Dawson, too, but to a lesser degree. Even so, I've developed feelings for many of them.

I'll miss Sebastian for sure. His sweet innocence, combined with his cheerfulness, was always welcome. Even the quiet way of his older sister, Sadie, was welcome. Even though she said little, I'm convinced she saw a lot, taking in her surroundings and staying alert. And always being there to help her mom.

Leanne can be difficult, but she seemed to soften in recent days. Whether from being so sick or from her new relationship with Donnie, something has changed in her. And yesterday, when she talked about Jameson needing to know Jesus, I saw a different side of her.

Sebastian had told me that his mom used to believe in God, but that God abandoned her while they were walking before, and now his mom no longer wants anything to do with Him.

Then he dropped his voice to a whisper and said, "But I know He didn't. I know God is still helping us. We arrived safe in Wyoming because of Him, and now we'll go to my mom's aunt's house and God will guide us the whole way." Oh, but to have his faith!

Jennifer and her sons—the A Team—with their willingness to always do what was needed, combined with a strong faith, was always appreciated.

Kimba and Rey, and their children, were also a joy. Being always on their game, keeping us as safe as possible, made Kimba and Rey almost indispensable.

Part of me thinks we made a mistake separating. But the other part of me knows letting them continue on was the right thing to do. No one needs to be in peril longer than necessary. Even if the military is here, it'd be foolish to believe all the dangers of this new world suddenly subsided.

The short distance from the abandoned house outside of Lockwood to here showed us that. We were in the saddle until we got close to the checkpoint near the Lockwood firehouse, then walked the rest of the way.

Our passes from before were scrutinized and our belongings checked. We had to remove our sidearms and put them in our saddlebags or backpacks, while our rifles remained in our scabbards. While walking the horses through town, we saw two different fights break out among the weary refugees.

Once we reached the entrance to the interstate and went through another checkpoint, we were allowed to ride again. We took a moderate pace, walking along the soft shoulder as often as possible.

Entering the interstate was almost a different world than what we'd experienced on our way to Lockwood. Where we saw few people on the quiet country road, the interstate was busy, not only with people walking but also with military vehicles and even the occasional civilian car or truck. Like Kimba said, maybe having transportation again will help with the rebuilding.

I can't help but wonder how long it'll be until the reconstruction efforts reach Bakerville, or even farther south to my home in Lander. If the military can move in and make it safe for me to get to our ranch, that'd be a huge blessing.

"You think they'll be okay?" PJ asks.

"Our group? Kimba and Rey seem to know how to predict danger. It's pretty amazing."

"I was thinking specifically of the Dawsons."

"Oh. I don't know. They're certainly a mess, which is understandable but sad."

"Yep. I'm wondering if it was a mistake for them to leave Bakerville. At least we had a psych nurse there."

"They refused to talk to her," I say.

"Is that right? I guess that shouldn't surprise me. Victoria is . . . she's different. Strong one moment and then a wallflower the next. And the way she lets Jameson walk all over her, that's not right. At least Brett doesn't seem to needle her."

"I agree that Jameson's behavior isn't okay. But some of his behavior is typical. Christopher would grumble and complain when we'd ask him to do things—oh, and the eye rolls. I tell you. Those were something that'd drive Dale nuts."

I let out a small laugh. "Of course, then, it wasn't life or death. Christopher could not take the garbage out, and we wouldn't be much worse for it other than a full garbage can. Now, everything is so important, there's no room for slacking."

"You must be wondering how Christopher has held up these last several months."

I bite my upper lip as I let out a long breath. "He's slightly older than Jameson, yet younger than Brett and Axel. Jameson is . . . the way he is. But Brett and Axel seem to get it. I'd like to think Christopher will be more like them. What mom wouldn't?"

PJ stretches his long legs. Our seating is a log put in place by, we assume, the Army as part of our campsite. My tiny tent is set up, but PJ, who was originally sharing a tent with Donnie, is using only a tarp on the ground and his bedroll. When the weather allowed, he stopped sleeping in the tent, complaining about Donnie's snoring.

PJ insists he prefers the tarp because he feels less contained and stuck. If there was an emergency, he wouldn't have to struggle to get out of a tent. Apparently, from the looks of the park turned campground, most do not share his apprehension. There must be over a hundred tents.

We're on the far east side of the park, next to a road and a line of trees where we could set the horses up on a highline. They're the only horses in the campground tonight, but it's obvious there's been others. There isn't an abundance for them to graze on, but some. And since we're near a grove of trees, they've been nibbling there too.

What we really need is good hay. Although they had a nice field at the house we stayed when Robyn and Leanne were first injured, and some good tall grass along the way, it's been rough since reaching civilization.

The house we stayed in outside of Lockwood did have a couple of old bales in the barn, but we had to pick through them to get out the mold. Feeding like that is a risk, so we were super careful. We brought oats with us when leaving the mountain, but those are long gone, and we haven't been able to find more.

The tall grass along the interstate was a welcome treat for them and was part of the reason we went such a short distance today, since we allowed them ample time to stop and eat along the way. We're both hopeful that, once we're past Huntley, there will be more grazing opportunities for our geldings.

"Likely, a lot of it'll depend on what your son has endured. From what you've told me, he's in a good place. Isolated. Maybe not too many outside influences are giving them trouble."

"I hope so. I can't even . . . " I shake my head. "I try not to let my mind go to places where he's been in danger."

"Understandable. Won't be long— "

"Hey, man," a guy says, lifting his hand as he walks toward us.

My spine instantly straightens. His long hair and pockmarked face bear a close resemblance to one of the guys who kidnapped me on the day of the EMP. The same man who shot Dale.

I move my hand to my hip, feeling the weight of my pistol. My rifle is against the backside of the log, propped on a stick to keep the barrel out of the dirt. A quick glance behind me shows what I expect to see: PJ's rifle in an almost identical position behind him.

"Can we help you?" PJ asks, shifting slightly.

"Those your horses?"

"That's right."

"Beautiful animals. Looks like they could make things easier on a person. How far you going?"

"Far enough."

The guy lets out a hoot of laughter. "Glad to see you've got a sense of humor." He lifts his hand slightly, giving a little wave.

"PJ," I say quietly, as the wave results in four more guys walking in our direction from across the camp. Even from this distance, I can see they're as rough looking as this guy is.

"Listen," PJ says, lifting his hands, "we aren't interested in any trouble."

"Good to hear." The guy squats down, his stench filling the air. "Here's what's going to happen. My friends and I are going to take your horses—nice and quiet like so there's no one getting all riled up about it. We'll complete this transaction like gentlemen."

He gives a smile, showing yellow teeth with a gap in the front. In the next instance, he pulls his pistol, leveling it on PJ. "Right?"

With his friends still a hundred yards away, and his focus on PJ, I draw my pistol and shoot him in the cheek.

"Move!" PJ dives over the log we were using as a seat. A bullet slams into the log next to me as I follow his orders. The four are running toward us, shooting their handguns wildly as they advance. A lady yells and goes down. In a swift motion, PJ has his rifle up and returns fire.

"Go! Get to the trees."

Grabbing my rifle, I take off running to the tree line. As I'm moving, I swear I feel a bullet whiz by me. Titan and Lucky, who've both been around shooting most of their lives as hunting outfitter horses, are standing with their ears forward and their tails down, front legs slightly splayed.

While I want to go to them, turn them loose so they can find safety, I don't want to risk the shooters hitting them by mistake. I dart into the trees about twenty feet to their left. As soon as I'm behind a trunk, which is about half the size it should be to provide me any real protection, I take a knee and lean my left side against the tree.

With a deep breath, I search out PJ. He's still behind the log, now with his handgun up. I can't see any of the bad guys advancing toward him and the shooting has stopped.

"I'm here," I hiss. When he doesn't respond, I try again. "PJ, I'm at the trees."

Turning his body slightly, he looks for me.

"I'll cover you." I motion with my rifle.

He picks up his rifle, then launches himself off the ground. Head down, he runs toward me. He's taken only a few steps when a shot rings out.

I zero in on the shooter. He's using a tent as cover. With his shoulder and head in clear view, I squeeze the trigger.

A scream cuts through the air over the percussion of the rifle. I find the tent in my scope again. He's no longer there. As I'm looking for him, the tree I'm leaning against splinters, sending chunks into my hair.

I move back several feet as PJ slides into the tree line five feet to my left.

When another shot hits a tree to my right, I raise my rifle to fire back.

Click.

Empty.

Pulling out my pistol, I find the shooter as he moves toward us. I shoot three times, missing completely.

From beside me, PJ's 10-millimeter Glock sounds off several times.

I watch as the guy falls to the ground.

"You okay?" PJ asks.

"The horses?" I ask in a wobbly voice.

"Not hit. Ready to bolt."

"You?"

"Mad," he answers.

"How many shooters?"

"I took down two."

"I may have got one."

"Besides the first guy?"

I give a shrug. "There should be one more. Where's the Army?"

"Good question."

I instinctively duck as another shot sounds. "Do you see him?" I ask, scanning the campground.

There're several bodies on the ground. My heart drops as I realize bystanders have been caught in the crossfire.

PJ's 30.06 answers my question. A shot sounds, and PJ whispers, "Got him."

We sit in silence, hiding in the trees, looking for additional threats. It's many minutes before a voice comes over a bullhorn. "All aggressors are to lay their weapons on the ground. Do it now."

I stay put, waiting to see if any of the guys who attacked us stand up.

"I think they mean us," PJ whispers.

"What? No. He said aggressors. We didn't—oh . . . "

PJ calls to them, "We're coming out of the trees."

"Put your weapons down and come out with your hands up."

"Don't shoot!" I yell.

"Out. Now," the bullhorn orders.

"Nice and slow, Rochelle." PJ sets his rifle down, then puts his handgun next to it.

With a nod, I follow suit. Tears sting my eyes as I stand up. "Is it safe?" I ask in a hoarse whisper.

"I pray so."

Out of the trees, several people surround us, ordering us to the ground. I'm on my stomach as my arms are roughly pulled behind my back.

"We were defending ourselves!" I cry.

"Shut up," a man orders, shoving his knee in my back.

I let out a moan.

"Hey, we're not a threat," PJ says. "Go easy." He lets out an *oomph*.

"Please! We were only— " I cry out as the brute yanks my ponytail and increases the pressure on my back.

"I told you to shut your mouth." The man on my back moves off, jerking me by my arms. I let out a yelp as pain seers through my shoulders.

"Take them to the holding area," a deep voice off to the side demands. "We've got a mess to sort out here. I'll deal with them later." I look toward the voice to find a small man in Army fatigues shaking his head.

"How many down, Captain?" someone asks.

"Four dead, six injured, medics are with them now," the small man responds, motioning to the flurry of activity throughout the campground. With my ears ringing and my adrenaline pumping, I barely registered the cries and screams filling the air.

Nearby, a woman calls out, "We've got to get that bleeding stopped. Press harder." She's working on a man by a tent.

My mouth goes dry as I realize he's the one who was shooting at me. The one I hit.

"Is she a doctor?" I ask.

"I told you to keep your pie hole shut." My captor gives my arms another yank.

"Easy with her," the captain orders. "Do you need a doctor, ma'am?"

"They didn't start it," a shaky female voice calls out. She's near us, at the next tent over where they're working on the bad guy, but on the other side of the tent. She's sitting on the ground, tears streaming down her face, a man lying in her lap. A dead man.

"I saw what happened. Me and my husband were sitting here watching the sunset. The guy there— " She points to the man I shot in the face, sprawled on the ground.

My eyes dart to him, and I immediately feel sick to my stomach. *I did that. I killed him.* I swallow the bitter bile at the back of my throat.

"I'll be over to get your statement shortly, ma'am," the captain assures her.

Ignoring him, she rushes on. "He went over there, walking like he was all that. My husband knew the guy was trouble. We knew it as soon as we saw him. Then he told them he was going to take their horses and whipped out his gun."

She shakes her head in disbelief. "It all happened so fast. We didn't even see the other guys, the ones coming at us. We saw the gun—she shot that one. Then the other guys were shooting and my husband . . . he's dead. What do I do now?" A whine escapes her.

"Those others, they didn't even care. Just started shooting, not giving a whit about who they hit." She drops a kiss on the dead man's forehead.

My heart aches for the woman as gratitude soars through me. "See?"

"I'm sorry for your loss, ma'am," the captain says. "We'll help you with your loved one." He turns to the soldiers. "Get the prisoners moving."

"But— " I cry.

"Shh," PJ cautions.

The captain turns toward me. "I heard what she said. We'll get to the bottom of this. But for your safety, we're going to secure you."

For our safety? None too gently, the soldiers march us to the side road.

"Our horses?" PJ asks.

"Shut up," the guy leading me growls, while the one with PJ says, "Captain will have someone take care of them. They'll be fine."

Our pace is fast and awkward, my legs threaten to give out as I'm overcome with exhaustion. Tears sting my eyes and wet my cheeks. They hustle us down the side road, then turn north onto the main road through town.

There're several uniformed people standing guard, their rifles ready to take out any threat.

We walk for many blocks, most of which are a blur to me, before we reach a large building. From the looks of it, it's some kind of manufacturing plant. Inside, there're more uniforms.

"We're putting them in the holding cell. Open it up," the guy leading PJ says to the soldiers at the door.

One of the men quickly complies, and we're led into a small, dark room. The gruff guy leading me shoves me into one of the chairs. "Don't move a muscle." His voice is a harsh whisper.

An involuntary shudder runs through my body.

"That's what I thought." He gives a bitter laugh. He uncuffs my left wrist, running a hand up my arm, lightly brushing my skin with his rough fingers.

I stiffen and stare straight ahead.

Leaving the handcuff on my right hand, he hooks the other end to the chair leg, again messing with my arm in the process. Then he puts his hand on my thigh. "There now. That should keep you."

I close my eyes.

The man shoves me to the ground, roughly grabbing my leg and shackling it to the woman next to me. "Are you okay, Mommy?" a small voice asks. "Did they hurt you again?"

"Mommy's fine. You're doing so good, Sweetie," I tell my young daughter, Cheyre. "You're being so brave." I croak out the words, my voice taxed and scratchy.

My head aches. Every inch of my body hurts.

Through a bloody lip, I smile at my child. She's on the bed across the room with another girl around her age. At least they aren't in chains too.

I turn my head, looking for my older daughter, Kerryanne. Like me, she's chained, connected to the girl next to her. One leg has a metal cuff around it; the chain's attached to the floor with an eyebolt.

Kerryanne has a black eye and a bruise on her cheek, but at least she's escaped the worst of the atrocities.

A far away voice says, "Someone will be in to talk with you soon. I'm sure we'll get it sorted out and you'll be on your way."

"Rochelle, are you okay? Rochelle?"

"She doesn't look so good."

"Something's wrong with her!"

"Humph. She's fine."

"Did you get her cuffs too tight?"

"I'm telling you, she's fine. Probably just faking it, trying to get your sympathy."

"She's not fine! Look at her!"

"Uncuff her."

"Not happening. She's a prisoner."

"Are they going to kill us?" Kerryanne asks.

"No," I declare with more conviction than I feel. "We're going to get out of here. We'll be fine. Then we're going to find your brother and—"

"And what?" she asks. "Dad's dead. We're dead, too, Mom. They should've just shot us. I wish they would've."

"Don't say that!" Cheyre yells. "Mommy says we'll be okay. All of us."

One of the other women starts to hum. The tune is familiar, but I can't place it until someone else adds the words, "I once was lost, but now I am found . . ." Others join in.

We keep our voices low, but our captors still hear, banging on the door, telling us to shut up.

"See? She's fine. Humming to herself."

"She's not fine. She's . . . she had a rough time when this all started."

"We all had a rough time, buddy. Why do you think I'm with these guys?"

"Uncuff her."

"C'mon, man. She's faking it."

"Do it."

"Fine. But you get to tell the captain. Make sure he knows it was your doing."

The hand runs up my arm again. I flinch as he touches me. "Please don't hurt me," I whisper. "Don't hurt us."

"Nutty as a fruit cake, this one. Probably snapped and shot the place up."

"That's not what happened! Rochelle? You're okay. He's taking the handcuff off. You're okay."

A door slams. I cover my ears with my hands. They're back, coming for one of us again. Not Kerryanne! Not Cheyre! Please, Lord, protect my girls.

Chapter 16

"Rochelle. You're okay."

They never call me by my name. They've never even asked it. None of us have real names in here. Just degrading terms. Words to demean and cheapen us. To make it clear we're subhuman. Even my little girls.

"Rochelle, I'm here with you. You're safe."

The fog begins to lift. It's still dark, pitch black. I'm on a cold tile floor. This isn't the room. The room had wood floor—subflooring, with remnants of staples and tufts of padding from where the carpet was ripped up.

I run a finger gently across my lip. It's chapped and rough, but not bloody and raw.

I'm not in Prospect. We're not being held by those men. Cheyre and Kerryanne are safe with my friend Sylvia in Bakerville.

"PJ?" I ask softly.

"That's right, Rochelle. It's PJ. I'm here with you. Are you . . . are you okay?"

A sob escapes me. I curl into a ball, relishing in the sensations of the cold tile as it pulls me back to the present.

The Army has us. I killed a man, maybe two. They put us in handcuffs, but I'm okay.

I sob for many minutes as PJ makes soothing sounds. PJ Cameron. He's been so good to me, risking his life to help me find my son.

Not like Fred Lassiter, my so-called husband who said there was no room in our lives for Christopher. It'd mess up his plans of a perfect family, and people would start asking questions.

Besides, Christopher was old enough to be on his own. That's what Fred said.

But not PJ.

As soon as I told him I was going after Christopher, he volunteered to help me. Fred was out of my life by then, discovered as the rat he is.

When I finally regain control, I look around the dark room. My eyes are adjusting, and I can make out several forms. Chairs.

There was light from the hallway filtering in when the soldiers brought us in here. I was cuffed to one of the chairs when . . . I shake my head. I'm not going to think about that.

I look for the chair they sat PJ in. "Are you still handcuffed?"

"My right arm is attached to the chair leg. The chair is bolted to the floor. You're better?"

"I'm sorry about that." Embarrassment washes over me. "I didn't . . . I didn't know that was going to happen."

"You have nothing to apologize for. I can't . . . I'm so sorry I couldn't help you. I should've realized what being captive may do to you."

I move to a sitting position, pulling my legs to my chest. "I killed that man."

"You did what you had to do. God was truly watching over us. The scoundrel was so focused on me, he didn't even notice you."

"And the others. They were . . . that was awful. They were just shooting anyone in their way."

"It was bad. At the time, I was so focused on you getting to safety, I'm sad to say I didn't even notice the man who was hit or any of the others."

"You think they killed others? Besides for the husband of the lady who was telling the Army guys what happened?"

"It sounded like there were injuries, but I don't know how severe."

"It was such a beautiful sunset." I let out a sigh. "I hope— "

Footsteps echo in the hallway.

"Are they coming?" I whisper.

A rattling noise is followed by the door opening.

A flashlight catches me in the face; I cover my eyes and look to the floor.

"The captain's ready for you," a voice says. It's not the gruff, revolting guy from earlier, but I'm not sure it's the other one either. To be honest, I barely remember what the one who was escorting PJ looked like.

PJ is unattached from the chair and recuffed with his hands behind his back. They usher us down the hall. Unlike before, my arms are left free. They take us into a new room that's lit by gas lanterns, their hiss breaking up the silence.

"Unhook him," the captain orders. "Please have a seat, ma'am." He motions to the chair. As soon as PJ is loose, he says, "Sir," then points to a second chair.

The captain is already sitting, facing us, with a table between. It's an interview room, like I've seen in hundreds of police shows.

"I'm Captain Sawyer. Are you okay, ma'am?"

I lift a shoulder in response. "Are you letting us go?"

He tilts his head. "We have several witness statements. All corroborate you being attacked."

"Great," PJ says. "Then we'll be on our way. Our horses are where we left them?"

"I had my men take care of them. We're patrolling the area, making sure no one else gets any similar ideas."

"Were there many others," I ask.

"Pardon?"

"Like the woman's husband hit in the crossfire?"

"One other death. Several injuries."

"And the man by the tent? The one the woman doctor was working on?"

"Didn't make it."

I drop my eyes to the table.

"It's full dark now," Captain Sawyer says. "And your tent is shot full of holes. We can set up a spot for you to sleep near the infirmary."

PJ turns to me. "Why don't you take them up on that? I'll stay with the horses. Then, tomorrow morning, we can assess the situation and head on to Shepherd."

"Shepherd?" the captain asks.

"That's where we're going," I say. "It's just up the road from here."

The captain shakes his head. "You might want to rethink that."

"Why's that?" PJ asks, reaching for my hand.

"The town emptied out. There's a— " He pauses a moment and looks toward the ceiling. "There's a faction nearby. They've made it difficult for us to determine exactly what's going on. We've heard rumors, but . . . " He lifts his hands.

"Faction?" I ask, struggling to keep the emotion out of my voice. "Like a gang?"

"Something like that."

"What are you going to do?" PJ asks.

"Right now? Not much. But at some point . . . " He lifts his hands even higher. "We've heard from townspeople that they've taken over a feedlot. Before we showed up, they were trading with those here in Huntley. But now, they've shut everything down."

"So, wait." My voice cracks, betraying my concern over Christopher. "If they were trading with the people here in Huntley, then why do you call it a gang?"

"They were trading. *Were.* When we showed up and went to make arrangements, they warned us off."

"Maybe they don't like the Army." I think of the disgusting guy who was feeling me up. There's probably more like him.

"Seems so. And we'd be happy to let them be, but the cattle are a commodity. That trade needs to be established. Why are you going to Shepherd anyway?"

I blink my tears away. "My son is there. *Near* there. He was away at camp when all this happened."

"Camp Ah Nei?"

PJ's grip on my hand increases, reminding me he's here with me. *Here for me.* "Y-yes," I whisper.

"Do you know anything about the boys at the camp?" PJ asks.

"Just what we've heard from the people here. They're part of it. The town of Shepherd, along with the boys' camp and those living in the area, have all banded together."

"They're alive then?" I ask. "The boys?"

Captain Sawyer gives me a kind smile. "From what we know, they've been faring well. They opened up the feedlot and have been free ranging the cattle."

"And you know this how?" PJ asks. "From the people here in Huntley?"

The captain bristles. "Seems even the people here may not like the Army much. Most have been pretty tightlipped, but a few—those who understand we're here to help—provided information as to what's happening."

I furrow my brow as I try to sort out why the townspeople wouldn't have been happy to see the Army arrive. After almost a year of lawlessness, the military coming in and helping reestablish society should've been welcome.

"They won't talk to you." PJ nods. "Will they let us find her son?"

"Don't know. They've got the place buttoned up tight. You'll be going in at your own risk."

PJ turns to me. "Rochelle?"

"I'm not going home without him."

"Would you deliver a message for us?" Captain Sawyer asks.

"That depends on the message," PJ says roughly.

"Only that we wish to establish communications. We can work this out. We must work this out."

"Sounds a little like a threat."

"It's not a threat. We have no choice but to find an equitable division of the livestock and any other resources. I'm sure you know this, but there's still a considerable amount of people in Billings and the surrounding area."

"About that . . . " PJ taps his fingers on the table. "How'd Billings fare? We tried to ask at the checkpoint in Lockwood, but they either don't know or aren't saying."

"Those numbers are still coming in."

"You're not saying either?"

"What about other places across the US?" I ask. "We've heard bits and pieces, but we don't know anything solid."

He scrubs his hands across his face. "No one's talking about the actual numbers. We don't know—probably won't ever really know. If I had to guess, I'd say Billings itself will be about a third, maybe a quarter of the population it was before the planes were taken down."

"A quarter?" I gasp. "It had over a hundred thousand people. Are you . . . that can't be right."

"The truth is," Captain Sawyer says, lowering his voice, "as far as cities go, they've done better than most. Those not wiped out by the bombs were still . . . decimated. You folks were fortunate to be here. Montana, Wyoming, Idaho, most of the Midwest really, wasn't hit as hard. And since the cities were smaller, other than Denver, it was not as severe."

"Where's the president? Do we have a capitol right now?"

"They're not saying. After the assassinations, we don't know much about him, or anyone left in Congress. They're in hiding."

I give a nod. It seems like so long ago. And it really was. Before the EMP, many of our nation's representatives and senators were murdered. While it was shocking at the time, it was just another blip in a terrible series of attacks.

We never even knew who was killed. There was a brief address on it by the president, but no names were mentioned. I consider asking the captain if he knows who was assassinated but decide it still won't matter much. Not as far as getting my son back and our day-to-day survival.

"You want us to tell the group outside of Shepherd they need to share their cattle?" I ask. "What's in it for them?"

"We'll pull them into the fold, provide protection for them like the town of Huntley has."

"Protection?" I scoff. "Is that what you call what happened to us?"

"We have some details to work out on how to keep people passing through safe."

"Yeah. I'd say so. Has something like this not happened before?"

"Not to this level. There've been spats, and some theft, but we haven't had an actual shootout."

"Unless there's something else," PJ says as he stands, "I'd like to get Rochelle settled and see to our horses."

Although I want to return to camp and help PJ with the horses, plus get nightclothes, he convinces me to stay. That and the fact that the room begins to spin when I stand up.

"Let's get you a bunk," Captain Sawyer offers.

Down the hall, he introduces me to one of the nurses, who ushers me into a small closet off the building's cafeteria, now being used as their hospital.

"I'll see you in the morning." PJ smiles, his gaze holding mine. "Get some rest."

After he and the captain leave, the nurse says, "Here's a set of scrubs. There're washcloths in the cabinet and warm water in the cooler. Here's a basin so you can clean up a little." She gives me a kind smile.

I glance toward the mirror on the wall. Even in the soft light of the lantern, it's plain to see I'm a filthy mess. My face is caked in dirt, except the spots where my tears have made clean streaks. There are twigs in my hair, and even a small cut on my forehead. I look down at my hands. They, too, are disgusting with encrusted dirt. How'd I not notice this?

"Thank you. I'm a bit of a wreck," I say to the nurse.

"This is one of our on-call rooms, so you might hear one of us pop in for a little shut eye during the night."

My eyes go wide.

She lifts a hand. "This is the female room. The men have a separate space."

I let out a breath. After my breakdown earlier, I'm not sure how my mind would handle waking up in the middle of the night with a strange man in the cot next to me.

After she leaves, I change into the clean clothes and wash up. It feels amazing to settle into the thin mattress with an honest to goodness pillow, instead of the wadded-up coat I've been using since we left the mountain. Turning on my side, I tuck my head under the pillow, breathing in the smell of bleach.

Even though I'm exhausted, I struggle with sleep. The images of what I did today are too fresh. Lifting my pistol and shooting the guy was pure instinct. I don't even know if it was a conscious thought. His gun went up, pointing at PJ's head, and that was it.

Pow.

Something switched inside of me. From deep within myself, I knew it was him or us.

He would've shot PJ and then me—or worse. Either way, I'd never see my children again. Kerryanne and Cheyre would never know why their mom didn't come home with their brother. And Christopher would never know how desperately I tried to get to him.

Thinking of my son brings a smile to my face. The Army may be unhappy about the townspeople of Shepherd banding together and taking over the large feedlot on the way to Camp Ah Nei, but I'm ecstatic about it.

When we drove Christopher to camp last spring, the feedlot must have had over ten thousand cattle. While Huntley is farmland that started as an irrigation project, thanks to its proximity to the Yellowstone River, Camp Ah Nei and the feedlot is high prairie with native grass, sagebrush, and scrubby evergreens. It isn't great for growing crops but is perfect for ranching.

Turning the feedlot cattle loose and managing them well over the several thousand surrounding acres would provide my son, the rest of the camp boys, and any of those living in the area or moving from the tiny town of Shepherd—which couldn't have had more than two hundred people—plenty of meat to get through the winter. It may not have been an exciting diet, but they'd certainly survive.

And with the rural area surrounding Camp Ah Nei and Shepherd Ah Nei Recreation Area, an off-road vehicle riding area of about fifty miles of trails on over a thousand acres, and a second portion of about four thousand acres for hiking, horseback riding, mountain biking, and more, it's a great place to ride out the apocalypse.

Christopher always had a great time at camp, reporting of days filled with dirt bikes, horses, hikes, mountain biking, and, his favorite, airsoft wars. They'd have competitions among themselves—scrimmages for practice—then would participate in a multi-team event near the end of the six-week camp against other airsoft clubs in the area.

While he loved the airsoft events, those are definitely a thing of the past, a thing for fun and not survival. Now we carry rifles and sidearms loaded with live ammunition.

Ammunition that can easily take a person's life.

I pray Christopher hasn't been exposed to that side of the apocalypse.

Chapter 17

Even with the mattress and comfy pillow, I tossed and turned through the night. When someone near my door declares it's oh-five hundred in a booming voice, I stumble off the cot. My entire body aches, and there's a pounding behind my left eye. A glance in the mirror tells me I look almost as bad as I feel.

Finger combing my hair, I put it in a single braid and then wrap that into a bun, tucking the ends under and securing with the two bobby pins I had in my hair yesterday. I change out of the loaner clothes and back into my dirt-crusted denims and long-sleeved button shirt.

I'm lacing my boots when one of the nurses pops her head in, the same one who helped me get set up in their on-call room last night.

"I thought I heard you up and about. You getting ready to head back to the campground?"

"I am. You're still on duty?"

"I'm off in about an hour."

"Was there . . . everyone from last night is okay?"

With a raise of her eyebrow, she asks, "Do you know how to find your way back to the campground?"

That's a good question. With captive status on the way here, and my adrenaline surging from the shootout, I wasn't paying very close attention to how we got here. The look on my face must have answered her question.

"I'll take that as a no. Let me find someone to walk you back."

The soldier she finds is young. Too young. I'm not even convinced he's shaving yet. He sets a brisk pace and only walks me as far as the block before the park, then points as he gives me directions. I don't even have my "thank you" out of my mouth before he's turned and jogged away.

I take in the chill of the early morning, thankful I was wearing my zip-up fleece when everything happened. Although the afternoons have been warming up nicely, mornings and evenings are still cold. And from the look of the clouds, we'll see weather today. A thunderstorm looks to be brewing to the west.

Stepping onto the predominately brown grass of the spacious former town park, I'm surprised by how empty it is. Where was once a tent city, there's now only a handful of campers remaining.

I smile at the horses, happily munching on something. We were assured they were okay, but it was still a niggling worry of whether they really were.

A few yards away, PJ's moving around our camp, packing things up in preparation of leaving.

The smile he gives makes my stomach do a flip. "Hey, you look like you got a little rest."

Considering how terrible I know I look, I just give a shrug. "Some, yeah." My eyes move to my tent, spread out on the ground with several strips of black on it.

He kneels by the tent and pokes at one of the strips. "Electrical tape. The captain offered it for the holes."

"Good. That'll help. Looks like we might be in for rain."

"Looks like it. At least your plastic tarp didn't get shot up. Unfortunately, one of the tent poles was nicked. It didn't break, but it's bent and weak. I added several layers of tape. Still . . . we'll need to be careful when setting it up, and maybe start looking for a replacement. I heard some good news from the captain."

"You did?"

"He said they're working on clearing out the troubles around Laurel. He thinks we'll be fine going down Interstate 90 to there, then taking Highway 212 to Joliet."

"That's great," I say, with a squeal of excitement in my voice. "That'll save us so much time."

"We'll have you back with your girls in no time."

"You think we'll have any trouble getting Christopher?"

He lets out a long, slow breath. "I've been wondering that too. My guess is it'll be fine. Sounds like they had a good relationship with Huntley until the Army showed up."

"What's with that?"

"The animosity? Don't know. It seems people here may not have been too excited about them taking over the town either."

"Yeah, but why?"

He lifts his hands and shakes his head. "I'm not sure. Maybe they don't like the captain's plans to take whatever action is necessary to feed the region."

"You think it could get bad, that the Army might attack them?"

"The thought crossed my mind. Captain Sawyer seemed a reasonable sort, but we don't know if he's the one making the decisions. Asking us to talk with them leads me to think they're still looking for a compromise. For how long . . . " He lifts his hands. "It's good we're here and getting Christopher out of there. No tellin' how bad it could get."

"They'd wipe them out, right? Would a bunch of ranchers be any match for the Army?"

"That's the age-old question, isn't it? The right for ordinary citizens to bear arms against a tyrannical government has been debated for how long? Remember that senator from . . . oh, I don't know where . . . saying how it didn't matter whether we had guns or not, that the government had nukes and would use them on any troublemakers?"

I shake my head. "I don't remember hearing about that, but . . . this isn't the same, is it? They're not tyrannical by asking them to share what they have with others who have nothing. People are starving. You heard him. Up to three-quarters of the people in Billings have died. Don't you think starvation was probably one of the reasons?"

"Really? You don't think forcing someone to give up what they own is tyranny?"

"I think it's called being a good human! How many of those starving are children?"

"And we know they were willing to trade. They'd been working with this town. They just don't want to be told they have to give." I narrow my eyes at him. "People are dying."

PJ lifts his hands. "I'm not disagreeing with you on that, Rochelle. I believe they should have a choice. When my family joined the people of Bakerville, we were given a choice: contribute to the good of the community and move up the mountain, where it'd be defensible— *safe*—or don't contribute and stay with those who decided to not move."

PJ gives a shrug. "Or we could find someplace else to live. Of course, our choice was partly decided for us by their community rules, but it was still a choice. Is the Army giving those folks a choice? It didn't sound like it to me."

"They should *want* to help."

"And I say they have proven they do. They've traded with Huntley."

My back stiffens, and I raise my chin. "I'm not an idiot."

"I know that— "

"And I'm not going to talk to you about this anymore." I turn my back on him as I say, "They're being selfish. You can think whatever you want. Now can we finish packing up and go get my son before the Army decides to attack?"

I bend down by my tent and start rolling it up. We work in silence for many minutes as each of us takes care of gathering our goods and filling our saddlebags.

I make a point of avoiding the log we were sitting on last night, the grass surrounding it rust colored from blood. With the dew of the morning, it looks wet. Fresh. Even from several feet away, the metallic smell fills the air.

I squeeze my eyes tight as the memory of the bullet hitting him overcomes me.

You did what you had to do, Rochelle.

He would've shot PJ. Then me. Or . . . he might not have killed me right away. It could've been like before. I shake my head. Never again. I will fight to the death rather than be taken captive again.

After a bit, PJ says, "I cleaned the rifles and handguns last night. The captain had his men put them in the tent."

"That was good of him."

"Yeah. I half expected they'd confiscate them. He walked me back last night, made sure everything was here and all was well—or as well as it could be." He hands me my rifle. "I reloaded it. The magazine is full, nothing in the chamber."

"How are we on ammo?"

He tilts his head. "We'd better pray we don't have any more gun fights like that one. For the rifles, we each have a full magazine and the full sleeves on the stocks." He points to the nine-round buttstock ammunition carrier. "Each of our Molle cases are still full—they hold twenty rounds. But the box has only five cartridges left."

"Do you still have your second magazine?"

"Yep. Loaded up and on my belt." He points to a small black pouch.

I do some quick calculation. Five rounds in the magazine, nine in the stock sleeve, twenty in the Molle, which we keep attached to our backpacks—that's thirty-four rounds of 30.06 each, plus an extra five-round mag for PJ. And five left in the box in one of the saddlebags.

"How many rounds did we shoot?" I ask.

"Rifle rounds? I emptied both magazines. You emptied your single magazine. So . . . fifteen between us. My Glock was full, with one in the chamber, so sixteen there. Then five from my second mag. You shot three from your pistol."

I shake my head. "I had no idea we fired so much. We didn't . . . it wasn't our bullets that caught any of the bystanders, right?"

"No. And the captain agreed. Those murderers were shooting at anything. Completely wild."

"I was sure I didn't shoot at anyone who wasn't shooting at us, but . . . " I lift a shoulder. "Replaying it in my mind has been hard."

"Yeah. Same here. I've harvested plenty of wildlife. But it's completely different shooting and killing a human. It's hard to get used to. By the way, I don't think I've properly thanked you."

"Thanked me?"

"For saving my life." He gives me a smile while lifting his bushy eyebrows.

"I . . . I didn't even really think. It was just— "

"Instinct? That's the second time your instincts have saved my life. I'm glad you go with your gut."

Last winter, when we were on a hunting expedition, a bear came out of nowhere. Its massive paw took PJ down with one swipe. It was my rifle that immediately came up and stopped the attack. PJ was still injured, but at least he lived through it.

That was the beginning of whatever it is he and I have going on between us. Friendship, for sure. Romance, maybe at some point. Obviously, after my breakdown last night, I'm still a wreck from my past.

"I, uh, I should probably apologize for last night."

PJ wrinkles his forehead at me.

"You know . . . in the room they took us to."

"Oh. Why would you need to apologize?"

"For freaking out like I did."

"That's not something to apologize for. I'm just . . . I'm sorry there wasn't anything *I* could do to help you."

"You were there for me. I could feel you there."

"I truly believe God will use the nightmare you endured, Rochelle. He already has. You may not see it, but you're an inspiration. With everything that happened to you, you still praise the Lord. Oh, I know you've had times of doubt, wondering how God could allow it. But you overcame those doubts. You follow Him. You love Him, and it shows. You're an amazing woman." He steps closer to me, putting a hand on my shoulder.

As his eyes meet mine, the flutter in my stomach returns. His hand moves from my shoulder to my cheek. My breathing stops as he leans toward me. I can almost feel the warmth of his lips when I pull back.

"I— " Shaking my head, I step away. "I'm sorry. It's . . . I'm not . . . " I drop my gaze and lift my hands. "I'm such a mess, PJ."

"I'm sorry, Rochelle. I shouldn't have . . . I should've asked first. I know we're just . . . we're friends. Always friends."

I stare at the toe of my boot. "My heart *feels* like we're more than friends. And I want to be. I'm just . . . not ready. Not yet anyway."

"I'll wait." His eyes meet mine and he gives me *that* smile. "Now, let's get our packing done and find your son. And pray they're welcoming to us when they realize we're not planning to take their property."

Chapter 18

In the years Dale and I have been taking Christopher to Camp Ah Nei, we've always stayed on the main roads, driving through the town of Shepherd. That was the plan PJ and I had, too, until he spoke with Captain Sawyer.

The captain said the entire area up to Scandia Road and then C A Road, where the feedlot and camp are located, are cleared out. He suggested an alternate route, which is about four miles shorter. Although I'd love to bring Lucky up to a trot and get there within the hour, we maintain our even walking pace.

At just past the two-hour mark, we near the intersection with Scandia Road.

PJ motions with his hand to the junction about a hundred yards ahead. "Looks clear."

"Should we get off the horses?"

"Let's stay on. It'll be better for a quick getaway."

My heart pounds, both from nervousness of what lies ahead and excitement from being so close to my son. "Give me a minute. I need to get this coat off."

"It warmed up nicely for sure."

Even with the clouds building in the west, the sun is beating down on us. PJ took his coat off not long after we left the town of Huntley. With a slight breeze, I was still cold. Now my nervousness and excitement contribute to my feeling of too much warmth.

Tucking my fleece under my saddlebag, then tying the arms to the bag straps so it doesn't slide off, I let out a loud breath.

"You okay?" PJ asks.

"Yep. I'm just . . . ready." My body releases an involuntary shiver.

"You sure you want your coat off?"

I release a nervous laugh. "Maybe not. I'll probably want to stop in five minutes and put it back on. But for now, let's ride."

"Works for me."

In this wide-open country, we don't even need to turn onto Scandia Road to see the roadblock set up on C A, the road that leads to Camp Ah Nei.

"Here we go," PJ says as we approach the intersection. "Put a smile on your face and let's look friendly."

"You want me to do the talking? Like we did at the military checkpoints?"

"Might as well."

We go only a dozen or so feet when PJ whispers, "Shooters behind those strawbales in the fields on both sides of the road."

"What do we do?"

"Keep our hands away from our guns and don't make any sudden moves. Maybe they'll see we're not a threat."

I swallow the lump in my throat and take several deep breaths. Seeing movement behind the blockade, I whisper, "I'm going to call out."

"Yep. I'll keep praying they're not jumpy."

Pasting a smile on my face while trying to appear relaxed, I call out, "Hello! We're friendly."

There's no verbal response, but we see obvious movement from the haybales in the field and the roadblock.

"Try again," PJ whispers.

"My name is Rochelle Bennet. My son was at Camp Ah Nei when . . . when everything fell apart."

"Keep your hands where we can see them," a deep, booming voice orders. "Stay on your horses and keep coming, nice and slow."

"Y-yes, okay," I reply.

"We're okay," PJ whispers. "We'd do the same thing if we were them."

When we reach the intersection of Scandia and C A, the voice, though still deep and booming, yet unmistakably female, calls, "Far enough. Now slide on off those horses. Leave the rifles where they are, and don't even think about touching your sidearms."

"We won't. Like I said, I'm here for my son. That's all."

"Great," she responds without enthusiasm. "Then maybe we won't have to shoot you."

When we're on the ground, she tells us to step away from the horses and to move away from each other. Immediately, there are two people by our sides and two young girls—barely in their teens—holding our horses' reins.

PJ smiles at the one nearest him. "They ground tie. They'll stay put."

We're told to keep quiet and hold still while two men disarm us.

"What else you got?" The one who took the gun from my holster asks.

"Knife in my boot and a folding knife in my pocket."

"What about you?" He points at PJ.

"Same."

"Let them keep 'em." The woman steps out from where she was crouched behind the roadblock.

She's short. Seriously short, like under five foot. Although she's short, she's not petite. Even in the apocalypse, she's bordering between pleasantly pump and decidedly overweight. Pear shaped and in her late thirties to early forties, her distaste at our arrival is evident.

Dressed in much the same manner as me, with jeans and a button-up shirt topped by a shearling vest—and an impressive leather shoulder holster under her left arm—she strides toward us with a decided swagger, oozing confidence. I give her a smile, which she ignores.

"Now, tell me again why you're here."

I clear my throat. "My son. He's at Camp Ah Nei. His name is Christopher Bennet."

"And?"

"And . . . I'm here for him."

"Oh, you are, are you?" She lets out a laugh. More of a cackle, really.

My eyes dart to PJ.

With a furrowed brow, he gives me a slight shake of his head.

"Um . . . yes?"

The woman shakes her head. "You do realize I've been providing for your son—and all the other boys at that camp, along with the people of the area, for almost a year now?"

"I tried to get here sooner— "

"Right. But then your car stopped working and you were too lazy to walk. I get it."

I bristle at her tone. And her words. "The car did stop working." I meet her stern gaze. "And I did start walking. It's just . . . I've had a few delays."

"Oh, yeah? Like what?" She leans casually against the barrier and picks at a nail.

"Really?" I stand straighter. "You want to quiz me? I'm here now. For my son."

She narrows her eyes at me. "You his daddy?" She points to PJ.

"No, ma'am."

"Mm-hmm. Who are ya' then?"

"PJ Cameron. I'm helping Rochelle get here and get home. *With* her son." He gives her a nod.

"If I didn't know better, Mr. PJ Cameron, I'd think that might be a threat. But seeing how that'd be stupid on your part, I'm sure you didn't mean anything by it."

"We just want my son," I say in a rush. "We're not here to cause any trouble."

"See, though, here's the problem with that. I know which boy is yours. And to be quite frank with you, I don't have much desire to let him leave."

Tears prick my eyes as a pounding begins in my head. "I don't . . . I don't understand," I whisper.

"He's one of my best soldiers. And now that the Army is here, well, I just don't think it'd be smart to lose him."

"Give it a rest, Mom." I turn my head in the direction of the voice. A boy around Christopher's age steps from the trees along the ditch. "You know he, along with all those camp boys, want nothing more than to go home."

"Did I ask your opinion?" The woman glares at him.

"He's right, Rogue," the man who took my gun says.

"I didn't ask you either. Just because I let you put your boots under my bed on occasion, doesn't mean you get an opinion in how I run things. At least Skull is my blood."

I glance to the man standing next to me, watching as the pink of embarrassment tinges his ears. What have we got ourselves into?

"So, I don't suppose you're willing to just ride out of here?" The woman glares at me.

I shake my head.

She sighs. "Guess that leaves me two choices then. Let you take your son. Or shoot you where you stand."

It's completely quiet. Even the wind stops blowing as the seconds tick away. With a shake of her head, she says, "Suppose, if I shot you, he'd hear about it and, well, that wouldn't be good."

Hope soars within me as I give her a smile. "Thank you."

"Don't thank me yet. I might still change my mind. Skull, send someone after The Ritz. He's on watch at the other end."

"Ace is there too," Skull says. "You want me to bring him?"

"Not until Ritz confirms who she is." She points a stubby finger at me. "He knows you, right?"

"Douglas Ritzdorf? He knows me." I nod. Doug and his wife, Candice, run the camp.

This woman's need to have my identity confirmed sounds a little ridiculous. Do they have lots of people stopping by demanding to see their sons?

Keeping my mouth shut about this seems the smartest course of action. From my brief interaction with the woman—did the man call her Rogue?—I'd say she's on the verge of being completely unhinged.

"Welp, then. We'll just settle in and wait." She motions to Skull, who disappears into a grove of trees, returning after a moment on horseback. He spurs his gelding into a trot, taking off up the road.

The wind kicks up, bringing a chill to the warm day. The rain clouds I've been watching build since daylight are moving in quickly now. With the way it's brewing, it's going to be a gully washer.

We need to get Christopher and get away from here, maybe find a house or a barn to stay in tonight. With the temps dropping, there could even be snow mixed in. This late in the year, a wet and heavy snow can do considerable damage, bringing down trees and tents that have been shot full of holes.

And a house will be great for catching up with Christopher. From what I'm seeing here, just in these few minutes we've been at the blockade, this woman rules with an iron fist. Was she always like this, or have their experiences in the months since our world fell apart created the person before me?

I'm not who I was before this either. That woman was strong and confident. That woman knew where she was going in life. Now I'm a scared little rabbit fledging out an existence. Surviving.

There's been a few bright spots, but it's been a day-to-day grind. Living on the mountain gave my girls and me security. We were safe and fed.

These people look like they've been eating well too. None are underweight; their skin's supple and smooth. Not like Leanne, who's nothing but wrinkly skin and bones, or David the Pharmacist and his family with loose and chapped skin.

I watch as the woman puts a thumb to her mouth. She works the nail a minute, then spits the debris off to the side. No one talks. Her people all seem to be content to just wait.

Many more people have stepped into view. I'm surprised to realize that, other than her and the two men who disarmed PJ and I, and are still standing next to us, the rest are all youth.

Children.

One of the girls that stepped out of the trees looks to be around Sebastian's age—only eight or so—and she's toting a rifle almost as long as she is tall. She even looks like she knows how to use it.

A dozen more kids, only slightly older than her, are also in view. I look toward the field where PJ first saw the sentries stooped behind strawbales. Are they children? It's hard to be certain from this distance, but none look overly large. Of course, they could just be short like their leader.

When you get right down to it, we had children ready to defend our people on the mountain too. Even though it was a rule that only those sixteen and older could be full militia members, junior militia started at fourteen. And training in hand-to-hand combat and shooting skills started even younger.

On this trip, Sadie and Nate both started taking watch, sharing a .22 rifle. But we didn't have children lugging around guns as big as themselves.

"Mind if we grab our jackets?" PJ asks as a gust of wind blows through, moving my ball cap slightly.

"As a matter of fact, I do. Toughen up, buttercup." The wind lifts her long braid off her shoulder and whips it in her face. She grumbles a few choice words and wraps her braid in a knot, then tucks it under the collar of her shirt. She zips her heavy jacket to her ample chin.

In the distance, two horses crest the hill, moving quickly.

Like the others in this group, Doug Ritzdorf looks good—physically, anyway. There's something else though, a vacantness to his eyes. Even though he's smiling at me, it's with his mouth only.

He slides off his horse. "Good to see you, Mrs. Bennet."

"You too. Please, call me Rochelle."

He dips his head before turning to the woman. "Skull said there's a problem?"

"Ya know her?"

"Of course. She's Ace's mom."

Ace?

"She's here to collect him."

"Well, that makes sense. It's going to storm. Should we invite them in? Get him packed and ready to go so they can take off when the weather breaks?"

"Ace is one of our best. You know we have a war ahead of us, the likes of something we've never seen. Those Army guys— "

"Whether Ace is here or not won't matter much when they show up and won't take no for an answer. We need to do what we discussed— "

"Enough! I give you the courtesy of allowing you to voice your opinion as one of my lieutenants. But keep in mind, you are not in charge here."

I open my mouth as PJ clears his throat. I glance to him. He gives a motion, one from our militia training that translates to *keep quiet.* I lift my chin in response.

"Never meant to imply I was." Doug smiles at Rogue. His voice is light. Calm.

"You two see any Army people on your way here?" the woman asks, pointing to PJ and me.

"We did," PJ answers.

"Where?"

"Huntley."

"I know that. On the way between there and here?"

"There's a squad camped off . . . what was it, Rochelle? Fran Road?"

"Frey Road?" Doug offers. "Camped in the field right before Yeoman? They've been there awhile."

"Sounds like where we saw them."

"We know about those," she says. "None closer?"

"No, ma'am," PJ responds.

"Good. Figured, if they were moving in, our scouts would've hightailed it back here with a warning."

"You have scouts?" I ask.

"'Course we do."

I look to PJ, waiting for him to deliver the message the captain gave us. He raises his eyebrows at me.

"What do you think?" Doug asks, directing his question to the woman.

"Bring 'em in. Take them to your place, and get Ace so he can reunite with Mommy."

The way she says mommy, in a cruel and mocking tone, makes me want to punch her in the throat.

"Stiletto, Venom, you two take the horses. Tank and Scorpion, keep close to Mom and her boyfriend. 'Course, I'm sure they're not going to cause us any trouble, right?"

"No trouble." I shake my head. "I'm just— "

"Yes, yes. You're just here for your son. I've heard."

Chapter 19

"Well, let's get a move on it," the woman says. "I don't have all day to be escorting you through my territory."

"I'll take them," Doug offers. "If you want to stay here— "

"Not a chance. Let's get a move on." She motions to the men who took our guns. "Hurry it up."

Though most of her people stay at the roadblock, several of the younger kids seem to want to follow us.

The woman turns, bellowing over the wind, "You all have jobs to do. Get back to them."

They quickly scurry away, going back into the trees or crouching by the barrier.

"Skull! You get your horse and go after Ace. Don't tell him why, just tell him to get to Ritz's place."

"Stay calm," PJ whispers. "We'll have Christopher soon."

"And we'll get him out of this place. Something wacky is going on here."

"No talking." The guy escorting us taps me on the shoulder.

I don't know if he's Tank or Scorpion, since the woman—whom Doug Ritzdorf called Rogue—didn't differentiate which was which. I don't really care either. All the nicknames and child soldiers—what has Christopher gone through in the last year? He's no stranger to guns; we used them on our ranch for running off predators, and Dale used to take him hunting. But the lack of adults at the barricade is wrong. What are they doing that's so important they're putting eight-year-olds on the front line?

Rogue turns around, meeting my eye. "You got a problem, girlie?"

I answer with a slight shake of my head.

"Didn't think so."

The first few raindrops, big and fat, hit before we're halfway there. The wind's so swift, PJ and I remove our ball caps and tuck them under our arms.

Rogue and her group have their coats buttoned to the top. Some have hoods in place and others have their hats pulled down tight. At Doug's insistence, we were allowed to put our heavy coats on shortly before the first drops hit. Although it's obvious Rogue's in charge, she does seem to listen to Doug. At least slightly.

By the time we're at the driveway to Camp Ah Nei, more than a mile and a half from the barricade, the fat rain is a stinging slush. And Rogue isn't happy about it. She's let off a string of colorful words.

I'm no prude. Having grown up on a ranch, I know plenty of interesting words. They're especially brought out at branding time when nothing ever seems to go as smoothly as it should.

But she'd give every cowboy I've ever known a run for their money. And though I don't know many sailors, I'm confident she'd make them blush.

Things at Camp Ah Nei look much the same as they did when Dale and I left Christopher here last summer. There're a dozen small cabins nestled in the trees, much like the one I lived in over the winter. The spacious main house, where Doug, his wife, and little girls live, plus where all meals and many indoor activities for the camp take place, is in the clearing. It's surrounded by several barns and outbuildings, along with corrals for the horses dotting the landscape. Now there are also cows roaming around, dozens of them.

"Tank, help the girls put the horses in the barn," Doug says.

Rogue releases a huge, over-the-top, dramatic sigh. "Might as well. S'pose they'll have to stick around with the storm."

"Do you think he's here?" I ask Doug as we get within steps of the side door.

"He should be."

With tears in my eyes and my heart pounding in my ears, I'm a step behind Doug as he opens the door. Rogue seems to understand my need to get to my son and makes no effort to stop me or tell me to stand back.

"Hey, Ritz," a deep voice says. "Did you call me back because of the weather?"

I step around Doug, willing my eyes to quickly adjust to the darkness of the room.

"Not the storm, Christopher."

"Why're you calling me that. You know I go by— "

I raise my gaze to meet his eyes.

He's taller than me by several inches. And his black hair is too long, curling over his collar and shadowing his eyes. What was a whisp of a mustache last summer, barely peach fuzz, has filled in to cover his entire lip—still feathery but darker.

The voice coming from his mouth isn't the same pitch as it was last June. It's deeper and fits his new taller physique. He's even filled out some. He's not heavy by any means, but he's bulkier. I take it all in during the half second it takes for him to realize I'm standing next to Doug.

"Mom?" There's a catch in his voice.

Not trusting my own, I nod and open my arms. He flies into them.

"I can't believe you're here. I kept hoping, but after a while . . ." He lifts his head, looking at those gathered around us.

"It's just me," I whisper.

His face crumbles. "Dad?"

"Gone. I . . . we lost him the day of the EMP."

"How?" He sounds like the boy I dropped off at camp.

"Shot. It was quick."

"The girls?" he asks in a whisper.

"Fine, fine. They're back home . . . um, where we've been staying, with some friends. They can't wait to see you."

Chewing his lip, he motions with his head. An unruly hank of hair covers one eye. "I can't believe you're here." He looks over me. Taking in my well-worn jeans and half chaps. "Did you ride?"

"Most of the way. They took our horses to the barn."

Christopher's eyes immediately go to PJ. "Who're you?" Christopher asks in his new man voice.

PJ steps forward and offers his hand. "PJ Cameron."

"Why are you here?" Christopher shoves his hands in his pockets.

"Well, shoot, Ace." Rogue smirks. "Pretty clear your mom's got herself a new beau."

"Is that true?" he asks, his green eyes meeting mine. I see so much of his father in him. The way he holds his head. The set of his jaw. The quickness to judge.

I lightly shake my head. "PJ brought me to get you. It's not . . . out there isn't safe. Especially not for a woman alone."

His shoulders relax. "I understand. I can't believe you're here." He throws his arms around me again. After a moment, he releases me and turns to Doug. "Looks like it's going to storm awhile."

"Yeah, maybe through the night. We'll find a place for them to stay. Why don't you take 'em to the kitchen, have a seat at the table. I'd like to talk to Rogue for a minute, then we'll join you."

Christopher leads us into the warm house. There's been some changes since I was here two years ago. That was for an end of camp party. I helped Candice Ritzdorf with taking out the food. At that time, it was a lovely, large kitchen with new appliances and granite countertops. Now there's a woodstove where the fridge stood. The counters are cluttered, full of goods and supplies.

"Where's Candice?" I ask.

"Dead. She fell off her horse. Broke her leg, a hip. She was a mess. Lingered for six weeks or so. That was a hard time."

That explains the sadness in Doug's eyes. "Their girls?"

"V is on watch on the north end."

"V?"

"Vanessa. That's what we call her now—V."

"On watch . . . " I repeat, thinking of the last time I saw the girl. She was only seven or eight. "And Beatrix?"

"She must be here. The fire was going when I came in, and there's a pot of bones on the stove."

I blink my eyes, trying to comprehend what he's saying. "Beatrix does the cooking?"

"Some. Most of it, maybe." He shrugs. "We all do what's needed. Ritz didn't want her messing with the fire, but she's learned well."

"She's, what, four years old?" I whisper, feeling PJ's hand briefly touch my shoulder before he pulls out a chair at the table for me.

"She's almost six. And with her mom dead, as well as most of the other adults . . . we do what's needed." He drops his head. "They're going to miss me."

"What happened to the adults?" PJ asks, slipping into his own chair.

"Some bast—um . . . *hoodlums* went through last summer and wiped out the town of Shepherd. Killed all the men and older boys— the ones around my age and up—and most of the women. They took a few with them, some of the older girls too. But the young kids, they locked them in the school and left.

"Rogue and her husband went into Shepherd to do some trading. They found the bodies. The kids had been locked up a few days by then. Some were already dead. They brought them all back here.

Some were so dehydrated and had gotten so hot, there wasn't anything that could be done for them.

"Mrs. Ritzdorf was still alive then. It was nuts, and sad, trying to take care of the ones who were really sick and crying when they died. The men rode into Musselshell, it's north of here. You know, on the other side of the rec area?"

I close my eyes, visualizing a map of Montana. "I know where it is. What about Roundup? Isn't that just west of Musselshell?" Roundup is one of the towns Kimba, Rey, and the rest of our group will travel through on their way to Lewistown and then on to Great Falls.

"They didn't go there. Just cut through the recreation area, checking the houses along the way. They were hoping to get some help. Maybe find a doctor or a nurse—anyone really."

"Did you go with them?"

"Not me. That was early, when the adults still treated us like kids. They didn't find help. What they found—oh, it was bad, Mom." He looks at me, steeling himself.

"Musselshell was hit too. Only . . . they didn't get there in time. The kids were locked up like the others, but only two were still alive. We figured they hit them first, then went to Shepherd. Doug and another guy brought them home. One died later, but Rafe, he made it. He lives here too."

"That's good." I struggle to keep my voice even and matter of fact, the way Christopher does as he tells his story.

"They went from Musselshell east a ways, checking houses along the way, finding a few kids still alive. At some point, they stopped finding bodies, so they turned around and came home. When it was all said and done, there were a lot of kids found and brought back. We had *a lot* more kids than adults. Then Mrs. Ritz, Rogue's husband, and a few others died. Some people even took off, just left without a word. Now there's only nineteen adults."

Rogue strides in. "We've got a hundred and forty-three children with at least two more on the way. Ace here, he's one we depend on." She slides a chair from the table, moving it several feet away before sitting. I half expected her to spin it around and sit down backward just to prove to us what a rebel she is.

Christopher drops his head. "Mom, I need to stay. I need to help them."

"You're going with your mom," Doug leans against the doorframe, crossing his arms. "But what we'd like, what would help us, is if you all can take a few of the children."

"The young ones," Rogue says.

"The young ones," I echo. "I don't— " I look to PJ. *How can we do that?*

"How many and what ages?" PJ asks.

She holds up four fingers. "More trouble than they're worth."

"They're babies." Doug moves closer to the table. "Not yet even two years old. Christopher told you what happened? Did he tell you that, by the time we found the children, most of the babies were already . . . they were dead. The murderers left them to die. They couldn't make it quick and easy. They— " His voice halts in a choking sob.

"And someone always has to watch them." Rogue throws her hands up.

"Who takes care of them now?" I ask.

"Mainly Reba," Christopher says. "But whoever isn't on sentry duty or watching cattle also takes a turn."

Rogue taps the table. "You should take Reba too. She's seventy-eight and— "

"She'd never go," Doug interrupts. "But the babies, they need to go. Also, Marnie and Renée."

"Who?" Christopher asks.

"Ditto and Rabbit."

His mouth makes an *O* shape. "Yeah. They should come with us. They can help."

"And I want . . . " Doug's voice cracks. He coughs. "You need to take Rafe and Beatrix."

"You want me to take your daughter?" I ask.

"I want you to take both my daughters, but Rogue won't agree. She wants to keep Vanessa as one of her toy soldiers." His voice drips with venom.

"Douglas," Rogue warns, "you're walking a thin line."

"So what? What kind of life are we giving these kids? None. I'd send them all away if I could. We're just going to get them killed."

With pursed lips, Rogue gives him a hard look. "We have a right to protect what's ours. My husband gave his life to make sure we could feed these people, these kids. Your kids too—your daughters and your camp boys. Ace here, he's been an asset. So have most of the others, but we even care for the ones who've been dead weight. Like Zero, who did nothing but knock up Ditto and Rabbit."

My eyes dart between my son and the two adults. *What is going on here?*

Sensing my confusion, Doug says, "Not everyone's equipped to deal with the world we've found ourselves in."

"Most of us weren't equipped," PJ says.

"True." Doug dips his chin. "Robert, or as he became known, Zero, was one of my camp boys. It was his first year. His parents were having trouble with him and thought we could iron out some of his rebellion. And it might have worked, had things not gone the way they did."

"The kid was a liar and a cheat." Rogue slaps the table, causing me to jump. "He'd disappear from sentry duty or cattle watch. Did nothing but sleep and eat—and argue. Then he started romancing the young girls. We found out about that too late. Marnie is only twelve. Our best guess, her baby will be here in September. Renée will be fourteen before her baby gets here a few weeks later. There might be others too. I've noticed one who's looking a little chunky around the middle."

"Who's that?" Doug asks.

"Aspen."

Doug shakes his head. "She's even younger than the other two."

Christopher tightens his jaw. "I told her to stay away from Zero."

"What is it you want us to do with these children?" PJ asks.

"Take them somewhere safe—*safer.*" Doug answers. "Where they have proper adult supervision."

"Why don't you take them to Huntley? The Army— "

"No. Not Huntley. It's too close." Rogue leans back in her chair. "They can't know where the kids came from. If those brownshirts knew we were defending what's ours with mostly kids, they'd swoop in here and take it all. The Army shouldn't even be here, you know. They're not supposed to be on US soil. They're breaking all sorts of rules."

I look to PJ, wondering if we should tell her what the Marines told us. He stares straight ahead as Rogue continues her tirade.

"As it is, we're going to have a hard time keeping what's ours. And I'm not giving it up."

I trace my finger across the tabletop. "Or if they knew how many children you have here, they'd offer help—set up a good trade and maybe even give you some actual soldiers to help protect and tend the cattle."

"Yep." Doug nods. "We've discussed that. We know that, at some point, we'll have to work something out."

"Not happening." Rogue leans forward, glaring at Doug. "These are my cattle. My husband's family owned this business. They homesteaded the land, making it something out of nothing. The finishing pens became our bread and butter. That was Derek's dad's doing, and when he died, we kept it going. When this is all over, I still need a business in order to survive. Plus, I'm passing it on to my son. I'm not giving it up."

Doug gives her a long look and a slight shake of his head. "Getting the youngest out of here will help. It's just too much. And taking the pregnant girls will give their babies a better chance. And Rafe and Beatrix."

"I still think those two should stay," Rogue says.

"They're going."

She raises her hands. "Fine. Fine."

"You do realize we only have two horses." PJ lifts a hand. "As it is, we planned on alternating riders. With everyone else— "

"Bea has a pony." Again, Doug's voice cracks with emotion. "I have one for Rafe too. I'd prefer you not pass her off to the Army. If you could find a family for her—Rafe too—I'd be grateful. Maybe someday . . . " He chokes on his words.

"We have a small amount of spare gear," Rogue offers. "I'll even give up a couple of horses. None that are too impressive, of course, but they should get you down the road."

"And we have dried beef to send with you," Doug adds, as he swipes at his eye.

I look to PJ. He tilts his head and lifts a single shoulder. "The older girls, they'll be able to help with the youngsters? And exactly what are the ages?"

"Who knows?" Rogue throws up her hands.

"The youngest was only a few months old when we found him," Doug says. "He's not yet walking, but we think he should be. My guess is he's just over a year."

Rogue's demeanor seems to soften. She gets a faraway look. "Been a long time since my son was that age. Don't remember it being so much work. You met him—he's the one I sent after Ace."

"The one you called Skull?"

She straightens, once again looking hard. Fierce. "That's what he prefers. Just like *he* prefers Ace." She points at Christopher. "Almost everyone has shed their old persona and became who they believe they should be. Though some, like Ritz here, still think of themselves by their real names. In those cases, we may or may not call them by the name they prefer."

"Yeah." Christopher nods. "Like Zero wanted to be called Subzero because he thought it sounded bada—um . . . tough. But we all switched it to just Zero because of how he was—a big fat zero."

"And where is he now?" I ask, wondering what kind of trouble we might have if we take away the girls carrying his children.

"Gone. Disappeared one day."

I catch a quick look that passes between Rogue and Doug. Disappeared, or forced out? From the looks they're giving each other, my guess is they sent him packing. Or worse.

"Do we have a deal?" Rogue asks.

"We'll do it. Right, Mom?"

"How many horses?" PJ asks. "And you said their condition isn't great. What are we talking?"

"I'll show you the ponies," Doug says. "They're probably making friends with your horses right now. I think we can get three horses so each of the older girls and Christopher have one. The toddlers can either ride double or maybe we have backpacks for the smallest ones."

PJ nods. "And the condition of the horses?"

"You won't want to run any races. And I'm not sure all of them will make it back to Lander. And even though we talked about you not taking them to Huntley, we heard there's also military around Billings. That'd be better. The horses can get there. The ponies should make it all the way. Do you know a family Bea and Rafe can live with?"

I bite on my lip and shake my head. "I haven't been in Lander since the morning of the EMP. We spoke with you the night before, left that morning for here to pick up Christopher. We were about halfway between Meeteetse and Cody when the EMP hit. We started walking.

Dale was killed that day. My girls and I ended up in Bakerville, north of Prospect and on the Montana state line. You know the place?"

Doug shakes his head.

"They're still there, staying with friends. I think I can find a family to take them in."

"Will we go home?" Christopher asks.

"We will. As soon as it's safe to travel."

"And when will that be?" Rogue asks.

"Soon? The military is stabilizing things."

"Humph. You think so?"

"I'd like to think they will. We were in Lockwood. We heard they had some troubles, but the Marines have many of the problems under control. And they've made the interstate safe to travel."

"Yeah, well, we'll see. I wouldn't get my hopes up if I were you. This thing needs to burn itself out."

Chapter 20

The rain turned into a full-on thunderstorm, with lightning streaking through the night sky. PJ is bunking in the barn—his choice. Doug and his group have hay and even oats, giving our horses some extra nutrition.

Unlike our home on the mountain that had community meals, each of the houses here does their own thing. According to Christopher—I refuse to call him Ace—beef is their main food, along with last year's field corn and oats.

Every few days, Rogue has someone drop off raw ingredients, and each household does what they want with them. Beatrix and Rafe, ages five and four, do much of the cooking in this house when they're not tending the on-site garden or working in the fields.

They've planted hay, corn, oats, potatoes, and more for harvest this fall. Children just older than the babies going with us spend most of their time working in the fields.

I can't stop staring at my amazing son. He's grown so much in the past year, but I can still see my little boy. We're sitting in front of the fireplace in the living room. We'll bed down here tonight, allowing Christopher to catch me up on his life.

"We mostly eat boiled meats and corn. It's easy. Before Candice died, she made sure Bea knew how to safely light the woodstove and use a knife. They've had to grow up way too fast. All the kids here have."

Tonight's dinner was broth with what was left of the meat. It seems today is the last day of rations and they should get more tomorrow. Of course, on her way out, Rogue made a point of telling us our arrival messed up today's work.

Christopher thinks rations will be late showing up. "Not the first time," he said. "There's always something going wrong with the butchering."

I still haven't seen Vanessa. According to her dad, she's probably at the lookout, waiting for a break in the weather. He left about an hour ago on one of the horses to run errands and meet up with her.

Beatrix, Rafe, and many of the other camp boys all wandered through at some point for their meals, then disappeared. Christopher introduced me to everyone, but I didn't even try to keep people straight.

I recognized a few of the camp boys from previous years, but they have many of the young boys from the towns living in the cabins too. While not actual camp boys, it seems they're referred to that now since they live at former Camp Ah Nei.

Christopher said five parents arrived before the EMP. He hopes the boys who left made it home. The rest are like him, the parents—Doug and Candice too—thought it'd all blow over in a few days and things could go on like normal and be like every other summer.

For the boys, it *was* like every summer. When the attacks started, they did little to alter their day-to-day activities.

They didn't even know about the EMP since they were in the recreation area riding horses when it happened. Doug checked his phone for the time; it was dead, but he thought he'd just forgotten to charge it. Even when they got home, they had no idea until Rogue's husband came up later on a rickety old dirt bike.

The EMP wiped out most of the dirt bikes and quads in the area, but a few of the older, simpler ones were still running. There was even a newer four-person utility terrain vehicle—a UTV, or what many people call a side-by-side—that wasn't affected by the EMP.

"We get a lot of use out of that thing," Christopher says, "the side-by-side and the few old pickup trucks and cars that still work. Although, fuel is getting to be an issue. The UTV and quads do better than the old trucks, so we use those. And the horses too. We had to move out of the cabins during the worst of the winter. They aren't insulated and only had electric heaters."

"Where'd you sleep?"

"Some slept in here, making beds on the floor like we are. Some of us slept in the barn. It wasn't too bad with the horses."

"We had a guy where I was staying that had a room off one of the livestock sheds. He said he didn't even need a fire. Lots of body heat from the animals."

"It's good they took you in after Dad died. Just like what Rogue did for everyone here. I know she comes off a little . . . strong."

"She seems a little . . . " I pause as I search for the word I want. "Like the stress has got to her?"

"Humph. It's gotten to everyone. She's really great, Mom. Everyone loves her. Part of me hates to leave— "

My eyes go wide as he rushes on with, "I mean, I want to go with you. But there's a friendship here. More than that. We all work together. And we know Rogue is the reason we're doing so well."

"What about Doug?"

"Him too."

"I mean, he doesn't really seem to like Rogue very much."

"Oh, he does. He's just . . . they got in an argument or something. He's still mad."

"About?"

He shakes his head. "The Army. He wants to surrender. She doesn't."

"What do the others living here think?"

"Think about what?"

"Do the rest not have a say?"

"It's not like that. Rogue's in charge. We understand that, and we'll do what she wants. Doug knows that too. She just wants everyone to live. We understand that. And we know she'll do what's needed to keep us alive. There's been so much death. Too much."

We sit in silence for many minutes while I consider what it might be like living here, with Rogue having the final say in everything. And from the sounds of it, Doug going against her would not only result in her wrath but the wrath of the entire community.

"What happened to Rogue's husband?" I ask.

"Shot."

"Were you attacked?" I ask, concern filling me to the core as I imagine him in danger, as I imagine the things he may have experienced.

"That's not how he died. His friend shot him. They got in an argument, and *bam*. He pulled out his gun and shot Rogue's husband dead. He realized what he did and then shot himself. It was a bad day. Reba, the lady we told you about who cares for the babies? She was the shooter's mom. He and Rogue's husband knew each other forever—even went to school together. No one even really knows what the fight was about."

"That's terrible. People don't always act rationally."

"You didn't tell me about Dad. Who did it?"

I chew on my upper lip and close my eyes. "A stranger."

"A stranger? Were you attacked?"

"Sort of, yes."

"What happened," he asks, his voice barely above a whisper.

"It was bad, Christopher. Your dad was murdered. Your sisters and I were kidnapped." I struggle to keep my voice even, to report just the facts. Not too many facts, though. My son doesn't need the details.

"Did they . . . did they hurt you, Mom? Kerryanne and Cheyre?"

"Not much, no." A lie.

"How'd you end up in—what was the name of the town?"

"Bakerville. That's . . . " I let out a sigh. "It's a long story. And it'll probably be hard for you to hear."

"I want to know."

"And I'll tell you. But you need to understand, I did what I had to do to protect your sisters. To keep them alive. To stay alive myself so I could find you again. That was my entire goal, getting us back together."

"PJ, is he actually your friend? Or did he— "

"Friend. A true friend. He wasn't involved in the bad stuff." As I give him the briefest details of the kidnapping, being purchased by Fred Lassiter, my forced marriage, and the abuse, I watch as his face colors and his eyes grow hard.

"I'll kill him." He clenches his teeth. "I'm going to hunt him down and kill him. The ones at the . . . the house where he found you. I'll kill them all. You watch. I'm going to do it."

"That's how I felt too." I reach for his hand. "I've struggled with my anger, still do sometimes. But the Lord has helped me."

"The Lord? Doubtful."

"I know it seems that way. But I've— " I let out a small laugh. "In the worst of this, with everything that's happened, I've found God. Found Jesus."

"I don't think . . . if there's really a God out there, I doubt He had anything to do with helping you. You helped yourself."

I give him a smile. "It may seem that way. But the truth is, God's become an important part of my life. Even now, coming here, His hand has been in it all along. He's provided protection and— " I hesitate as I remember shooting the man in the campground. "And He helped me when things weren't going well."

"Did something happen on the way here?"

"You know what kind of world this is? Off this hillside?"

"I know from what happened in Shepherd and the other towns. We talk about what it's probably like. Lawlessness. And we've had some troubles here."

"Were you attacked?"

"There was . . . we had a group try and steal cattle. And another group—can we talk about it later? Sometimes . . . " He lifts his hands.

"Yeah. Sometimes it's hard to think about the things that have happened."

He gives me a nod before whispering, "I hate it."

I wrap my arm around him, pulling him close. "It's been terrible. But I've found God spreads His wings and pulls me toward Him. Kind of like I am with you now. He shelters me, giving us His Son— "

With a shake of his head, Christopher pulls away. "That's just a crutch, Mom."

"Jesus?"

"Yeah. You provided your own protection. PJ said he's with you to protect you. I didn't hear him spouting about Jesus."

"Jesus is the most important person in PJ's life and has been for many years."

"Oh, please. What kind of a real man . . . you know what Dad said. Church was fine for special occasions, but we needed to make our own way in the world."

"Sometimes, I wonder if your dad would still think that. With everything that's happened, would he see his need for Jesus?"

"Not even. Dad's a real man."

"Believing in Jesus, following Him, doesn't make PJ any less of a man."

"We'll see," he scoffs.

"Just because PJ believes God is in control, doesn't mean he's just meandering through life letting whatever happens happen."

We sit in silence for many minutes before Christopher says, "Tell me about Cheyre and Kerryanne. Do they like where you're living?"

"They do. It's different for the children than here. We still have school."

"Pshaw. I don't miss that. I hope you don't think I'm going back to school."

"You're fifteen, school will be different for you than the younger ones. Older kids are part of the junior militia— "

"Now we're talking."

"They get to choose an apprenticeship. Kerryanne plans to join the medical team. In fact, she's probably already on it since she turned fourteen after I left. That's when the training starts."

"You have a doctor?"

"We did. He died in November. But we have a couple of nurses who are very well trained. When a bear attacked PJ, they took care of him."

"A bear? A *grizzly* bear?"

"A black bear. We don't know why it attacked."

"Do you think the nurses can deliver babies?"

"They have, two so far. One of them was PJ's niece, and there were a couple of women pregnant when we left. Do you want your friends to come back to Bakerville with us?"

"I want all of them to come with us."

"That'd be . . . hard."

"You've told me before that hard things are worth doing."

"I did?"

"Well, something like that." He shrugs. "Wait until you meet the babies. And Ditto and Rabbit, you'll like them."

"It's hard not to like babies," I agree. "I can't make any promises right now. We need to see how the horses look, see how they'll do. It's a hundred miles to Bakerville. And then, what happens when things are safe enough for us to go home to Lander? Will you want all of them to go with us?"

"After this is over, Ritz will want Bea back. But Rafe, he's become like a little brother to me. We could adopt him."

His suggestion hangs in the air as we sit in silence. I did notice that Christopher and Rafe got along particularly well. And Rafe and Beatrix, though they look nothing alike, are almost like twins, even finishing each other's sentences.

Rafe with his dark, curly hair and dark eyes and Bea with stick-straight hair so blond it's almost white and pale green eyes—they couldn't look more different from each other, but they act so much alike. While Christopher may wish to adopt Rafe, the best thing would be to keep those two together and let Doug bring Rafe back with Beatrix.

Clomping at the side door brings me to my feet.

"Relax, Mom." Christopher releases a small laugh. "That's probably just Ritz bringing V home."

"Oh, yeah." I sit back down, giving my own nervous laugh. "Jumpy, I guess."

"Seriously."

After a few moments, Doug pokes his head around the corner. "You're still awake. Do you want to say hello to Vanessa?"

I stand. "Yes, sure."

The girl I remember from last summer looks much the same in stature, but like her dad, she has a sadness about her that's amplified by her red-rimmed eyes.

"Hello, Mrs. Bennet. I'm glad you're here to take Ace—I mean, Christopher home."

"Thank you, Vanessa. It's nice to see you again."

"I wish— " She looks at her dad, and fresh tears begin to fall.

"I told her about Bea and Rafe going with you." Doug's voice is horse. "She's—*we're both*—having a difficult time with it."

"I understand." I know my own heart would be breaking if I were him. A piece of me has been missing as long as Christopher and I have been separated. It won't be any easier for Doug. Or for Vanessa. "Do you want to reconsider?"

"No." It comes out harsh, full of anger. "There's no life for them here. Vanessa knows that, too, don't you?"

"Mm-hmm." She mutters. "I wish . . . Dad, we should go too."

"We've discussed this. We can't leave." He wraps an arm around her shoulder. "It's coming down pretty good out there, cold enough it's snowing. I stopped at the barn and talked with PJ. He thought you might need tomorrow to get ready and then plan to leave the next day."

"We discussed that. If you don't mind us staying?"

"Not a problem. You'll need time to get everything together, maybe more than just a day even."

"I'm ready," Christopher says. "I've got everything. I put it in two pillowcases and used some rope and bungees, made a good saddlebag. And I'll wrap up my blankets into a bedroll. It'll work."

"I'm sure it will. We'll get everything sorted, get the things you all need. We'll look over the map too."

"The map?"

"I think I have a better way for you to get home, a shorter way. Should shave some time off."

"Really? Okay."

Christopher and I return to our nest of blankets. We visit awhile longer before our conversation lulls. Soon, I hear his soft rhythmic breathing. I smile to myself. My son is safe.

Chapter 21

I'm up long before daylight. The fire has burned down, but there are enough hot coals to easily bring it back to life.

I'm at the kitchen table, sitting in the dark, with just the company of the flames, when Doug stumbles in. "You're up early," he says, sinking into the chair next to me.

"Did you sleep much?" I ask.

He shrugs. "I'd offer you coffee, but we haven't had that for months."

"Same. Although, we did have some people show up at the lodge who'd found a few unopened containers."

"You did? Was it amazing?"

"We only had it one morning at breakfast, and it was too weak for my taste. I think they're saving the rest for a special occasion."

"Like what?"

"Who knows?" I chuckle.

"The place you've been staying, it sounds nice. Peaceful."

I let out a breath. "We've had our troubles. But I suppose it's better than most. You could come with us."

"I can't leave the rest of my camp boys. There're too many youths here I'm responsible for. You taking Bea and Rafe will help me. It'll help all of us."

"You're sure about this? I know what it's like not to be with your child, to not know— "

"It's not safe here. Nell—that's Rogue's real name, what she used to go by before her husband died and she became . . . the way she is, completely single minded. She still thinks she needs to leave something for her son. Even though she doesn't believe this is over yet—even, or maybe especially, with the military here—she's convinced one day things will return to how they were."

"You don't think they will?"

"Do you?"

I glance back at the woodstove, watching the flames take a log. "Like they were? No. Not in our lifetime at least. Maybe our children will see it. Even though the president says he's rebuilding, and the military is here, I think it'll be slow. Will we ever have computers at our fingertips again? Will everyone have a car or three in their driveway? I don't know."

I take a deep breath. "And I'm not even sure we should go back to that. These last several months, after many terrible things, I've learned to embrace the simpleness of our new lives. My daughters and I have grown extremely close. There's no hustle and bustle to get in the way. I see it with other families too. They're living in the moment instead of waiting for the next thing."

"It's good you have that. And that's what I want for my girls. It's not like that here. We're struggling. Truth is, we have too many cattle, too much work, too many children, and too little time. Giving up half the cattle to the Army, or even more, would be smart. We'd still have plenty of food for the rest of our lives if we managed them well. But Rogue won't hear of it. She won't listen to any of us, won't listen to reason."

"Why don't you all leave? Take the kids and go to Huntley?"

He lets out a long breath. "Most wouldn't leave. They're dedicated to Rogue."

"Christopher seems to think she's pretty great too, but he's leaving. Maybe they'd surprise you."

"Even if they did, she'd never allow it."

"What's she going to do? Shoot you?"

"Yes."

The word hangs in the darkness. The log cracks, causing me to jump.

"You don't really believe that?" I ask, my voice barely a whisper.

"I do. And before you say it, no, I can't shoot her first."

"I wasn't going to say that."

"Oh, well. Okay."

"But . . . why not?"

He lets out a low, humorless laugh. "Not only has there been entirely too much killing, if I did that—killed her—I'd be dead too. She holds a . . . power over them. They're dedicated to her. And to her son. I wouldn't stand a chance of getting out alive with my children."

"Your camp kids, the ones you say you need to stay here and protect, they would— "

"No, probably not them." He blows out a breath. "I know it might not make sense to you, but I need to stay here. Are you still willing to take Bea and Rafe?"

I bob my head up and down. "We said we would. But it sounds nuts. All of this."

"Yeah, no doubt. You taking Bea and Rafe will help me more than you know. They'll be safe and maybe . . . anyway, I'll grab the stew out of the mudroom, get it warming up for breakfast."

Doug slides his chair back. "I have sentry duty at noon, and we have much to do this morning. They'll bring the babies and girls over at some point so you can meet them, then we'll figure out everything you need. I know people will have started getting things together last night. Rogue was going to meet with a few of them to make sure."

"I don't understand her."

"Rogue?"

"Yeah. One minute you say she'll shoot you if you leave, the next minute she's gathering things to make the journey easier. Is she— "

"Nuts? Yeah. A little. But who isn't these days? When Candice died, I pretty much lost my mind and went through life in a fog. Was it the same for you when you lost your husband?"

"The same, yes."

"Christopher told you how Rogue's husband died? It was hard on everyone."

"It does sound awful. But she's . . . extreme."

"No doubt. We walk on eggshells around her, never knowing what'll happen next. But she'll make sure you have what's needed to get the kids somewhere safe. For all her faults, she means well. And she takes her position as provider of our group seriously."

"If you say so," I answer with a shrug. I'm glad I'm here for Christopher and can get him away from this mess. Walking on eggshells with an unstable person is no way to live.

I know this from my time with Fred. Sometimes, he'd be kind and almost loving. Other times, he was a monster. And he could turn on a dime. That's definitely no way to live.

As the sun begins to rise, PJ makes his way into the house. The rest of the house is up soon after, and the camp boys start coming in for their breakfast of stew.

"I'm supposed to help with the cattle today," Christopher says. "I'd still like to. Unless you need me to get things ready?"

While I don't want him out of my sight, I give a slight nod. "How long will it take?"

"Most of the day. I know I'm leaving, but if I don't do this, they'll be shorthanded. They'll make do after we leave, but . . . " He lifts a shoulder. "I don't want to shirk on my duties."

My heart swells with pride. My concerns that Christopher may be reacting to the apocalypse in the same way as Jameson Dawson seems unfounded. A pang of guilt runs through me. Judging Jameson isn't entirely fair. His circumstances are considerably different from what Christopher has encountered.

"Sure. That makes sense."

He gives me a quick hug before pushing his hat on his head and taking off. Unlike PJ and I, who chose ball caps for this trip, Christopher is wearing a typical cowboy hat—the rather nice fur felt Gus Crease hat Dale bought him last spring before he left for camp.

Dale and I argued about that hat. Christopher outgrew the hat he'd worn the year before, a simple straw hat perfect for summer and economical for a still-growing boy. Dale thought it was time for him to have a real hat. A man's hat.

Dale never wore straw, no matter the weather. He wanted the same for Christopher. I'll admit, it turned out to be the right choice. The now well-worn hat was needed over the winter and still has plenty of life.

After the breakfast rush subsides, I help Rafe and Bea with the dishes. Vanessa goes back to bed, tired after being up so late. PJ and Doug sit at the kitchen table, looking over the map.

"Looks like it'll shave off a couple of miles." PJ traces his finger along the route. "Rochelle, pop over here and take a look?"

Instead of heading east, back to Huntley, we'd go west and connect with Highway 87. It's the same two-lane road we were on while heading into Billings, the same road our friends planned to use to head north to deliver Leanne and her children to Lewistown. We'll go south, into the city.

"Dale and I drove that way before," I say. "It's not much shorter, is it? Only a few miles?"

Doug points to the map. "Yes, but on horseback, three miles is about an hour. Every mile will count. You're going to be stopping a lot more than you would if it was just you, PJ, and Christopher. Those babies . . . "

"Yeah, good point."

"You're sure about the roads being safe? Interstate 90? We could route you around most of the city."

"From the sounds of it, the highway and interstate are the most secure," PJ says. "The Marines and the Army are both patrolling."

"All right. This way is probably best, and not going back through Huntley may lead to less problems in the long run."

"We aren't going to divulge what you have here." PJ leans back in his chair, crossing his arms.

"Not intentionally."

PJ narrows his eyes. "What're you saying?"

I point to the map. "Going this way is fine with me. Three miles less is smart. And with Interstate 90 being under military control, we'll cut off even more miles than our trip here."

PJ softens his shoulders. "That's true, at least twenty."

"And it sounds like the problem between Laurel and Joliet should be cleared up, right?" I ask. "By now, they should have that whole area under control?"

"That's what it sounded like to me," PJ agrees, once again leaning forward to study the map. "Should be fine."

After finalizing the route and finishing the dishes, we go to the barn to meet the horses. The morning is overcast and still cold, and it looks like it could start raining again at any moment. Even with my heavy jacket on, the moisture seeps in and chills me to the bone.

I hope Christopher is warm enough working cattle. He was dressed in a lined denim jacket with a hooded sweatshirt underneath. Surely that's enough.

"PJ saw the ponies last night." Doug motions to a small paddock by the barn. "I have saddles for both."

"Beatrix and Rafe ride?" PJ asks.

"Yeah. She's been riding Sally for a couple of years now. We bought her for Vanessa." Doug gestures toward the pony, based on her size, she's possibly a Welsh or cross with a Quarter Horse.

"And that's Jazz." He motions to the small, dappled buckskin Shetland. "They're both really good on the trail. We had an overnight trip last summer before all this happened and took Jazz to carry a little extra gear. You won't have any trouble. They know what to do on hobbles and lines."

"They're friendly for sure," PJ says as the two ponies, along with half a dozen other full-size horses, including Lucky and Titan, make a beeline to the rail, eagerly accepting nose rubs.

Doug spends several minutes introducing us to his small herd. "And this is Whiskey. He'll be going with you." He points to a senior horse with white speckles on his belly and blaze on his face.

The horse looks better than I expected. The way they were talking last night, I was sure we'd be getting the worst of the worst—nags and swaybacks. But this guy isn't bad. PJ calls him a plug, a multipurpose equine plugged in to any job needed. A utility horse.

"You know anything about the other two horses we'll be given?" PJ asks.

"Not for sure," Doug says. "But I have a few ideas. I expected them to be here by now."

"You have a saddle for Whiskey? And the others?"

Doug gives a brief shake of his head. "We're working on it. Rogue said you can ride bareback."

My eyes go wide. Bareback for a ride around the corral is one thing. A hundred miles bareback is something else. Stupid and dangerous are the words that immediately come to mind.

"I know, I know." Doug raises his hands. "She may live on a ranch, but she doesn't ride. She's scared of horses, in fact. But don't tell her I told you that." He gives us a serious look.

"I have my grandpa's saddle that should fit this guy. It's in the barn. I haven't done much with it other than soap and oil it a couple times a year. Let's get it out and see how it is. The cinches were replaced a few years back and were okay the last time I looked at them. Of course, that was before all this started."

"All right," PJ says. "And the other two?"

"They'll bring saddles with them. I'm not sure what exactly, but we'll make sure they're safe."

The saddle, a rose tooled roping saddle, was probably a beauty in its day. Years of neglect have left it lackluster. He did have it covered well, and the fleece is fine. And as he said, the cinches look okay.

I want to ask if he's sure about parting with it since it is an heirloom, but since he's sending his daughter with us and knows he may never see her again, giving up the saddle seems minuscule.

PJ moves it around a bit. "Seems solid."

"You thinking the blaze horse and this saddle for Christopher?" I ask.

PJ shrugs.

Doug nods. "Probably. The horse's name is Whiskey. He belongs to Reba. She was riding him through the neighborhood until right before this all happened."

"Reba as in the elderly lady caring for the babies?" I ask. Not mentioning she's also the mom to the man that killed Rogue's husband and then took his own life.

"Yep. I talked to her last night, after getting Vanessa. She was happy to give him to you, said to use whatever was needed to care for her babies."

"How's he on a line? Hobbles?" PJ asks.

"We'll have to try him. I don't know if she's ever used him for anything other than riding around the neighborhood."

"That'll be important," PJ says. "I'll need to work on the saddle too. You have saddle soap and neat's-foot oil?"

"Yep. Let's take it inside. You can work in the kitchen and heat the oil on the stove that way."

"Good plan."

PJ is lugging the saddle to the house when the noise of a small motor approaching causes me to turn. A quad pulling a trailer turns into the driveway.

Chapter 22

"Probably the gear." Doug motions in the direction of the quad. "Want to help me, Rochelle?"

I glance to PJ and motion to the saddle. "You got this?"

"I'll get it in the house," PJ says. "Then I'll be back out to help."

The trailer, driven by Rogue's son, is full of different supplies, including the sorriest looking saddles I've ever seen. One even has chunks out of the cantle and teeth marks from being chewed on!

"Really, Charles?" Doug asks.

"It's Skull," he says, pointing to his head. "Remember? Hey, you get what you get. It's not like we can spare anything decent."

"Reba was more than happy to let them take the saddle she has for Whiskey."

"And you know Mom said no. At least the pads are decent."

"What else do you have?"

"Stuff for the babies. Bedding, clothes . . . I don't know. Looks like a couple of backpacks. Saddlebags. The horses are on their way. I passed them down the road."

"You know which horses?"

"One from Linden and one from Brooks. Not the worst we have."

"Well, that's something then." He looks at the saddles again. "If we can clean up the saddles, hopefully they'll be a good fit."

PJ returns to the yard, looks at the saddles, and shakes his head. "Doug, while I appreciate you all are doing the best you can to get us what we need, these . . . " He points to the dilapidated saddles. "We have to be safe."

"I know, I know. We'll get them out, check the tree and make sure they're sturdy. If those are good, the rest is all cosmetic, right?"

PJ snorts. "Not exactly."

We've just emptied the trailer, moving everything to the barn, when the horses enter the driveway. Instead of riding them, they're being walked.

"Uh, oh," PJ mutters.

Even from a distance, it's easy to see that, if they're not the worst they have, they're close to it. One is a definite swayback. It's not severe, but it is noticeable.

"Ach, Charles . . . " Doug shakes his head.

"Hey, what do you want from me?"

"I know this isn't your fault."

"That's right." The boy climbs back on the ATV, roaring it to life. He's smart enough to take it slow by the old horses. Even so, one of them noticeably reacts.

"Great," PJ mutters.

We wait in the yard for them to approach. Like Whiskey, the new arrivals are old.

"Howdy, folks." A man in his early to mid sixties tips his hat. "Would you like to meet your new friends?"

He strokes the chestnut mare along the neck. "This is Miss Ellie. She's been with me forever. My old cutting horse. Retired now, of course. She used to be a hoot to ride and could really put on a show. Even in her twilight years, she's still responsive. She's not only for looks, but she's also a worker. You can hobble her or put her on a picket or highline. Ground tie her even. My grandkids loved riding her, and she'll know what to do on the trail. Be right proud to have her help get those babies to families who'll love them."

"She's beautiful." I step close and caress her nose. "Hello, Miss Ellie."

"And that one we call Big Steve." He motions to the other horse, the swayback.

"You think he's part Clydesdale?" I ask.

"Or Shire, maybe," PJ offers. "He's tall."

"Maybe," the other man says—a teenager really, maybe a year or two older than Christopher. "He's some kind of draft horse for sure. We don't know much about him. He was at one of the houses where they found bodies. Guess the bandits realized he wouldn't get them too far, so they left him. We've been feeding him up, and he's been ridden by some of the younger kids."

"Someone started calling him Big Steve," the teenager continues, "and it stuck. He's absolutely dog gentle and a bit of a deadhead, so you won't have to worry about him taking off. I checked him on a highline after we heard about this yesterday, kept him next to Miss

Ellie for a couple of hours, and there was no trouble. I haven't tried to hobble him. We think he'll be fine for Renée. She's still pretty tiny."

Swayback or not, this is a big horse. I've yet to meet Renée, and he could easily overwhelm her if she's inexperienced around horses.

"And you should be able to have one of the toddlers on with her," the older man says. "His swayback isn't terrible. Long as you take it easy . . . s'pose you planned that anyway."

"We do." PJ looks less than convinced.

Worn out horses, worn out saddles . . . I'm beginning to think we'd be better off on foot.

"It means a lot to us. To some of us." The old man's eyes mist. "You taking the babies, helping the girls that are in trouble. The young 'uns, they're our future. I pray someone is making sure my grandkids are being cared for if their mama and papa can't do it." He pulls a hanky from his pocket and loudly blows his nose.

"Where are they?" I ask.

He swallows hard. "Outside of Indianapolis. Praying for them is all I can do."

"Praying is everything," PJ says.

"Amen to that."

After getting the new horses into the paddock with Whiskey, the ponies, Doug's horses, and our horses, Doug lets out a noisy breath. "Miss Ellie should be fine. Big Steve, though— " He raises his hands. "I'd let you take Candice's horse, but we need him for working the cattle. Sorry we can't do better."

"Yup," PJ says. "We'll see if we can make this work."

Doug excuses himself to do some things inside before his sentry duty. PJ tells him we're going to check the horses, make sure they can do what we need.

"Should we start by working with Whiskey?" PJ asks. "See how he does on a line?"

It only takes us a few minutes to determine this gentle old horse has been well loved and well trained. PJ puts Titan's hobble on him; the nice leather one PJ uses when saddling and tying the lead rope isn't an option, and ground tying doesn't seem smart. The hobble is a strap that links the two front legs together, restraining the horse. Whiskey doesn't balk at all.

"Well, that's something."

"He's been hobbled to saddle?"

"Maybe he was more of a working horse than Doug knows. We'd hobble when we were working cattle. There aren't a lot of tie options in some parts of the prairie. And not all horses are obedient to ground tying."

We brush him while he's hobbled, waiting to see how he does.

"Well, there you go." I laugh. "He's yawning, so I guess he's not too upset about this."

"True enough. He's looking pretty relaxed."

We spend many minutes with Whiskey, checking his feet, testing him with one of our saddles, and more. After we're satisfied that he'll be fine for the trail, we move on to Big Steve, the swayback. He balks slightly at the hobbles, then seems to relax.

"He's not quite as comfortable as Whiskey," PJ says. "We may need to work with him a bit. Get that girl on him, the one they said is skinny. When are they supposed to show up?"

"Doug didn't say." A gust of wind whips my hair into my face. "Looks like it's getting ready to storm again. Should we put Steve away and check Miss Ellie?"

"We might have time for a quick once over, the ponies too."

Miss Ellie is everything the old man said she'd be. She's a total dream. Sally and Jazz, the ponies, are also fine. We're putting Jazz back in the paddock when the rain starts up. PJ and I move into the barn to keep from getting soaked.

"We'll have to find some cotton rope to make some hobbles."

"What about picket lines?" Picket lines, like highlines, are a way to secure the horses together. The picket lines work well when there aren't trees around. We use stakes with swivels and keep the rope at ground level.

"Not sure."

"Could we see if Doug has tent stakes we could use?"

PJ moves his mouth around, biting on the tips of his mustache as he considers. "I'd feel better about having something with swivels. We could check and see what he has, but if nothing's suitable, we'll hobble for them to eat and then use a highline at night when it's appropriate. We'll keep Titan and Lucky on pickets. It'll work."

I think over PJ's plan. Although we can hobble anywhere, trees are needed for highlines. And trees aren't always easy to find in this area.

"You're sure?" I ask. "We could just take Titan and Lucky, swap off riders and have everyone else walking."

"We might end up walking anyway. These three horses aren't spring chickens."

With all the new gear in a pile in the garage, we start sorting it while we wait out the rain. PJ checks the saddles first, tsking over the condition of both. He soon determines they're okay. The saddles are probably safe, provided we can get replacement cinches for the one that has bites taken out of it.

They've also given us bedding, tents, toiletries, clothing, assorted packs, a single-burner propane stove with two one-pound canisters—still new—and several other useful items. There's even supplies to put together a grooming kit for the horses: a curry comb, dandy brush, body brush, face brush, finishing brush, a couple of rags, hoof pick, rasp, and nippers.

"Well, lookie here." PJ smiles. "Someone was thinking."

"Is that a two-horse kit?" I ask, as PJ pulls out two swivels like we use for our highlines.

"Four." He pulls out two more. "There's even a couple of saver straps to protect the trees. Now if there's just trees where we need them, we'll be in business."

"Can we use the stakes we have and add the lines to them?"

"Might have to. We'll figure it out." He digs through a few more things before saying, "There's no food."

"Maybe they'll bring it later?"

"Maybe."

Next, I grab a burlap bag. Inside are several odd-shaped small chunks. At first, I can't make sense of what I'm looking at. Then it becomes clear.

"Check this out." I hand the bag to PJ.

Opening it, he pulls out one of the pieces. "Well I'll be. Used salt and mineral blocks. Someone knows their stuff."

Salt is something we desperately need. Not just for seasoning food but also for keeping the horses and ourselves healthy, especially as the heat of summer is approaching. We left the mountain with what we thought was a decent supply of salt. With all the meat preservation we did, it was gone quicker than we expected.

The horses' need for salt may be even greater than ours right now. While they do get salt and trace minerals from plants in the wild, it's probably not enough for the work they're doing. Each evening, when we put them to graze, we hand feed them a small amount. They lick it off our skin like it's candy. Having these well-used blocks is certainly a blessing.

Not only can the horses use the animal blocks, but we can pick off small bits of the salt blocks for our own use. No matter that cow, horse, deer, and other animal tongues have licked these in the past. The apocalypse isn't a time to be squeamish about things like that.

When we have things somewhat arranged, PJ peeks out the door, declaring the rain is light enough we should make a run for it.

Back in the house, Doug has already left for his sentry shift. We start work on the saddle brought in earlier, the one belonging to Doug's grandpa. He's left the saddle soap and neat's-foot oil on the table.

PJ lets out a long, noisy sigh. "There's no way we can be ready to leave tomorrow."

"The rain— "

"Not just that. We've got too much to do. This saddle needs several days of oiling—and it's the best of the bunch. We need to meet the children, get them each on the horses and see how they do. That Miss Ellie, I know the man said his grandchildren rode her, but he also said she was a cutting horse. Those can be rather . . . "

"Spirited?" I offer.

He tilts his head. "I was going to say broncy, but spirited works. The good ones know their job, but they tend to have a mind of their own too."

I give a nod. I don't know much about horses used in cutting competitions. But I've watched the sport and found it beautiful. The precision between horse and rider is amazing.

And PJ's right. We need to make sure Miss Ellie—all the horses— are suitable for the children. They need to ride, and we need to watch them. And we need to practice with the babies onboard.

"You think she'll understand? Rogue? Will she let us stay a couple of days?" I ask.

"We'll see. I'll talk to Doug as soon as he gets here. Or someone else if they show up before him. He said they'd be bringing the children over to meet us today, right?"

We spend the day working on the saddles. When there's another break in the weather, PJ brings in the chewed-up saddle, which we think is sporting dog bites. It's nothing short of a mess. We trim the worst of it, then find replacement cinches in Doug's barn. They're also well used but are an upgrade from what was in place. Like many ranchers, he seems to have a habit of never throwing anything away—a habit we're grateful for.

By midafternoon, PJ, who has been expressing his frustration with a series of sighs, lets out an exaggerated groan.

"You okay?" I ask.

"Isn't there some saying about being only as good as your gear?"

"Is there?"

"If there isn't, there should be."

"Are they safe? The saddles and the horses?"

"We'll know more once we see how the children ride. With the babies, we won't be able to put on many miles each day anyway. We'll check the saddles each time we stop."

The rain continues through the day. It's after six before the camp boys start coming in for dinner, prepared by Rafe and Bea, with my minimal assistance, using freshly delivered meat and corn.

Even though I'm not convinced having kids their age doing the cooking is a good idea, I must admit they seem to be cautious with their work. And I'm also thankful for their maturity. It'll make our days on the road easier. We've yet to meet the babies or the teenage girls. I'm hopeful the girls will be half as capable as these children.

About an hour before sundown, Christopher and Doug return.

"The girls and babies should be here shortly." Doug dishes up a bowl of stew. "But I told Rogue you should probably wait out the weather. She agreed you should stay another day or two."

"We were talking about that," I say. "We want to get the children on the horses and see how they do."

"Yeah, that's smart. While I know Rafe and Bea will be fine, I'm not sure about the older girls. And riding with the babies could be a challenge. Did you work with the horses much?"

"This morning," PJ answers. "Before the rain started coming down in buckets again."

"Staying a few more days is probably good," Christopher agrees. "It'll give everyone a chance to rework the schedules to take me out of rotation."

It's not long after when the door opens and Rogue marches in, followed by her son, one of the men from the roadblock, and the children who will go with us.

It's a whirlwind as we meet the babies—two boys and two girls—and the older girls. Marnie, the taller of the two, has a very slight pooch. Not something I'd associate with pregnancy as much as being a well-nourished adolescent. She's also less than thrilled about leaving and makes it known.

Renée, accurately described by the young man who delivered the horse as tiny, is more than tiny—she's waiflike. Her pregnancy isn't at all apparent. She's also quiet and says little. I have no idea if she's happy to be going or if she's opposed to it, like Marnie.

The babies are just as adorable as Christopher said they'd be. Rogue was probably right on with the age of the youngest. The oldest of the four, a boy, is big and may be closer to three than two. The girls are between the two boys in age.

"I've decided it'd be foolish for you to leave tomorrow," Rogue declares.

Doug raises his eyebrows at her. "They'll need a few days. PJ brought up a point about making sure everyone was comfortable on the horses."

"I can ride a horse," Marnie says.

"And you?" I ask, turning to Renée.

Without raising her head to meet my gaze, she lifts a shoulder.

"She'll be fine." Marnie touches Renée's arm.

Rogue plops down in a chair. "Take a couple of days and get everyone set. Won't help us any if someone falls off the horse just down the road. We're still putting the food together anyway. How long you think it'll take you to get where you're going? A week?"

"Humph," PJ snorts. "A week of food should get us through the city at least. After that, we can start trapping and harvesting. Anything you can spare will be appreciated."

"By the way, they live here now." Rogue points to the girls and babies. "Do what you need to do to get ready. We'll increase the rations enough to cover the extra mouths. S'pose we ought to feed you and your man too." She gives me the stink eye.

"Thank you, Rogue," I say.

"You are not part of my unit. You may call me Mrs. Schoenfelder."

"Oh, sure, of course," I sputter. A quick glance at PJ shows he's attempting not to laugh. What a strange one she is.

Later, after Rogue and her troupe leave, Christopher bunks in his cabin and I sleep in the living room with the girls and babies. I'm pleasantly surprised when they all settle right in.

Sleep is slower for me and interrupted several times. Having not been around babies in a while, I find myself waking up each time one of them makes a noise. When the youngest one lets out a whimper, I decide it's close enough to dawn to get up and start the day.

Chapter 23

I change the baby into a fresh, homemade diaper—much more of a semblance to an actual diaper than the ripped sheets I used for Robyn—cooing and talking to him through the process. He responds with a belly laugh. Holding him on my hip, I rinse the dirty diaper, then swish a little soap on it. While the older two are becoming potty trained, they still wear diapers at night. The youngest are in diapers full time. We've been given three dozen diapers, a generous amount.

Too generous, according to PJ.

"Where are we going to keep them all?" he asked. It's a legitimate question.

PJ and I have our backpacks, the saddlebags, pommel bags, and bedrolls. It's been a good setup. Bea has decent gear of her own, which Doug gathered last night to show us. It's very much like ours: a rucksack, a pommel bag, and saddlebags—a really nice setup for a girl who's used to trail riding with her family.

The girls and Rafe were each given small backpacks. Saddlebags for them are similar to what Christopher did: pillowcases or sheeting bundled and tied.

At least Doug found carriers for the babies. One of the few women in their community suggested cloth wraps. She still had one from when her own child was an infant, which she brought over and showed us how to use. It worked well enough, and she said she could make two more out of a flannel sheet, stitching the rough edges to keep it from fraying.

Someone else came up with a cheap baby backpack, which the youngest fits in . . . for now. If he grows much more, we're going to have troubles. Just like if Marnie's and Renée's waists expand too much, carrying the babies could become a challenge for them.

After looking over everything last night and seeing the size of the girls and the babies, we decided book-sized backpacks made sense to use as saddlebags. Since Christopher's horse and saddle are the soundest, he'll get those—one tied to each side with his bedroll under her cantle.

Doug even managed to come up with a scabbard for him and gave him the rifle he's been using on watch—a .308. Surprisingly, Rogue, or *Mrs. Schoenfelder*, is okay with him not only taking the rifle, but Christopher and each of the teen girls were given handguns and a decent amount of ammunition.

Another day of cold, drizzly rain leaves us stuck indoors, oiling the saddles, packing, and preparing.

As soon as breakfast is done—more soup—we begin checking the horses. We start with PJ testing Whiskey and Miss Ellie. Both do fine as he puts them through their paces. With Big Steve's swayback, we don't want to risk PJ riding him.

"Should I try?" I ask.

"Yeah, better you do than if we put the girl on and he bucks her right off."

"You think he's got any buck in him?"

"Doubtful, but he may surprise us."

He doesn't. I spend several minutes working with Big Steve. He's a gem, perfectly mannered and responds well to all commands. His height almost makes me feel like I'm flying.

"All right," PJ says. "Let's get the children on them. Maybe start with Christopher. He's on watch at noon, right?"

Christopher and Whiskey work together like they were made for each other.

"Who's going to ride with me?" Christopher asks after several minutes.

PJ taps his finger to his beaded chin. "I was thinking the biggest one. Either with you or with Rochelle." He turns to me. "What do you think?"

"Mikey?" I ask.

Found in one of the farmhouses, his father murdered and his mom missing, no one knew his name. They started calling him Mikey, and it stuck.

"I thought I'd take him, and maybe Christopher and Whiskey could take Jack."

"Jack'll ride in the backpack, right?" Christopher asks. Jack, the youngest, was found in the school in Shepherd, and some of the older children believe it's his actual name.

"You okay with that?"

"Sure. Let me put the pack on and see how it works. You think I should put the backpack on with Jack in it and then get on the horse?"

"Might as well." PJ nods. "I'll help you, make sure you have your balance."

"I'm sure I can do it on my own."

"All right, then. I'll stand by in case you need me."

I help Christopher get the backpack on, not an easy task to sort out the straps, then we get the baby. Getting him in the pack and the two on the horse goes fine. PJ, as promised, stands by to help but isn't needed.

Once on Whiskey, Christopher lets out a breath. "It's not bad. My balance feels a little off. And, uh, I can see the need for having someone standing by while mounting up. It's a little shaky."

They ride around the yard a bit. Jack laughs and seems to love it.

"Looks like you'll both do fine," PJ says. "You're sitting good in the saddle. I'm going to give it another oiling after you're done, but it cleaned up nice."

"It feels good," Christopher agrees. "What do you think, Jack? You having fun?"

Jack lets out a squeal and a laugh, then sneezes all over Christopher's neck.

"Ewww. That was gross."

After Christopher and Jack are finished, we move on to Marnie, putting her on Miss Ellie. With using my hands as a step, she has no trouble getting on and sits easily.

"I could've saddled her too," she says, after I comment on her familiarity with horses.

"Ready to try it with the kiddo?" PJ asks.

"Which one?" she asks.

"The older of the two girls? Esme?" I suggest. Like Mikey, Esme's name was given after she was found. She, too, was the only one at her house and was in bad shape when they brought her here. Reba's responsible for nursing her back to health.

The other girl, Harper, was one of the children from the school in Shepard where Jack was found. Like Jack, Harper is believed to be her real name.

"Sure, fine." Marnie nods.

With the homemade baby wraps delivered late last night, and a lesson on how to use them, we take one and fiddle with it for several minutes until we have it positioned around Marnie.

"Will that be okay?" I ask.

"Should be fine. Unless . . . " She tilts her head. "If I get much fatter, it might not work as well."

"You're not fat," I say quietly.

"Whatever."

"We can rewrap it so Esme can ride on your back."

"Yeah, okay."

Esme and Marnie ride around, with the baby loving it and Marnie laughing along with her. When I go inside to get Renée, she's holding Jack.

"You ready to give it a go?" I ask.

"He's sick," she says.

"Sick?"

"Started sniffling and coughing. I think he has a fever."

I move to them and put my hand on his forehead. He's warm.

Marnie and Esme come in, Renée repeats to her about Jack being sick.

"I'll keep him." Marnie opens her arms to take the baby. "Go see your horse. He's nice. You'll like him."

Renée looks unsure—scared even—as she gives a slight nod.

When she's standing near Big Steve, she goes pale. "He's too . . . much. Too tall."

"Let's just get to know him," I say. "Even though he's big, he's sweet as can be. I rode him."

We spend quite a bit of time letting her touch him and get comfortable before she climbs up.

After a while, PJ asks, "You ready to try it?"

"Is it safe? With my baby?"

PJ looks to me. I rode through most of my pregnancies. But I'd been riding since I could walk. My doctor told me she didn't recommend riding after the first trimester. "When are you due?" I ask.

With a shrug, she whispers, "Around the middle of October. That's what Reba thinks, anyway."

I do some quick calculating. She's about eighteen weeks—if Reba's calculations are correct—so she's into her second trimester. But what choice do we have? If we take her to the military in Billings, she'll only need to ride for a few days. If, like Christopher wants, we take her to Bakerville, she'll need to ride until we get the wagon in Joliet, which will likely be a couple of weeks.

"I rode through each of my pregnancies. Riding isn't really the problem. Falling off is."

She gives a nod. "I should make sure I don't fall off?"

"That'd be best," PJ agrees. "Not just because of your condition, but because falling off is never fun. This boy here— " he strokes Big Steve on the shoulder " —he's about as calm as they come. Definitely a plodder. No buck in him at all."

"All right," she says quietly. "I'll do it."

In the saddle, she's stiff and awkward. Big Steve is patient and wonderful. Eventually, as PJ leads the horse, she begins to relax. She even smiles.

After a half hour or so, I ask, "Do you want to try it with a baby?"

"Maybe I'd best carry the last baby," PJ offers.

"No, I'll do it," Renée says. "It's bad enough Ace will be carrying a baby and won't be able to move fast. We need you in case . . . " Her voice trails off.

"She's right," I agree. "With the baby on my chest, I won't be able to shoot the rifle."

"I think we ought to practice," PJ says. "Put that contraption on and put something baby sized in it. Do some of our shooting maneuvers from militia practice and the ones we worked on with Kimba and Rey."

"You can't shoot while holding a baby." Renée shakes her head.

"We might not have a choice."

~~~~~

Jack's sniffles and low fever turned into a full-blown cold, and the weather continued to be drizzly off and on. Rogue allowed us to stay until the weather cleared and Jack was better. During our time, we continued to work on the saddles and make sure all of the children were comfortable on the horses.

A week and a day after we first arrived at Camp Ah Nei, baby Jack is well enough to travel. The saddles are as good as they're going to get, and our gear is well stocked. Renée, with baby Harper in the sling, are riding Big Steve like champs. Renée's nervousness over the massive
~~~~~

horse has subsided, and it's clear she and the horse have made a connection.

We're not leaving a moment too soon. Yesterday, a group of soldiers showed up.

Rogue's watchers arrived shortly before the Army, allowing everyone to prepare. PJ and I stayed at the house with our group, minus Christopher, who went to his preassigned position. It was a harrowing time, waiting to see if they'd attack.

They left an ultimatum: cooperate or else. After their appearance, Rogue made many noises again about losing Christopher. This time, he seemed to understand that her desire for him to stay was not going to change whatever the outcome may be. If the Army attacks, one fifteen-year-old boy won't save the day.

We're finishing our packing when the neighborhood starts showing up to say their goodbyes. Marnie and Renée may not have originally wished to go, but several others make it quite clear they'd love an invitation to leave with us. Rogue has a conniption fit, calling them several names—names children and even adults should never be called, including ungrateful, selfish, mooches, and much worse.

"That's enough." Doug turns on her. "You brought this on yourself. If you didn't act like the Iron Lady, maybe they wouldn't want to leave!"

"You don't get to give me lip in front of everyone," she hisses.

"You know what—" He stops midsentence. I watch as his shoulders drop, followed by his head. "You're right, Rogue. Please forgive my outburst."

I'm close enough to hear her harsh whisper. "Listen, you insolent little twit. I won't be talked down to in front of my crew. Got it?"

He bends his head and gives her a weak smile. "I was out of line. It won't happen again."

She visibly softens. "I suppose it's hard for you today, with Bea and the boy leaving. Ace too. It's not too late to change your mind about your daughter going. She can stay."

"No, it's best this way. What about Aspen? Did you find out about her, um, situation?"

"She's denying everything, said she's not pregnant and started crying when she thought she'd have to leave. She's got a little sister here, you know."

"I know. We could send both of them. Find another horse— "

I look to PJ, who gives a slight shake of his head. While I feel bad for the girl, especially if she is in the family way like the others, I don't know if we can take anyone else with us.

As it is, the four toddlers are going to stretch us thin. And this is something that should've been sorted out in the days we've been preparing and waiting for Jack to recuperate, not at the last minute.

"They'll stay here," Rogue says. "We'll deal with it when the time comes. Let's get a move on. Everyone's just standing around here. We have work to do."

Doug turns to me. "You think you have what you need?"

"We'll be fine. Thank you for the dried meat and grains. That'll help."

"Let's get you all loaded up then." Rogue's impatience is evident.

"Before we do," PJ says, "I'd like to ask for God's blessing on our travels. Anyone who wishes to join us in our petition, please bow your head." He gives me a smile.

I glance to Christopher, who rolls his eyes and shakes his head.

PJ pauses a beat to allow people to adjust.

"Father God, You've been our beacon throughout this journey. You've brought us safely here, helped us find Christopher and comforted Rochelle's heart—refilled it with the love of her child. We, once again, humbly ask You to give us traveling mercies. Help us all as we make our way back to Wyoming. Please be with these children on the road. Help the young ones to . . . well, Lord, I don't really know what all we'll need help with, but You do.

"We need You now as much—*more*—than ever. And please be with those here as they face the days ahead. We know You have a plan for the future. Help each person present reach out to You and listen as You share that plan. We pray these things in Jesus' precious name, amen."

A chorus of amens follow. Not from Christopher. Or Rogue. But from many of those gathered.

"Now that you've got that out of the way . . . " Rogue makes a shooing motion with her hands. "Time to hit the road."

With the wraps and babies in place, and Christopher carrying Jack in the backpack, we mount up. Bea and Rafe are helped onto their ponies, feet firm in their stirrups, riding helmets on their heads. Both Doug and Vanessa are struggling with their emotions. Vanessa hugs her sister and Rafe several times.

"You'll be going down to Shepherd and then going on 87 from there, right?" Doug asks.

"Yup," PJ says. "It's smart to cut off those miles."

Rogue, again, reminds us they have plenty of work to do.

"Thanks for your hospitality and sparing the gear." PJ holds out his hand. "We sincerely appreciate it."

She reluctantly reaches out. "Yeah, well, glad you're taking the young ones."

She gives his hand a single pump before striding to her ATV. She doesn't hesitate to fire it up and take off.

With final goodbyes, we start off down the long driveway.

"Bye, Bea!" Vanessa hollers. "I love you. You too, Rafe. Bye, everyone!" There's plenty of tears from Bea and the older girls. Rafe makes a point of holding his head high, but I still see the moisture in his eyes.

The babies are excited, making plenty of noises over their horsey ride. Mikey, the one I'm carrying, has a great vocabulary and talks about the horses, the cattle, the trees, the birds, and more.

"Talkative thing, ain't he?" PJ asks as we turn from C A onto Scandia Road.

"Seems pretty happy too. Reba, the lady caring for them, she's done great."

"I'm surprised we never met her."

"She didn't want to say goodbye," Marnie says. "She'll miss them too much. Besides, she still has the others with her."

"The others?" I ask.

"The ones just a little older."

"There's a dozen or so between two and six. We're only taking the very youngest."

"Oh . . . of course," I mutter, remembering how Christopher said the children around that age help work the fields.

We ride in silence, with only Mikey and the other babies chattering, until we reach the intersection of Scandia and Shepherd Road.

We've gone slightly past the intersection when Rafe points ahead. "Is that V?"

Along the side of the road, just ahead, is a full-sized horse and a small rider. She lifts a hand in greeting. It's for sure Vanessa.

"Is everything okay?" PJ asks as we get close enough to talk.

"I'm coming with you."

"You are?" Bea asks, her voice full of excitement. "Dad too?"

With a shake of her head, Vanessa says, "Just me. He won't leave the others. He's worried about what *she* might do."

"How'd you get here?" I ask.

"Overland. There's trails that are a shortcut." She shrugs. "He said you'll need help. But when the trouble is over, I'm coming back to him. You'll bring me back, right?"

"I'll make sure of it," Christopher assures her.

With one of his now-famous sighs, PJ asks, "How's your gear?"

"Good. Dad had it ready for me. Sent me with a shotgun too." She motions to the scabbard on the offside of her horse. "He said to tell you it's only a 20 gauge, but there's plenty of shells for it. He thought you could teach me how to use it. It might come in handy."

"He's right about that," PJ says.

He and I had spoken to Doug about all the hunting we'd done on our way here. We'd lamented slightly about losing the two shotguns, them having gone with our friends heading north. The rifles are great for wild game and for long-range shooting if we need them, but the shotguns were necessary for the fowl and great for self-defense.

"As soon as everyone left, he got the saddle on and sent me off. Told me to ride fast." She nods. Like Bea and Rafe, she's in a riding helmet. She turns to Christopher. "You promise you'll bring me back? 'Cause I'm not leaving unless you do."

"I promise." He lifts a hand in a pledge. "I know what it's like not to be with family."

Doug's insistence of going over the map and ensuring we were taking this route makes perfect sense now. He'd planned this all along, planned to send Vanessa on the trails to meet up with us. I pray the fallout won't be too much.

Our goal for the day is only to get near US Highway 87. We'll camp there for the night, in as secluded of a location we can find in this flat land, maybe even in an abandoned house with a barn for the horses.

Then, tomorrow, we'll take 87 toward Billings, probably stopping at the first military camp. Neither PJ nor I are overly excited about that after what happened in Huntley. Avoiding those places would be best, but there really is no option. We'll definitely be more on our guard than we were before.

From there, we'll be in the city for a couple of days as we make our way through Billings. We plan to check on orphanages for the babies, though, now, after spending several days with them, that doesn't sound like a great idea. I'd rather choose families for them to live with. Maybe there's someone in Bakerville willing to take them in.

After getting through Billings, we'll head west on Interstate 90—provided the report is still favorable for safe travel on the road between Laurel and Joliet. If not, we'll continue south on 87 to Pryor and cross back the way we came. As long as we can get to Joliet where the wagon is, we'll be good.

The wagon.

Will that be a help or a hindrance? Although it does make us a target, once we're out of heavily populated areas, it should be a help. Renée, Marnie, and the babies can ride in the wagon. Getting the pregnant girls off the horses as soon as possible is a good idea. We'll pony their horses and use them to carry gear. It's a good plan.

A really good plan.

But PJ and I both know how plans can change. Especially at the end of the world.

Chapter 24

"I'm so glad you're here." Tamra pats my arm. "And just in time too. The rain is really starting to come down."

We rode the last hour into Joliet in a fine mist, drenching our filthy clothes and soaking our horses. Nothing new. The last several weeks, since we left Camp Ah Nei, have been one rain-soaked ride after the next. Even though I've changed into somewhat dry clothing—yoga pants and a T-shirt that have been crammed at the bottom of my saddlebag and are only slightly damp—the smell of wet horse lingers on my body. It's permeated into my skin after too many wet days in the saddle.

A bath. I'd love a long, hot bath, where I can just lie back and soak, luxuriating in the warmth of the water, staying in until my skin wrinkles and every bit of the trail is removed. When was the last time I had a bath? Well before the attacks last summer, even before we took Christopher to summer camp.

No. That's not true. When Dale and I dropped Christopher off at Camp Ah Nei, we came up alone. Kerryanne and Cheyre stayed with friends so we could take a night to ourselves in Billings afterward. A romantic night away, such a rarity in our long-married life.

We made the most of it, splurging and getting the best room the hotel offered: a king suite with both a jacuzzi tub and a balcony, which overlooked the interior courtyard of the hotel.

We had laughed about the balcony. While it was a selling point at the front desk when the clerk asked if we wanted an upgrade, it wasn't terribly practical. The interior courtyard was lovely to look at, with a fake stream and fake waterfalls, along with a koi pond and half a dozen public hot tubs. It was also noisy with kids running around on their way to the pool and the game room. Oh, we didn't mind, but it wasn't a great addition to our romantic interlude. The jacuzzi tub, however . . .

"Do you think you can stay a couple of days?" Tamra asks. "Rest up a bit?"

"Probably only long enough for the rain to let up. Being this close . . . I'm ready to see my girls. I *need* to see them, to be a family again."

"I suspect they'll be plenty surprised when you show up with not only their brother but also nine other children."

"No doubt. I just . . . PJ and I, we couldn't leave them at the orphanage. They had one at the Metra Arena, and the people running it are doing the best they can, but we just couldn't do it."

"Getting through Billings sounds like it was quite the ordeal."

"Very much so."

As we thought, our plans of an easy trip were derailed. We left Doug and Camp Ah Nei on May 23. Today is June 12. It took us almost three weeks to travel less than sixty miles.

The military campgrounds set up along the way were mostly safe and even suitable for the horses—some with paddocks set up for the new Cavalry being formed, and they were opened to be shared by civilians.

The first campground, on US Highway 87 just outside of Billings, was the only one I'd describe as rough. And we were there for six days! The military stopped all travel through Billings while they had an operation going. We didn't get the details of exactly what the operation was, but until it was over, we had to stay put.

From there, we only made it as far as the MetraPark Arena, where the Montana State Fair and other big events used to be held. Now it's a huge aid station with camping, medical care, meals, the orphanage, and more. And we were forced to stop for a full week as they, once again, suspended all movement from the Metra to Interstate 90.

Being stuck was awful—especially being stuck with around a thousand other people. At least we were in a section with other horsemen that was well protected.

When we finally got back on the road, we reached I-90. There were campgrounds set up every few miles. We aimed for ten miles a day, the limit we could ride with the young children and senior horses, and would stop when we'd reach a suitable encampment.

Thanks to constant patrols, there were no issues along the interstate. I'd like to say the Marines were the reason for this, but it was the new Cavalry and the Civil Air Patrol—the group of mostly young, mostly volunteers we first met in Lockwood.

Like the CAP, the Cavalry also consists mainly of new volunteers. One man called them the new Rough Riders. And from what I gathered from the actual military personnel we talked to, they're not a welcome addition. Many times, we heard them referred to as vigilantes. Even the official volunteers seem to think the Cavalry is trouble, and they had plenty of less than favorable comments about them.

Once we reached Laurel—only twenty miles and what should've been a two-day ride from Joliet—we were stuck again. This time, we found out it was because of troop movement. We stayed at the city park along the Yellowstone River for three nights before we were allowed to travel again.

"There's a couple here in Joliet who were trying to adopt before all this happened," Tamra says.

"Oh?"

She lifts a shoulder. "Things are so different now that I don't know what they'd think about it. And the town, they might have . . . concerns. I'll admit, a few townspeople were less than happy about me and my girls showing up."

"Is it getting better? With the military around?"

"There's been a lot of change just in the time we've been here. The first day we heard the helicopters flying over—wow! That was something. My mom, the girls, and I were working in the garden, turning the soil so we could plant. All of a sudden, we heard the *whoop, whoop, whoop.*"

"Debbie was scared," Tamra continues. "She went diving to the ground. Even though she's heard helicopters before, at least I think she has, it'd been so long and our world is so crazy now. Beth, though, she knew what it was. She couldn't decide whether to be scared or excited. Mom and me too. We wanted to believe they were *good.* But with everything we've been through, it was hard."

"I know. It's amazing how much things seem to be returning to some semblance of normal, like helicopters and airplanes, even the military vehicles, but still things are so different. Did you see the Cavalry?"

"They haven't been through here, but we've heard about them. We heard they're looking for horses. Did you have any trouble with them wanting yours?"

"No trouble. Of course, our old nags and ponies aren't exactly primo specimens."

"Right?" She laughs. "But Titan and Lucky are beautiful. And the one girl you have with you, her horse looks good."

"Vanessa. Yes, thanks to her dad sneaking them out."

"That's quite a story about what they're doing there. Child soldiers. That's like something from a different continent. And that lady . . . what a nut."

"Christopher respects her. The girls too. But I think they do see, especially now that we're gone, how things weren't right. Respecting Rogue is one thing. Being grateful to her for all she's done is understandable. But some of them almost seemed to worship her."

"Why? That makes little sense?"

I shake my head. "I don't know. In some ways, it reminds me of how I was with Fred. How . . . " I chew on my upper lip as I think of my words. "How he was terrible to me. But I still went out of my way to try and please him, to keep him happy."

"I guess, unless we're in the situation, it's hard to judge, especially with so many of them being young. They're impressionable."

"True. Doug and the few adults there are definitely outnumbered. Christopher told me the first day I was there how they'd do anything for her. I don't think Doug could stage a coup and expect it to go well. He knows that too. Sending his children away seemed like the best option."

"And maybe now that he doesn't have their safety to be concerned with . . . " She tilts her head.

"Yeah. PJ half expects he'll take as many of the boys he can, the ones not fully loyal to Rogue, and show up in Bakerville one day. He had PJ map out several routes there."

"Do you think it's happening in other places too? Children being used as soldiers?"

"PJ and I've discussed it. He thinks there's probably little pockets all over the US where the adults are gone, murdered or whatever, and the children are fending for themselves. Or like outside of Shepherd, the children far outnumber the adults. I understand why Rogue is doing it . . . to a point. But I don't like it. Especially not ones as young as Vanessa. Can you imagine Debbie toting a gun around?"

"My dad's been helping her learn the .22."

"Cheyre used to shoot on the ranch, had her own pink Crikett .22. Dale gave it to her when she turned five," I say. "Teaching them how to shoot, learning to be comfortable with the rifle and safe, it's different than what's happening there and what may be happening in other places. Those children are their first line of defense."

"True," Tamra says.

"I just hope the Army in Huntley doesn't go in guns blazing after the cattle. If they do . . . " I shake my head. "We've been gone so long now, they may have already. Their threat sounded serious."

"I hate that our military is threatening our citizens. It's bad enough that we're hearing the rumors about the other countries and their intentions."

I respond with a slow nod. The ham radio operators in Joliet are hearing some disturbing things. Not through any official channels, like the announcements from the president, but things being passed from one operator to another.

When we were living on the mountain, we'd hear others broadcasting on occasion but never strong signals from any distance. Here, a lot more information's being relayed not only from different parts of the country but even throughout the world. And it sounds terrible.

After the United States was devastated, other countries also fell apart. There's talk of skirmishes and full-on wars in a variety of places—even a nuclear event in the Middle East. In one of the early addresses from our president, he'd said he was working with other countries to come to our aid. But from the sounds of it, the rest of the world isn't in much better shape than we are.

We sit in silence for several minutes, each of us lost in our thoughts.

"I could ask my dad about the family looking to adopt," Tamra says. "I mean, if you *want* me to."

Do I want her to? We've been together for weeks now, riding, eating, talking, even laughing. Even with the long delays, the journey has gone better than PJ or I could've hoped. There's been no real danger. In some ways, we've been like a family on a long road trip . . . the 1800s version of a road trip.

"As much as I already love them all, it's not feasible for me to have a dozen children. Or to take that many to Bakerville. They already have too many orphans. And Marnie and Renée will be having their own babies in a few months."

"I was surprised how well the town of Joliet has done. They haven't seen as much violence as we did. No internal issues. No outside attacks. I guess they're in a good location to be protected."

"It's surprising, too, considering the troubles all around. With the bandits just on the other side of Rockvale— "

"Did you hear how they ended them?"

"I didn't hear. They just told us when we camped on the Yellowstone River in Laurel that the road was cleared—old Highway 310, anyway. The new highway was still a work in progress."

"The old highway is better anyway." She smiles. "We heard it wasn't the military, but rather a group of ordinary folks who banded together. They used snipers and whittled away at the outlaws bit by bit. Had them so scared they wouldn't show their faces."

"I'd like to think the lawlessness is going to subside. That the reconstruction efforts will give people hope, and they'll realize they don't have to steal and kill people for whatever they can get."

"The president's announcement from last week sounded promising. Did you hear it?" she asks, leaning forward.

"They had a handwritten transcript in one of the camps. It was in line with what we saw and experienced in Billings, with the military taking over, eliminating bad guys, and trying to get the lights on. Not that the lights are on yet, not around here anyway."

We sit in silence for a few minutes—a rare treat for me. The children are all in the kitchen with Tamra's mom and daughters.

The large house masks the sound between that room and the upstairs bedroom the babies, young children, and teen girls are sharing with me. Christopher and PJ will sleep in the den on the first floor tonight.

And if the rain has stopped, we'll start the final leg of our journey tomorrow. Lucky and Titan will pull the wagon as we travel the remaining fifty miles to Bakerville. A week or so on the road, and then I'll be back with my daughters. My children will be together again.

"PJ and Christopher seem to get along well," Tamra says.

"At the moment. It was tense when we first showed up at Camp Ah Nei, and also the first couple of days on the road. Christopher was hurting over the knowledge his dad is dead, plus the sudden change in his life. He went from being a . . . a warrior of sorts to realizing PJ was in charge of our group."

"Just PJ?"

"No. Me too, of course. We're pretty equal in things. But following my lead, as his mom, was certainly easier on him than following the lead of a stranger. Someone who just happened to show up with his mom. Someone he didn't entirely trust. And he isn't at all impressed with PJ's faith, with starting each day with prayer and ending each day with nightly Bible readings and prayer."

"Those Bible readings and prayer were such an important part of our trip to Joliet. Learning about God and prayer . . . it changed my life."

I reach for her hand. "And now?"

"Now I understand. When you used to say how important God was to you, how He'd changed your life, I thought you were a little . . . " She makes a whirly bird motion with her finger by her temple.

I can't help but laugh. "You thought I was nuts!"

"You'd better believe it! But now I understand. And when we finally got here, finally got home to Joliet and I was back with my parents, everything really started to make sense. Especially discovering my mom and dad had also been led to the Lord. Debbie now too. Beth . . . well, she's asking questions and wants to know more."

"That's great! Knowing the Lord is life changing."

"It's been—well, amazing. Such terrible things have happened, but something so good has come of it."

"Same for me. Learning to trust in God has been one of the best things to come of this disaster."

"Trusting Him to get us through each day, it's not an easy thing to trust. Have you told Christopher about . . . everything?" Tamra asks. "Oh, wait, am I supposed to call him Ace?"

I snort. "Ha! I don't. I don't call the other children by their nicknames either. I suppose I understand the appeal of it, but I just can't get used to thinking of my son as Ace. And yes, he knows."

"How'd he take it?"

"About as you'd expect. He was mad for me and mad for the girls, especially about the way it changed Cheyre so much. You know how we used to call her Sweetie and Kerryanne was Kitty? Christopher gave them those nicknames. But with Fred and how he was to my girls . . . the way he said their names . . . they won't go by Kitty or Sweetie anymore."

"That makes sense, I guess."

"Christopher promises, if he were to ever meet up with Fred Lassiter, he'd kill him. He added a few additional choice words during his tirade."

"What Fred did to you and the girls . . . I'm so sorry I never saw it."

"You have nothing to apologize for. I let you see what I wanted you to see. I had to. I was so afraid of what he'd do if anyone knew I wasn't marrying him of my own free will."

"At least he's gone and you won't have to worry about Christopher meeting up with him."

I close my eyes. "Gone, yes, though I do wish he wouldn't have just disappeared. I wish I knew where he was."

"Surely he'd have left the area?"

"Would he? He worked in Prospect, had friends there."

"You think he went to Prospect? The town's a wreck with the stuff happening there."

"Sounds like Fred would be a perfect fit. Knowing how he is . . . " I lift my hands.

"Yeah, he'd fit in with all the other outlaws and murderers. Probably even have good friends who'd— " She shakes her head.

"Sometimes I wish they would've . . . " I lift my eyebrows and cock my head.

"Killed him?" she whispers.

"No, I don't think that's what I wish. Locked him up? Yes, definitely. Anything other than him escaping and killing the men with him in the process."

"I've been reading from the Bible, the one Jennifer gave me. Last night I read about not repaying evil for evil. Trying to live in peace with everyone. How we're supposed to feed our enemies, give them water. Revenge is for God, not us. While I like the sounds of that, how does that work with someone like Fred? Someone who did such awful things? Someone like Jackson?"

I give a small shake of my head. Like Fred, Tamra's second husband did terrible things.

"I mean," Tamra continues, "I guess the Lord did get vengeance on Jackson since he met his end in an avalanche. But those families of the women he killed, do they feel like they were shorted? Like they should be the ones getting revenge?"

I gaze at my friend as tears fill her eyes. She and I have been through so much. Fred Lassiter and Jackson Nicholson were friends. She married Jackson and I married Fred in a double wedding last September. The big difference: she loved Jackson. It might not have been a passionate, consuming love, but it was a love based on comfort and understanding. Before Jackson became her husband, he was her brother-in-law.

When Tamra's husband died in a fire, Jackson was there, providing a safety net for her and her daughters—his nieces. Marrying him made sense. Especially in today's world. At the time, she didn't know he harbored deep, dark secrets. Similar secrets to what Fred carried.

Fred purchased my daughters and me. Jackson was a serial killer. He killed three women after the apocalypse began, and it's believed he killed at least a half dozen more before our world fell apart. Tamra knew Jackson for over fifteen years and never suspected a thing.

I shake my head. "I don't know. I imagine some would, yes. Others may be happy to let the Lord do His work."

"And you? If you saw Fred on the street, would you . . . "

It takes me several moments before I whisper, "I'm scared of him. Even now. I'm afraid, if I saw him, I might be too frightened to do anything."

Chapter 25

"It seems like we were just here," PJ says as he brushes Titan. "'Course, there's not a foot of snow on the ground now."

We're camped about a mile outside of Belfry, Montana, at a newly established camping spot. Though we were here not that long ago, it was back in March when winter was in full swing, and back when Belfry was on its own. Since then, they've joined forces with Bridger, Fromberg, and Joliet to form a partnership for mutual aid.

We stayed in Joliet longer than expected, thanks to the rain continuing for a couple of days. When it finally stopped in the early morning hours on a Tuesday, we waited until midday for the ground to dry up. When we left, it was without three of our babies.

Jack and Harper, the two youngest, stayed with the family Tamra told me about. They were ecstatic about the opportunity to have a family. Not just one child, but two. A boy and a girl. And, thankfully, there was much support from the rest of the town.

In the years before, there'd been fundraisers and other events in support of their pursuit of adoption. And they were terribly close to becoming parents when the world fell apart. They'd matched with a birth mother in Billings. Unfortunately, contact was lost, and they don't know if she and the baby made it through the worst of it. Or if they were part of the casualties, thanks to violence and hunger.

A second couple, parents to a young girl born shortly before the attacks, took in Esme. The birth of their daughter had gone wrong, resulting in the mom needing an emergency hysterectomy. Adopting Esme gives them the family they'd always hoped to have.

Though we all miss the babies, we also know they'll be loved and well cared for. Part of me wishes we could've found a home for Mikey too. But most of me is glad we didn't. With him as my riding partner from Camp Ah Nei to Joliet, we've developed a bond. I can't deny I love him.

I love Jack, Harper, and Esme also, but I know this is the best choice for them.

Marnie, Renée, and Mikey now ride in the wagon. We talked about leaving Big Steve in Joliet, but we've all grown rather fond of the old horse, so he walks behind Christopher and Whiskey on a lead rope. Miss Ellie is ponied by Vanessa and her horse, Buddy, and Bea and Rafe are still riding their ponies.

We camped partway between Joliet and Fromberg that first night, then halfway between Fromberg and Bridger the next night. When going through Fromberg, we learned the military convoy that stalled our progress when we were in Laurel had stopped in Fromberg for several days. The town was still riding high on the visit and the supplies left behind.

Arriving in Bridger the next day, we were surprised by an old friend at the town barricade.

We'd met Scruff back in March, only a couple of days into our trip. He was traveling from Texas to Canada, where things were rumored to be normal. He joined our group, and we traveled together until Bridger.

He was shot in an altercation there—the same one that left Robyn with a dislocated shoulder and Donnie McCullough with a permanent scar along his scalp from a bullet graze. Scruff was healing well when we continued our journey without him. I'd thought for sure he'd have continued on his way, but he seems to have fit in well with the small town and is still there.

Scruff told us about the military staying in Bridger for several days—mainly Marines and a few of the new volunteers, the Auxiliary group—saying they restocked supplies and helped everyone with morale. Their town was still enjoying the items left behind and was still celebrating. So much so, Scruff invited us to stay in Bridger and join in the memorial service scheduled for the next night.

The service was in honor of one year since the planes were shot out of the sky, starting the downward spiral that has changed our country forever. It was a somber event, filled with lots of patriotism, song, and prayer. It was well worth the delay. Even so, it was good to get back on the road and make our way closer to Bakerville and my girls.

"It's nice here." I motion to the bank of the Clarks Fork of the Yellowstone. "It was a good place for them to set up a campground."

"And quiet compared to the military campgrounds back on I-90. They've done a nice job with it. I have to admit, I'm glad to be away from the crowds."

"I wonder how they're doing in Belfry?" I ask, remembering the people we met when we were here months ago. We ended up staying a couple of days then. Donnie McCullough had been shot in the hand after we were attacked down the road. Their small medical team treated him.

"You mean overall? Good is my guess. Otherwise, we would've heard of it. A couple more days and we'll be home. I bet you can hardly wait to hug your girls."

"I'm already forcing my excitement down."

"Have you thought much about the other children?"

"Continually."

"I'm sure my sister-in-law and brother would be happy to help with them."

"Don't you think they have their hands full after taking in the children who survived the Bakerville massacre?"

"Yeah, I guess that's true." PJ talks softly to Lucky as he lifts a foot to pick his hoof. I'm finishing up with Rafe's pony. We've groomed and checked the rest of the horses and have them on picket lines or hobbled.

Although the children usually take care of their own horses, we're handling it today and letting them enjoy the river and rest. Even Christopher, who doesn't shirk on his duties, agreed to take a break with the younger ones, watching over them to make sure they stay safe.

"We could get married," PJ says softly. "Give them a proper family."

My hands continue to move, one hand with the finishing brush, whisking away the final bits of hair, dirt, and debris, and the other hand moving along the pony's body, comforting him, keeping him calm as I work.

"You don't have to answer me right away. Just think about it."

"You know I'm still married to Fred, even though it wasn't by choice."

"There was nothing legal about that marriage."

"Legal or not, he disappeared. Escaped when being taken to jail. Wouldn't I still be married?"

"Did you consider yourself married? Did you believe there was a Godly Covenant to it? And that's what marriage should be—a sacred bond, one that both parties go into willingly, with God at the center."

With my heart pounding, I ask, "Why would you want to marry me?"

He releases a small snort. "I'd think it's fairly obvious by now, Rochelle. I love you."

A scream echoes through the silence.

"Mikey!" I yell, dropping the brush. "That was Mikey."

"Go! I'll get the horses secured and be right behind you."

I sprint to the riverside where the shriek originated. As soon as I reach the upper bank, I see them twenty feet below me on the soft beach-like area. All the kids are standing there, pointing at something.

Christopher sees me and raises a hand. "It's okay, Mom. Another dead rabbit. It just scared him is all. Right, Mikey?"

"Ki-cat on dirt," Mikey points while jumping up and down.

"What is it?" PJ asks from behind me.

"Dead rabbit. They're okay." With my adrenaline still racing, I raise my voice, "Why don't you all come back up here. We'll have some dinner. The pheasant should be about ready."

The geese that were plentiful through here during the winter have moved on. There's still the occasional honker or duck on one of the numerous small ponds or the river, but not like it was. We were fortunate to find a bevy of pheasants. And thanks to the shotgun Doug sent with Vanessa, Christopher brought one down in an open field a few miles back.

We're grateful to have the bird. We'd anticipated an increase in food to hunt as we moved away from the populated area of Billings. But that hasn't been the case.

Between Joliet and Fromberg, we figured we'd be able to get a couple of rabbits, but all we found were dead ones, at least half a dozen that we could see near the road. One looked like it'd been in a fight— even had a bloody nose. And now, there's another dead one here where we're camping. I'm starting to wonder if they have some kind of a plague. Could they get the Chronic Wasting Disease like the deer herd has?

After dinner, Renée, always eager to help, asks if she should get water from the river for washing up.

I pat her arm. "You stay here and keep the babies entertained. I'll get it."

"You want some company?" PJ asks.

I watch as Christopher bristles at the question.

"No, I'm good."

With a single bend of his neck, PJ says, "All right. I'll get the horses on the highline."

"I'll help with the horses." Marnie grabs a sweatshirt to fight off the early evening chill. Even though she may not be eager to help with dishes or other domestic items, she's always happy to work with the horses. And unlike Christopher—who they still call Ace, which he prefers—both she and Renée have dropped their nicknames.

Like Marnie, I grab my own fleece jacket. These late June days are plenty warm, but as soon as the sun starts to drop, there's a chill in the air.

"Can you get a jacket on Mikey?" I ask Renée.

"Sure. You think it's going to rain tonight?"

I look to the western sky. There're a few darker clouds. "I wouldn't be surprised. Hopefully it's just a sprinkle. Be right back."

Should I do it?

That's the question on my mind as I make my way down the embankment to the edge of the river. Should I marry PJ?

He said he loves me. And I believe he truly does. But . . . a year ago I was with Dale, happily married and still in love after almost seventeen years. The anniversary of his murder is in only a few days. With his death, my life changed in an instant.

Everything except my love for him. It's still there. It always will be.

PJ knows this. He understands, having lost his own wife and child years ago. The love never leaves.

I'm not naive enough to think that there isn't something between PJ and me. The way I feel when he smiles at me. The kindness he shows, not just to me but to others. The way he is with the children. While he knew it'd be a lot for us, and it has been, he barely hesitated to bring them. The way he treats Christopher, too, says much about him as a man.

He knows there's still animosity there, some distrust on the part of my son, but he doesn't push. Instead, in his quiet way, he allows Christopher to continue to be the man he's becoming, the man he was forced to become as a child soldier under Rogue's reign.

PJ lets him keep the good parts of that growth while helping him realize the parts that weren't needed. And he lets Christopher see—not just see but experience—that a real man can have a heart for God.

I turn and look back at the camp. Not only is Marnie with PJ at the horses but so is Christopher. PJ sees me and lifts a hand. I return the gesture before starting the decline toward the river.

But is it really fair to PJ? To marry him after what happened to me after Dale died, after what happened with the men at the house, after Fred forced me to be his wife? PJ's told me before it doesn't matter, that it doesn't change how he feels about me. He's told me he respects me. And I do believe he loves me.

I stoop down and fill the first container. After we lost most of our water jugs when Robyn and the others fell in the creek, finding replacements has not been as easy as expected. All we could find were a few old soda bottles along the road that got us to Camp Ah Nei.

At least Rogue and her people made sure we had enough containers to get home. This one, a two-liter soda bottle, is the largest and is what we use to fill with water for washing dishes and other cleaning needs, like diapers.

Mikey is doing well during the day, but nighttime's are still iffy. We left most of the diapers with the family in Joliet, keeping only four. We'll need to make more diapers for Marnie's and Renée's babies.

"Hello, Rochelle."

My stomach drops as I let go of the bottle. I watch it float away, not daring to raise my head.

"Are you not going to say hello to me, to your long-lost husband?"

"Fred," I whisper. With tears running down my face, I lift my chin. "You're not my husband. You're nothing to me."

He's standing two dozen feet away from me as he lifts the muzzle of his pistol and aims it right at my chest. "I'm everything to you. I own you and your little brats. Too bad you left them behind with Sylvia Eriksen."

I feel the color drain from my face.

Fred lets out a cruel laugh. "That's right. I know all about it. You see, I found a couple of your neighbors when they attacked the town of Prospect. I took them in and asked a few questions. They didn't want to answer at first, but I was very convincing, even had a friend helping me. They told me all about how you went after your son. We've been waiting here, knowing you'd come through Belfry at some point. Patience. That's definitely one of my virtues."

"You tortured someone to find out about me?"

"Yep. When they attacked Prospect."

"I don't . . . I don't know what you're talking about." My voice is barely above a whisper.

"I guess you don't. You left your little mountain hideaway before all the fun started. You missed out on a lot, Rochelle. But not to worry. We'll get you caught up. You and me, we're going to finish what we started. We'll get your two girls and make that family we dreamed about. I must admit, I was sad to discover you weren't already carrying my child. I was sure we'd made a baby that last time. But not to worry, we'll get it done.

"In fact, maybe we should bring one of those pregnant girls along with us. Then, if you can't give me the child you promised me, we'll at least have a surrogate available. We know she's fertile. I heard that man with you reading the Bible. Is that what you are now? One of those Bible thumpers? They did that in the Bible, you know. When the woman was barren, they'd get the servant girl to provide the children. Yeah . . . that's what we'll do."

It's clear to see Fred's mental health has deteriorated, even beyond what it was when I last saw him.

I clench my fists. "You won't touch either of them." An unwelcome quiver to my voice betrays my fear. I take a deep breath. "And my children are not—*will not*—be your family."

"That's where you're wrong, sugar. Now stand on up, and we'll get moving."

"I won't— "

I watch as he spins slightly, grabbing at his leg as the sound of a shot fills the air.

"Mom! Get down!"

Fred whips his pistol toward the top of the hill, popping off three quick shots.

Putting one knee on the ground, I pull my sidearm. "Fred!"

He turns to me. Seeing the gun, he lets out a cruel laugh. "You can't. I own you."

I squeeze off the first round, then keep squeezing until the slide stays open. My Glock is empty. An instant later, I've popped in the second magazine, ready to shoot again.

"He's down," PJ calls to me from the top of the bank. "Step back and I'll check him."

Sixteen 10-millimeter rounds from a Glock 20 . . . checking him isn't really necessary. Overkill, that's what it was. I more than stopped the threat. I was excessive.

"You need to get up there." PJ skids down the hill. "Christopher was hit."

Chapter 26

"He's hit? Christopher's hit?"

"Holster your weapon, Rochelle. Then go to your son. Marnie is putting pressure on it."

I'm up the hill in a moment, swiveling my head, trying to find him.

Marnie lifts her chin toward me. "Here! Rochelle, it's . . . it's bad."

"Not that bad," Christopher says through gritted teeth. "Just my arm."

I kneel at his side. Marnie lifts the towel off slightly. He was hit directly above the elbow.

And she's right. It's bad.

I can see bits of bone among the mangled flesh.

"Marnie," PJ says, suddenly at my side. "Get Lucky and Titan ready to hook to the wagon."

"I'm okay, Mom," Christopher assures me as a shiver runs through his body.

PJ pulls a bandanna from his pocket. "Keep pressure on it. What happened to the other one?"

"The other one?" I ask, as I shove Marnie's sweatshirt tighter against Christopher's arm to stem the bleeding.

"The tracks show there were two guys on the river. Did only one attack you?" He squats next to me, wrapping the bandanna around Christopher's arm above the wound. He pulls it tight. Too tight. Christopher cries out as PJ cinches it. It's a tourniquet.

"If you put on the tourniquet— "

"It can't be helped." He gives the bandanna another slight yank. "Is that okay?"

Pale faced, my son gives a slight nod.

"All right. We'll get the bleeding stopped and get you some help. Rochelle? The other guy on the river?"

"Just Fred. He was alone."

"Fred?"

I look up from Christopher's arm and meet PJ's eyes. "Fred Lassiter," I reply, remembering that PJ didn't know him. PJ arrived in Bakerville after Fred escaped.

"Mom?" Christopher whispers. "What was he doing here? Did you kill him?"

"Don't worry about that now."

Fists clenched, PJ stands. "I'll get the wagon. You'll need to take him into town on your own—uh, take Marnie to hold him while you drive. The lady who took care of Donnie when we came through here before, she'll know what to do. I'll pack up the kids, and we'll be right behind you. The tracks show Fred wasn't alone, and we can't risk them— "

I move a strand of hair out of my son's eyes. "You'll be okay, Christopher. We know people here. They'll help us." I bite my lip, remembering how the woman who cared for Donnie only had basic medical training and limited supplies.

Please, Lord, please help my son.

It's only a few minutes until PJ is back with the wagon. We move Christopher into the back. He's sweating and pale but doesn't cry out with the motion. Marnie climbs in next to him.

Even with the tourniquet, there's still blood. Too much blood. We've added a towel on top of the jacket, and Marnie's keeping pressure on it, which isn't an easy task considering the amount of damage.

I'm in the wagon seat, reins in hands, when PJ calls, "Go! We'll be right behind you. Remember, they'll have a roadblock set up."

I bring Titan and Lucky to a trot. "Hold on!"

Within minutes, the roadblock comes into view. I yell out, "We have an injury! Gunshot wound! A boy! We need help!" I slow the horses slightly and continue to yell—screech, really, the panic in my voice overcoming anything that sounds like normalcy.

Someone yells back for me to stop the wagon.

"Whoa," I say to the horses, slowing them. "Did you hear me? We need help!"

"Ma'am! Stop. Now."

"You'd better stop," Marnie hollers.

I stop the horses and yell, "Please. My son's been shot. I need help!" There's some scrambling and muttering from the roadblock. "Please!"

"Where's the shooter?" someone asks.

"Dead. Your medical team. We need their help or— " My voice falters.

"Come forward," someone says. "Let's take a look."

Once we're at the blockade, a man puts down the gate and looks at Christopher from afar. "How're you doing, son?" he asks.

"Hurts. Bad."

Tears stream down Marnie's face. "He needs help."

"I've been through here before," I say, my voice high and squeaky. "You had a hospital set up at the Blue Rooster. They treated my friend."

With a nod, the man starts barking orders. "Pennington, you run ahead and tell them to get ready for a gunshot to the left arm." He hoists himself into the wagon and tells me to go on but keep it below a trot.

It takes only a minute to get from the roadblock to the restaurant through the tiny town of Belfry. There're three people waiting in the parking lot, two are holding an old door.

As soon as I stop, the lady who helped Donnie several months ago asks, "How bad is it?" as she flips down the tailgate.

"As bad as I've ever seen," the man in back answers as I climb out of my seat.

The door quickly becomes a stretcher, as the lady asks Christopher his name.

Instead of Ace, he gives his birth name.

"All right, Christopher. I'm Rhiannon. We'll get you inside and fix you up." She turns to me. "You related?"

"I'm his mom." My voice is hoarse, scratchy.

She looks to Marnie. "Can you handle the team?"

Marnie nods. "The rest of our group will be here shortly too."

"All right, Mom, you can come in with us for now."

The two men take the stretcher on each end. The man who rode with us holds the restaurant door. Inside, one section has been arranged with standard beds. On the other side of the room is a higher platform, which they quickly take the stretcher to, laying it on top—the operating table.

I stay back far enough to be out of the way but still present.

Rhiannon makes a face as she gets her first look at his arm. "You must be pretty tough to not be passed out."

"Hurts bad . . . lots of blood."

"Yeah, there is. My friend Lance is going to get an IV started. He has a bag of our finest ready for you."

"Okay, good." Christopher's voice fades away as his eyes close.

I step toward him.

"He's okay," Lance, the one starting the IV, says with a nod. "He passed out from the pain."

"Can I get you a chair, ma'am?" the man from the roadblock asks. I give a weary nod as he pulls a wooden kitchen chair toward me.

The other man, the one who was carrying one end of Christopher's stretcher, says, "I'll step outside, see if she's okay with the wagon."

After a few minutes, Rhiannon looks to Lance. "The bone's shattered."

"Is there anything you can do?" Lance asks.

She turns slightly toward me. "We don't have many options."

"What are you saying?" I ask, looking from her to the two men.

"The arm's a mess. There's too much damage for me to do any sort of repair."

"And?"

She looks back at Christopher and gently wipes the hair from his forehead. "His arm needs to come off."

"What? No. He's just . . . he's just a boy."

"And I think, if everything goes well, he'll live to grow into a man. If we take the arm."

"And if you don't?"

She gives a slight shake of her head. "There's too much damage. The bone fragments . . . he'll get an infection."

"And if you take it? Will he get an infection?"

"He might. It's a risk. We'll do everything we can to prevent it."

I stare at the wall behind her. There's a mural of the mountains in the distance—the Beartooth Mountains.

I've been here before, when this was still a restaurant. We had lunch here on one of our trips to Billings. No. Not to Billings, to Camp Ah Nei, the first year Christopher went. He'd been invited by a friend. What was his name? Shane? Shawn?

The boy broke his leg the week before and couldn't go. Christopher wanted to cancel, but we convinced him it'd be an adventure. He loved it, which is why he's gone back each year since. Shane or Shawn moved away before the school year started. They didn't stay in touch, but many times, Christopher has said how glad he was he told him about Camp Ah Nei.

"Do it," I whisper. "But please. *Please.* You need to save him. I can't—please."

"We'll do our best. I promise you that. Lance and I, we'll do what we can."

I close my eyes, trying to remember what I know about this woman from when she treated Donnie. "You're not a doctor."

She gives a slight shake of her head. "EMT."

I swallow hard. "And him?"

"I'm her assistant," Lance says.

"Have you done this before? Either of you?"

Rhiannon gives me the tiniest of smiles. "I've read about it. And I have the supplies needed. The Marines were here last week. They gave us a few things we were missing or low on. We can do this."

"Perhaps it'd be best for you to wait outside," the man from the roadblock says. "Or even— "

The front door opens with a squeak. A head pops in and asks, "Rhiannon?"

"Yeah, Dad. C'mon in."

"A man is with me from the boy's group."

"It's okay."

I stand up, moving quickly toward the door. PJ is barely inside when I throw myself into his arms. He strokes my hair as I sob out what I know about Christopher.

"You can do this?" he asks, his voice cracking.

"I'll do my best," Rhiannon says. "I'll do everything I can to save your son." She turns to Lance. "We'll need to move him to the surgery room. Pennington, get washed up. You're helping us."

Rhiannon gives us a few minutes with Christopher, who's still passed out, before we're gently ushered out. All the children and horses are in the parking lot of the former restaurant turned hospital.

Rhiannon's dad, who we met on our way through Belfry back in March, says, "Sorry about your son. We've got a house we can put you up in until he's, um, recovered. My daughter, she'll do her best. Don't you worry none about that."

"Thank you." PJ offers the man his hand. "The man who shot him, he's still on the bank of the river."

"Heard you say so at the roadblock. We already sent someone to take care of the body."

"There was someone with him, two sets of footprints," PJ says.

"Another threat?"

"I didn't see anyone else." I shake my head. "Only— "

PJ touches my arm. "She only saw the man who shot her son. She took care of him."

With a nod, the man says, "We'd best be careful then. Bunch of crazies around. Thought it'd get better with the Marines about."

"Did they leave supplies?" PJ asks.

With a nod, the man talks about the string of military trucks that came through, leaving MREs and medical supplies just like in Fromberg and Bridger. "Even got some prenatal vitamins. Maybe your girls need those." He wrinkles his brow.

Though Marnie and Renée were not noticeably pregnant when we left Camp Ah Nei, the days on the road have changed things. There's now no doubt they're expecting, Renée especially. With her tiny frame, she now looks like she has a basketball under her shirt. Marnie's bump is more spread out and even, but it's still apparent.

"You know," the man says, "I remember you two from when you came through before. But weren't you with a group of adults then, had a man who was shot in the hand? Had a few kids with you, too, right?"

"We were," PJ says. "Good memory. I'm PJ Cameron. This is Rochelle Bennet. I'm sorry, but I don't remember your name."

"Michael Carpenter," he says, reaching out his hand. "Where's the rest of your group?"

"Our friends continued north. They were going to Central Montana—Lewistown and Great Falls." He motions to me "We were after Christopher. He was away at camp when everything happened last year."

"Ah, well. That explains it then." He looks to Marnie and Renée.

Standing tall, blood still on her hands from helping with Christopher, Marnie says, "It's very kind of you to offer vitamins for us."

Michael looks back to PJ and me. "Is there something fishy going on here?"

"What?" I ask, barely able to comprehend the conversation happening around me.

"Nothing fishy." PJ lifts his hands. "The children—all of them—were at the camp and the surrounding neighborhood. They asked us to help with them."

"Is that right, Miss?" he asks Marnie. "Are you . . . okay?"

She narrows her eyes. "If you're asking if they're kidnapping us, the answer is no. We— " she points to Renée " —want to be with them. It's a whole lot better than where we were. We're fine."

"Okay. Good enough," he says. "Let's get you settled. Sun's going to be down soon."

"How will I know about Christopher?" I ask.

"We'll keep you updated. It'll probably be a while before they're finished working on him."

Michael walks alongside the wagon, taking us toward the roadblock before turning on the apparent main street in town. After that, I pay little attention until we stop.

"This should be fine. The yard is fenced out back. We've got some hay. I'll have it brought over for your horses. Keep 'em in the yard. Let's get you inside. Then I'll check on your boy."

I'm completely numb as PJ leads me into the house.

"The faucets don't work," Michael says. "I'll bring some water back. You can wash up a bit at least."

I look down at my bloody hands and give a weak nod.

Michael shows the others the house, while I stand in the living room.

PJ rests a hand on my shoulder. "I'm going to get the horses put up. We have a couple of water bottles still with water in them. Why don't you and Marnie get washed up?"

"Yeah. Okay."

Renée helps us wash our hands. We hold them over the sink, and she dumps the water over the top. "Here, I have soap." She shows a hotel-sized bottle of shampoo.

After we've washed, Marnie asks, "Do you want to change, Rochelle?"

Somehow, my pack has been brought in and is in one of the bedrooms. Marnie grabs clothes from her bag and goes into the bathroom.

When we're both in clean clothes, Renée gets Mikey ready for bed and has the younger children put on their nightclothes. Vanessa, Bea, and Rafe have all been quiet and helpful, though it's obvious they have been crying. Even Mikey knows something isn't right.

PJ is soon back inside, and he also gets cleaned up. Mikey's asleep in the bedroom. The rest of us are in the living room when there's a knock at the door. I jump to my feet as PJ answers.

"Sorry for the delay, folks." Michael steps inside. "It's getting ready to rain. We had to batten down the hatches. I stopped off to see about your boy. They're about halfway finished. It's going well so far."

"Thank you," I say weakly.

"We brought some hay over. I've got someone putting it in the garage. He'll throw them a few flakes.

"Thank you." PJ nods. "We appreciate it.

"And it seems the man who shot your boy, a few people recognized him. Came into town a couple weeks back, along with another guy. One of my men says they were asking about a group they thought might have come through a couple months back. Specifically, they were looking for a woman who seems to fit your description, ma'am."

I stare at the floor.

"Did you know the man who attacked you?" Michael asks.

PJ moves next to me. "She knew him. He'd been causing her trouble. He was brought up on charges for it. But he escaped custody, killing his guards."

"You had history. Knew him. Is that why you turned him into Swiss cheese?"

"Is there a point?" PJ asks.

"Just wondering why you didn't say you knew him, that's all. And I'm wondering who the other guy is that he was lying in wait with."

"Her son had just been shot. We don't know who the other guy is. Never saw him."

"That right, ma'am? You never saw the other guy?"

"I . . . I didn't even know there was a second guy. Not until PJ told me he saw tracks."

Michael crosses his arms. "We don't want trouble here."

"I didn't know he was here." My words rush out in a jumble. "Fred told me he tracked me down. That some people from our town—he kidnapped them. Tortured them. He found out I was going after Christopher, going after my son. He figured I'd come this way. Fred said a friend helped him with the torture, to find out where I was. But I don't know who that was or anything about him."

"How'd he know you were gone?" Renée asks.

"I don't— " I shake my head. "I didn't think to ask. But . . . " I close my eyes. Maybe he was spying on us? I look to PJ. "He knew about Sylvia watching the girls. He had plans for us to go get them, to be the family he always dreamed of having. "PJ! We need to get home and make sure everything's okay. My girls . . . "

I cover my face with my hands as I sink into the couch, tears streaming and my heart pounding.

PJ sits next to me, pulling me toward him.

Many minutes later, I get my emotions back under control.

Sometime during my breakdown, Michael moved to a chair. "Where'd you say home is?"

"Not far," PJ answers. "Bakerville."

"Bakerville, huh? You've been up in Billings how long?"

"We left mid-March. Took a while to get where we were going."

"So you don't know about Bakerville being involved in getting rid of that guy in Prospect."

"We don't know anything from home."

"They did a good thing. He was a blight on the region. Planned to take over the entire area. We can all breathe a little easier now."

"Are you talking about Richard Majors?" PJ asks.

"Yep. Him and his son. They're done for. Thanks in part to the people of Bakerville."

"Do you know much about what happened?"

"Some. Rumors mostly. Seems there was a rebel faction, along with your people. The Marines that stopped in here are heading that way. They'll help the town of Prospect get back on their feet."

"Fred said something about that," I say. "About an attack on Prospect."

"I'll make sure our patrols know about the other guy. We'll keep an eye out for him."

"You have a description?" PJ asks.

"Not much. Two of my guys talked with him. Unfortunately, one of them went to Bridger to work out a trade. The one still here, he's not big on details. All he really said is he was a dandy."

"A dandy?" Renée asks.

"He was wearing a dress shirt and tie! Can you believe that?"

Chapter 27

After Michael leaves, Renée asks, "Should we pray?"

PJ takes my hand, giving it a squeeze. After a round robin of prayer, in which each of the children voice their heartfelt love and concerns over Christopher, begging God for His help, we say our goodnights as they leave to bed down in the room with Mikey.

"You should try and get some sleep." PJ motions to the couch.

"Not until we know how the surgery went."

"At least stretch out."

"Who was with Fred?"

"I can't think of anyone like that from Bakerville."

"I think he may have been living in Prospect. Fred, I mean."

"You mean after he . . . uh . . . "

"Escaped? Murdered the men who were transporting him and escaped? Yeah, then."

He's dead. Fred is dead, and I killed him.

Closing my eyes, I take a deep breath. When I heard his voice, my heart felt like it stopped beating. How could he be there? How could he be on the edge of the river, essentially in the middle of nowhere? From the extra details Michael provided, he was lying in wait.

PJ stares at the ceiling for a moment. "Richard Majors was usually in a tie. Even after the EMP. He'd dress like a— "

"Dandy?"

"I guess."

Richard Majors was the man who took over Prospect, killing the elected mayor and hundreds of others. But Michael made it sound like the rebels, along with help from Bakerville, eliminated him. What if he got away?

As PJ suggested, I do lie on the couch. While I don't actually sleep, I'm relaxed enough that the knock at the door causes me to jump.

"Relax," PJ says. "I'll answer it."

Instead of Michael, it's his daughter, Rhiannon, the EMT turned surgeon.

I sink back into the couch.

Stepping just inside, she removes her damp hood. The promised rain has arrived. She gives me a cautious smile. "It went well. You did a good job in the field, which helped immensely."

"You took his arm?" I ask.

She nods. "The bone above the wound was clean. He has a drain in. Now we wait and watch."

"Can I see him?"

"We'll keep him sedated until morning."

"You have medicine for that?"

"Thanks to the Marines, we do. If this would've happened two weeks ago . . . " She shakes her head. "I started him on a course of antibiotics. Oh, and this is for you, for your group."

She hands me two bottles, one of prenatal vitamins and one of children's chewable vitamins. "Have the girls had medical care?" she asks.

"Thank you. We were going to stop at one of the military hospitals, but they were afraid they'd be forced to go to the orphanage."

"We have doctors at home," PJ says.

"Doctors?" she asks.

"Nurse practitioners," I say. "And a veterinarian."

"That's helpful. They'll be good for following up with your son too."

"You think the Marines stopped in Bakerville?" PJ asks.

She shrugs. "Not sure. Maybe. They stopped in the other towns between here and Billings. I'll start easing up on Christopher's sedation doses around five a.m. You can come over any time after eight."

My eyes bore into hers. "But you think he'll be okay? He'll live?"

"I'm hopeful. And we're praying too. Most of the town is, the ones who believe anyway. Even many who don't. If you— "

"We're praying," PJ says.

"See you tomorrow. Try and get some rest so you can be fresh for him in the morning. It may be a rough few days."

I stay on the couch. My sleep is light and interrupted. Every time I open my eyes, PJ is awake, quietly walking the room, peering out the windows. Keeping watch. I finally give up on sleep and offer to take over watch so he can rest.

"I'm too keyed up," he says. "I'll nap later, when Michael's people are able to watch over you."

"You don't think Majors—if that's who was with Fred—would come after me? I don't even know him."

"But if he was with Fred, saw you shoot him . . . he might want revenge."

"It makes no sense. If he was there when I shot Fred, why didn't he shoot me?"

"Good point. Still, I want to be cautious."

~~~~~

The children are up, the horses are tended, we're dressed, and we've eaten leftover pheasant soup—which Renée packed away before the shooting began—well before the appointed visiting time.

PJ's still worried about the other guy, the dandy, and doesn't want me walking to the hospital on my own. He's also worried about leaving the children at the house alone.

"I'll see if I can find Michael or one of the other townspeople and have someone stay with the children."

"You know Renée and I were part of Rogue's soldiers before you found us, right?" Marnie asks.

Vanessa crosses her arms, doing her best to look fierce. "Me too. Only the little kids like Bea and Rafe weren't part of her crew."

PJ rests a hand on her shoulder. "I know you can handle yourselves. You proved that yesterday. Remember, you'll also have Mikey to keep out of trouble."

"We'll keep him in the bedroom." Bea points to Rafe. "He'll help, too, and we know what to do."

Marnie motions to Renée. "And we'll keep watch. We have our pistols and the shotgun. Doug gave us some of the double aught and the buckshot. I'll load it with that."

"I put the self-defense rounds back in after Christopher got the pheasant," PJ says.

"Okay, then we're set. Tell Christopher were thinking of him."

"Praying," Renée corrects. "We're praying for him."

"Yeah." Marnie nods. "That too."

Leaving the house, I look around the neighborhood. Nothing seems familiar. "Do you know how to get there?"

"Down this street, left at the main street. Then it's only a block or so to the highway. You want to take the horses?"
~~~~~

"No. I'm fine to walk. I just . . . getting here was a blur. I'm glad you were paying attention. Do you think he'll be awake?" I ask as we leave the front yard.

The small town has decent-sized yards between the houses and an abundance of trees, stretching to the sky and providing a full canopy over the neighborhood.

"Sounded like she'll keep him on painkillers of some sort, but he'll be around enough for you to visit."

The walk takes about fifteen minutes. When we're almost there, walking along the highway the former restaurant turned hospital is located on, PJ stops and looks around.

"You know what? I think we took the long way here. Look at that big elm tree?" PJ points to a tree behind a building on the highway. "Didn't we walk by it? Just a couple of doors down from the house we're staying in?"

"Maybe?"

"I guess I wasn't paying much attention last night either. I should've realized where we were. Speaking of not paying attention . . . " He motions with his arm. "I didn't even notice the old restaurant we stayed in last time we were in Belfry is being torn down."

"I wonder why they're doing that?"

"Hard telling."

At the front door of the hospital, I ask, "Should we knock?"

"Let's just see if it's open."

With a squeak and a creak, the door easily sways outward.

As we step into the vestibule, a voice calls out, "There you are."

"Yes," I say. "Um, I'm sorry. I've forgotten your name."

"I'm Lance. Rhiannon just ran home for a minute to change her clothes. She said to have you come in."

"How is he?"

"We're keeping the pain under control. He's woken up a few times and asked for you."

There's already a pair of chairs by his side, the side without the missing arm. They've moved him from the tall surgical table to one of the regular beds across the room. He's pale—too pale. Even his lips are nearly white, almost invisible against his face.

I bite my lip as I look to Lance. He gives me a slight smile. "He lost quite a bit of blood. Plus, it's a trauma to his body. He'll get his color back."

A blanket is pulled up, covering the injured arm almost to the shoulder. It's elevated slightly, and the outline of his bicep is there, then the blanket goes flat. I swallow the gasp that threatens to escape. Sliding into the chair closest to his head, I motion PJ to sit next to me.

I have Christopher's hand in mine as PJ rests a hand on my shoulder. "He's going to be okay, Rochelle."

Tears stream down my face as I nod my response. We sit silently for many minutes.

In many ways, I'm taken back to those days of caring for Robyn, of waiting for her to wake up, to say something. I give Christopher's hand a slight squeeze, causing him to stir.

He lets out a groggy moan.

"Is he in pain?" I ask.

From across the room, Lance says, "Probably not yet—not much anyway."

"Mom?" His voice is weak, hoarse.

"I'm here." I squeeze his hand.

"Water?"

In an instant, Lance is by the bed and offering Christopher a drink from a straw. "Better?"

"My hand hurts."

I loosen my grip. "Sorry. I might have been squeezing too tightly."

"The other one."

I look to Lance and mouth, *"He doesn't know?"*

"Christopher," Lance says, "do you remember when we were talking to you earlier? Rhiannon and I introduced ourselves? Told you we'd done surgery?"

"I remember. She's pretty."

Lance lets out a laugh. "She is."

Christopher scrunches up his face. "My arm. The bullet. My elbow."

"Yeah," Lance answers.

"My arm is gone."

"It is," Lance agrees, his voice cracking slightly.

"Why does my hand hurt?"

"Rhiannon said— "

"Oh." Christopher clenches his eyes shut. "Hurt earlier too. She called it . . . "

"Phantom pain," Lance says.

"Mom? My arm's gone."

Christopher begins to cry—soft, silent tears at first and then louder, racking sobs. Painful sobs that cause him physical pain.

Helpless to do anything, I lean across his body, hugging him as best I can.

"Mom," Christopher whispers. "You're crushing me."

With an awkward laugh, I peel myself off and return to my chair. The groan of the front door announces a new arrival.

"Good morning," Rhiannon calls out in a cheery voice. "How's my best patient?"

Christopher gives her a shy smile. "My mom tried to suffocate me."

"Oh?"

"Hugging," I say quickly. "I was hugging him."

Rhiannon goes to a basin across the room. After washing and putting on gloves, she steps over to Christopher's bed. "I'm going to take a look."

"Okay." He closes his eyes.

After a few minutes, she declares things look good. "It's what I'd hoped to see. We have a drain in, and it's . . . " She shrugs. "Well, it's draining."

"What you hoped to see? From what you've read?" I ask.

She answers with a smile and a nod. "I think we're okay. He'll need to stay here for— " she shrugs. "Days. I don't know how many. Then you'll probably want to wait several more days, weeks maybe, before you finish your journey. I know, with being so close, it's going to be difficult. If you want to go on— "

"I'm not leaving," I say.

"I didn't figure, but if you did want to go and check in and then come back, that'd make sense."

PJ turns slightly toward me. "Rochelle, I'm going on to Bakerville."

"What?"

"I need to make sure they know about the other guy. We don't know if he's a threat to your girls."

I blink as my eyes fill with a fresh batch of tears. "Do you think— "

"Probably not." PJ puts his hand on my arm. "But just in case. Also, if it is Richard Majors, then we should let them know. Michael said they were involved in the assault on Prospect. He could want revenge."

"Richard Majors?" Lance asks. "He's dead."

PJ cocks his head. "You're sure?"

Lance looks to Rhiannon, who gives a shrug before saying, "That's what we heard. Why would you think he wasn't?"

"Michael said the guy with Fred—the one who attacked us—was wearing a tie. Majors was almost always in a tie."

"Hmm. I don't know. It would be weird for anyone to be wearing a tie these days."

"When would you leave?" I ask.

"As soon as I can get Titan ready. Without the wagon and the children, I can be there in just a few hours. I'll check on your girls, let them know what's happening, and be back tomorrow. The day after at the latest."

I look back to Christopher. His eyes are closed, and his easy breathing suggests he's asleep.

"It's a good idea." I long to go with him, to hug my girls. But I won't leave Christopher's side.

Chapter 28

I've been watching and waiting for PJ to return. He left the day before yesterday. He promised he'd be back no later than today. Christopher's color has significantly improved, and they're keeping his pain well under control.

He sleeps most of the time, which should help with his healing. When he's awake, his emotions are all over the board, bouncing between accepting the loss of his arm, to grieving, to being full of anger.

The rest of the children and I are still living in the little house, which is almost directly behind the hospital. Instead of walking down the streets and the highway, we use a nearby path that cuts through and saves time.

Marnie, Renée, Vanessa, and I swap duties of watching the children or sitting with Christopher; although, I'll admit to being the one with him most of the time. It's definitely the way I want it.

I'm at the house now while Renée sits at the hospital. Yesterday, Rhiannon asked if we wanted her to examine Marnie and Renée to see how their pregnancies are progressing. She quietly told me, at their young age, there could be complications.

"I know," I said. "But what can we do?"

"Not much. But let me at least check them out. Maybe we'll be able to determine something. You might even want to take them on to Prospect, get the Marines' help. They've got Navy docs with them."

"Maybe," I agreed, thinking back to the doc who examined Robyn.

Renée enthusiastically agreed to the exam, while Marnie rolled her eyes and said, "Might as well."

Afterward, Rhiannon seemed happy enough with their health, saying everything seemed well. The girls are healthier than she expected, and the babies had strong heartbeats. She'd even felt Marnie's move.

"I wondered if you'd been feeling movement," I said to Marnie. I'd wanted to ask her before if the baby was moving, but I know it's not something she's interested in discussing. This baby is little more than an inconvenience to her.

"I thought it was gas or something," she answered with a shrug. "Rhiannon is the one who thinks it's the baby."

"Do you agree with their estimated due dates?" I asked, turning to Rhiannon.

"Seems to be what they think. Marnie at the end of September or maybe even early October, and Renée a few weeks later. Right, ladies?"

Marnie shrugged while Renée said, "That's what Reba thought."

"Rochelle's going to find someone to take my baby," Marnie said. "So it doesn't much matter to me when it's born."

Rhiannon looked to me as I nodded. "We'll find a good home for him or her."

"And you, Renée?" Rhiannon asked.

"I don't know yet."

"You have plenty of time to decide. There is . . . " Rhiannon hesitated as she bit her lower lip. "I wanted to ask about radiation fallout. Was there much where you were living?"

Renée and Marnie shared a look and then both shook their heads.

"We didn't know each other then," Renée said. "We didn't meet until after the nukes and EMP. My parents were still alive, and when we heard the alert, we went to our root cellar. My dad made us stay there a couple of days. I was hiding there when my parents were killed. We were all supposed to go to the root cellar if strangers showed up, but I was the only one who made it."

As Renée began to cry, I wrapped an arm around her and held her close.

"We didn't have a root cellar or anything like that," Marnie said. "Didn't even know about the nukes since our phones never started working again and we didn't get an alert. I don't know if there was fallout. Does it matter?"

"I'm not sure," Rhiannon said.

"They weren't pregnant then," I said.

"Right. But there are some concerns that people who received a dose of radiation could've—you know, this is probably nothing we need to worry about."

Even though Rhiannon said not to worry, I have. Could their babies have trouble from radiation received before conception? As I put my hair in a bun, I think about Marnie and her wish to put her baby up for adoption.

She's so young. They're both young. Too young. Neither of them ever mentions the boy Christopher called Zero—the one responsible. And what about radiation affecting him? Does it just need to be the mother, or could he contribute to birth defects or other issues the babies may experience?

Shaking off these thoughts, I head to the living room.

"You're leaving?" Marnie asks.

"I'm going to go sit with Christopher. I'll send Renée back."

A roll of her eyes is the only response.

"You okay?"

"Bored."

"Yeah, I get that. PJ should be back today. Maybe then we can figure something out so you can— "

"What? So I can what?"

"I don't know, Marnie. Being here while Christopher heals enough to travel isn't fun for any of us."

With pursed lips she gives me a brief nod.

"I'll be back in a couple of hours, then you can take a turn sitting with him, okay?" I ask.

"Whatever."

When I walk into the hospital, Renée lifts her head from the book she's reading aloud to Christopher.

"Hey, Mom," he calls. "Is PJ back yet?"

"Not yet. Should be any time. What are you reading?"

Renée lifts the large book for me to see the cover. The Bible.

I raise an eyebrow.

"It wasn't my idea." Christopher points to Renée. "All her. But I'll admit, it's not terrible."

"I told him how we're always praying and how the Bible says we should do that. So we were trying to find the verse about it, but I keep getting sidetracked."

"There's several verses that talk about praying and being in constant communication with God. You know my good friend Tamra that we stayed with in Joliet? She had many questions about prayer when we were traveling together. I spent some time searching out different verses in the Bible to share with her. But I think one that really fits for— "

I pause for a moment as I think about how I want to word my next sentence. Not coming up with anything, I give a slight shake of my head.

I give Christopher a smile and touch Renée's arm. "When we left the mountain and started traveling together, Tamra had zero interest in God, Jesus, or anything she considered churchy. And now . . . well, you met her. You know she's a Believer and Jesus is Lord of her life."

"Yeah." Christopher winks. "She yapped on and on about it."

"The changes in her . . . they're amazing. Truly a miracle. Anyway, when we were in Joliet, she and I were talking about Romans, which caused me to begin reading the book. There's a passage I read recently about being faithful in prayer."

"Romans?" Renée asks.

"It's in the New Testament. First the Gospels, then Acts. Romans is after Acts."

She takes a minute and flips to it. "Which chapter?"

I think a minute, recalling where I'd read it. Was it in the same chapter Tamra and I were discussing about not taking revenge on our enemies?

Ha. That didn't work out so well. I've spent hardly any time thinking about killing Fred. Where the people I shot in the campground replayed over and over in my mind like a movie, I hardly remember anything about Fred's death.

I didn't look at his body afterward, instead going quickly to Christopher. And since then, my son's recovery has been my concern.

"Mom?" Christopher asks.

"Oh, um, maybe twelve?"

Renée flips the pages again before finally stopping. Moving her finger along the page, she reads, "Be joyful in hope, patient in affliction, faithful in prayer."

Christopher shakes his head. "That's not saying to pray without ceasing."

"Isn't it?" I ask. "Doesn't faithful in prayer suggest that we should be doing it faithfully? Constantly?"

"If you say so."

"I like it," Renée says. "I like the rest of it too. Joyful in hope. Patient in affliction—what does affliction mean?"

"I'm pretty sure that's what's happening now." Christopher lifts his good arm, pointing to the missing one. "I'm afflicted with having only one arm."

Part of me wants to laugh. The other part wants to cry. "Affliction is something that causes hurt or pain."

"See? It is causing me hurt *and* pain. Only I'm not sure how I'm supposed to be patient in my affliction. That implies that if I wait long enough, my circumstances will change. They won't. My arm isn't going to magically grow back, no matter how patient I am."

He's not wrong. How is he supposed to be patient in his affliction?

While I consider his words and attempt to come up with something comforting, Renée says, "That's true. Same for me. My affliction— " she points to her growing stomach " —won't change either. Someday I'll have my baby, but I'll still be in the same circumstance."

Christopher harrumphs. "That's not the same. Not even close."

"Why not?" she asks. "Losing your arm is terrible. It really is. But you're alive. You can still have an amazing life with only one arm."

"What do you know about having only one arm?" Tears well up in his eyes as he blurts out the question.

"Nothing. But I know about affliction. I know about . . . " She drops her voice to a near whisper. "I know about thinking the worst possible thoughts. You think I wanted to keep living when my parents were murdered? Then when I found out I was pregnant, I . . . I thought about terrible things. There're all kinds of afflictions. Not just the one you have."

He turns his head away from her as he attempts to roll his body.

Renée scoots her chair back and sets the Bible on it. "I'm sorry if I upset you. I just think you're a great guy, Ace . . . Christopher. You've always been nice to me, to all of the kids. You . . . you can get through this affliction." She gives me a wobbly smile, tears running down her face, before saying she's going back to the house and will see me later.

As she goes out the door, I slide into her chair. Christopher continues to stare across the room. I hate that my son is going through this, that he lost his arm. But I'm also eternally grateful that our God is so good Christopher *only* lost his arm. He could've—maybe even *should've* in today's world—lost his life. I truly believe, with God's help, Christopher can get through this.

Just like I made it through my affliction: being kidnapped, raped, and beaten. And then sold to Fred, who continued the abuse. While my affliction may have been temporary, it does still have lasting results, as evidenced by my flashback when PJ and I were held in Huntley. Will those incidents continue? I pray not. I want to be joyful in hope, patient in my affliction, and faithful in prayer.

"That was pretty mean of her." Christopher turns back toward me. "Mean?"

"The way she thinks losing my arm isn't a big deal—comparing it to having a baby. It's not even the same thing."

I chew on my upper lip as I consider my response. "Losing your arm will change your life."

"See? You should've told her that."

"Having a baby will change her life too."

"Not in the same way. It's . . . it's different. Everyone will look at me like I'm a freak."

"How old is Renée? How do you think people look at her?"

His brow creases. "But she won't always be pregnant. I'll always be a one-armed freak."

My heart breaks. I run my hand across his forehead, moving the strands of hair that are always flopping in his eyes. "But she'll always have *been* pregnant. Marnie, too, even though she doesn't want to raise the child. It's changed her. It's changed both of them. Losing your arm will change you."

"It already has."

"Yes. But I'm with Renée and believe you will get through this affliction."

"Sure, Mom. I'll be patient in my affliction." He closes his eyes before saying, "I'm tired and need to sleep."

The front door opens, and Renée pokes her head in. "He's back! PJ's back! And he brought another wagon."

Christopher's eyes pop open. "You should go see what's going on."

"You're okay?"

"It's not like I'm actually alone. Rhiannon and Lance are both here somewhere."

"Right here," Lance pops his head from what used to be the kitchen.

"I'll be right back!"

From the parking lot, Renée and I watch as PJ rides Titan alongside a team and wagon. I squint to make out who's sitting in the seat of the wagon.

"There's another horse too," Renée says. "See?" When one of the team moves slightly, I see a second rider behind the wagon. "Do you know them?"

"I'm sure I do. As soon as they get closer . . . " I lift my hand above my eyes, shielding from the glare of the sun. "That's PJ's brother in the wagon. And one of his nephews, Dax, is on the horse."

"They probably didn't have any trouble at the roadblock, right? Do you think they had to pay a toll?" Renée asks.

When Belfry joined forces with Bridger, Fromberg, and Joliet, the road connecting the four towns became a toll road. When we came through here before, just Bridger and Fromberg were connected by the toll road. While a toll sounds drastic, the benefit of somewhat safe travel is worth it.

"I think we owe more than a toll for what this town has done to help us," I say.

As soon as PJ sees me, he lifts his hat in a wave—now a proper cowboy hat instead of a ball cap. Even from this distance, I can see his huge smile. My stomach does that weird little flip flop.

I never answered him . . . when he asked me to marry him.

Renée and I wait in silence, listening to the hooves knocking on the pavement as they get closer. Knowing PJ, they probably drove in the gutter most of the way to protect the horse's legs, choosing the soft shoulder instead of the unforgiving concrete.

PJ pulls ahead of the wagon, trotting the last bit. "How's he doing?" he asks as he slides off Titan.

"Good. He's doing really good. Rhiannon says he's healing nicely."

PJ's standing in front of me, only steps away.

I lift my arms slightly, hoping he'll take the hint.

With a smile, he closes the distance, pulling me tight. With his mouth by my ear, he whispers, "I've been praying for him. For you too."

"I'm okay." I pull back to gaze into his eyes.

"Truly?"

My stomach does a flip flop. "I missed you."

"Why'd you bring them with you?" Renée asks.

PJ holds my gaze for another beat before releasing me and saying, "I thought it might be best if they took you and the others on home while we wait for Christopher to heal enough to travel."

"I don't . . . but . . . " Renée stares at the wagon that's turning into the driveway, with the horse by its side. "We don't *know* them."

"Hi, Dusty, Dax." I wave at the men. "I'd like you to meet— " Just then, a little head pokes out from the wagon. "Cheyre?" I whisper.

"Surprise, Mom!" she yells, beaming and waving. "And look!" She pulls Kerryanne up also.

Shaking her head, Kerryanne says, "She made us hide, to surprise you."

I'm quickly at the side of the wagon, reaching for them. "I can't believe you're here!"

"Sylvia came too." Cheyre points. "See?" She grabs my friend Sylvia Eriksen and pulls her close to the edge.

"Hey, Rochelle." Sylvia waves.

"Is it— " I turn to PJ. "This is okay?"

"We figured it was safe enough. With the military around, it seems okay."

With the wagon gate open, I help Cheyre down, hugging her tight in the process. PJ offers Kerryanne a hand. Then I get in my hugs with her, and then Sylvia.

"You've grown." I pull Cherye into another hug. "You too, Kerryanne."

"Not much." Kerryanne shrugs.

Cheyre beams. "I know! Sylvia had to find me longer pants. And she cut my hair. See?"

"It looks great."

"I wanted it curly like hers. She put curlers in it, and it was all bouncy and spirally, but then the curls all fell out. I want it curly all the time. Maybe you can give me a—what's it called, Sylvia?"

"Permanent. But remember, we talked about this."

"I know." Cherye lets out a long sigh before turning to me. "I asked her to make my hair curly and black like hers, but she said there isn't stuff like that right now."

"How's Christopher?" Kerryanne asks, her face pinched. "PJ said he was hurt but will be okay? Where is he?"

"I want to see him," Cheyre says. "He might not recognize me, though, since I've grown so much."

"He'll recognize you," I say, hugging her again. I look to PJ. "Did you . . . "

"I told them it was Fred who attacked you and Christopher. I figured the details were best coming from you."

Kerryanne looks from me to PJ, then glances at Sylvia. From the look on my friend's face, PJ did tell her.

"What's going on?" Kerryanne asks.

I take a deep breath. "I'm going to tell you something that's going to be hard to hear. It's going to sound scary and . . . and terribly sad. But I promise, it'll be okay."

Cheyre points behind me. "Is it about her?"

I turn to follow her finger. She's pointing at Renée.

"Oh! Sorry. No, that's my good friend Renée. She's coming back to Bakerville with us. Did PJ— "

"I thought that'd be best coming from you too."

"Renée, these are my daughters, Kerryanne and Cheyre."

Kerryanne stares directly at Renée's stomach, while Cheyre doesn't seem to notice. That makes sense, considering she's so young. Kerryanne, at fourteen, is well aware of what Renée's swollen stomach indicates.

"Hi." Renée gives them a shy smile. "I'll, uh . . . I'm going to go back to the house. See you there?"

"We'll be there soon."

"Mom?" Kerryanne asks. "What— "

"We'll talk about Renée in a bit," I say. "First, I need to tell you about Christopher. About his injuries."

"PJ said he'll be okay."

"He will." I put my hand on Kerryanne's shoulder. She really has grown in these past three and a half months. She's now almost as tall as I am. "But before you see him, I want you to know that when he was hurt, when he was shot, the bullet hit his elbow in such a way that it was severely damaged. They couldn't fix it, so they had to— " I swallow hard and fight my emotions. "They had to remove his arm."

"They took his arm off?" Cheyre asks.

Kerryanne shakes her head and drops her eyes. "What's his prognosis?" she asks, her voice barely a whisper.

"Good, it's good. He's getting excellent treatment."

She gives a nod. "What'll he do? The way things are . . . "

"He'll adapt. He'll learn to do what's needed with just one arm. He's alive. That's what's important."

"Can we see him?" Cheyre asks.

"Of course. Are you ready, Kerryanne?"

"Are they managing his pain?"

I smile at the professional tone to Kerryanne's question. "You've started your apprenticeship with the medical team?"

She gives a slight nod. "Some. It's mostly bookwork right now, but I've learned how to take vitals. His pain?"

"They have him on painkillers to help, not as much now, just when it starts to get bad. He's doing okay."

"Did the Army guys come here?" Cherye asks. "They came to Bakerville. They brought medicine and even some food. Kelley and Belinda were so happy, they cried."

"It was the Marines." Sylvia wraps an arm around Cheyre. "And PJ said they stopped here too. Praise God for that."

"I'm ready," Kerryanne says. "Let's go."

I glance to PJ. He gives me a smile. "Take the girls in. We'll wait."

"Sylvia?" I ask.

"I'll wait. I'm sure Dax can use my help with the horses."

"If you want to help." Dax's cheeks color slightly.

I shoot PJ a look, who responds with a shake of his head. *Dax and Sylvia?*

I'm barely inside the hospital, leading my daughters, when Christopher says, "Sounded like a party out there."

Cheyre pops around me and yells, "Surprise!" as she rushes to his side.

"What?" Christopher cries. "What are you doing here, Sweetie— I mean, Cheyre? Kerryanne too?"

"Yep. PJ said we should come see you, that it might make you heal faster."

With his eyes brimming over, he says, "He might be right."

After many minutes of catching up and telling Christopher how they got here and who's with them, Cheyre turns serious. "Mom says you don't have an arm now."

"Yeah," he answers.

"Can I see it?"

"You want to see my stump?"

With an impish grin, she lifts a shoulder. "Will you get a hook like that guy we used to see in the restaurant?"

Christopher lets out something resembling a laugh. "How do you even remember that? I'd forgotten— "

"I remember too." Kerryanne smiles. "When we were much younger, we'd see him around town. What was his name, Mom?"

"Mr. Ballard," I say.

I'd completely forgotten about him, but memories of Mr. Ballard come rushing back. He was a friend of my dad's who lost his arm during the final days of Vietnam. When Christopher and Kerryanne were young, they were mesmerized by his hook. Just like most of the kids in Lander.

And Mr. Ballard had great elaborate stories to go along with the missing arm. He'd tell tales of the superhuman things he could do with the hook. Christopher and Kerryanne would grab coat hangers and make their own makeshift hooks. He died about three years ago. We, along with most of the town, attended his funeral. Like Christopher, I'm surprised Cheyre remembers.

The children spend a few minutes discussing Mr. Ballard. Part of me cringes at the conversation. Especially when Cheyre again asks Christopher if he'll get a shiny silver hook. And then she reminds him that if he does, he should never try to pick his nose with that hand.

He gives a hoot of laughter. "Thanks for the advice."

I take a step toward the door. "I'm going to tell PJ they should head to the house. I'll be right back."

"Mom?" Christopher calls. "Tell him thanks, would you? And I'd like to meet the rest of your friends."

From the table at the side of the room, Lance says, "You'll probably be able to see them at the house if they're planning to stay a day or two. Rhiannon may release you tomorrow and let you heal up there, with one of us popping by a few times a day."

Chapter 29

"I really appreciate this, Sylvia." I release her from a hug. "It's . . . it'll be great."

"This was the plan PJ proposed, so it's no problem at all. Just think of it as a vacation."

"In Belfry, Montana?"

"Well . . . it'll be good to have this time together. And it'll give Christopher and his sisters a chance to get to know each other again, and let him get to know PJ better."

I bob my head. PJ, his brother, and his nephew moved to a house up the street. PJ will stay there, while my three children and I stay in the original house, waiting for Rhiannon's approval to travel.

"And then— " Sylvia gives me an exaggerated wink " —the vacation will be over. Once you get back to Bakerville, you'll have a houseful to take care of!"

"That's for sure! And you think it'll be okay? The community is fine with the additional children?"

"Do you think they'd turn them away?"

I lift a shoulder.

"Don't worry." She pulls me into a hug. "This is part of God's plan. And we know children are a gift from God. All will be well."

"You sound more like your mom every day."

With a laugh, she says, "There's a time I would've thought that an insult. But now . . . " She lifts her hands. "I'll keep the children and babies with me until you get back. Renée and Marnie will help, so it won't be too difficult. Then we'll find you a house. Phil has a few in mind."

Sylvia's stepdad, Phil, and her mom have lived in Bakerville for years and know the community well. And with the loss of so many since this all started, empty homes shouldn't be a problem. An empty home large enough for a single woman with nine kids might be a challenge. Then, when the babies arrive . . . we'll work it out.

Single woman.

Last night, I told PJ I can't marry him. Not yet.

Even with the issue of Fred Lassiter and my sham of a marriage no longer hanging over me, the timing isn't right. Christopher is hurting too much, both physically and emotionally.

"I bet I know what you're thinking about," Sylvia says with a twinkle in her eye. "You know what I think."

"Oh yeah. Just like you know what I think about you and Dax."

Her eyes drift to the man getting the horses ready. She's almost a decade older than him, but things like that no longer matter, if they ever did.

"He's a good man," she whispers. "Just like his Uncle PJ. But this isn't about me. You, however . . . " She gives me a quirky smile and waggles a finger at me. "You and PJ are perfect together. You have so much in common. He loves you. He loves your children. You love him—don't deny it.

"I won't," I whisper.

"Your children love him—the girls, anyway. And Christopher, he's coming around. I think he probably thought of PJ as a threat, for your affections. Especially since he wanted to be the man with his dad gone."

"Are you using your mom's psych teachings?" I ask.

"Maybe a little." She laughs. "He's doing okay, though. Christopher will be okay."

"I keep hoping that, when we're in Bakerville with a few others his age, that'll help too. Even though we didn't have the same setup of using the very young for defense, there're several that he'll relate to, right?"

"I'm sure there are. And with the final battles against Prospect— " She lets out a long sigh. "It could've been much worse. We were very blessed to lose so few. I think we all just want peace now."

"And you're positive Richard Majors was not the man that was with Fred here in Belfry?"

"Positive. It's widely known he didn't survive."

"But who could it have been? PJ said Majors was always wearing a tie—even a suit most of the time."

"I've been thinking about that. Dax said there was a guy who had shown up in Prospect around the time Majors took over. He was always in a white dress shirt, slacks, and a tie. Could've been him."

"Who was he?"

"Dax didn't know for sure. He talked with some of the rebels after the assault was over. One man who was a captain in Majors's army—but was really working against Majors—said that they called the guy Doc, and he was used to torture and brainwash people who seemed to be having doubts about the good things Majors was doing."

"*The good?* Yikes. That sounds— "

"Nuts? Yeah. Anyway, Dax said maybe it was him. Besides, didn't Rhiannon's dad say they saw the man walking toward Billings?"

"Yes, that's true. Michael said one of the guys who had originally talked with Fred and the tie wearer met him between Bridger and Fromberg. Michael's man went to work out trades. And when he was coming back, he ran into—what'd you say his name was? Doc?"

She gives a nod.

"If it was this Doc guy, then he's on his way north."

"Well, whoever he is, if he was with Fred Lassiter, he's bad news. I hope he doesn't cause any trouble."

"Are you ready, Miss Sylvia?" Rafe asks, carrying his backpack to the wagon.

In the few days since Sylvia arrived, Rafe has made it clear he thinks the sun rises and sets around her. He's always going out of his way to talk with her or have her read to him. It's terribly sweet.

"Just about. Dax and his dad are finishing getting the horses ready. Then we'll go."

Bringing the second wagon was brilliant on PJ's part. We'll have the original wagon for taking Christopher home, while they can take Mikey and the pregnant girls.

Sylvia is riding Whiskey while ponying Big Steve. Dax will pony Miss Ellie. Vanessa, Beatrix, and Rafe will ride their equines. That means, when it's time for us to make our way back to Bakerville, we only have the team and wagon to worry about.

A short while later, after waving goodbye to our friends, my children and I settle into the little house. With just the four of us— and PJ stopping by often—it truly does feel like a vacation in many ways. While PJ is working with the townspeople, helping them with their winter wood and food supply, I'm doing little but lounging and enjoying my family.

I feel a little guilty that I'm taking it so easy while PJ works so hard. When he arrived with the wagon from Bakerville, he'd brought back supplies and goods to give to the town as payment for taking care of Christopher, but he wanted to do more.

In this arid land, a reliable water source is needed for trees. As is common in towns, the residents had been planting and caring for trees since the place was established over a hundred years ago . . . but they definitely don't have an abundance.

For firewood, the townspeople have been using fallen and dead standing trees they found in town and along Bear Creek, on the northern edge of town, before venturing farther north to the Clarks Fork River and Silver Tip Creek just beyond. Now their wood supply has essentially dried up.

They've started taking down unoccupied houses and buildings, like the former casino/restaurant we stayed in on our way through here in March. They'll use the lumber for firewood and are saving anything else they can for other uses. With the limited number of trees, it makes sense.

Even though part of me knows I should be helping, especially since it's my son who PJ is reimbursing the town for his treatment and care, I know I'm where I need to be.

There were so many difficulties in the early days after Dale was murdered. I was focused only on survival for me and my girls. Then, after Fred was out of our lives, I was in recovery, trying to get past the things that happened, plus doing the work needed to keep us fed and warm. And planning to find my son.

Now, after much time and difficulties, we're together again. And even though I didn't deny my feelings for PJ when Sylvia asked, I also know the timing isn't right. As much as I may want to marry him, I need to think about Christopher.

Kerryanne and Cheyre had a year to adjust to their dad's death. For Christopher, the news is only a few weeks old. While he may have worried his dad was dead—his sisters and me also—he didn't know for certain until I told him. And grieving for his dad was quickly followed by losing his arm. He doesn't need his mom entering into a new marriage right now.

~~~~

"I'm amazed with how well you're healing." Rhiannon removes her latex gloves with a snap. "Everything looks great. Your
~~~~

movement—just everything. I think we can start talking about you going home."

"You mean to Bakerville," Christopher says. "We aren't going to my real home until . . . who knows when."

"Sounds like that may be a reality soon. The new battalion—or whatever they call their group—said they're working to stabilize the entire states of both Montana and Wyoming before the end of the year. With the volunteers they're picking up, they could do it."

Yesterday, the military came through Belfry again. Or at least some military. Unlike the last time, when it was mainly Marines with a few of the volunteer units, this time it was mainly volunteers—the Auxiliary—with a handful of actual military.

This group was headed to Prospect to take over for the group that went there a few weeks ago. Those currently in Prospect will move farther south to Cody.

We spoke with a captain, an actual Marine, who said they're continuing to make progress securing the interstates in Montana, with I-90 now safe for travel from Exit 484, near Hardin, Montana, all the way to Bozeman in the west.

Kimba and Rey plan to travel to Bozeman after delivering the others to their homes. Finding out things are secured to there is a welcome relief. I asked about farther north, if there were any updates regarding Lewistown—where Leanne and her children were going— but the captain didn't know.

Great Falls is still under Air Force control, which I thought was fantastic. But the captain didn't seem to think so, saying "I'm surprised the *Chair Force* was able to keep anyone safe."

Okay, then.

PJ asked the Marine if he knew anything about the rumors we'd heard via the ham radio while in Joliet. Was the rest of the world in as bad of shape as we are?

With a shake of his head, he said, "Rumors are running rampant. Truth is, we're all operating on a need-to-know basis. And what I know about is Montana and Wyoming. The rest of it . . . " He lifted his hands in surrender. "Your guess is as good as mine."

He then went on to tell us more about our area; although, afterward, PJ said he thought the captain probably does know more than he's telling but isn't allowed to discuss it for various reasons.

While we may not know what's happening in the rest of the world, what we've learned about Wyoming is definitely encouraging. South of us, Interstate 25 is also secured between Cheyenne and Casper. And, like Rhiannon said, they hope to have the entire state of Wyoming returned to lawfulness before the end of the year. Then we'll be able to go home to Lander.

But until that happens, I have no plans to put my children in harm's way again. Christopher may not be terribly happy about us returning to Bakerville, but he does seem to understand it's necessary.

Besides, with Marnie and Renée expecting, it makes sense to be with trained people who know how to deliver babies. The Bakerville nurses have now delivered three babies, since another one was born after we left the community. Thankfully, there have been no issues. And according to Sylvia, a fourth is due within a few weeks.

They'll be well experienced before Renée's and Marnie's babies arrive, which will alleviate some of my concerns. I must admit, Rhiannon's discussion over radiation fallout and how it may affect the babies is still something I think about.

By the time the babies are born and old enough to travel, we'll be back in winter. We'll need to wait until the worst of the weather subsides.

Leaving the middle of March in search of Christopher was a mistake. Had we waited another four weeks, our journey would've been just as quick without all the stalls to wait out the weather.

Spring of next year, that's the soonest we can go home to Lander.

Going back to Lander has been part of the discussion between PJ and me too. I feel a need to return to the ranch my dad started before I was born. If not for me, for my children. While I don't agree with the way Rogue is using the children as soldiers to preserve her husband's legacy and keep their feedlot a viable business to pass on to her son, I do understand.

PJ's response to my desire to go back to Lander was simple. "I'll go wherever you wish to go. My place is with you, Rochelle. God put us together for a reason. I'm not going to argue with that."

~~~~~

"There it is," PJ motions to the giant road sign in the near distance. "Welcome to Wyoming."
~~~~~

"Yay!" Cherye cheers.

"Won't be long now and you'll be back in your home state."

"Just wait, Christopher. You're going to love Bakerville," Cheyre gushes from her perch next to PJ.

"You know, you might be right," Christopher says, offering his sister a smile.

The last few days, I've started to see a change in Christopher. He's more like the boy he was when I left him at Camp Ah Nei last year.

There's still a hardness to him that wasn't there before, a hardness caused by the life he encountered in the past year—not just with losing his arm but also because of his deeds as part of Rogue's crew. Until recently, those deeds are things he'd chose to talk little about, dropping only hints of what he encountered during that time.

Our family time in Belfry made a huge difference. As the children got to know each other again, Christopher let his guard down. Still grieving over the loss of his dad and his arm, it'd start as the occasional smile . . . then a chuckle.

One night, after the girls had gone to bed, he opened up. "I know you have questions about Camp Ah Nei. About my, um, duties there. I want you to know that anything I did was to protect the younger kids. I figured that I'd want someone watching out for my sisters, so . . . " He lifted his hand. "Just like you, Mom. You did what you had to do to take care of Kerryanne and Cheyre. That's what I did."

After that night, a weight seemed to lift. The smiles became more frequent, and so did the laughter.

We left this morning in the predawn, when it was just light enough to see, and have kept the horses at a gentle walk through the day, stopping as needed for Christopher.

Even though he was deemed well enough to travel, the motion isn't without pain. While it'd be smart to divide this twenty-plus-mile journey over two days, at Christopher's insistence, we're determined to get home today.

Home.

Bakerville truly does feel like home, especially knowing the rest of my children will be waiting. And this is the perfect day to reunite. It's the Fourth of July, the celebration of American independence. We aren't celebrating with fireworks or barbecues, but it's still a day of observance.

We've met many other travelers along the way today. Most are walking, some are on horses, and we even saw a beat-up old car. Without fail, we've heard *Happy Independence Day* or *Happy Fourth* from each group.

When I traveled this road last, there was still snow on the ground as our little group of twenty-two made our way to Joliet, Montana, where Tamra was reunited with her parents. Now this usually arid location is a lovely shade of green, thanks to the ample amounts of rain and cool weather from the spring. The rains have now stopped, and the temperatures are climbing. So much so that when we do stop, we try to find shade—not an easy task when away from the river or other water sources. Trees don't grow freely in the desert.

I look to the mountains in the west, taking in the beauty of the area. It won't be long until we cross into Wyoming. Then we'll only have a couple of miles to the Bakerville turnoff. A few miles beyond that is Sylvia's place, where the rest of our family waits.

At our pace, we may be finishing the journey in the near dark.

PJ and I have taken turns driving the team, and we all swap around where to sit. With Cheyre and PJ in the seat at the moment, that puts Kerryanne, Christopher, and me in the wagon. We've been talking and even playing cards. I'm amazed at how Christopher has managed to adapt so quickly to having just the one arm.

"PJ?" Christopher calls out. "Can we pull off for a minute."

"Yup. Nature calling?"

"Just need to stretch my legs."

Pulled into a wide spot by the welcome sign, still on the Montana side, we're standing by the wagon. Christopher puts his hand over his eyebrow, looking to the mountains in the west. "It's a beautiful view. How're the sunsets?"

"Montana and Wyoming, the sunsets are always something," I say. "Sunrises too."

"I'll admit, in some ways, I'm not sure I want to cross the state line."

My eyes dart from Christopher to PJ. *What's happening here?* I want to ask.

PJ gives a slight shake of his head.

"Last time I was in Wyoming was over a year ago. My dad was still alive. And I had two arms. It feels . . . wrong to go back. I can't explain it."

"What are you saying?" I ask in a whisper.

"That it's weird. Totally weird. I miss Dad. I miss my arm. And somehow losing both seems terribly unfair."

He turns to me, tears moistening his eyes. "But at the same time, I seem to be . . . what was that Bible thing Renée read? I'm finding patience in my affliction? I might even be finding joy in my hope. But I don't know about the praying without ceasing part. I still struggle with talking to God."

Cheryre bobs her head up and down. "I talk to God. It's easy. Just pretend He's a friend you want to play with."

"I'm not sure that works when you're not seven," Christopher says.

"Have you tried?" Cheyre asks, wrinkling her forehead.

"Maybe not hard enough. I've been . . . mad. I've lost a lot, more than I think God should've allowed." He motions to his stump. "But I realize I've gained a few things too. I finally got that little brother I always wanted."

Christopher tweaks Cheyre's nose. "Not just one but two. Rafe and Mikey. And I now have way too many sisters." He lets out a laugh when Cheyre sticks her tongue out. "That does make me want to ask a question."

"What's that?" I ask.

He gives me a smile, then tilts his head toward PJ. "I'm just wondering when you two plan to get married?"

Continue the journey with Kimba, Leanne, Jennifer, and the rest of the group in Merciless Havoc: Montana Mayhem Book 3.

Find out more about Rochelle's struggles during the early days of the attacks in Christmas on the Mountain: A Havoc in Wyoming Novella.

Note From the Author

In the spring of 2021, we started finding dead rabbits on our small Wyoming homestead. A few weeks later, we received an email from the Wyoming Game and Fish Department inviting us to participate in a research study on how to prevent the spread of rabbit hemorrhagic disease (RHDV2) in the United States. While I'd heard of RHDV2 from a friend who was concerned her domestic rabbit might get it, I knew little about it and how it could affect the wild rabbit population. It was time to research!

RHDV2 is highly contagious, affecting both domestic and wild rabbits. It does not pose a health risk to humans. Many times, the only signs of the disease are sudden death and blood-stained noses caused by internal bleeding. A few of the rabbits we found on our place showed evidence of bloody noses. The disease is transmitted by direct rabbit-to-rabbit contact and also through an infected rabbit's excrement. It even lives on carcasses and can be spread by shared food or water. A person can spread the virus by carrying it on their shoes or clothing.

In this book and book 1, *Unending Havoc*, of my *Montana Mayhem* series, along with my original series, *Havoc in Wyoming*, I've gone in-depth about Chronic Wasting Disease, commonly called CWD. CWD is a prion disease that affects cervids (deer, elk, moose, reindeer, etc.), similar to scrapie in sheep and bovine spongiform encephalopathy in cattle (BSE, or "mad cow disease"). At the time of this writing, CWD has been found in 26 US states, Canada, Norway, Finland, Sweden, and South Korea.

CWD is believed to be transmitted through animal-to-animal contact and infectious bodily fluids such as saliva, urine, and feces. Once excreted, CWD prions can persist for years and are almost impossible to eradicate. The prions can also bind to certain plants and be transported to other areas while remaining infectious. CWD is not known to affect humans, but when BSE was first discovered in cattle, it also wasn't known to pass to humans. The "mad cow" epidemic from the late eighties through the nineties resulted in over 200 deaths.

While CWD and RHDV2 may not directly affect humans, the loss of wildlife (deer, elk, moose, rabbits) is certainly concerning—and would be even more so in an end-of-the-world situation.

As I put the finishing touches on *Ruthless Havoc*, our rabbit population is returning. Our hot, dry summer may have helped with curbing the disease in our area. But a new notice was released from our game and fish department recently, declaring they're tracking an outbreak of epizootic hemorrhagic disease (EHD), a virus that primarily impacts white-tailed deer and pronghorn. This outbreak may be caused by the drought we're experiencing.

It's widely believed in preparedness circles that wild game would be scarce in a catastrophic event. Usually the reasoning is because of overhunting by a starving population. In Wyoming, we have a joke that there's more antelope than humans. Officially, we have around 400,000 antelope and a whopping 580,000+ humans. But add in the 400,000+ deer and over 100,000 elk, along with a variety of other large and small game, and the wildlife sounds plentiful. But not if diseases are threatening the species. Soon, those living in wildlife-heavy areas may be in as much of a food desert as those in the city.

Some people in our traveling group left behind close friends or family when beginning their journey off the mountain. Read more about the adventures on the mountain, and before, in the *Havoc in Wyoming* series.

Havoc in Wyoming

Part 1: Caldwell's Homestead

Jake and Mollie Caldwell started their small farm and homestead to be able to provide for an uncertain future for their family, friends, and community. They have tried to plan for everything. They never planned on Mollie being away on business when the terrorists attacked.

Part 2: Katie's Journey

Katie loves living on her own while finishing up her college degree, working her part-time jobs, and building a relationship with her boyfriend, Leo. When disaster strikes, being away from family isn't quite so nice, and home is over a thousand miles away. Will she make it home before the United States falls apart?

Part 3: Mollie's Quest

Two or three times a year, Mollie Caldwell travels for business. Being away from her Wyoming farmstead is both a fun time and a challenge. They started their farm to be able to provide for an uncertain future for their family, friends, and community. The farm keeps the entire family busy, meaning extra work for her husband while she's away. This time, while on her business trip, terrorists attack. Her weeklong business trip becomes much longer as she tries to make her way home.

Part 3.5: Havoc Begins

Laurie Esplin is spending summer break from college in her hometown of Wesley. As far as she's concerned, this small town--full of kind people--is just about heaven on earth. Her fiancé Aaron makes it even better. When a series of terrorist attacks happen, Laurie is concerned but is positive they're safe in Wesley. She's wrong.

Part 4: Shields and Ramparts

The United States, and the community of Bakerville, face a new threat . . . a threat that could change America forever. As the neighbors band together, all worry about friends and family members. Have they found safety from this latest danger?

Part 5: Fowler's Snare

Welcome to Bakerville, the sleepy Wyoming community Mollie and Jake Caldwell have chosen as their family retreat. At the edge of the wilderness, far away from the big city, they were so sure nothing bad could ever happen in such a protected place. They were wrong. Now, with the entire nation in peril, coming together as a community is the only way they can survive. But not everyone in the community has the people of Bakerville's best interest at heart.

Part 5.5: Havoc Rises

Newlyweds Shelby and Grant Cameron are expecting their first child. But their excitement over the upcoming birth is shadowed by a series of terrorist attacks. Shelby's concerns are increased when the town's hospital burns down. Their small Wyoming town begins to pull together as plans are made for the future. Things are going well until one fateful night when everything changes.

Part 6: Pestilence in the Darkness

Surrounded by danger, they band together with the community of Bakerville to move to a new defensible location. But they weren't prepared to have to give up so much for the security they so desperately need. And they quickly learn trust must be earned, not freely given.

Part 6.5: Havoc Peaks

When their small community in Oregon is overrun with refugees from the nearby cities, Clarice and her family assume they will band together with their neighbors. As the other families mysteriously disappear, it soon becomes evident the only option is to leave. But the only safe place they know is over 1000 miles away. Will the journey prove too dangerous?

Part 7: My Refuge and Fortress

When Jake and a group of hunters return to Bakerville and find their former neighbors slaughtered, they realize there is a new, even more deadly threat. Will their reinforced location be secure enough? And what about the radio announcement from the president? Will his promise of help arrive in time?

Find these titles on Amazon:
www.amazon.com/author/milliecopper

Acknowledgments

Thanks to:

Ameryn Tucker, my editor, beta reader, and daughter wrapped in one. I had a story I wanted to tell, and Ameryn encouraged me and helped me bring it to life.

Dee from Dauntless Cover Design.

My husband, who gave me the time and space I needed to complete this dream and was very patient as I'd tell him the same plot ideas over and over and over.

Three more daughters and a young son, who willingly listen to me drone on and on about story lines and ideas while encouraging me to "keep going."

My amazing Beta Readers! Thanks to April, Barbara, Becky, Carol, Doc, Ilona, Jim, Katrina, Linda, Glen, Marquita, Nancy, Paul, Tammy, Tonya, and Tracy for your help in creating the final story. Your insights and abilities to see the things I miss are very much appreciated! And a special thank you to Tim, specialist in all things that go boom, for always answering my questions and pointing out things I wouldn't even think about.

And to you, my readers, for spending your time with our band of weary travelers. If you have five minutes, you'd make this writer very happy if you could leave a review. I appreciate you!

About the Author

Millie Copper, writer of Cozy Apocalyptic Fiction, was born in Nebraska but never lived there. Her parents fully embraced wanderlust and moved regularly, giving her an advantage of being from nowhere and everywhere.

As an adult, Millie is fully rooted in a solar-powered home in the wilds of Wyoming with her husband and young son, milking ornery goats and tending chickens on their small homestead. In their free time, they escape to the mountains for a hike or laze along the bank of the river to catch their dinner. Four adult daughters, three sons-in-law, and three grandchildren round out the family.

Since 2009, Millie has authored articles on traditional foods, alternative health, homesteading, and preparedness-many times all within the same piece. Millie has penned five nonfiction, traditional food focused books, sharing how, with a little creativity, anyone can transition to a real foods diet without overwhelming their food budget.

The twelve-installment *Havoc in Wyoming* Christian Post-Apocalyptic fiction series uses her homesteading, off-the-grid, and preparedness lifestyle as a guide. The adventure continues with the *Montana Mayhem* series, scheduled for release in the summer of 2021.

Find Millie at www.MillieCopper.com
Facebook: www.facebook.com/MillieCopperAuthor/
Amazon: www.amazon.com/author/milliecopper
BookBub: https://www.bookbub.com/authors/millie-copper

www.ingramcontent.com/pod-product-compliance
Lightning Source LLC
Chambersburg PA
CBHW061613190726
48288CB00007B/2297